MISSION:
IRRESISTIBLE

ALSO BY LORI WILDE

Charmed and Dangerous
License to Thrill

"WHEN I GET OUT OF THE CAR, I WANT YOU TO SLIDE BEHIND THE WHEEL AND DRIVE IMMEDIATELY TO THE NEAREST POLICE STATION."

Harrison ducked his head and fumbled for the door handle. *Round the back of the Volvo, shove up the trunk lid, grab the tire iron, and start swinging.*

Cassie unsnapped her seat belt, leaned across the console, and planted a kiss on his scarred cheek.

He was so startled that he jerked his head toward her, and her mouth slipped from his cheek to his lips. Lush and full and ripe and sweet. Throbbing and heated and humid. His mouth sizzled as Cassie's tongue glided over his lips. Nibbling, licking, tasting, teasing.

And then a fist knocking hard against his window slammed Harrison back to reality. He jerked his head toward the driver's-side window, expecting to see a knife-wielding carjacker, a brass-knuckle-wearing loan shark, or members of the Minoan Order . . . their faces hidden behind Minotaur masks.

PRAISE FOR LORI WILDE'S PREVIOUS NOVELS

LICENSE TO THRILL

"With a sassy, in-your-face style, reminiscent of Janet Evanovich, Wilde has created an unforgettable heroine."
—*Booklist*

"Steamy."
—*Cosmopolitan*

more . . .

"Hilarious as well as romantic."
—The Pilot (NC)

CHARMED AND DANGEROUS

"With a deft hand, Wilde blends humor and suspense, passion and mystery into a story both charming and dangerous."
—BookLoons.com

"An exhilarating romantic suspense."
—Midwest Book Review

"A plot that is sure to win [Wilde] more readers."
—The Pilot (NC)

"Fans will take immense pleasure [in] this FBI art romance."
—Harriet's Book Reviews

"Quite the exciting romp. Fans will be charmed."
—Romantic Times BOOKclub Magazine

"Lovable . . . Wilde has a unique voice that will soar her to publishing heights."
—Rendezvous

MISSION: IRRESISTIBLE

LORI WILDE

WARNER
FOREVER

NEW YORK   BOSTON

Cover design by Shasti O'Leary Soudant
Cover image by Scott Cunningham/Getty Images
Book design by Giorgetta Bell McRee

Warner Books

Time Warner Book Group
1271 Avenue of the Americas
New York, NY 10020
Visit our Web site at www.twbookmark.com.

Printed in the United States of America

First Paperback Printing: May 2005

10   9   8   7   6   5   4   3   2   1

To my cousin Ginna, you're the best!
Love you bunches.

To the people who painstakingly helped me brainstorm this book—Carolyn Greene, Jamie Denton, and Hebby Roman. Thank you for your high tolerance for my whining. Your insight and talent astound me.

And to my research team who came through like gangbusters—Fred and Maxine Blalock. Keep surfing the Net!

MISSION:
IRRESISTIBLE

PROLOGUE

Egypt, Valley of the Kings
Sixteen years ago

Who is my father?"

It was late. The oil lanterns burned low, casting flickering shadows against the walls of the tomb of Ramses IV. The air smelled of dirt and musty decay. Nothing met sixteen-year-old Harrison Standish's question but the sound of a shovel steadily scooping sand.

Except for the armed security guards posted outside the pyramid, he and his mother, Diana, were the only ones left at the excavation site. The rest of the archaeologists, dig workers, and college students had long ago returned to their quarters at the university compound.

They were searching for the lost grave of Ramses's oldest daughter, Kiya, and her lover, Solen, a Minoan scribe sold into slavery to the Egyptians. According to lore, Solen and Kiya had been separated by Ramses's vizier Nebamun. The Egyptian title of vizier was a very important position, administratively just under the pharaoh himself. In fact, a vizier could even be elevated to pharaoh, often by marrying into the royal family.

For his loyal service, Ramses had promised Nebamun Kiya's hand in marriage, but when the vizier found her in Solen's arms, he poisoned them in a jealous fit of rage.

Nebamun had buried each lover separately with one-half of a magical brooch amulet in an attempt to avoid the curse Solen cast upon him with his dying breath—even though he'd been too superstitious to destroy the amulet entirely. Mythology held that if the two rings of the brooch were ever brought together again, Solen and Kiya would be reunited in the Underworld, and Nebamun's descendants would be forever damned.

For months Diana had been working from dawn until midnight. She was immersed, focused, fixated on her goal. She glanced over at Harrison. Her eyes shone with a feverish light.

He pushed his glasses up on his nose and held his breath. Would she answer him this time?

She did not. Her jaw tightened and she returned her attention to what she was doing, squatting on the ground, meticulously sifting through sand.

"Was my father Egyptian?" he asked. "Is that where I get my coloring?"

Scrape, scoop. Scrape, scoop.

"Mother?"

"He was an asshole," Diana said. "You're better off not knowing him."

"What about Adam's father?" Harrison asked, referring to his younger half brother.

"What about him?"

"How come he gets to know his dad?"

Diana groaned, rocked back on her heels, and lifted a dirt-stained hand to brush a lock of blonde hair from her forehead. "Because Tom Grayfield insisted on being part of Adam's life."

"And my father didn't insist on being part of mine?"

It was a rhetorical question. The absence of a father was explanation enough.

"No. Your father was already married. Already had a son. Although I didn't know that when I met him." The bitterness in Diana's voice echoed throughout the cloistered chamber.

"Oh."

He swallowed the ugly information. His biological father was married to a woman who wasn't his mother. His father had another son. A son he obviously liked better than he liked Harrison.

Disappointment weighted Harrison's shoulders. Slowly, he rose to his feet.

"Look, son." His mother's tone softened. "You've got to trust me. For your own good, stop asking questions."

"But I need to know the truth."

"Why?"

"Because everyone deserves to know where they come from," he said.

"Does this have something to do with your little friend Jessica? Are her hoity-toity parents refusing to let you date her because they don't know your heritage?"

His face flushed hot. He fisted his hands.

"I must be right," Diana scoffed. "You're blushing."

He did not reply. He was too angry, too frustrated, too confused. He sucked his emotions deep inside his lungs, held them down with the indrawn breath, and stared at his mother. He couldn't believe she had withheld such vital information from him for so long.

"I deserve to know. I'm sixteen now. A man."

"Okay." Diana relented after a long pause. "I'll tell you this much. Your father was born of noble blood, and he holds a very powerful position."

Harrison expelled his breath along with his emotions. He felt as drained as if he'd sprinted fifty miles without stopping.

And as empty.

"Did you ever love my father?" he asked.

Diana snorted. "Love is for suckers. What you're feeling for Jessica is nothing more than raging hormones and teenage angst. Take my advice. Forget about her. Concentrate on your work, your schooling. Science will free your mind. Not love."

It was as if his mother had sliced open his head, peered inside his brain, and voiced his greatest fear out loud. He loved Jessica with an intensity that scared him, but he didn't like out-of-control feelings. They clouded a man's reason, and he thought of himself as a reasonable man.

But his heart refused to stay silent. Something unexpected inside him rebelled against logic. Something wild and scary and exhilarating.

"You're wrong. I love Jessica, and she loves me."

Diana shook her head. "My poor, naive boy."

"If you don't believe in love, then how come you've spent your entire life searching for Kiya and Solen to prove the legend of the star-crossed lovers?"

"Is that what you think we've been doing?" She looked surprised.

He shrugged. "What else?"

"Harrison, all these years I've been trying to *disprove* the legend."

"I don't understand." He frowned. For as long as he could remember, his mother had been consumed by the story. How could he have been so mistaken about her motives?

"Haven't you been listening?" Diana clicked her tongue. "There's no such thing as soul mates and undying love. No such thing as love at first sight, or even second sight, for that matter. It's all romantic bullshit concocted to entertain the masses. When we find Solen and Kiya and join the two pieces of their amulet together again, absolutely nothing is going to happen."

He blinked at her, incredulous. "You dragged Adam and me to Egypt when we could be having a normal life, staying in one place, making friends, all to prove nothing?"

"Exactly! Now you understand."

"Nihilism. How Nietzsche of you, Mother."

"Don't get smart."

"Why not? Apparently intelligence is the only quality you value." Harrison pivoted on his heel and stalked toward the exit.

"Where are you going?"

"Back to the campus. To see Jessica. To tell her how much I love her. Because I'm not bitter like you. I do believe in the legend of the star-crossed lovers. I do believe in love."

"Don't do it, Harrison. It's a mistake," she called after him, but he just kept marching.

Tonight he would take a chance. He would give Jessica the promise ring he'd been carrying in his pocket for three weeks. Waiting for the courage to speak what was in his heart.

In the illumination from the fat yellow full moon high in the velvet-black sky, he rode his bicycle into town. His stomach was in his throat. He wanted this. He did, he did. He was no longer afraid.

I love you, Jessica.

Thirty minutes later, he pedaled through the gates of the university, his pulse pounding in his ears. He parked his bike in front of the girls' dormitory.

He intended to sneak around the side of the building and throw pebbles at her window to wake her up, the way guys did in romantic movies. He stuck his hand in his pocket, fisted his fingers around the delicate promise ring. The smooth feel of it gave him courage.

Jessica, Jessica, Jessica.

He started across the veranda, but then he spied a couple locked in an embrace on the porch swing. He shuffled to the right, giving them a wide berth, but a familiar scent caught his attention and stopped him in midstep.

Cherry blossom cologne. Jessica's signature scent.

He froze, rooted to the spot, to that horrible moment in time. Harrison stared while the young lovers kissed.

They must have sensed his presence, because they raised their heads, and in the bright moonlight he saw clearly the thing he most did not want to see.

Jessica in the arms of another guy.

And not just any guy, but his half brother, Adam.

The emotions were too much to handle. Betrayal, anger, disappointment, bitterness.

He shut down his feelings. Shut down his heart and stalked away.

"Harrison, wait," Adam cried out. "It's not what you think."

But it was. They both knew it.

At that moment Harrison realized his hand was still clenched around the promise ring. With a curse, he pulled it from his pocket and flung it into the darkness.

Mother had been right all along.

Love was for suckers.

CHAPTER
1

No question about it. The mummy was following her.

Cassie Cooper slipped past King Tut, who was chatting up Nefertiti beside the lavish hors d'oeuvre table, and cast a surreptitious glance over her shoulder.

Yep.

There he was. Peeking from behind the Sphinx's chipped nose, his mysterious dark eyes following her as she meandered around the main exhibit hall of the Kimbell Art Museum.

Stifling a triumphant grin, she readjusted her Cleopatra Queen of the Nile headdress, which kept slipping down on her forehead and mussing up her wig. Just to tease, she moistened her lips with the tip of her tongue.

Who was lurking beneath the swaddling linen?

Her pulse quickened. She had a lot of admirers. No telling who was in the costume.

Maybe it was an old flame. Maybe a new one. Maybe it was even a stranger.

Goose bumps dotted the nape of her neck.

A mystery. How exciting.

Don't let yourself get diverted. Forget the distractions; you've got a job to do.

The voice inside her head sounded exactly like her straight-arrow twin, Maddie.

Cassie sighed in wistful longing. Apparently she missed her sister's lovable nagging so much that her own conscience had taken over the job. She was happy Maddie had married her true love, hunky FBI agent David Marshall. What she wasn't so thrilled about was David's getting promoted and dragging Maddie off to live in the urban wilds of Washington, D.C.

Focus on your goal.

Okay. All right. She was focusing.

Cassie turned her back on the mummy and managed to tamp her libido down a smidgen. If she had any hope of landing her dream job in the public relations department of the Smithsonian, she would have to make sure this charity masquerade to promote the legend of the star-crossed Egyptian lovers exhibit went off without a glitch.

After getting laid off as the PR director for *Art World Today* magazine four months ago, she'd been grateful just to get her old job back at the Kimbell, but now her wanderlust had kicked up again. She was hungering for something new and different. Cassie wanted the change not only because bagging the Smithsonian represented the pinnacle of her career, but also because she would get to live near her twin again.

Unfortunately, achieving her dream job would require a glowing recommendation from her new boss, Phyllis Lambert. And old Prune Face was not her greatest fan. In fact, if Cassie hadn't been instrumental in helping capture the charming art thief who had robbed the Kimbell the previous year, she knew Lambert would have convinced the board of directors to show her the door.

She must perform flawlessly. All she had to do was keep her mind off Mummy Man and firmly fixed where it belonged.

On the party.

With a discerning eye, she assessed the room. Exotic Egyptian music trickled through the state-of-the-art surround sound system. Large navy blue banners with ivory lettering adorned the walls of the exhibit hall. Underneath the lettering on each banner was the amulet's double-ring emblem, encircling an embossed silhouette of two lovers kissing beneath a blanket of golden stars.

"UNDYING LOVE," declared the banner along the north wall. "INTRIGUE" bordered the south. "DANGER" flanked the west. "BETRAYAL" along the east wall, completed the quadrangle.

Tuxedoed waiters moved throughout the assembly carrying trays of champagne. Armed security guards manned the exits. Caterers dished up bacon-wrapped water chestnuts, assorted puff pastries, grilled prawns, Russian caviar, and the finest pâté.

Cassie had spared no expense. A hundred patrons of the arts had shelled out a thousand dollars apiece to witness the reunion of the ill-fated lovers separated in death for the past three thousand years.

Great. Perfect. Everything was running like a precision Swiss timepiece as they anticipated the arrival of the guest of honor, the illustrious Dr. Adam Grayfield from Crete, who was bringing with him Solen's portion of the exhibit.

Until then, Cassie found her concentration drawn irresistibly over her shoulder again. She scanned the guests, searching for the mummy.

Impromptu romance had landed her in trouble more times than she cared to count, but she couldn't seem to help herself when it came to the first rich blush of potential amour.

Putting an extra wiggle into her walk just in case the mummy happened to be watching, Cassie sashayed over to where several high-profile patrons, an eminent Egyptian from the Ministry of Antiquities, and various members of the press were clustered around a red velvet cordon. They were oohing and aahing over the feminine segment of the main attraction.

Princess Kiya's sarcophagus and the section of amulet found among her artifacts.

The amulet, displayed on black velvet draped over a granite pedestal, was nothing spectacular to look at. After all the fanfare, seeing the amulet in person was a bit of a letdown. The talisman was a simple half-dollar-sized copper brooch, and there was a small jagged tear in the pliable metal ring where a second circle had long ago been ripped away.

Kiya was patiently awaiting the return of her Minoan lover, Solen.

Tenderness clutched Cassie's heart. Damn, she was a sucker for romance. But secretly, while at the same time she dreamed of finding her own true love, deep down she was conflicted about the reality of such intimacy. The whole one-man-for-the-rest-of-your-life thing gave her the heebie-jeebies. For crying out loud, how did a girl ever know for sure if the grass wasn't greener in another pasture?

From her peripheral vision she caught furtive movement through the crowd. The mummy was creeping closer. He was most definitely following her. He edged around a collection of canopic jars before ducking behind a guy in a hawk mask dressed as Horus the Sky God.

Aw, he was shy. How sweet.

She was normally attracted to bold, daring types, but there was something about shy guys that made her feel all soft and squooshy and maternal inside.

Face it, Cassie, Maddie's voice teased inside her head. *You have a talent for finding something to like about any member of the opposite sex.*

True enough. She did love men.

Well, except maybe for the annoying Dr. Harrison Standish skulking at the back of the room. He was petulantly tossing from palm to palm that odd miniature replica of an ancient Egyptian battery that he always carried with him. She tilted her head and met his gaze. He glowered at her through the smudged lenses of his round, dark-framed glasses.

Dr. Standoffish. That was what Cassie called him behind his back.

The truth was, the guy intimidated her with his intellect. He was a Rhodes scholar, and he used so many big words, she often felt the need to lug a dictionary around with her just so she could figure out what he was saying.

Harrison had arrived from Egypt the previous Monday with Princess Kiya and her artifacts in tow, giving Cassie dark and brooding looks right from the beginning. Two years ago he had resurrected Ramses IV's oldest daughter in the Valley of the Kings, and ever since then he had been diligently searching for her eternal soul mate, Solen.

But Dr. Adam Grayfield had beaten Standoffish to the punch. Harrison had to be irked over Dr. Grayfield's coup d'état. Perhaps that was why he was so pissy.

Standoffish was younger than she had expected. His

youthful face placed him in his early thirties, but still, he seemed much older. Stodgy. Set in his ways.

And Cassie was stuck with him.

He was the sole reason the Egyptian government had allowed the exhibit into the United States. The Kimbell had gotten lucky because Standish was a Fort Worth native, and he'd chosen to host the exhibit in his hometown.

Cassie and the obstinate Egyptologist had had several heated disagreements over the publicity of the star-crossed lovers. She'd had to remind him on more than one occasion of the politics of economics. If he wanted more grant money for his digs, then, like it or not, Harrison would have to play footsie with both the media and the museum's benevolent benefactors. You'd think after so many years in the archaeology game, the guy would have already bought a clue or two.

They'd also argued over his refusal to wear a costume for the masquerade party.

The spoilsport.

Cassie might have won the publicity war, but Standish had triumphed in the costume department. As usual, his dark hair was disheveled, looking as if he'd combed the unruly locks with a tuning fork.

He was attired in his quintessential nerdy professor clothes. Rumpled orange-and-white-striped shirt, hideous purple tweed jacket with worn leather elbow patches, a god-awful chartreuse bow tie, and five-pocket, pleated, baggy khaki Dockers. Hadn't anyone ever told him that pleats were out, out, out?

And omigosh!

She just now noticed he was wearing one brown tasseled loafer and one black one. The clueless guy had to be either color-blind or severely fashion-impaired.

Or both.

What a geek.

Cringing, Cassie rolled her eyes and prayed that no one else had noticed. He was destroying the exotic atmosphere of ancient Egypt she'd worked so hard to re-create.

His gaze held hers, and Cassie forced herself not to glance away. She didn't exactly know why, but something about the man made her jittery. Maybe it was the way he habitually handled that toy of his. Or perhaps it was because he seemed immune to her charms. She was accustomed to batting her eyelashes, crooking her little finger, and having men fall at her feet.

But not this dude. He just kept scowling and tossing that stupid artifact reproduction.

Did he want a staring contest? Was that the deal? Oh, he had sure picked the wrong gal for that. She was the master of the staredown. The only one who could trump her was Maddie.

Let's have a go at it, Poindexter. Cassie narrowed her eyes and sank her hands onto her hips.

He didn't blink.

Neither did Cassie.

She'd heard Standish was known as old Poker Face around the digs, but she wasn't intimidated. The game was on.

He narrowed his eyes.

She responded in kind.

One minute passed.

Two.

Then three.

Okay, now she'd see how he responded under pressure. She stuck out her tongue.

Real mature. He cabled the message with his eyes and

didn't crack a smile. Apparently he wasn't going to let the sight of her tongue unnerve him.

She laughed, flipped her straight dark wig over her shoulder, and gave him a quick flash of her natural blonde hair beneath. The peekaboo was no accident. His face flushed as if he was having thoughts he had no business entertaining.

"Ahem." Phyllis Lambert cleared her throat. The middle-aged curator was also dressed as Cleopatra, but Phyllis didn't possess the pizzazz to pull it off.

"Uh-huh," Cassie mumbled without glancing over at her boss. She didn't want to break eye contact with Standoffish and default the game.

"If you're all done exchanging meaningful glances with Dr. Standish, might I have a word with you, Cassandra?"

Meaningful glances? As if!

First off, she wouldn't be caught dead flirting with a pointy-headed intellectual like Einstein Poindexter Standoffish. Second, before Cassie could ever successfully flirt with him, he would have to read the comprehensive volume of *Flirting for Dummies* cover to cover.

Twice.

From what she had seen of Standoffish so far, the dude possessed few social skills and zero talent for coquetry.

"Cassandra," Lambert repeated.

No one except the annoying curator ever called her by her given name. Not even her own mother when she was displeased with her.

Cassie directed her gaze to the potato-chip-thin woman who wore too much makeup and not enough clothing. Powder foundation had settled into the numerous wrinkles lining her disapproving mouth. The air-conditioning was cranked a couple of degrees too low, providing indisputable evidence that the fifty-something Lambert wasn't wearing a bra under her flimsy white gown.

Not that her "girls" needed a harness, but barf, this was a classy event. At the very least, a couple of strategically placed Band-Aids were in order.

Be nice. Lambert has the power to make all your dreams come true.

Or crush them into dust.

Cassie forced a smile and ignored both the curator's comment about exchanging meaningful glances with Dr. Standish and her unbound ta-tas.

"How may I help you, Phyllis?"

Lambert pursed her lips and tapped the face of her wristwatch. "The presentation starts at eight o'clock. It's now fifteen minutes until the hour, and there's no sign of Dr. Grayfield. Have you heard from him?"

Seven-forty-five. Really? Time flew when you were being shadowed by a mysterious mummy.

Cassie frowned. Where *was* Adam?

He had called her from New York the previous afternoon, promising that he and Solen would arrive at the Kimbell with plenty of time to set up for the reunification ceremony. Even if Dr. Grayfield appeared right now, fifteen minutes wasn't nearly enough time to get things set up and rolling.

She had offered to send a car and an assistant to help him unload the crate at DFW Airport, but Adam had refused. For the sake of secrecy, he'd insisted on handling the details himself. Because she was a big fan of the dramatic, Cassie had acquiesced. In retrospect, it wasn't such a hot idea.

Had something happened to him? Could he have been robbed? Accosted? Worse?

Anxiety clutched her, but then she blew out her breath and brushed her fears aside. Her twin sister, Maddie, was the worrywart, not she.

Everything would be fine.

Adam would show. No doubt he just wanted to make a grand entrance. And who could blame him? He had a big surprise in store. Imagine being the first person ever to decipher the hieroglyphs of the ancient Minoans, on top of discovering the lost tomb of Kiya's beloved Solen.

Cassie felt especially honored because she was the only one Adam had told about the hieroglyphs. He'd said it was on a need-to-know basis, and because she was in charge of the party, she was the only one who needed to know in advance that he had an addition to the program. He'd sworn her to secrecy. Which wasn't a problem. She liked being in on secrets.

From over Phyllis's shoulder, Cassie spied the mummy again. He was waving, trying to get her attention. When his dark, enigmatic eyes met hers, he inclined his head toward the exit door leading to the garden courtyard. Was he telling her to meet him outside?

A sudden thought occurred. Could Adam Grayfield be the mummy? He'd told her he would be wearing a special costume. Was he playing flirtatious games with her? Or did he have an urgent message to relay?

"Well?" Phyllis demanded.

"Hmm?"

"Have you heard from Dr. Grayfield or not?"

No point putting the woman in a snit before there was something to snit about. "I heard from Adam."

Last night, Cassie mentally added. "Everything is on schedule."

"He better be here by eight." Phyllis tapped her watch again. "Because if anything goes wrong tonight—"

"Nothing," Cassie interrupted the curator, "is going to go wrong."

"Then do me a favor and put my mind at ease. Locate Dr. Grayfield."

"Okay, fine."

Jeez Louise, don't get your panties in a bunch.

"Go. Now." Phyllis made shooing motions.

"I'm going, I'm going."

Cassie started after her purse, where she'd stashed her address book. She had taken only a couple of steps before Lambert dropped the nuclear bomb.

"Oh, and Cassandra," Phyllis called after her.

Cassie forced herself not to sigh. She turned around and plastered a perky smile on her face. "Yes, Phyllis?"

"If you return without Dr. Grayfield and the remainder of the exhibit, you can kiss your coveted recommendation to the Smithsonian good-bye."

CHAPTER
2

Dr. Harrison Standish hated parties.

No, *hated* was too mild a word. He loathed them, despised them, abhorred them. He would rather have a root canal, a major tax audit, and a prostate exam—all on the same morning—than attend one of these exorbitantly expensive, butt-kissing cultural affairs.

He'd already scoped out every exit so he could make a quick and clean getaway as soon as feasibly possible. He never went anywhere without an escape route mapped out.

Worst of all, it was a masquerade party. How pathetic—a group of grown people dressing up in silly costumes, pretending to be some ridiculous characters from history or literature. And as the icing on the cake, there in the center of the room, glomming on to attention, was the flamboyant Cassie Cooper. Looking as if she owned the world in her regal Cleopatra costume, heavy eyeliner, and thick dark wig. The kohl made her big eyes look even wider than they were, emphasizing that compellingly innocent-yet-naughty quality of hers.

Harrison was irritated with himself because each time

she sashayed by, every intelligent thought bounced right out of his head, to be replaced by a drooling, Cro-Magnon, monosyllabic beat.

Me want.

This wasn't like him at all, dammit. But whenever Cassie appeared he could not seem to stop himself from fantasizing about her. And he hated his unexpected weakness almost as much as he hated this party.

He had to stop thinking about her because she was, quite frankly, the most mesmerizing yet infuriating woman he had ever met. He could not afford the luxury of falling under her spell. However, it was far more than her fair complexion, light-colored eyes, and voluptuous figure that drove him around the bend.

Her scattered thought processes made no rational sense. Just when he thought he had her figured out, she would do something totally illogical. Harrison suspected the woman possessed a serious case of adult attention deficit disorder.

She strutted across the room, hips swaying with primal rhythm. In his head he heard the hissing whispery sound of metallic brushes whisking over brass cymbals, reverberating with each roll of her fabulous ass. *Tss-tta-tss-tta-tss.*

A guy could get whiplash from watching her.

The woman was nimble. He would give her that. She was Lepidoptera *Danaus plexippus*, flashy, colorful, flitting from flower to flower. Here, there, everywhere. Never lingering in one place, always on the move.

Working with her over the course of the past nine days had been a royal pain in the butt. Whenever she wanted to get her way on an issue, she would ply her womanly wiles. Flirting, teasing, cajoling.

Harrison had pretended to be underwhelmed by her charms, even though he was as bedazzled as the stammering college students helping them set up the exhibit. But he refused to let her know the extent of her power over him. He'd learned from hard experience you couldn't trust lust.

Face it, Standish, it's just been too long since you've had sex.

The pressure of celibacy, that's all this was. Because he and Cassie were total opposites in every way imaginable. She was a bubbly optimist. He was an eternal pessimist. She was sensual. He was cerebral. She was a romantic. He was a cynic. She was laid-back. He was tense. She sought the silver lining. He was always waiting for the other shoe to fall. And whenever he looked into her eyes, he could tell exactly what she was thinking.

Nerd. Dork. Geek.

Harrison knew, without a word being said, what kind of man she normally went for. Suave, debonair, charming dudes with expensive sports cars, ostentatious wardrobes, and toothpaste-commercial smiles.

Guys like his devilish half brother, Adam. Who upstaged him at every turn. The way she had gone on and on and on all week, chattering about how excited she was that Dr. Grayfield was coming to the Kimbell, really stuck in his craw. What was he? Chop suey? He was so irritated by her obvious adoration of Adam that he hadn't even told her they were brothers.

Harrison ground his teeth. He was trying to suck up his disappointment and be the bigger person. So what if Cassie seemed enamored of his half brother? So what if Adam had found Solen before he did? No big deal. Adam and his gregarious personality had been able to raise the financial backing while introverted Harrison had not.

Story of his life.

But he was suspicious of his brother's financial support. Although Adam's father, Ambassador Tom Grayfield, was rich, Adam, forever the rebel, raised his own money so he wouldn't have to do things his father's way. In the past, Adam hadn't been too choosy about where he got his funding, often running afoul of loan sharks and other unsavory characters.

Harrison would hate to see his younger brother in trouble again. Because as much as they disagreed, they did share an unbreakable bond. They'd both survived a nomadic childhood with Diana Standish.

Besides, he didn't care about the fame that came with finding Solen. The discovery was what mattered. Not their sibling rivalry.

Where was his brother, by the way?

He glanced around the room. Adam should be making his grand entrance anytime now. He was all about grand entrances and grand gestures and grand romances that flared hot but never lasted.

All style and no substance. Come to think of it, Adam was essentially a masculine version of Cassie Cooper.

Harrison snorted. What a spectacular pair those two would make.

The yin and yang of glitz and flash. If Adam and Cassie ever hooked up, it would be like spring break, New Year's Eve, and Mardi Gras all rolled into one. Of course, when reality reared its inevitable head, bye-bye hot tryst. Neither one of them had the staying power for cleanup after the party was over.

"Excuse me, young man," said an elderly woman with

an Isis headdress. She was peering at the display of an ancient Egyptian battery found in Kiya's tomb. "Do you know what this is?"

"It's called a *tet* or a *djed*." He pointed to the label mounted on a plaque above the display. "A wireless battery."

"They had batteries in ancient Egypt?"

"Yes, ma'am, they did."

"What did they use them for?"

"We don't know for sure, although there's a lot of speculation. Some believe it was for religious rituals, others think it was used for medicinal purposes."

"Really?"

Harrison's personal theory was that the ancient Egyptians used the djed as a transmitter of electromagnetic waves. He'd been very excited about finding one in Kiya's tomb and had even constructed a miniature replica of his own so he could test his theories. "Would you like to see a reproduction?"

"Why, yes." The aged Isis peered at him curiously as Harrison placed his homemade djed in her hand.

"It has a bit of a phallic appearance, doesn't it?" Isis ran her hand along the tube.

"Uh, yes, ma'am."

The woman gave it back to him and winked. "Very interesting."

He pocketed the djed and decided to move away from the exhibit to forestall future questioning. He strolled over to the central display, eyeing Kiya's sarcophagus and the amulet. Ahmose Akvar, exalted son of a former Egyptian prime minister and himself a high-ranking official with the Ministry of Antiquities, moved to stand beside him.

Ahmose wasn't much older than Harrison, and while they possessed similar olive-toned complexions and were about the same height and build, the resemblance ended there. The Egyptian's features were much more patrician than Harrison's, and he wore tailor-made silk suits and expensive Italian shoes. Ahmose was there to make certain nothing happened to Kiya. Over the years, many precious relics had been stolen from the Valley of the Kings, and the Ministry of Antiquities took their artifacts very seriously.

Ahmose shook his head. "You know, Dr. Standish, I am worried about the lax security."

"Lax security? There are armed security guards posted at every exit."

"Yes, but I did not realize the amulet would be displayed right out in the open. It should be in a locked case."

Harrison had similar reservations concerning the display, but Cassie had insisted that the guests, who had paid an excessive amount of money to attend the event, would demand to see the amulet without the restriction of a locked case. Against his better judgment, he'd allowed her to have her way, simply so he wouldn't have to watch her lips plump up in a pout. Those pouty lips clouded his reason every single time.

God, he was a fool.

"As you know," Ahmose said, "I've never approved of reuniting the star-crossed lovers. What if something unexpected occurs?" The Egyptian's English was flawless. He held a bachelor's degree from Harvard and a master's from Oxford.

"Don't worry. It's just a myth. There's no magic, no charm, no curse. Nothing to be afraid of."

The furrow in Ahmose's otherwise smooth brow deepened the longer he stared at Kiya's sarcophagus. "There are more things in heaven and earth than mortal man understands, my friend."

Terrific, here was another gullible believer in that idiotic star-crossed lovers legend. "I didn't realize you were such a sentimentalist, Ahmose."

"You do not know everything there is to know about me, Dr. Standish."

Apparently not. Harrison had presumed that Ahmose was a man of science. Instead, he had just discovered he was as susceptible to the ludicrous fairy tale as everyone else.

"No need for alarm," he reassured the Egyptian. "Everything is under control."

Well, except for the small detail that his brother had yet to show up with Solen's remains for the reunification ceremony. What was taking Adam so long?

Ahmose glowered. "For your sake I hope you are correct, Dr. Standish."

"That sounds like a threat. Are you threatening me, Ahmose?" Harrison squared his shoulders.

"It is not a threat. It is a guarantee. If anything happens to the amulet, the djed, or any of Kiya's artifacts, your visa will be rescinded and you will never again be allowed inside Egypt."

Alarm shot through him. Surely Ahmose couldn't be serious about this.

"Nothing's going to happen," Harrison reiterated.

Why was Ahmose acting so strangely? He wasn't by nature a dramatic man. Usually the Egyptian was quite reserved. His dark mood seemed infectious. The crowd shifted restlessly. People peered at their watches and mumbled negative comments.

"Dr. Standish?"

Harrison glanced over to see one of the young college students who had spent the past week helping him and Cassie assemble the exhibits. The lanky kid's name was Gabriel Martinez, and he had a rare enthusiasm for archaeology. Harrison had considered inviting the young student to participate in his next dig.

"Yes?"

"A man asked me to hand this to you." Gabriel passed him a white business-sized envelope with Harrison's name printed in block lettering. It looked like Adam's handwriting.

"What man?"

"That dude over there." Gabriel pointed.

"Where?" Harrison squinted at the crowd.

"In the Indiana Jones hat."

The Indy hat stood out among the cluster of Egyptian headdresses. Immediately, Harrison knew whose head was under it, because he'd been there when his brother had bought the hat on a trip to London.

But Adam wasn't hanging around. He was headed for the front entrance at a fast clip.

Where was he going?

Clutching the envelope Gabriel had slipped him, Harrison jostled through the throng. He didn't want to shout and attract undue attention, but he didn't want Adam to get away either.

"Excuse me," he apologized as he careened into Isis, whose oversized headdress bobbled precariously. He'd had his gaze so fixed on keeping the Indiana Jones hat in sight that he hadn't seen her meander into his path. He zigzagged around her, just as the moving Indy hat reached the foyer.

The crowd was even thicker here because this area was much smaller than the main part of the exhibit hall. He had to move quickly, or his brother was going to disappear. To hell with his dislike for drawing attention to himself.

"Adam!" he called.

People turned to stare. Harrison pretended not to care that he was being watched. He had never been a center-stage sort of guy, and collecting stares made him uncomfortable.

The front door opened.

"Wait!"

The hat disappeared and the door clicked shut.

Harrison was still a good twenty feet and twenty people from the entrance. What parlor game was his brother playing? From the time they were small kids, Adam had had a penchant for pirate treasure maps and secret spy codes and fantasy role-playing.

His fondness for outlandish pranks and schemes lasted into adulthood and frequently plunged him into trouble. One year, when they were collage students on a dig site in Peru, Adam had cooked up a scheme to fake a famous religious artifact. It had started out as a joke. He'd never meant for people to take it seriously.

For several days he was touted in the media. He achieved instant celebrity status and actually started to believe he'd honestly found a real artifact. He had a way of buying into his own bullshit. When the artifact was proved a fraud and Adam found himself threatened with legal action, Tom Grayfield rushed in, threw his money around, and hushed everything up.

Adam had confessed to Harrison that those few days

of notoriety had been well worth the ass-chewing he'd received from his old man.

Was his brother up to his old tricks? Could he have faked Solen's discovery? But that was impossible. Solen's tomb had been authenticated by highly trained specialists. Experts Harrison knew and trusted. Still, he wouldn't put it past his brother to pull some crazy publicity stunt.

He reached the door, pushed through it, and ended up on the sidewalk outside the main entrance of the Kimbell. The streetlamps glinted off the smudged lenses of his glasses and the reflected glare blocked his view.

He whipped off his glasses and wiped them on his shirttail. One of these days he was going to have laser eye surgery and throw the damned spectacles away forever. His brother had been nagging him to do it for years. Adam was fond of saying, "Girls don't make passes at guys who wear glasses."

Still rubbing his lenses, he squinted into the darkness. The grounds were empty. The street was deserted except for a nondescript white delivery van parked at the corner. No one else was around.

Adam had vanished.

Where'd he go?

He heard the roar of a motorcycle engine, and just then a souped-up Harley, customized with lots of chrome and specialty tires, zipped around the corner. The powerful machine buzzed past him on the street, Indiana Jones seated behind the handlebars.

Quickly jamming his glasses back on, Harrison waved his arms. "Adam!"

His brother never glanced back.

                    *   *   *

The balmy April night air greeted Cassie as the double-glass door snapped closed behind her, muting the laughter and voices from inside the museum. Suddenly, she felt very far away.

Isolated. Alone.

Tingles skated up her spine.

Her breath came in short, raspy gasps. Anticipation escalated her excitement. She looked right, then left. Where had the mummy gone?

Maybe she'd misunderstood his intentions. Maybe he'd been signaling to someone else. Nah. She knew when a guy was sending signals. And the mummy had been telegraphing her big-time. Who was he?

Old boyfriend? New boyfriend? Friend? Lover? Enemy? Adam Grayfield?

The suspense was excruciating. And totally irresistible.

Ambient lighting from quaint low-voltage streetlamps illuminated the courtyard. Well-manicured trees and dense shrubbery cast dark shadows over the walkway.

"Yoo-hoo." Cassie wandered around the maze of chest-high bushes. "Anybody here?"

No sound except for the echo of her high-heeled sandals clicking against the flagstones.

What if Adam *was* the mummy? What if he needed to tell her something important about the exhibit? What if someone had been following him, and he had dressed up like an extra from an old Hammer Films horror movie so he wouldn't be recognized?

"Don't be silly," she growled under her breath and plopped down on a stone bench. More than likely the mummy was just teasing her, heating things up a notch, escalating their flirtation. "Everything is just fine."

To prove it, she would call Adam right now. She took her cell phone from her purse, along with a tin of cinnamon Altoids and her address book. She looked up his number, punched it in, and then popped one of the curiously strong breath mints.

The phone rang. Once, twice, three times.

"Come on, Adam," she muttered. "Pick up the phone. Lambert's looking to serve my behind on a platter over you."

When his voice mail answered after the tenth ring, Cassie sighed and switched off the phone without leaving a message. She stuffed the cell back into her purse and crunched the remainder of the cool cinnamon mint between her teeth.

A rustling noise emanated from the bushes behind her. Her stomach nose-dived. She turned her head and saw the mummy silhouetted in the light.

"Hello?"

He shuffled toward her.

"Adam?" She stood, dropping her purse on the ground beside the stone bench. "Is that you?"

He nodded, or at least she thought he did. His head barely moved, but she could have sworn it was a nod.

"What is it? Is something wrong?"

He made a rough, gurgling sound.

Cassie sank her hands onto her hips. "I have to tell you, this isn't earning brownie points with me. Everyone is waiting for you inside the museum."

He lumbered closer, his hands outstretched, reaching for her. He mumbled something indecipherable in a foreign language. She was fluent in Spanish, but he certainly wasn't speaking that. Neither was he muttering French or Portuguese. Greek? Latin?

"Adam," she repeated. "Is that you?"

Maybe she'd made a boo-boo and this wasn't him after all. She'd never met Adam in person.

"Beware . . . ," he whispered hoarsely, and then he started coughing.

"Are you okay?" She took a step toward him. "Do you need a glass of water?"

"Beware . . ." He raised a linen-wrapped hand to his throat and coughed again.

"Beware of what? Dry crackers?"

He repeated the foreign phrase.

She strained to listen. If she squinted real hard and turned her head in his direction, it sort of sounded like he was saying, "Wannamakemecomealot."

"Pardon?"

"Wannamakemecomealot."

"Oh, I get it, you're flirting with me." She grinned.

During their numerous transatlantic telephone conversations over the course of the past few weeks, as they made preparations for the exhibition, Cassie had nonchalantly let it slip that she adored surprises and fantasy role-playing games. Perhaps Adam had taken her suggestive comments to heart and decided to use the occasion of their first face-to-face meeting as an opportunity to seduce her.

Too fun.

"Let me guess. You're pretending we're in jeopardy. Bad guys are after us. Danger heightens the sexual attraction," she said. "It's a good game. You really had me going there for a minute."

He drew in another gurgling breath. He was doing a great job of sounding creepy.

"Is it the vizier's men? Are we pretending to be Kiya and Solen? Are they after us?"

"Beware of the . . ." He wavered on his feet, just inches from her.

Was he drunk? She hoped he wasn't drunk. She didn't like drunks.

"Spit it out, man. Stop being so cryptic. I know it's a game, but I can't get into it if you don't move things along. I have a short attention span. Everybody says so. Beware of what?"

But he didn't answer.

Wait a minute. Something wasn't right.

Ever since her near-drowning accident as a kid when she had spent three months in a coma, she occasionally experienced a weird sort of hotness at the very base of her brain. The sensation almost always preceded an unexpected turn of events. And right now her medulla oblongata was sizzling like skillet bacon.

Her nerve endings scorched a heated path from the nape of her neck to the tips of her ears. Burning, tingling, stinging.

Run, leave, get out of here.

Suddenly, the mummy pitched forward and Cassie thrust out her arms to catch him before he smashed face-first onto the stone walkway.

And that's when she saw the wicked, black-handled paring knife protruding from his back.

CHAPTER
3

An ominous feeling swept over Harrison. Something wasn't right, but he had no idea what was going on.

Stay calm, stay cool, stay detached from your feelings. He repeated his life mantra and exhaled slowly. Gradually his sense of dread abated.

That's when he realized he was still clutching the envelope Gabriel had given him. He ripped the flap open and dumped the contents into his palm. For some strange reason, he had expected to see Solen's half of the amulet. Instead, he was puzzled to find an airport baggage claim ticket.

Huh?

What was his brother trying to tell him? Why had he given the envelope to Gabriel rather than delivering it himself? What did the ticket mean? Had Adam left Solen and his artifacts in baggage claim at the DFW airport?

But why?

Considering Adam's look-at-me personality, whipping up an elaborate exploitation of the reunification ceremony was not a far-fetched notion. Harrison had a flash of insight. Although Adam claimed to believe wholeheartedly in the legend of the star-crossed lovers, his innate fear of ending up with egg on his face like Geraldo Rivera with Al Capone's empty safe could explain his motives. Adam would have to make sure *something* happened when the pieces of the amulet were joined together.

Harrison pulled out his cell phone. He hadn't talked to his brother in so long he'd forgotten his number, and it took him several seconds to remember it. Adam's voice mail answered, and Harrison left a message for him to call ASAP.

He wondered when Cassie had last heard from his brother and decided to go ask her. On the way to the courtyard, he palmed the ticket into his jacket pocket. He shouldered past King Tut, who was lip-locking Nefertiti behind a replica of a Minoan sailing ship from 1100 BC, and moved toward the side entrance.

He stopped with his hand on the exit door. Did he really want to meander into the courtyard and find Cassie in flagrante with a mummy?

If the door handle had been made of plutonium, he couldn't have jerked his hand away faster. He stepped back.

The room was uncomfortably hot and getting hotter by the minute. The party was too loud. He was breathing too fast. He felt claustrophobic. More than anything, he longed to be alone in a library studying ancient Egyptian lore, or knee-deep in sand at a new excavation site.

Calm down. Don't let the crowd rattle you.

He got his breathing under control just as a woman's screams erupted from the courtyard, and then the lights in the museum went out.

And all hell broke loose.

*   *   *

Panicked, Cassie backpedaled. The injured mummy slumped to the ground. She turned and ran full-out for the museum, her shoulder throbbing from the weight of his body, her nostrils filled with the smell of his blood.

Sprinting wasn't easy, considering the most rigorous exercise she got on a regular basis was blow-drying her hair straight, but she was scared witless and wanted out of there.

Now.

She reached the entrance and the lights winked out at the same time. The entire building was plunged into instant darkness. She couldn't see whose chest it was that she slammed into when she barreled through the door, but she could tell it was a masculine one.

Strong male arms embraced her.

Safe.

She couldn't see anything. The room was totally black. She heard people gasp. Then came the exclamations of fear and concern. Everyone was in a tizzy.

But she was all right. She felt the hardness of the man's honed chest beneath her fingers and she trembled, not with fear, but with something just as elemental.

"I'm here," he said.

It was almost as if he were inside her head and his mind was wrapped around hers. As if their hearts were beating to the same tempo. As if his breath were hers and hers his.

Bizarre.

Something about him arrested her. Something about his calm-in-the-storm aura filled her with a strong sense of déjà vu. She'd never felt such a compelling mental connection to any man in her life. She hadn't even believed such a bond was possible. And yet, here it was. Deep inside her, something monumental stirred. Something long-buried. Something hoped for and dreamed of but never dared spoken aloud.

Soul mate.

All the headlong giddiness and impulsiveness that had defined her life to this point vanished. As if for the first time since birth, she was sobered.

This was no mere flirtation. This was no simple tease. This was no ordinary male-female reaction.

Her skin tingled as the warmth of his breath feathered the minute hairs on her cheek. Her heart lub-dubbed frantically. The rough material of his jacket lightly scratched her bare arm. His masculine scent, an odd but pleasing combination of sand, soap, and old parchment paper, soothed her.

He smelled intriguingly like the Prado museum in Madrid where Cassie had worked as a foreign exchange student when she was in college. Bookish, old-worldly, solid. He was as hard and firm as she was soft and pliable. He tightened his grip on her shoulder, squeezing gently.

Her trembling increased.

"Cassie," he murmured. "Don't worry, I've got you. You're all right."

His voice was rich and earthy. He sounded the way mushrooms tasted, she found herself thinking dizzily—*shiitake, cremini, enoki, portobello, chanterelle.* But unlike mushrooms after a rain, his words did not sprout willy-nilly. He did not speak again, even while others crashed into things around them, cursing and complaining.

He was a rock. Gibraltar. Atlas.

Strong, present, unmoving.

She heard Phyllis Lambert urging everyone to stay

still and remain calm, reassuring the panicky crowd that the backup generator would kick on momentarily. But Cassie wasn't listening to the curator. She wanted to hear *him* speak again.

She curled her fingers around his wrist and whispered, "I'm scared."

"Nothing to be afraid of." His tone was low, measured, controlled. "I've got you."

His quiet, deliberate words inspired her. She fought an urge to beg him to fling aside those precise vocal notes and let loose in a careless, heartfelt rush of verbiage. She wanted to hear him breathe a cornucopia of language. Each sound falling upon the next, like kernels of corn slipping through a tin funnel.

Speak to me. Talk. Feed my ears.

Her twin sister, Maddie, teased her because she compared so many things to food, but Cassie embodied sensual experiences. She saw nothing wrong in associating a man's virile baritone with the lush sumptuousness of delicious mushrooms.

She loved to taste and smell everything. To lick and sup and dine. It was probably the main reason why she wore a size 14 instead of a 9. But who cared? She'd take sated over skinny any day. Plus, she'd never had any complaints about her cushy upholstery from her numerous suitors.

Cassie felt the heat of his hand at her waist, the pressure of his hip resting against her pelvis. She was disoriented, lost. All senses distorted. Thrown off balance by the lack of sight.

That had to be what this feeling was all about. It couldn't be anything more.

Could it?

Sounds were either too distant or too close, smells too sharp or too muted. The lingering cinnamon taste on her tongue was too immediate and too raw. The texture of his nubby jacket beneath her fingers too authentic and yet at the same time too surreal.

Her mind spun topsy-turvily.

For the moment, she forgot there was a mummy lying in the courtyard with a knife in his back. She forgot all about the botched party and the missing guest of honor and the nervous horde surrounding them. She forgot about everything except the feel of this stranger's virile arms around her and the echo of his sexy voice fading from her ears.

She was lost in time. Lost in the moment. Lost in the dark. It was the most erotic sensation she'd experienced in recent memory. Her reaction to the stranger was potent.

Whoa. Wait a minute.

Hadn't he called her by name? He couldn't be a stranger. He must know her. Who was he, her mysterious protector?

The pulse in her neck kicked.

At that precise moment the lights flickered on, and she found herself in Harrison Standish's arms.

Holy crap.

She stared at him.

No, it simply could not be. She could not be having such stunning feelings for this geeky intellectual who dressed funny. Somewhere, somebody's wires had gotten seriously crossed.

Harrison peered at her curiously through the lenses of his dark-frame glasses as if she were an interesting fossil he had just excavated.

"You," she whispered.

Immediately they jumped apart as if they had received a simultaneous electrical shock. Cassie couldn't have been more disconcerted if she had discovered she'd been French-kissing a boa constrictor.

Harrison glanced at the ceiling, the floor, out the glass door leading into the courtyard. Everywhere but into her eyes.

Everyone else seemed startled by the light as well. People stood around blinking and rubbing their eyes and shaking their heads.

And then Cassie remembered why she'd run screaming into the museum in the first place.

The mummy. His cryptic message. The knife.

"Murder," Cassie croaked. "In the courtyard. There's been a murder."

The mummy lay in the courtyard, barely breathing. In his palm he clutched a half-dollar-sized copper circle that exactly matched the ring in the museum display.

He had to hide the amulet. The consequences would be dire indeed if he failed.

Because *they* were coming for him. *They* would stop at nothing. And *they* would assassinate anyone who got in their way.

The pain was so blinding he could barely see, but he could not get caught with the amulet. Desperately, he tried to raise his head, to look around for some kind of hiding place.

His gaze fixed on a bright red shoulder-strap purse resting against the stone bench.

There. Perfect.

Not much time. Hurry, hurry.

But each tiny movement jarred his back, stabbed throughout his entire spine. His body throbbed and ached and burned. He drew a shallow breath and his lungs cried out.

Fight it off. You can't fail.

Gritting his teeth, the mummy pulled himself up on his elbows and dug them into the cobblestone walkway. Painstakingly, inch by awful inch, he dragged his body forward.

He didn't know if the streetlamps had flashed off in unison or if he had suddenly gone blind, but all at once he could not see.

He bit down on his bottom lip, urging himself onward. Go, go, go.

In the distance he heard noises, loud voices, crashing sounds. But he wasn't concerned with that. One thing dominated his mind.

Get rid of the amulet.

The pain was so agonizing that he didn't know if a minute had gone by or if it was a millennium, but at long last his hand reached out and struck against the supple leather handbag.

He fumbled inside.

His hands, wrapped in white linen like mittens, were clumsy and cold from shock. His search yielded a zippered compartment.

He opened the hiding place and slipped the amulet ring inside the pouch. He zipped it shut again and then shoved the purse as deeply as he could reach into the nearby bushes.

Later he could come back for it.

If there was a later.

He lay there panting, hoping he had outsmarted his attackers. Sweat dripped into his face; salt burned his eyes. He blinked even though he could not see.

And that was when two pairs of rough, careless hands reached down, grabbed him by the upper arms, and hauled him away in the darkness.

All the occupants of the exhibit hall erupted into the courtyard.

Osiris, Horus, two Nefertitis, three King Tuts. Anubis, Seth, Isis, and Ra. Harrison lost count as the courtyard filled up with more than a hundred curious guests. All the gods and goddesses of ancient Egypt converging upon Fort Worth, Texas.

And then he caught sight of Ahmose, the real Egyptian royalty, standing off to one side.

Harrison followed the group, but his brain was back there in the dark, holding a trembling Cassie close to his chest. He would have bet hard cash she was truly frightened and not putting on, but he wasn't about to place his trust in her.

Still, her sweet, delicate perfume enthralled him, clung to his clothes. She smelled like a garden, a bouquet, a spring event. Like some ripe, rich fruit in full bloom.

A scent like, oh, say, cherry blossoms?

The unexpected memory of that long-ago night in the Valley of the Kings when he had caught Jessica smooching Adam washed over him, and Harrison remembered why he'd started out to the courtyard in the first place.

To find out if Cassie knew what was going on with Adam.

But that had been before he'd held her in the dark, before the lights had come on and she'd looked both shocked and disappointed to discover he was the one holding her.

To Harrison's own mind, in the darkness, he had been someone else. Someone more like Adam. An easygoing guy with a fun-loving grin. A swashbuckling hero who knew how to dress, could court the ladies as easily as he could pick out the right wine for a gourmet feast, and wasn't so color-blind he couldn't tell blue from green.

Enough.

He had to stay mentally tough. He couldn't forget the woman was the antithesis of everything he valued.

"Well?" Phyllis Lambert said to Cassie. "Who got murdered? Where's the body?"

The crowd murmured, echoing the curator's questions. The courtyard was empty.

No body. No blood. No sign of a struggle.

Harrison pushed his glasses up on his nose and watched Cassie peer down at the cobblestones where she stood near the hedges. She looked confused.

And heartbreakingly vulnerable.

She nibbled her bottom lip and shifted her weight from foot to foot. She kept bobbing her head as if to convince herself she was right and everyone else's eyes were deceiving them.

"He was here before the lights went out, I swear," she declared. "A guy in a mummy costume, and he had a knife sticking out of his back."

"So who was this mysterious stranger?" Phyllis sank her hands on hips so narrow her palms slid right down her outer thighs.

Harrison had never seen Cassie distressed. He had the strangest urge to shove himself between the two of them and tell the curator to step off.

"I don't know," Cassie admitted.

For a minute the earnestness in her voice almost had Harrison believing that she was telling the truth, that there really was a backstabbed mummy crawling around in the bushes.

"You expect us to believe some guy with a Ginsu in his back just got up and toddled off?" Phyllis tapped her foot.

"I never said it was a Ginsu. It very well could have been a Henckels. I really didn't look that closely."

"That's not what I meant," Phyllis snapped. "Where's the damned mummy?"

Cassie's eyes widened. "Why don't we search the courtyard? He could be lying in the shrubbery, slowly bleeding to death."

Several people made a move to do just that.

Her urging aroused Harrison's suspicions. Why was she so interested in having the guests search the courtyard?

Had Adam planted a surprise? Was Cassie in on his publicity stunt?

"I found a purse," Osiris said, pulling a leather handbag from the bushes. He stood on tiptoe and peered down over the back of the hedge. "But I don't see any dead mummies lying around anywhere."

"That's mine." Cassie snatched the purse from him. "Thank you."

"Where's the blood?" Phyllis demanded, clearly growing tired of the charade. "Do you see any blood?"

"He wasn't bleeding much. The knife blade must have stanched the flow."

"A likely story." Phyllis narrowed her eyes. "What do you take me for? An idiot?"

"It's true. I came out here to meet him and . . ."

"You came outside to meet a man you didn't even know, when you were the hostess of the party and I explicitly told you to locate Dr. Grayfield?"

"I thought the mummy *was* Dr. Grayfield."

Now that was total bullshit.

Harrison stroked his jaw with a forefinger and thumb. He knew full well Adam couldn't have been in the mummy costume, because he'd been tearing through the exhibit hall in his Indiana Jones hat not fifteen minutes earlier. There hadn't been nearly enough time for him to park his motorcycle, swaddle himself in linen, run to the courtyard, get stabbed in the back, and then disappear again.

"Now why on earth would a man of Dr. Grayfield's distinguished stature slink around the courtyard in a mummy outfit?" Phyllis questioned.

Cassie's face flushed. "We've sort of been flirting with each other over the phone for the past few weeks while we made plans for the exhibit."

It figured. Harrison snorted silently. Adam was probably pulling some kind of stunt to impress Cassie. She was the kind of woman men did foolish things over.

"I've had it with your impetuousness," Phyllis snarled. "You know what I think?"

Cassie shook her head. Gone was her normally ebullient smile, and Harrison couldn't figure out why that would cause his stomach to knot. Impatiently, he shoved aside the unpleasant sensation.

The crowd shifted, glancing from Phyllis to Cassie and back again, waiting to see what was going to happen next.

"I think you made the whole thing up because you're

a drama queen who can't stand it when you're not the center of attention."

"No." Cassie's bottom lip quivered.

"And I never believed that line of malarkey you fed the FBI last year when you took off with that art thief. I think you were in on the deal all along, and when it looked like you were about to get caught and hauled off to prison, you pretended you were on the good guys' side."

Harrison couldn't tolerate watching anyone get raked over the coals, but neither did he like confrontation. Normally, he just walked away from a fracas. But with every passing moment, he was becoming more and more certain that Adam was involved in some kind of publicity exploit gone awry.

One question remained. Was Cassie part of Adam's scheme or not?

She looked pretty innocent with her wide, susceptible eyes and her silly Cleopatra wig knocked askew. Had Adam set up this mess and then disappeared on her? Or was Cassie a consummate actress who knew exactly what she was doing to elicit sympathy?

Either way, Adam had flown the coop, leaving only the baggage claim ticket in way of explanation. He'd put Harrison in something of a bind.

If the reunification ceremony didn't come off as scheduled, the Egyptian government would get testy. And if the Egyptian government got testy, the university backing his excavations would end up looking bad. And if the university ended up looking bad, he could kiss his funding good-bye.

Dammit, Adam. Thank you so much for screwing me over yet again.

"I wanted to fire you the minute I took over this job,"

Phyllis continued to harangue. "But the board of directors wouldn't allow it. Well, this time you've gone too far. You're out on your keister, Cooper."

Cassie gasped. "Ms. Lambert, please, you don't know the whole story. Let me explain."

"I don't want to hear it." Phyllis held up her palm in a talk-to-the-hand gesture.

Harrison couldn't allow Cassie to get fired. He might regret his decision later, but he had to do something to bail her out. He had to make her beholden to him. Then she couldn't refuse to answer when he asked her some very pointed questions concerning her involvement with his brother.

"Excuse me, Ms. Lambert." Harrison cleared his throat and fiddled with his bow tie. He had no idea what he was going to say.

"What is it, Harrison?" Phyllis's tone quickly changed from waspish to syrupy.

The curator had to suck up to him. Without Harrison there would be no Kiya, no star-crossed lovers exhibit. No one hundred well-heeled guests willing to shell out a thousand dollars apiece to see the show.

"Call me Dr. Standish," he said sternly. He didn't like brownnosers.

"Of course," Phyllis replied. "If that's what you'd prefer, Dr. Standish."

"I do prefer."

The guests had gone curiously quiet. One hundred bated breaths.

Waiting.

Quick! Astonish her with your brilliance.

Damn. He was lousy under pressure.

It turned out he didn't have to dazzle her with bullshit.

At that moment a security guard came rushing from the building. The man pushed through the crowd, panting and gesticulating wildly. "Ms. Lambert, Ms. Lambert!"

"What is it?" Phyllis snarled

"Come quickly. Kiya's amulet. It's been stolen!"

CHAPTER
4

The myriad gods and goddesses filed back into the museum with a grim-faced Phyllis Lambert marching at the head of the pack. Cassie brought up the rear, anxiously nibbling her bottom lip.

Which wasn't like her.

She never lagged behind and she rarely fretted, mainly because she didn't like thinking about anything that bummed her out. Plus, she hated chewing off her lipstick because she indulged too lavishly at the Neiman Marcus Lancôme counter. At twenty-eight dollars a tube, she'd learned to make her lipstick last.

But she'd just been fired. She was out of a job. So long, Smithsonian. Good-bye, Maddie.

Cassie swallowed the lump in her throat and told herself she would not tear up. She wasn't about to give Phyllis the satisfaction of making her cry.

Just ahead of her in the multitude, she spied Harrison and her heart thumped illogically. She didn't even like the guy. Why was her pulse speeding up?

As if sensing her gaze on the back of his head, he turned and glowered at her. Apparently he wasn't any fonder of her than she was of him, but he had stepped in and interrupted Phyllis when she'd been reading her the riot act.

The question was, Why?

She searched his face, looking for answers, but found none. The man was a master at hiding his emotions. Which in this instance was probably a good thing.

The entire group skidded to a halt in front of Kiya's now-empty display case. Phyllis took one look, narrowed her eyes, and spun around.

"Cooper!" she bellowed.

Cassie took a deep breath, marshaled her courage, and stepped forward. How much worse could it get? She had already been canned. What else could the irritable curator do to her?

"What is it, Phyllis?" she asked, making sure her tone sounded light, casual, and untroubled as she toed off with the woman.

"Now I realize what you were up to." Lambert shook a finger in her face. "Screaming and claiming there had been a murder in the courtyard. You were creating a distraction, luring us outside, while your accomplice shut off the electricity to deactivate the security alarms and stole the amulet."

The crowd inhaled a collective gasp of surprise. She could feel a hundred pair of staring eyes.

"Oh, no," Cassie denied. "You're wrong. That's not what happened at all."

She had been quite mistaken. Things could get worse. A lot worse.

"Detain her," Phyllis barked to the security guard, "while I alert the police."

The brawny security guard moved to firmly take hold of Cassie's arm.

"What a minute," Harrison blurted, nudging aside the guests until he was standing beside them. "Phyllis, obviously you didn't get the memo."

The curator looked puzzled. "Er, what memo?"

Cassie gaped at him, totally confused. What was he talking about? What was going on? Why was he trying to help? The guy hated her. She narrowed her eyes suspiciously.

Harrison sent her a look that said, *Just go along with me on this.*

As a rule, she wasn't a liar. She did not prevaricate without a darned fine reason. And she wouldn't allow someone to step in and take the blame for her. Especially not someone like Standoffish, who wasn't even pleasant to her under normal circumstances.

"Phyllis, I don't know what memo he's talking—," she started to say, but then Harrison gently but firmly trod on her toe.

Shut up, his chocolate eyes insisted.

Hey, hey, hey!

Purposefully, she jerked her foot out from under his brown tasseled loafer. She couldn't believe he was behaving so out of character. What was up?

"What Cassie means is that she doesn't understand why you didn't receive your memo," he said, muscling in and interrupting her in midsentence. "She sent it four days ago, after we cemented the plans."

"Clyde, did you get their memo?" The curator glanced over at her executive assistant, a pie-faced balding man in his early fifties.

Clyde Petalonus was dressed as George of the Jungle

in a cheetah-spotted loincloth with artificial kudzu vines draped around his neck. Poor Clyde didn't really have the figure for the ensemble. Cassie presumed he'd either gotten his Brendan Fraser movies mixed up, or his sense of geography was so terrible he actually thought there were jungles in Egypt.

"Sure thing. I got the memo," Clyde lied.

His reply took Cassie by surprise.

Why was Clyde lying? She knew he liked her and that he really disliked Phyllis. The curator had the annoying habit of sending him on "essential" errands the minute the man sat down for a meal in the employees' lounge. And the sneaky woman would always wait until Clyde had a cherry Pepsi poured over ice and his sandwich unwrapped or his frozen Hungry Man zapped in the microwave before she sprang the urgent assignment on him. But that wasn't explanation enough for him to risk his job over her.

She looked at him, and he gave her a quick smile that said, *Don't worry, I'll cover for you.* But she was worried. Why would he cover for her?

Maybe he wasn't covering for her. Maybe he was lying to protect himself. He was in charge of overseeing the crew that had set up the lighting for the exhibit. Maybe he was afraid Phyllis would accuse him of some culpability in the crime when she got done chewing out Cassie.

She might get fired, she might even get accused of stealing the amulet, but she knew she was innocent. Whatever Clyde's and Harrison's motives might be, she simply could not allow them to prevaricate on her account. She'd done nothing wrong. Phyllis couldn't pin a thing on her.

Could she?

"What memo?!" Phyllis's voice jumped an octave, and the tip of her nose turned blotchy red. "What are you talking about? What did this memo say?"

"Interactive murder mystery theater," Harrison supplied. The tone of his voice was calm and steady, but Cassie caught the jerk of a subtle tic at his right eyelid. He was nervous.

A general titter of delight undulated throughout the gathered crowd.

"What a marvelous idea," murmured Lashaundra Johnson, a reporter for the Arts and Entertainment section of the *Fort Worth Star-Telegram*. Lashaundra had written a feature on Cassie last year after she'd helped the FBI capture the art thief.

"I adore murder mystery theater," exclaimed a very prominent, very moneyed museum patron dressed as Isis. "Will there be prizes for the winner?"

Murmured speculation rippled throughout the room as the guests eagerly exchanged ideas and discussed suppositions. Harrison's fabrication was a huge hit.

"I don't understand." Phyllis impatiently tapped her foot. "Explain it to me."

"Give us more details," one of the King Tuts said. "Who is the mummy? Why was he in the courtyard? How is he connected to the legend of Kiya and Solen?"

"Wait, wait," Nefertiti said. "I'll need a pen and paper to keep this all straight."

"Me too," piped up Horus the Sky God.

"But what about Dr. Grayfield?" Phyllis asked dubiously. "What about the reunification ceremony?"

"Oh, that's not tonight." Harrison shook his head. Cassie admired his grace under pressure. To the casual observer he seemed totally composed, but she noticed he was squeezing his replica djed so tightly the muscles in his wrist bulged.

"Not tonight?" Phyllis repeated and frowned.

Not tonight? Cassie wondered.

"It's all in the memo." Harrison gave Phyllis a gosh-are-you-out-of-the-loop expression.

On the surface, he did not look like a man whose life's work had just jumped off that display case and walked out the door. He was pretty darn good at bluffing. But Cassie detected the telltale signs. His lips were pressed thin, and she saw a single bead of sweat glisten on his forehead.

"Let me get this straight, Dr. Standish. What you're telling me is that the amulet is not really missing. No one stole it?" Phyllis asked.

"That's correct."

Cassie adjusted her cumbersome headdress. What had happened to the amulet? She shot him a surreptitious glance, and the look he returned was so desperate that she knew for certain the amulet *had* been stolen and he was covering up the theft.

But why?

Because of her?

But that made no sense. Harrison barely knew her, and until tonight he'd acted as if he didn't care for her methods or her personality.

Was he simply using this opportunity to steal the amulet for himself? But why would he do that? He'd discovered the amulet. If he'd wanted to steal it, wouldn't he have done it when he first excavated it?

Should she back him up in the lie or blurt out the truth? What were Harrison's motives? Who had stabbed the mummy? Who was the mummy? Who'd turned off the lights? Who'd stolen the amulet? And most of all, where was Adam Grayfield? Things were weird and getting weirder by the minute.

"Where is the amulet?" Phyllis inclined her head toward the empty case.

"It's secured in a bank vault. The amulet on display was a copy made for the sake of the murder mystery theater. It was all in the memo."

"I wish I could see this memo. Clyde, do you still have your copy?" Phyllis crossed her arms over her chest.

"I deleted it from my e-mail," Clyde said.

"Since there doesn't seem to be a copy of this elusive memo, then you won't mind taking me to the safety-deposit box at the bank vault tomorrow morning and showing me the real amulet, Dr. Standish."

"I wish I could, Ms. Lambert, but Adam Grayfield has the key. He'll bring both halves with him to the reunification ceremony," he said.

"Dr. Grayfield is in on this too?"

"You could say it's his brainchild."

Was Adam party to this farce? Cassie frowned. Pondering these questions was giving her a headache. She didn't like thinking this hard.

"Oh. Well. Then I'll take you at your word." Apparently Phyllis was willing to give them enough rope to hang themselves. "What happens next?"

"The guests will have a chance to solve the mystery on their own, and then when everyone returns with their guesses, we'll give out the prizes and have the reunification ceremony," Harrison supplied.

Cassie realized he was trying to buy them time to figure out who took the amulet. She only prayed it worked before Phyllis became suspicious and called the police. She didn't know who Harrison was protecting or why, but if she went along with his plan, she would be up to her eyeballs in the conspiracy with him.

And the last thing she wanted was to be eyeball-deep in anything with the contentious, but oddly compelling, Harrison Standish.

She had to speak up.

But how?

"And when is everyone supposed to return for the re-unification ceremony?" Phyllis raised an eyebrow.

"Anyone who's interested in returning for the second part of the show will meet back here on Saturday night. Eight o'clock," Harrison said.

"What about the logistics of all these people returning?" Phyllis waved a hand. "Will there be another party?"

"Absolutely." Harrison nodded. "It was in the memo."

Another party on Saturday night! Cassie didn't have the budget for a second party, and it was only three days away. Would they be able to find Adam and the amulet in seventy-two hours?

"But I can't make it on Saturday," one of the King Tuts whined. "Will I get a refund?"

"This event is a charity fund-raiser for the Kimbell," Harrison said. "You're one of the most influential men in Fort Worth. Surely you will still want to make your contribution, even if your schedule doesn't permit you to return for the second party."

That shut King Tut up and put an end to a possible mass rush for refunds.

"Dr. Standish," Cassie said. She took his elbow and

squeezed it meaningfully. "May I speak with you in private about our mystery theater?"

"Right now?"

"Yes, right now."

"Phyllis," Harrison said and smiled at the pickle-faced woman, "could you give us a minute?"

"Of course." The curator's return smile was frosty. Clearly, Phyllis didn't want to go along with their story, but the guests were so excited about the murder mystery theater concept that she had little choice.

"Out in the courtyard, Standish," Cassie hissed.

She flounced away through the murmuring crowd. Harrison followed at her heels.

"What gives?" she demanded once they were outside. "What's with this interactive murder mystery theater crap?"

"I'm trying very hard to save your skin, along with my brother's miserable hide."

"Who in the heck is your brother?"

"Adam Grayfield."

"For real?" That was a shocker. Charming, romantic Adam was kin to this pigheaded cynic? The plot thickened. "But you have different last names."

"He didn't tell you?"

"If he'd told me, then I wouldn't be surprised that you two were siblings, now would I?"

"We're half brothers. We have the same mother, different fathers."

"That's all well and good, but please don't do me any more favors. I didn't ask you to do me any favors. Why *are* you doing me favors?"

The man was a certifiable nut job. Why was he under the mistaken impression that she needed saving? And even if she did need saving, she wasn't his to save. If she *was* searching for a Sir Galahad, she certainly wouldn't turn to Sir Gripes-a-Lot as a consolation prize.

Harrison's jaw hardened in that stubborn clinch she'd come to recognize and dread over the course of the past nine days. Whenever he set his mandible at that fight-or-die angle, Cassie had learned she was in for a protracted battle.

"I know what Adam's up to, and the way you've been waxing rhapsodically about him all week makes me wonder if you two might be in on this together. As far as I know, you might even be his lover."

"How can I be Adam's lover? I've never even met your brother in person, you ass," she snapped.

Harrison's cheeks flushed. Was he embarrassed over his false accusations? Or was he mad because she had called him an ass? He was lucky she hadn't called him worse.

"Besides, I have no clue what you're talking about," she finished.

"I'm talking about you two staging a publicity stunt involving Solen and Kiya as a way to milk the museum benefactors out of more money to fund Adam's future excavations."

"You are a petty, suspicious man, you know that?" Even though she felt a little guilty for sounding so harsh, Cassie refused to budge. She crossed her arms over her chest and glowered at him. To think that for one brief millisecond back there in the dark she had actually been sexually attracted to him.

Heaven forbid.

"I'm not petty and suspicious," he denied. "Not at all. But I do know my brother. He's a trickster. He loves games and treasure hunts. When it comes to Adam, I know exactly what to expect. You, Miss Cooper, are the wild card."

"I might be wild," she agreed, "but I don't pull stunts to dupe people out of their money. And I can't believe you think so little of your own brother."

Cassie was breathing hard and she didn't know why. For the longest moment, they glared at each other, gazes locked, temperatures rising.

"Why don't you try to call Adam and see if you can wring a confession from him?" she challenged.

"I will." Harrison took out his cell phone and punched in his brother's number. Voice mail answered. He hung up.

"Is he still incommunicado?"

"Apparently."

"Guess you'll just have to take my word for it that your brother and I are not in cahoots."

She could tell he didn't want to buy it, but at last he relented. "All right, I'll take you at your word, and I apologize if I offended you in any way."

He did have the good grace to look chagrined, and when he humbled himself he was less like a high-minded pompous ass and more like a real human being.

"Your apology is accepted," Cassie relented, uncrossing her arms.

"Thank you for not holding a grudge."

"Don't get too comfortable. You're on probation with me." She shook an index finger at him.

"As are you with me." His eyebrows bunched darkly. "I don't trust you."

"I don't even like you." She hardened her chin.

"Nor I you."

"You're arrogant and judgmental and contentious."

"And you're self-centered and overly opinionated and self-destructive."

"Obviously we don't get along." She wondered why she was so breathless.

"Not so much." He frowned and shook his head. He looked a little winded too.

"Great, as long as we have that established, could you clue me in? Where do you think your brother might be? Seeing as how my livelihood is on the line and all."

"Adam was here just a little while ago."

"You saw him at the museum?"

Harrison nodded.

"Did you talk to him?"

"I tried. He ran outside."

"Why'd he do that?"

Harrison shrugged. "I don't know. I thought you might have the answer."

"Not me. What did you do?"

"I followed him. Just as I hit the street, he took off around the corner on a custom Harley. He had Gabriel Martinez slip this to me."

Harrison pulled an envelope from his pocket, extracted a small rectangle of paper, and waved it under her nose.

"Looks like a baggage claim ticket from American Airlines," she said.

"Exactly," he crowed, like he was Columbo or Hercule Poirot or Perry Mason. Her mother was a huge mystery buff. Cassie had cut her teeth on late-night Charlie Chan reruns and could recite verbatim every title Agatha Christie ever wrote in order of publication date.

"I had to tell the white lie in order to buy us time with

Phyllis, so we could figure out what the baggage claim ticket means," Harrison said.

"It means there's baggage at the American Airlines terminal that needs picking up." What was the deal? She thought the guy was supposed to be some kind of Mensa genius.

"But whose baggage? And why hasn't it already been claimed?"

Cassie shrugged. "I dunno."

"If we get the baggage," he continued, "we might find the answer to Adam's whereabouts. Or a clue to who took the amulet, but we don't have time for honesty. Police rigmarole would slow us down for hours."

"There's something more you're not telling me. You're not too upset about the missing amulet. You're thinking that Adam's the one who took it, and you don't want to get him into trouble."

"No, I'm just good at cloaking my panic."

"Had me fooled."

"Actually I'm praying like hell that Adam *did* take it. If the amulet is truly missing and it's not part of my brother's crackpot ploy, then my life's work has vanished in a whiff of smoke." He snapped his fingers. "The Egyptian government is going to be extremely unhappy with me. If the amulet is not recovered, I'll lose not only my funding, but my visa to Egypt. My entire future is on the line."

"So that's your real motive for lying. To save your career. This isn't really about your brother. This is personal."

"Yes, okay," Harrison admitted. "It's personal. What's wrong with that? But I'm not as selfish as you want to believe. Even though the amulet represents everything that

I treasure deeply and hold dear, that's not what's important. The real travesty would be the loss of a precious artifact that gives us new insight into the ancient Egyptian culture. There's nothing more important to the future than an understanding of history. I've devoted my life to it, and I'll do anything to preserve it."

"Even lie?"

"Even lie."

Cassie blew out her breath, letting everything he'd told her sink in.

"Meanwhile, your boss is getting edgy." He nodded toward the exhibit hall. "So like it or not, we're in this mess together."

She peeked over his shoulder to see Phyllis standing behind the glass door, hands on hips, lips pursed disapprovingly.

"I'm not in the habit of lying," she whispered. "Not even to keep myself out of trouble."

"I don't lie either, dammit. But this is important. I just blurted it out. Believe me, I'm not an impulsive guy. I hate this as much as you do, probably more so. But this has to be done. For me, for my brother, for Egypt, for Kiya and Solen, but most important, for humankind."

What a moving speech!

She'd had no idea such passion lurked beneath his cool exterior. The moonlight glinted off Harrison's honed cheekbones, giving him a surprisingly knavish appearance in spite of his scholarly spectacles. An unexpected shiver tripped down her spine.

"You're cold," he said and removed his jacket.

Before she knew what he intended, he'd already slipped the hideous purple tweed jacket over her shoulders. She wanted to protest and hand it back to him, but she was cold. The jacket smelled of him, and the pleasantness of his scent caught her off guard.

She stuck her hands in his pocket and felt a cylindrical tube. It was the replica he'd made of the djed found in Kiya's tomb. Harrison had once told her that he was determined to discover the true use of the djed. Considering the size and shape, Cassie often wondered if it hadn't been anything more than an Egyptian sex toy, although Harrison would probably be horrified if she suggested such a thing.

"Please," he said. "I know this is not an optimal situation, but just go along with me."

"I'm sorry." She shook her head. "I can't lie."

"What happens," he asked softly, "if my brother has stolen the amulet and you're left holding the bag? You two planned this event together. You expect Phyllis to believe you weren't part of it? Especially after that stabbed, disappearing mummy escapade you pulled."

"I didn't pull anything. A mummy *was* stabbed in the courtyard."

"Either way, Phyllis is gunning for you."

"You noticed that too? I'm not just paranoid?"

"Who could miss the animosity? She almost hisses whenever you walk by."

Well, thank you very much. At least someone else had confirmed Cassie's suspicion that Phyllis hated her guts.

"Would Adam hang me out to dry?" she asked. "He doesn't seem the sort of guy who would do something like that."

"I would hate to believe it of him, but honestly I don't know. The murder mystery theater is our best temporary solution. If Adam is just pulling a publicity stunt, we successfully nip it in the bud. If not . . ." He didn't complete the sentence, leaving the rest of his unspoken words up to her vivid imagination.

Cassie's pulse spiked and a surge of excitement shot through her. Her exploits with the art thief last year had given her a taste for crime solving.

"All I'm asking is for three days to locate my brother," Harrison continued, "and straighten this whole thing out. It's probably a simple misunderstanding."

"And what happens if we can't find Adam or the amulet by Saturday?"

"I'll report it to the police and explain what happened. I'll tell them I coerced you into going along with me. In the meantime, you'll still have your job, and the guests will get a big kick out of playing sleuth. And if everything turns out okay, I'll make certain you get that recommendation to the Smithsonian. Adam's father is Tom Grayfield, the U.S. ambassador to Greece, and he has a lot of influence in Washington. He could pull strings."

"I don't know what to do."

"Whichever way you decide to go," Harrison said, "lie or tell the truth, you're already in trouble."

That was true. Even though she wasn't involved with the theft of the amulet, Phyllis was ready to hang her from the highest tree based on circumstances alone.

"So what do you say?" He argued a good case, but she was still afraid to trust him.

"I'm not sure I can."

She saw that he wasn't a man accustomed to asking for favors. But she could also see he was very worried about his brother and his career. She was worried too. Empathy could do terrible things to a woman.

"And if everything doesn't turn out the way you foresee it?" Cassie murmured, bracing herself for the answer she did not want to hear.

Harrison grimaced and shook his head. "Then we're both royally screwed."

CHAPTER
5

Royally screwed indeed.

How had he gotten entangled in such an abysmal state of affairs?

Impulsive behavior didn't solve problems, it created them. Rational men thought before they spoke. Tonight, he had been anything but rational, and now he was paying the price.

Following the disappearance of Kiya's amulet, Ahmose Akvar had taken him aside and privately reiterated his earlier warning: *If anything happens to the amulet, your visa will be rescinded and you will never again be allowed inside Egypt.*

Exiled.

For Harrison, who had devoted his life to the study of ancient Egypt, banishment from his adopted country was unimaginable. To top things off, Phyllis Lambert had cornered him and issued a similar veiled threat, whispering that if she discovered he was covering for Cassie, she would report him to the head of the archaeology department at the University of Texas at Arlington, where Harrison taught as an adjunct professor. Hinting that she would make certain he lost his job.

Thanks a lot, Adam. I hope you have a damn good reason for absconding with the amulet. Because if you're not in trouble now, you will be when I get my hands on you.

The guests had finally departed the museum after Cassie's briefing. She'd concocted a spur-of-the-moment murder mystery tale so brilliant in detail, she'd mesmerized even Harrison. Her cock-and-bull story was one-third legend of the lost lovers, one-third reality, and one-third creative fabrication. Grudgingly, he had to admit the woman, however irritating, possessed an incredible talent for adapting to shifting circumstances.

A skill he sorely lacked.

He resented his need for her help. If he had his way, he would ditch her posthaste and go in search of Adam on his own.

But other than Gabriel Martinez, who'd merely been given the white envelope from his brother, Cassie was the last known person to have spoken at length with Adam. And even though she professed otherwise, Harrison still wasn't sure he could trust her.

Was she lying to protect his brother? She claimed they weren't lovers, and for some asinine reason he wanted to take her at her word.

It was all too coincidental. The mummy stabbed, his brother missing, the lights going out, the theft of the amulet. Cassie had to have more information than she was letting on, whether she consciously knew it or not.

"Hey, Harry, why so down in the mouth?"

They were the last ones left in the building except for the armed security guards and the janitors. Phyllis Lambert had just walked out the door with one last ominous word of warning that they had better produce the amulet come Saturday night or there would be hell to pay.

"Excuse me?" He scowled.

Cassie slung her purse over her shoulder, and she was still wearing his jacket. "You look like your best buddy just ran off with your wife and squashed your favorite puppy under the tires of his jacked-up monster truck on their way out the gate."

"Colorful analogy," he said. "If somewhat country-and-western-songish in nature. But I don't have a wife. Or a puppy."

Or a best buddy.

His friends were his colleagues. Outside of work he didn't hang around with the guys. He didn't enjoy shooting pool or drinking beer or yelling insults at football players on television. Harrison knew he was an odd duck, but he couldn't help the way he was. He liked being alone with this thoughts and his books. His time was precious. He didn't waste it on trivial pursuits.

Or trivial emotions.

Cassie rolled her eyes. "It was a joke, for heaven's sake. Ha-ha-ha. Lighten up, dude. Do you always have to take everything so literally?"

"I don't know any other way to view the world." Harrison held the exit door open for Cassie to walk through.

"I take that as a yes." She sighed.

"You find my objectivity tiresome?"

"Exasperating," she said. "There's no fun in logic."

"Maybe not, but there's logic in logic."

She gave him a sidelong glance, and he did his best to ignore the suggestive look she angled his way. He wasn't getting involved with her on a personal level. No way, nohow.

"Then again, I'm guessing you've never been accused of having too much fun."

Harrison ignored the comment. Ignored her. Well, as much as he could. Ignoring Cassie was a bit like ignoring a major force of nature.

The security guard locked the door after them and Harrison realized their cars, his ten-year-old Volvo and Cassie's late-model Mustang convertible, were parked at opposite ends of the lot. He couldn't distinguish shades of colors well, but he would bet the baggage claim ticket in his pocket that her car was a flaming "ogle-me" scarlet.

"So what's the plan, Stan? What's on the agenda, Brenda? Where do we start to sleuth, Ruth?" She was jumping around, swinging her arms, acting like a nervous thoroughbred eager to shoot from the starting gate.

"Are you always so hyper?"

"Always," she promised.

"Remind me never to give you sugar."

"As if I'd remind you of that. Chocolate is my middle name."

"Explains the hyperactivity," he muttered.

"Anyway, what's the scheme, Kareem?"

"I've calculated that the best use of time would be to head for the airport tonight and check out this baggage claim ticket. Put our heads together and see if we can determine what might have happened."

She gave him a thumbs-up. "I'm with you."

"Whose vehicle should we take to the airport?"

"Not mine, unless you don't mind stopping for gas," she said. "The empty light flashed on just as I was pulling into the parking lot this morning."

"You don't fill up when your gas gauge gets to the halfway mark?"

She squinted at him, incredulous. "Good God, no. Do you?"

Yes, he did, but Harrison wasn't about to admit it when she was staring at him like he had just sprouted a second head. He had a momentary flash of insight into Cassie's driving. He could just see her careening down the highway, talking nonstop on her cell phone, rock music blasting from the stereo speakers, her eyes everywhere but on the road. Anyone that drove around with their empty light flashing had to be an irresponsible driver.

"Never mind," he said, taking her elbow and hustling her toward the Volvo. "I'll drive."

"Oooh, Harry." She batted her eyelashes at him. "I never imagined you were the forceful, take-charge type."

"Knock off the eyelash batting. It won't get you anywhere with me."

"You think I'm flirting with you?"

"Yes."

"Please, don't flatter yourself. I flirt with everyone. You're no more special than the checkout boy at Albertsons."

Harrison's cheeks burned. She did flirt with everyone. "Just don't do it with me."

"Don't worry, chum. The last thing on earth I'd want is to 'do it' with you."

Dammit. She'd twisted his words.

"Listen, since we're forced to spend time together, could you please keep the sexual innuendos to a minimum?" he said.

"Aww, whazza matter, Harry? Get up on the wrong side of the bed this morning?"

When and why had she switched from calling him Standish and started addressing him as Harry?

"Stop calling me Harry," he growled. "I don't care for that particular moniker."

"Harrison's too uptight."

"I like uptight."

"I never would have guessed."

"You're big on sarcasm too."

"When it suits me." She stroked her chin with her thumb and index finger pensively. "Hank, then? You like Hank better?"

"Hank is a nickname for Henry, not Harrison."

"Yeah, but I could call you Hank if I wanted to, right? It's a free country." She blithely waved a hand.

"Don't call me either Harry or Hank." He gritted his teeth. "It's Harrison. Just Harrison."

"Okay, Harry's son." She shrugged and grinned mischievously. "Whatever you say."

With a grunt of displeasure, Harrison thrust a hand in his pocket, plucked out his keys, and opened the passenger door so she could slide in. *I won't throttle her, I won't throttle her, I won't throttle her.*

She wasn't worth a murder charge. That much was certain. Normally he was slow to anger, but there was something about this woman that rubbed him the wrong way.

Unfortunately, his testosterone was shouting, "Wrong way, right way, who cares, just as long as she rubs you."

He slammed the door after she got in. Briefly, he closed his eyes and swallowed hard.

Stay calm, stay cool, stay detached from your feelings.

The chant soothed him the way chocolate chip cookies soothed a carboholic. He felt his anger lift as he mentally disengaged from the moment. With a cool inner eye, he watched himself walk around to the driver's side and then ease behind the wheel.

That was better. No pesky anger to muddle his thinking.

"Hey, Harry," Cassie said huskily, her voice a velvet stroke against his ears as he started the engine.

"It's Harrison." He forced himself not to clench his teeth over her use of the unsavory nickname. Clenched teeth indicated irritation, and he wasn't irritated. He was aloof, far above his base emotions. This flighty woman couldn't touch him.

"Anyone ever tell you that you're really cute when you're pissed?"

"I'm not pissed," Harrison denied, and told himself the sweat pooling under his collar had absolutely nothing to do with her frank teasing.

"Coulda fooled me," she said lightly. "Oh, by the way, we have to stop off at my apartment."

"Good grief, what for?" Against his better judgment, he glanced over at her.

She had her stiletto sandals peeled off and her feet propped up against the glove compartment. He hated that she had her bare feet on his dash, but at the same time he loved the sight of her delicate toes, painted a light, pearly hue, wriggling in the dome light.

"I can't go to the airport dressed like this." She blithely swept a hand at her skimpy Cleopatra costume. The skirt hem had ridden up when she'd sat down, exposing a long expanse of round feminine thigh.

He swallowed hard. "You know, this is rather urgent. We've got less than seventy-two hours to find my brother and solve this mystery."

"I hafta go home and change. Hang a left at Seventh

Street. My apartment is on the next road over." She had a point about traipsing around in public in that diaphanous Cleopatra garb.

"My brother's missing," he said. "Kiya's amulet's been stolen, and my life is unraveling before my very eyes."

And, he mentally added, *I'm stuck with a free-spirited fruitcake of a woman.*

"It won't take ten minutes, I promise."

He wanted to be adamant and say no, but Cassie was so damned irresistible with her perky, expectant smile and her goofy, yet strangely winsome ways, he found himself doing exactly as she asked.

Five minutes later they were at her apartment.

"To speed things up, I'll just wait for you in the car."

"You're gonna sit out here in the dark all by your lonesome?" she picked at him.

He patted his dashboard. "I can listen to NPR."

"What is it, Harry? Are you just antisocial, or are you too scared to be alone with me?"

"I'm in a hurry, that's all."

"Prove you're not scared of me. Come up to my apartment."

He gritted his teeth. Damn, the woman could vex a Zen monk. To prove her wrong, he shut off the engine and followed her up to the second-floor landing.

It had been a long time since he'd been alone with a woman at her place, especially a woman as sexy as this one; maybe he was a little nervous. But he didn't want her to know that. He tried his best to look composed and nonchalant, but ended up tripping over the doorsill because he was too busy watching her derriere sway.

Cassie put out a hand to stop his forward momentum. "Are you okay?"

He nodded, feeling like he was back in high school, standing at his locker next to the gorgeous prom queen who dated the first-string quarterback that used to beat him up on a regular basis.

Would he ever stop feeling like a wimpy nerd when it came to women? Probably not. Especially with a woman like Cassie who could have any guy she wanted.

She wrapped her hand around his bicep and her eyes widened with surprise. "Why Harrison, you dawg, you work out."

He shrugged and pushed up his glasses, unnerved by the teasing awe in her voice. "Now and again."

"Now and again doesn't give a man muscles like these." She squeezed his arm. "You're hitting the weights at least three times a week. I should know. My identical twin sister is an Olympic athlete, and she's a rock."

"I didn't know you had a twin," he said, mostly to change the subject, but also because he was fascinated to learn this tidbit. There were two of her?

"But Maddie and I are nothing alike. She just won a gold medal in track and field, and me, I'd rather get forty licks with a wet noodle than sprint from here to my mailbox. We're as opposite as twins can get."

Well, that was a relief. He couldn't imagine two identical Cassies let loose on an unsuspecting world.

"Have a seat," she said. "I'll go change."

"I don't need to have a seat. It's only going to take you a couple of minutes, remember?"

"Suit yourself." She waggled her fingers and ambled down the hall.

"Hurry. We need to get a move on." Harrison cleared

his throat and tried not to fidget. No matter how hard he fought to block the visage, he kept visualizing her slipping out of the silky white goddess toga-thingy she was wearing.

"You can turn on the TV if you want."

"We're not going to be here that long," he called as she disappeared into her bedroom.

He ended up plunking down on the couch because he didn't know what else to do with himself. Cassie's apartment was as harum-scarum as she was. The cluttered decor was in sharp contrast to his own austere living quarters, where everything was monochromatic and totally bric-a-brac free. His house contained no extras except for his home office, which was filled with neatly cataloged artifacts.

No doubt about it. He would go crazy if he had to live in such chaos. He resisted the urge to get up and start cleaning.

Knickknacks lay jumbled across every bit of available cabinet space. Porcelain kittens decorated a wall shelf. An overgrowth of ivy spilled from a plant stand and curled along the window ledge. In the corner stood three umbrellas, one of them open. Books sprawled on the bar between the living area and the kitchen, and a roll of unopened triple-ply toilet paper leaned against a bottle of extra-hold hairspray.

Clearly, she had never heard the phrase "a place for everything and everything in its place."

There was a half-finished jigsaw puzzle on the coffee table and a three-quarters-empty glass of chocolate milk. In a tote bag beside the couch he spied a half-knitted afghan. Twinkle lights were stapled to the mantel, and

Harrison didn't know if they were left over from Christ-mas or simply part of her willy-nilly decorating scheme.

He was beginning to see a theme emerging. Cassie had a difficult time finishing what she started.

He glanced at his wristwatch. Ten-forty. Time was wasting. What in the world was taking so long?

"Hurry," he hollered, and when she didn't respond, he took out his phone and tried to call Adam. Voice mail again. He left another message.

"Harry?" Cassie's voice drifted from the bedroom.

He jumped as if he'd been caught doing something il-legal. He closed his cell phone. "Uh-huh?"

"Um . . ." She paused. "Could you come in here a minute? I could use a hand."

She required his help in the bedroom? What did that mean?

In his head, he heard the sound track from one of those cheesy soft-core porn movies that came on Cinemax late at night. Not that he watched them. Much.

Dow-shicka-dow-now.

"Harry?"

"Ulp . . . er . . ." Jeez, he was sweating. He adjusted his glasses and shifted uncomfortably on the couch.

"Please," she coaxed in that breathless way of hers that could turn a man's insides to soup. "I'm in something of a pickle."

Dow-shicka-dow-now.

This was sounding more and more like a bad script for some X-rated flick. Why was his heart knocking like a jalopy engine? He hadn't violated his personal code of ethics.

Well, as long as you didn't count sexual fantasies.

"I need you . . . ," she wheedled.

His instincts urged him to hit the door at a dead run. If Cassie had hanky-panky on her brain and she intended on seducing him, there was no way he could resist. But why would she choose this moment to come on to him? Particularly when she didn't even seem to like him very much.

Hell, who could know why the loopy woman did anything?

"Harry," her voice drew him.

Mesmerized, Harrison left the couch and edged down the hallway.

Her bedroom door stood slightly ajar as he approached with the mind-set of a warrior going into battle. If she was stretched out naked across the bed, giving him a come-hither look, he would retreat.

Um-hmm, yeah, sure. Uh-huh.

He would!

And when was the last time a delicious woman threw herself at you? Yep, never. Dream on, Romeo. If Cassie is buck naked on that bed, with lust for you gleaming in her eyes, you ain't about to turn tail and run.

He reached the door and hesitated.

"Could you possibly hurry it up? I'm in something of a compromising position."

Holy jeez, she *was* trying to seduce him.

The hairs on his arms lifted. He felt simultaneously panicky and thrilled and immediately tried to squelch the feelings. But they were unsquelchable.

Are you a man or a mouse, Harry?

Aw hell, now she had him calling himself by that atrocious nickname. Conflicted, he just stood there.

From inside the bedroom he heard a thumping noise.

"Did you leave?" Her voice sounded faraway and a little tremulous now. Like she was sad or in trouble or both.

And that's what got to him. The lost-little-girl quality in her voice and the notion that she needed him.

Emboldened, he marched into her bedroom.

Only to learn she was nowhere in sight.

He glanced around at the unmade four-poster bed covered by a canopy of some sheer girly-looking material. At least ten different pairs of shoes littered the floor, along with a blouse or two. A plaid miniskirt was thrown over the television set perched on a wicker dresser in the corner.

Talk about your lurid Catholic schoolgirl fantasies.

He jerked his head away, desperate for something less provocative to stare at. Three curio shelves lined the north wall, all three stocked with a variety of scented Yankee candles, and even though they weren't lit, the scents were still potent. The cacophony of aromas assaulted his nose. Peach parfait, freshly laundered linen, hazelnut coffee, pineapple-coconut, summer rose garden.

Hadn't anyone ever told the woman you weren't supposed to hodgepodge scents? The smell was too sweet, too intense, too overwhelming.

Much like Cassie herself.

What he lacked in visual acuity, God had made up for by supplying him with a highly attuned sense of smell. To Harrison's nose, her bedroom smelled the way a thirty-piece orchestra would sound if all the instruments were playing a different tune at once.

Olfactory bedlam.

Squinting, he noticed a collection of mini-collages tacked onto the wall behind each candle. Morbid curiosity, the quality his mother had sworn would be his ultimate downfall, propelled Harrison toward the candle wall for closer examination.

The collages were displayed in three-dimensional, eight-by-ten picture frames. In the center of each assortment was a photograph of Cassie with a different guy. Various memorabilia surrounded the photographs. Movie tickets, sports team pennants, lapel pins, charms, scrapbook lettering, stickers, swatches of fabric, and even a Top Forty playlist for the time period.

He counted the candles and framed memorabilia. Eighteen. Six on each shelf.

What in the heck was this?

Suddenly, Harrison realized what he was looking at. The wall was a shrine. To the men Cassie had known. Startled, he leaped back and ended up stumbling over a silk pillow thrown haphazardly on the floor. He lost his balance and crashed into the dressing table, knocking over a lamp in the process.

"Harry, is that you? I thought you'd run out on me and left me stranded. Are you all right?"

"Fine, I'm fine," Harrison muttered. "But where are you?" He righted the lamp, ran a hand through his hair, and struggled not to think about the significance of her candle wall.

"I'm in the bathroom."

Not good. Not good at all.

"The bathroom?" he repeated, because he did not know what else to say. Goose bumps spread up his arms like a bad case of the measles.

The *dow-shicka-dow-now* music twanged inside his head again.

"Yep."

"Why are you hiding in the bathroom?" he asked, even though he did not want to know.

"Because I'm embarrassed."

"Embarrassed?" he echoed.

"Before you come inside, I gotta know something. Do you shock easily? I get the feeling you shock easily, and this is a job for a man who doesn't shock easily."

"I don't shock *that* easily." Good God, what was happening in there?

"You sure?"

"For heaven's sake, just tell me what's going on. Nothing could be as shocking as my imagination."

Her voice turned teasing again. "Harry, just what *are* you imagining?"

Enough coyness.

Mentally girding his loins, he prepared his eyes for whatever unexpected sight might greet them. He placed a hand on the bathroom doorknob and slowly twisted it open.

Cassie was standing beside the vanity, her back to him, her shoulders slumped. A pair of hip-hugger jeans and a long-sleeved T-shirt had replaced the Cleopatra costume. The tight pants molded snugly against her well-rounded bottom, and the pockets were boldly embroidered with the Cadillac emblems.

Instantly, he understood the message. Here was a plush ride.

As Adam would say, *bootylicious.*

No matter how hard he tried, he could not stop ogling that fabulous fanny. The Flemish artist Rubens would have salivated for the opportunity of capturing such a lovely backside on canvas. Harrison found his own mouth growing moist.

"Cassie?"

She did not move. "Before I turn around, you have to promise me something."

"What's that?"

"You won't laugh."

"I promise I won't laugh. Please, just let me see what's causing you so much distress."

Slowly, she turned toward him.

He was so busy watching her facial expression, which was a touching combination of embarrassment, chagrin, and discomfort, that at first he did not notice that her blue jeans were only halfway zipped up.

First his gaze hung on the tiny heart tattooed at the level of her hip bone. It was no bigger than his thumbnail, discreet, tasteful, and yet it was still a tattoo. Wild women got tattoos. Or at least that's what he supposed.

Sexual awareness so strong it jarred his fillings zapped from his brain straight to his groin. He'd never found tattoos sexy before. Why now?

Was this what she'd called him in here for? To show him her tattoo?

Dow-shicka-dow-now.

It was only when she shrugged helplessly and splayed her hands in front of her fly that he realized the silky material of her skimpy black thong panties was wedged firmly in the teeth of her zipper.

CHAPTER
6

I was trying to hurry up for you, and look what happened," Cassie said.

Harrison dropped to his knees in front of her, the manicure scissors she'd retrieved from her makeup vanity clutched firmly in his hand.

"I hate that you have to cut them," Cassie muttered. "These panties are from Victoria's Secret, and I'm not about to tell you how much they cost."

"The material is jammed in tight; there's no other way around it unless you can shimmy out of those jeans."

"Don't you think I already tried that? The zipper isn't down low enough for me to edge the pants over my hips."

His breath was warm against her skin as he leaned forward and grasped the zipper. Cassie looked down at the top of his dark head planted startlingly close to her most private area. His hair grazed her bare belly and she just about came undone.

How did she keep getting herself into these sticky predicaments?

She closed her eyes against the hot, moist sensation

gathering low inside her. She was forced to brace her palms against the counter at her back to keep from toppling over on legs suddenly gone to Silly Putty.

What in the hell was the matter with her? Why was Harrison Standish, of all people, making her weak in the knees?

"Hold still," he muttered.

"I wasn't moving," she denied, not wanting him to know how much he affected her.

"You were swaying like a palm tree."

"Was not."

"I'm not going to argue with you. Just hold steady unless you want to get poked with these scissors."

She wanted to get poked, all right, but not with scissors.

Cassie!

She'd shocked even herself. How come she was so turned on? She had never been sexually attracted to a dude that she didn't even like.

It felt weird. It felt kinky.

It felt like sex outside in a lightning storm.

Unbidden, she had a sudden visual of the two of them doing the wild thing in a rowboat on a lake in the summer with a light spring shower pelting their heated skins.

Stop it.

The boat was bobbing. Birds twittered in the trees along the shore. The cotton-candy pink dress she wore was pushed up around her waist, the gauzy material clinging to her hard nipples as Professor Standish studiously explored every nook and cranny of her willing body.

In real life, his fingertips skimmed lightly over her skin and Cassie inhaled sharply. Yeah, baby. More of that. Oh, she was an unrepentant slut puppy!

"I'm sorry," Harry said rather gruffly. "I didn't mean to hurt you."

Hurts sooo good, her audacious side wanted to say, but luckily she was prudent enough to keep her mouth shut. Nevertheless, a shudder ran through her.

"You okay?" he asked, tilting his head to peer up at her.

"Just a little chilled with myself so exposed."

He made a noise that sounded like someone being strangled.

Turnabout was fair play. "You okay?"

"Just clearing my throat."

"You need a glass of water or something?"

"I'm fine," he mumbled. "I just want to hurry and get this over with."

Aw, don't hurry, whined her impish voice. *I like things nice and slow.*

Knock it off, she scolded herself. Think of something besides the fact his touch is so tickle soft it's giving you goose bumps.

Let's see. What could she think about? She wasn't much of a protracted thinker.

Hmm. She'd never noticed before how broad his shoulders were. He'd be a dazzler in a tux if he had a decent haircut and contact lenses.

There you go again, imagining him as a sexy stud. He's not a hidden hunk in geek's clothing. He's a nerd with a capital N.

Okay, okay. How's this? Think about the difference between Harry and Adam. While she had never met Adam in person, she knew ten times more about him than she did about Harry.

Adam was an outrageous flirt who loved to take

chances. And just like her, he enjoyed driving flashy cars really fast. His favorite food was lobster. His favorite color was aquamarine. His favorite video game was *Grand Theft Auto*. In high school, he'd won the starring role in *Damn Yankees*. And in college, his GPA had been the exact same as hers, 2.75. Adam read *GQ* religiously, owned the latest and greatest electronic gadgets, and he'd never once told her he had a brother.

What she knew about Dr. Harrison Standish could fit in a tube of lipstick. He was a bad dresser, and he mumbled under his breath a lot when things didn't go his way. He drove a white Volvo, and apparently he filled up whenever the gas gauge reached the halfway mark.

Ack! What a blah, safe car. Come to think of it, the Volvo was much too clean. No fast-food wrappers stuffed in the side door pockets, nothing cute dangling from the rearview mirror, no smushed bug guts on the windshield.

She would go crazy if she had to drive around in his spick-and-span-mobile.

"All done."

"Huh?" Cassie blinked.

Harrison had risen to his feet and was staring at her kind of funny. As if she had spinach in her teeth or something equally gauche.

"You're free. Panties clipped out of the zipper." Awkwardly, he handed her the manicure scissors.

She completely understood his awkwardness. She too was feeling decidedly ill at ease. Her idiotic hormones wanted to tango with Harry something fierce, while mentally she was much more in sync with his brother, Adam.

Her eyes locked onto his butt, which somehow managed to look sensational in spite of the baggy Dockers, as he walked out of the bathroom. She had to stop getting herself into these sticky predicaments.

At least for the next three days.

Across town in an abandoned warehouse, the man in the mummy costume slowly regained consciousness. The throbbing in his back was almost unbearable. Each tiny movement sent jolts of pain shooting down his spine. His lips were cracked, and his mouth was so dry that he could hardly swallow.

He frowned, and even that tiny movement caused intense pain. He realized he was lying facedown in metal shavings on a cement floor that smelled of rat excrement, and his wrists were duct-taped behind his back.

Not a good sign.

Nausea roiled his stomach. God, he couldn't puke. He must not puke. He moved his head to get his nostrils out of the metal shavings, before he accidentally inhaled them, and stared glumly across the floor.

The room was badly lit by a dim fluorescent bulb. He saw large sheets of corrugated tin stacked in piles all around him. Beyond the stacks he could make out heavy, double-rollered doors. The sharp bite of pain that blasted into his head wouldn't allow him to look any higher. He felt shapeless.

Boneless.

As desiccated as a mummy.

Pulp. Living mush. Mashed. Squashed. Pulverized. Hot. Red. Burning.

His back was a furnace. He could not think. Could scarcely breathe.

No.

He could not allow himself to be consumed. There was

something he must do. Something vitally important. Except he couldn't remember what it was.

Think.

But his mind was a blank. He closed his eyes. Think, think, think.

Where was he? Why was he here? Why did his back hurt like the belly of Hades?

He lay there for what seemed an eternity, his mind a sticky cobweb of jumbled thoughts. None of it connecting. None of it making sense. In his mind's eye he could see a red purse lying beside a stone bench, but he had no idea of its significance.

Awareness came and went in waves. First he was acutely aware of every physical ache, and then he would nod off, sleeping in brief snatches. Then he'd awaken, confused all over again.

Finally, there came a sharp intrusion to his mental meanderings.

He heard noises.

Footsteps.

Voices.

Low and argumentative. Originating from somewhere beyond his blurry field of vision. Speaking in a language he recognized, but not his native tongue.

Concentrate.

He strained to listen.

Greek. He recognized the language now. The men were speaking Greek. But they were too far away for him to hear what they were arguing about.

It's Greek to me, the mummy thought giddily and almost laughed.

Were they friend or foe? Considering he was tied up in a rat-infested warehouse stocked with sheet metal, it would be a good guess that they weren't his best drinking buddies.

Sweat trickled down his neck as they drew closer. Then the footsteps stopped just outside the door.

"Hold on to your temper this time, Demitri," a man who sounded like a bullfrog with a bad cold said in English. "You almost killed him when you stabbed him."

"I can't believe we are treating him with kid gloves," the man presumably called Demitri retorted. "He's trying to destroy everything."

Their voices sounded vaguely familiar. Especially the Louis Armstrong soundalike. But their identities wavered just out of reach. Maybe he didn't know them. He could be mistaken.

"Patience," said Croupy Bullfrog Man. "If you ever want to advance beyond apprentice then you must develop patience."

Who were these guys? Did he know them? Should he know them?

The mummy strained against the duct tape, but it would not yield. There wouldn't have been time to run even if the tape had given way. Plus, he wasn't in any condition to fight off a Girl Scout, much less two grown men.

He heard the mechanical whirring noise of the door being hoisted on its rollers. Squinting in the dimness, he saw two sets of feet round the corner of the metal stacks. One wore dirty Nike sneakers; the other guy had on patent-leather wing tips.

Wing Tips hung back.

Mr. Nike approached.

He had an awful feeling that the backstabbing, temperamental Demitri was the one in the sneakers. He closed his eyes, slowed his breathing, and pretended to be unconscious.

The tip of an angry Nike caught him hard and low in the rib cage.

The mummy grunted, biting his bottom lip against the pain. It wasn't only his ribs that took the jolt, but his entire spine.

The man squatted, peered at him. It was the face of a ruthless thug, scarred and hard. He grinned and licked his lips.

Alarm charged through the mummy. Even though he did not recognize the man, he had a sense that he had run afoul of this unsavory character in the past, and their encounter had not been cordial.

"Eh, you're not asleep," Nike said in English, then suddenly grabbed him by the neck and dragged him to his feet.

The mummy screamed in shock and agony. He'd only imagined that he had been in pain before. Nothing matched the fiery train wreck that was now chewing through his body like it was a toothpick.

"Take it easy, Demitri," Froggy croaked. "If he passes out again, it will be that much longer before we can coax his secrets out of him."

The mummy's eyes flew to the man illuminated in the path between the door and the stacks of metal on both sides of them. The man with the deep, hoarse voice of an ailing bullfrog. His coal-black eyes showed not the slightest glimpse of mercy. His face was as emotionless as marble.

He stepped closer.

Bullfrog Man was short and squat, barrel-shaped yet muscular. His dark hair was slicked back with something oily, and his mouth bore a nasty mixture of cruelty and intelligence.

"The sooner you talk, the sooner this will all be over." His English was heavily accented with Greek flavor. A gyro-eating, wing-tip-wearing, bad-cold-having bullfrog. "Where is the amulet?"

The mummy did not answer.

What amulet? He didn't remember anything about an amulet or who these men were, but something told him this question was vitally important. His head pounded. His gut roiled again.

Nike yanked his hair.

He yelped. Involuntary tears flooded his eyes. He couldn't help it. The pain was that bad.

"Please, don't make me ask you twice," Bullfrog said, pulling a pointy metal nail file from the pocket of his suit jacket and slowly dragging it across his nails.

The thought of what an evil man could do with a sharp metal fingernail file squeezed the mummy's breath right out of his lungs.

"I . . . I don't know," he whispered, his legs swaying as he struggled to remain standing. Demitri's breath burned hot against his neck. He just dangled there, too weak to fight.

Bullfrog nodded. Demitri pressed a thumb into the aching wound at his back.

Blistering tides of agony lapped over him. His knees gave way. His eyes rolled back in his head.

"Where is the amulet?"

"I don't know what you're talking about."

Bullfrog sighed and passed the metal file to Demitri. "You know what to do."

"Please," the mummy babbled. "I swear, I don't re-member. My thinking is fuzzy."

"Then Demitri will sharpen your memory for you. One way or the other, we will have both halves of the amulet. Never doubt that."

Demitri stroked the file against the mummy's cheek, stopping when he reached his eyes. "Where's the amulet?" he hissed, his breath thick with garlic.

The mummy whimpered. If he could remember, he would tell him. But his mind was a blank screen and the harder he tried to conjure something, the more elusive it became.

The file was at the corner of his eye now.

"Where's the amulet?"

Dear God! the mummy thought just before he lost consciousness. He couldn't remember anything. Not even his own name.

Not even to save his life.

CHAPTER
7

The American Airlines agent at the main ticket counter confirmed Cassie's inquiry. Yes, Dr. Adam Grayfield had arrived at DFW Airport on the eleven-twenty-five flight from JFK twelve hours earlier.

"What about Dr. Grayfield's cargo?" Cassie asked.

Harrison shot her a quelling glance. *Zip it*, his fierce glare warned.

She figured he was mad because she had asked the question before he could. Fine. She shrugged. No skin off her nose if he wanted to play big man in charge.

"What happened to my brother's freight?" Harrison addressed the man behind the ticket counter. "Did it arrive safely? Or did you lose it?"

The ticket agent—who looked like a strange cross between Bill Clinton and Mr. Rogers with his lush gray hair, hound dog nose, long slender neck, and wooly red cardigan—went on the defensive. Cassie recognized from his stiffening body language that his self-protective instincts were kicking in. Squarer shoulders, narrowing eyes, clenched jaw, petulant expression. She understood that a good part of the ticket agent's day must be taken up by people bitching about their lost or damaged luggage.

"As far as I know," the man said to Harrison in a tone as warm as an Alaskan glacier, "we've received no complaints from Dr. Grayfield."

"Did he pick up his luggage?" Harrison fished the baggage ticket out of his jacket pocket. "I have the claim stub."

"Then I'm assuming he did not pick it up. Check with baggage claim."

"Where's that located?"

"Near the baggage carousels, but they closed at ten and it's now eleven-thirty. Guess you'll just have to come back tomorrow morning." The ticket agent looked anything but disappointed.

"This is an urgent matter that can't wait until morning. Dr. Grayfield never showed up for an important engagement this evening," Harrison said.

"Not my problem," the ticket agent replied. "Now if you'll excuse me, it's time for my lunch break."

Cassie couldn't keep quiet. Not when the ticket agent was about to walk away. Not when they had less than seventy-two hours to find Adam and the amulet.

"Excuse me." She bellied up to the counter, not caring if Harrison got mad because she was taking over. She glanced at the ticket agent's name tag and gave him the friendliest smile she could muster. "Jerry."

Jerry stopped and turned toward her. "Yes?"

"Please excuse my friend. He's very irritable because his only brother is missing." She told him who Harrison was and explained about the star-crossed lovers exhibit, and she elaborated on how Adam hadn't shown up for the event.

"He has no right to take it out on me," the man grumbled and shot Harrison a dirty look.

Cassie nodded in agreement. "You're absolutely right about that, Jerry."

"I'm just doing my job."

"Of course you are." She lowered both her voice and her eyelashes seductively. "Could you please find it in your heart to check your computer and see if Dr. Grayfield's freight was picked up? It could be a clue to his whereabouts."

For the coup de grâce, she reached out and lightly touched Jerry's forearm.

The ticket agent stood up a little straighter. "I could do it for *you*."

"Thank you ever so much. I really appreciate your effort."

Jerry returned to his computer monitor and typed something in on the keyboard. "Dr. Grayfield's freight is still in the airport. It was never picked up."

"Is there any way that someone, a supervisor maybe, could open baggage claim for us?"

"I could ask, but don't get your hopes up." Jerry sounded doubtful.

She pursed her lips in the sexiest pucker she could muster. Pamela Anderson had nothing on her. "Please."

"All right," he agreed. "I'll call a supervisor and see if we can't get those bags for you."

She rewarded Jerry with a stupefying smile and a gentle squeeze of his forearm. She could practically see the man's knees weaken. "Thank you so much."

"No problem, Miss . . ."

"Call me Cassie."

Damn if Jerry's face didn't flush red and perspiration

break out on his forehead. Quickly, he grabbed for the house phone.

And that, Harrison Standish, is the way you handle people.

"You don't have to act like a centerfold queen to get people to do your bidding," Harrison growled softly in her ear while the ticket agent was on the phone to baggage claim. "I was handling things my way."

"And getting nowhere."

"I was about to demand to see his superior when you decided to butt in."

"Maybe you were, sugar," she whispered, keeping her smile pasted firmly in place even when she wanted to tell him to kiss her fleshy fanny. "But my way turned out to be faster and a whole lot nicer."

"And a whole lot more manipulative."

"A girl's gotta do what a girl's gotta do."

"You're justifying your means."

"What is your problem, Standish? Why do you care if I'm flirting with the guy to get my way? You reap the benefits."

"It makes me feel like a pimp."

"Well now, that sounds like a personal problem to me." She tossed her head. Give the man a palace, and he would no doubt bitch because it was too big and drafty.

Jerry hung up the phone. "The supervisor will be with you in a minute, Cassie. Why don't you have a seat? Can I get you anything? Cup of coffee? A soda?"

"I'm fine, Jerry, but thanks a million. You've been such a big help."

Cassie and Harrison seated themselves on the black vinyl chairs. She practiced smiling coyly, preparing to cajole the supervisor into opening the baggage claim office for them.

Five minutes later a tall, muscular brunette woman with plenty of sass stalked from behind a door marked "Employees" on the opposite side of the concourse. Her navy blue uniform fit her like a second skin, and her three-inch pumps made her long, lean legs look even longer and leaner.

Cassie disliked her on principle. So much for her plans to flirt her way into baggage claim.

The woman sauntered over to Harrison and extended a hand. "How do you do," she murmured in a silken voice. "I'm Spanky Frebrizo."

"Dr. Harrison Standish. And this is Cassie Cooper."

Spanky pumped his hand, but she never even glanced at Cassie. "I'm well aware of who you are, Dr. Standish. I'm a huge ancient Egypt buff, and I'm a big fan of the star-crossed lovers. I even attended one of your lectures at UTA through community education. When Jerry told me there was a famous archaeologist waiting to see me, I just about fainted."

Imagine that, Cassie mused. Harry had a groupie. She half expected Spanky to grab a Sharpie and write "I LOVE YOU" on her eyelids.

Harrison beamed. "It's always nice to meet someone with an interest in ancient Egypt, Spanky."

Spanky?

What in the hell kind of name was that anyway? It had to be a nickname. Cassie didn't even want to speculate on how the woman had earned it.

While Spanky totally ignored Cassie, Harrison explained the situation and their dilemma.

"I'll take you over to baggage claim," Spanky said.

"Anything I can do to help you, Dr. Standish." She turned and led the way.

Cassie mocked her behind her back, silently mouthing, *Anything to help you, Dr. Standish.*

She and Harrison were walking shoulder to shoulder a few feet behind Spanky. Harrison leaned over to whisper, "What's the matter?"

Cassie shot him an evil look.

"Jealous?"

Ha! Over Harrison Standish?

Why would she be jealous over a color-blind, pompous, nerdy professor who worked out regularly and was damned handy with a pair of manicure scissors? Okay, so maybe she was a teeny bit jealous. Big hairy deal.

Then suddenly she had an inkling into what he might have been feeling when she was flirting with Jerry. Ouch. The shoe didn't fit so well on the other foot.

"Here we are." Spanky unlocked the door to the lost baggage area, flicked on the light, and ushered them inside. "You can wait right here while I go see if I can locate the baggage."

"It's probably a heavy crate. You might need some help lifting it."

"I'm sorry, it's against our company policy to allow customers beyond the front desk." Spanky ran her gaze over Harrison again, and Cassie could have sworn the woman licked her lips. "But I suppose it would be okay to let you in this one time."

"Thank you, Spanky," Harrison said.

"But she has to stay here." Spanky indicated Cassie with a wave of her hand.

Bitch.

Cassie ground her teeth and glared while Harrison trailed off after Spanky. He cast a parting glance over his shoulder, giving her a what-can-I-do shrug. He might act innocent, but clearly he was enjoying turning the tables on her.

She plopped down on a bench. A few minutes later she heard whispering and giggling from beyond the shelves stacked tall with MIA luggage. She rolled her eyes and tried to ignore the churning in the pit of her stomach.

The giggling stopped.

A few seconds later Harrison reappeared. "By any chance do you have a Swiss Army knife?"

"Do I look like the kind of woman who carries a Swiss Army knife? If I needed to, say, oh, slice some Camembert, I'd just call in the Swiss Army."

"There is no Swiss Army," he said.

"Then what do they need knives for?"

"You're incorrigible."

"I know." She grinned. "What did you want the knife for anyway? You and Spanky aren't slicing Camembert back there, are you?"

Harrison looked at her like she was the weirdest person he had ever met. He just didn't get her sense of humor.

"The crate is locked," he said, "and I don't have a key, but I think if I had a Swiss Army knife or something like that I could pick the lock. It looks pretty flimsy."

"I have a fingernail file."

"May I borrow it, please?"

"It's gonna cost you."

"Don't be petty."

"Take it or leave it." She fished the file from her purse but held it out of his reach.

He sighed. "What's it going to cost me?"

"I want to be there when you open the crate."

He looked at her a long moment. "There's nothing going on between me and Spanky."

"Pfft." She waved a hand. "As if I care. I just want to know what happened to Adam."

"Me too," he said soberly. "Come on. If Spanky gets mad, then she just gets mad."

"Really?" Cassie's heart warmed.

He motioned for her to follow. Happily, she sprang to her feet.

"Cassie has a metal fingernail file," Harrison said when they reached Spanky and the coffin-shaped crate that was pulled out into the aisle.

Spanky frowned at Cassie. "I changed my mind. I don't think we should be breaking into it. If you don't have a key, you should come back when you get one."

"We have the baggage claim ticket. It's my brother's freight. I have a right to open it."

"Maybe so, but I don't have to let you open it on airport property."

"Spanky," Harrison said in a wheedling voice.

Cassie suppressed a smile. It was fun watching him try to flirt his way out of a problem.

"Solen's half of the star-crossed lovers exhibit is quite possibly in that crate," Harrison cajoled. "You would be the very first person to see it outside of archaeologists, scientists, and academicians. Patrons of the arts were paying a thousand dollars a head for a private viewing at the Kimbell."

"Really?"

"Really."

"Okay," she relented. "Go ahead and open it."

Harrison knelt on the floor beside the crate and worked

at the lock with the fingernail file. After several minutes, the cheesy lock finally clicked open.

He raised his head and met Cassie's gaze. They exchanged a look. What would they find?

Slowly Harrison raised the lid and sucked in his breath. Cassie peered over his shoulder to see what was inside.

Except for some sawdust, the packing crate was empty.

"Well, that was a big buncha hoopla over nothing." Spanky snorted.

Harrison was past the point of trying to get his needs met by charming the supervisor. He had to think. Kneading his brow with two fingers, he stared at the empty crate.

What was this all about? Had Adam screwed up with shipping? Had he somehow dropped the ball and lost Solen in transit? Was that why he hadn't shown up at the museum? Was it because he was too embarrassed to admit his mistake? It wasn't as if Adam was the most reliable person in the world.

And yet, in spite of his doubts, something told Harrison there was more going on here than met the eye.

"This sucks," Spanky complained. "You promised me something cool, and it's nothing but an empty box."

"Hush," he growled.

"Excuse me?" Spanky's eyes flamed.

"He told you to hush," Cassie said.

"Shut up." Spanky made a face at her. "You're not even supposed to be back here."

"What are you gonna do about it?" Cassie challenged, thrusting out her chest.

"Call security."

If their quarreling wasn't getting on his nerves, Harrison would have found Cassie's jealousy endearing. No matter how much she might deny it, she liked him. But as it was, he couldn't hear himself postulate.

"Stop bickering, both of you," he growled and glared up at them. "I'm trying to think."

Women. Throw in a little envy, and poof, you had a cat-fight on your hands. Amusing thing was, he'd never been the object of a chick brawl before, and it was something of an ego stroke. Too bad he didn't have time to enjoy being cock of the walk.

"But . . . ," Spanky started to protest.

"This is serious," Harrison said and pointed an index finger. "Not another word from either of you. Got it?"

Cassie and Spanky exchanged spiteful glances, but thankfully they fell silent.

Harrison ran his fingers along the crate. The outside of it was stickered with labels that proclaimed, *Fragile! Delicate! Don't mutilate!* But the shipping box was cheap, and the lock on it was even cheaper.

The Egyptian government had shipped Kiya's remains in an elaborate crate, escorted by Ahmose and an armed security guard.

Why hadn't Adam or the Greek government taken the same precautions with Solen? It made no sense.

Unless Adam had shipped the wrong crate. Unless Solen had never been in there in the first place.

If that was the case, where *was* Solen and his half of the amulet? And if Adam had screwed up, why had he given Gabriel the envelope with the baggage claim ticket to give to Harrison?

There had to be something he was overlooking.

"Harry," Cassie whispered. "Don't get mad at me, but the clock is ticking and we're running out of time. Maybe we should be on our way."

"No, not yet."

His gut told him there was a message in this box, and Harrison Jerome Standish was nothing if not methodical. He would not leave until he found the clue, and Adam knew that about him.

Damn you, Adam, and your silly games. If you've sent me on a wild-goose chase, I'll wring your neck when I find you.

He plowed through the fine wood shavings. Maybe there was a small artifact, something, anything, buried inside. Sawdust sifted through his fingers. He tossed it from the box, littering the floor, but he didn't care. He was frantic for evidence.

"Hey! Hey!" Spanky griped.

"It sweeps up," he said.

"I'm seriously starting to regret letting you in here," she muttered.

"See what happens when you let hormones do the thinking?" Cassie sassed.

"Oh, like you're one to talk, skank."

"Takes one to know one."

"Ladies!" Harrison shouted. "Shut up."

Minutes later, when he had most of the sawdust in a pile beside the crate, he was almost ready to admit defeat. The box was empty. There were no hidden secrets.

He sighed and rocked back on his heels, perplexed.

And then he remembered one of Adam's favorite possessions when he was a kid.

A box with a false bottom for hiding secrets.

CHAPTER
8

Without warning, the base of Cassie's skull started its precognitive burn. The freaky sensation always preceded some bizarre occurrence—say, for instance, a mummy stabbing. But she had never experienced it twice in one day. That fact by itself was disconcerting. And when the heat did not abate after a few seconds as it usually did, but actually blazed hotter, she got nervous.

She slapped a palm to the back of her neck and rose unsteadily to her feet. She'd been crouching beside Harrison, watching him dismantle the packing crate in the airport parking lot after Spanky had thrown them out of baggage claim for making too big of a mess.

"Harry," she said.

"It's Harrison," he corrected without looking up. He was intently trying to pry nails out of the board with his car keys.

"We have to get out of here," she said. "Something bad is about to happen."

"Uh-huh."

"Harrison." She raised her voice. "We gotta go."

"Look, look, Cassie!" He was so excited.

"Huh?" She wished she felt better so she could get into his enthusiasm. She'd never seen him looking so passionate about anything. But her head was so miserably hot that she longed to dunk it in a bucket of ice water.

"I was right." He beamed. "There is a false bottom."

"I've got a really bad feeling about this."

But he wasn't listening. He flung the strip of board across the parking lot and lifted something from the false bottom. It was bundled in sheepskin and tied with a cord bearing a wax seal. The seal depicted a Minotaur transposed over a double ring emblem.

"This is important." Her head was burning so hot she could hardly see, much less think.

"So is this." He carefully peeled away the sheepskin to reveal a papyrus scroll. The awe in his voice was perilously close to religious ecstasy. She had an artifact zealot on her hands.

"Dammit, man, listen to me!"

"What?" Finally Harrison raised his gaze and met her eyes.

"I know this is gonna sound crazy, but ever since I almost drowned when I was nine, I occasionally get these twinges."

"Twinges?" He pushed his glasses up on his nose with the index finger of one hand, while the other hand cradled his discovery.

"Premonitions. My brain gets really hot."

"You're joking." He was staring at her as if her mother had dropped her on her head one time too many when she was a baby.

"Nope, not kidding, and I've learned that if I ignore these twinges, it's at my own peril. We gotta get out of here."

"You're talking about premonitions when I have the find of the century in my hands?"

"Your brother found it first," she snapped, getting irritated with his one-track mind. "And if I don't sit down in a cool place soon, I'm going to pass out and crack my head open on the pavement."

"Okay, okay." He finally seemed to snap out of his artifact-induced euphoria. "I'll unlock the car door for you."

"Thanks ever so much." Feeling like a boiled jalapeño, Cassie sank into the passenger seat.

This will pass. Think of something pleasant. Think of your favorite things.

Like Kiss Me Scarlet lipstick and fusilli pasta and reruns of *Sex and the City*. Coffee ice cream and strolling the streets of Madrid and long soaks in the hot tub.

Oooh-no, not hot tubs. Don't think hot.

Cassie took a deep breath and waved a hand in front of her face in a vain attempt to cool herself. This was getting scary. She'd never had one of these ESP-induced brain hot flashes last so long. What she wouldn't give for a tall glass of sweet tea over crushed ice and an oscillating fan set to supersonic speed.

But the sense of urgency pushed at her, as overwhelming as the heat. "Get in the car, Harry," she barked.

He looked at the crate.

"Leave the crate. It won't fit in the car. You've got what you came for. Let's go."

"Okay."

Her face was sweating and she was panting hard. If the guy ever thought about getting married and having kids, he was going to have to learn that when a woman got that particular tone in her voice she meant business.

"Now!"

He wrapped the papyrus scroll in the sheepskin and got in the car. He glanced over at her as he laid his newfound treasure on the backseat.

"You're serious about this. You really are overheated."

"Damn skippy. I'm melting like a box of chocolates, Forrest Gump. Get the air-conditioning cranked."

They drove away from the terminal with the AC blasting as high as it would go. The nightmarish heat inside her head began to recede. By the time they were off airport property, Cassie was feeling almost human again.

"Take the next exit," she said. "There's a bunch of drive-through fast-food joints. I need a large Coke with extra extra ice."

"So these premonitions of yours, what happens when you get them?" he asked as he pulled up to the speaker at a Jack in the Box.

"The back of my head burns, and then something weird always happens. Get me a couple of monster tacos along with the Coke. No, wait, monster tacos have hot sauce on them, and the last thing I want is something hot. Just get me a grilled chicken sandwich and an order of curly fries."

He placed her order, plus he got a salad for himself and a glass of water.

"Sheesh, Harry, what's with the salad? Live a little, willya?"

"It's Harrison, and I prefer to watch my intake of fats and carbohydrates."

"Hey, with the kind of precognitive heat I've been feeling, today could very well be your final day on the face of this earth. Don't go out on lettuce and water."

"I'm happy with my choice of last meals," he said.

Cassie shrugged. "Suit yourself."

While they waited in the drive-through line, Cassie called home to check her messages to see if Adam had called, but her machine never picked up. She must have forgotten to turn the thing on. Terrific.

They got their food and Cassie tore into the sack. She peeled the paper from her sandwich and took a big bite.

"Hey, you can't eat in my car."

"Watch me. I'm starving."

"No one's ever eaten in my car."

"The old gal is like, what? Ten? I'd say it's way past time to pop her cherry. Wanna french fry?" She dangled a fry in front of his face.

"No, I do not want a fry."

"You might as well pull over and eat your salad. I've already contaminated your car by pigging out in it."

He considered her a moment, then to Cassie's surprise he pulled into the parking lot. With a resigned sigh he said, "Hand me the salad."

She passed it over to him and watched him carefully open the container and cautiously squeeze the packet of Italian dressing over his veggies. They munched in silence for a few minutes.

"How's your brain now?" Harrison asked in between bites. "Still fried?"

"Are you being a smartass?" She sized him up with a sidelong glance. "You don't believe me about the premonitions, do you?"

"Sorry. I'm a seeing-is-believing kind of guy."

"So tell me, Harry, what exactly *do* you believe in?"

"Harrison," he said. "I believe in the power of the intellect. In scientific method. In reason and logic and common sense."

"I take it you don't buy into the legend of the star-crossed lovers."

"I do believe that Kiya and Solen were lovers in real life. Hieroglyphic writing found in Ramses IV's tomb supports the story. But I don't believe that when the amulet pieces are brought back together Solen and Kiya will be reunited in some mythological afterworld."

"That's a shame," she said wistfully.

"What?"

"That you don't believe in magic."

"And you do?"

"Oh, sure. I believe in romance and magic and love at first sight and . . ."

"Happily ever after," he supplied.

"Oh, no, I don't believe in *that*."

"You believe in magic and in the legend of the star-crossed lovers, but you don't believe that people can find permanent happiness together?"

"For some people, maybe," she said. "But it's not my thing."

"Why not?"

"Because after a while things invariably get dull. The fire goes out. The passion dies down, and you're stuck with someone who leaves their socks on the bathroom floor and expects you to pick them up."

"Ah," he said. "I understand."

His smug expression irritated her. "What is it that you understand?"

"You're a commitment-phobe."

"I am not. I just don't want to be locked down."

He laughed. Really loud and long. "That's the definition of a commitment-phobe. Be honest with yourself. You like the thrill of romance but a real, honest-to-God, mature relationship based on mutual respect scares the pants off you."

Cassie felt as if he'd just driven a push pin through the center of her forehead. Ouch. He's got you bagged, tagged, and labeled, babe.

"Oh, like you're one to talk. When was the last time you even had a date, Harry? Much less a serious relationship?"

"I've been too busy for a relationship."

"You've been too busy? Doing what? It's been two years since you dug up Kiya." Cassie polished off her last french fry and took a long sip of her Coke. "What's been shaking since?"

"I've been looking for Solen."

"Unsuccessfully."

"Yeah," he said, sounding just a tad bitter. "Unsuccessfully. Thanks for reminding me. But I have also been working on the djed. I'm trying to figure out how it works and what the Egyptians used it for."

"You mean the dildo?"

"It's not a dildo!"

"It looks like it could be one."

"Well, it isn't," he snapped. "It's some kind of electromagnetic transformer."

"Hey, a dildo could transform me."

"You're impossible," he said.

"That's what they tell me."

He gathered up their empty food containers and stepped out of the car to deposit them in a nearby trash can. He got back inside, started the engine, and then motored toward the freeway entrance ramp without speaking.

Okeydokey. Apparently she'd made him mad by belittling his djed thingy.

"I apologize for the dildo comment," she said. "I was just teasing."

"Unlike some people, I'm serious about my work," Harrison grumbled.

"So what's this papyrus thing all about?" Cassie jerked a thumb at the backseat.

"I don't know. I recognized that seal, but is it a real artifact or something Adam's concocted? I didn't get to examine the writing on the scroll closely, but it looked like Minoan hieroglyphics, and no one has ever been able to translate them."

"Adam did."

He jerked his head around to stare at her. "What?"

"Yep. It was supposed to be a surprise. Adam was going to reveal his achievement at the reunification ceremony."

"But that's impossible. The Minoan hieroglyphics are untranslatable."

"Not according to your brother. He was very excited. Your name came up several times in our conversation, but he never let on that you were his brother."

"You're certain that he said he'd translated the Minoan hieroglyphics?"

"Positive."

"This changes everything. What else did he tell you?"

"All Adam would say is that the translation could alter the face of history. But you know your brother better than I do. I gather he leans toward the dramatic."

"That he does, but this time he might be right. It all depends on that scroll."

A car was following close on their bumper. The headlights reflected off the rearview mirror. The base of her skull warmed again, and she reached up a hand to massage away the tingling. Maybe it was just stress. Being around Harry was certainly stressful. Hopefully there was nothing ominous in the offing.

"I'm beginning to think this isn't a publicity stunt," Harrison said quietly. "I'm afraid Adam's gotten himself in serious trouble."

"What kind of trouble?"

Curiosity prompted her question, but it was more than casual interest that had her waiting for Harry's answer with indrawn breath. Maybe the smoldering premonition at the top of her spine wasn't for herself or Harry but for Adam.

"You saw the seal on the cord binding the sheepskin?"

Cassie nodded. "It was two circles with some Greek letters and a Minotaur on top."

"Not Greek letters. Minoan hieroglyphics."

"And?"

"The Minotaur over the double circles is the sacred crest of a three-thousand-year-old secret brotherhood sect that supposedly had perfected both the art of alchemy and the ability to control the weather. Adam's dad, Tom Grayfield, is something of an academic expert on the ancient order. I believe he even did his doctoral thesis on them."

"What were they called?"

"The closest we've come to correctly pronouncing their Minoan name is by using a Cretan intonation." Then he said something that sounded an awful lot like, "Wannamakemecomealot."

"Excuse me?" It wasn't that she hadn't heard him the first time. Cassie just couldn't imagine that she was hearing the same phrase twice in one night.

Harrison repeated himself.

"Omigosh, Harry." She splayed a hand over her mouth,

then whispered, "That's exactly what the mummy said to me before he collapsed."

"You're certain?"

Cassie inhaled sharply. "Do you think he was telling me that members of this cult were the ones who stabbed him? He said, 'Beware Wannamakemecomealot.' That was before I knew he'd been stabbed, and I just thought he was trying to be flirtatious."

"It seems a huge stretch, Cassie."

"Harry, the mummy was really weak. Barely breathing. I was so scared he was dying."

In the light from the headlamps of the car following close behind them, Cassie could see Harrison's jaw tighten. "Let's just hope you're wrong."

"Tell me more about this Wannamakemecomealot bunch," she said, quickly changing the subject. She didn't want Harrison dwelling on the fact that his brother might be dead. Best not freak out until there was something to freak out about. That was her motto. If you put off worrying long enough, maybe it would never happen.

"Many people in the archaeological community believe Solen was a member of this cult. Most scholars now refer to it as the Minoan Order. Causes fewer giggles in the classroom than 'Wannamakemecomealot.'"

"I can imagine." She snickered.

She wished that stupid car would pass or drop back. Wasn't the headlight glare bothering Harry? But he seemed totally wrapped up in his story, oblivious to what was going on around him. He had the most intense powers of concentration she had ever seen. It made her want to squirm.

Settle down. This is important.

Fighting her natural ADD tendencies, Cassie rested her

elbow against her knee, propped her chin in her palm, and forced herself to really hear what he was saying.

"Go on, sorry for laughing."

"When the Minoan Order was initially formed, they only used their metaphysical powers for good. 'Do no harm' was the foundation of their creed. Anyone discovered using their arcane knowledge for evil purposes was immediately stripped of their magic and exiled from Crete."

"Was that what happened to Solen? Is that how he ended up in Egypt? He did something bad and got banished?"

"No. At least not according to the hieroglyphics we found in Ramses's tomb, although we do know Solen was one of Ramses's scribes. He could have written his own version of history."

"So fill me in. What's the entire scoop?"

"Supposedly, here's what happened," Harrison said. "The village where Solen lived was threatened by a rampaging Minotaur, and even the strongest, most talented warriors could not defeat the beast. Solen was young. He was only fourteen, but he'd been studying metaphysics under a grand master. With the power he derived from his magic amulet and the purity of his soul, Solen was able to slay the Minotaur."

"What happened then?"

"The grateful villagers lauded him with praise and riches. But several young warriors in the Minoan Order were jealous of his triumph. They ambushed him one night, beating him until he was almost dead, but he refused to use his powers against them in anger. He would not violate the code, even to avenge himself. The men put him on a sailing ship to Egypt, where he was sold into slavery."

"Sort of like Joseph and his coat of many colors."

"Similar story, yes."

"From there Solen ended up in Ramses's household, where he fell in love with Kiya."

"And that was his downfall," Harrison said. "There was only one thing that would cause Solen to break the Minoan Order's code and commit an evil act."

"His love for Kiya," Cassie whispered and got goose bumps on top of her hot spot.

"Solen attacked Nebamun when he discovered the vizier had poisoned Kiya. They battled and Nebamun stabbed him with a dagger dipped in asp venom. With his dying breath, Solen cursed the vizier's descendants into eternity, just as Nebamun tore the magic amulet from his hands."

"Thereby preventing the curse from taking place." She sighed deeply and rubbed her palms together. "I love this star-crossed lovers stuff. It's so tragically romantic."

"You only like the legend because their romance ended passionately and luridly and before Kiya ever started to resent Solen for leaving his socks on the floor," Harrison teased.

"Oh, you." Cassie reached across the car to playfully swat him, but the minute her hand made contact with his solid shoulder she realized that touching him had been a major mistake.

He'd stopped at a traffic signal and as her fingers grazed his shirt, he turned to look at her. The reflection of the red traffic light illuminated him in a vermilion hue. He looked alien and unlikely and incredibly potent.

They stared at each other. All levity vanished in the heat of tension stretching between them.

His dark eyes glistened enigmatically behind his scholarly spectacles. For the first time, she noticed a small scar just below and to the left of his right cheekbone. The unexpected defect was intriguing and mysterious and darkly masculine.

Who was he?

She didn't know him. Not really. She was vulnerable. At his mercy.

She suppressed a shiver.

The nerd image was all a ruse, Cassie realized. A defense mechanism he hid behind. He cloaked his real self with thick glasses and bad clothing and disheveled hair. The real Harrison disappeared inside scientific method and mental analysis and complicated ideas. But there was so much more to him than his intellect.

Here, in the close confines of the car, she could feel the emotional surging of this heavier, earthier, more complex personality. She wondered if he even understood the dynamics of his secretive behavior.

She felt herself sucked in by the enticing vortex of unknown territory. They stared into each other, and her world spun.

The car behind them honked and they both jumped, brought back to their physical surroundings. The light had changed. Harrison put his foot on the accelerator, and the Volvo chugged through the intersection.

That furtive moment, the deeper connection, vanished like a whiff of smoke and everything was back like it had been. Neither one of them spoke of what passed between them, but Cassie could not tolerate the awkward silence.

"So this Minoan Order." She nervously licked her lips and then swallowed hard. "Whatever happened to them?"

"Not to get all *Star Wars* on you or anything, but the dark side won. When the elder members of the Minoan

Order found out what the young warriors had done to Solen, they stripped them of their powers and banished them from their homeland. But in exile, the warriors banded together. They sought revenge against the original sect for kicking them out. They murdered every member of the old order in their beds to steal their magic. But the new Minoan Order was now tainted with evil. They still had the ability to transmute base metal into gold and to control the weather, but every time they used these skills they grew weaker and weaker."

"Chilling story."

"Many scholars of ancient history feel that Solen held the key to the group's alchemical talents. Some think the power was in his amulet."

"Do any practitioners of the Minoan Order exist today?" Cassie asked.

"The general consensus is they were wiped out by the Greeks," Harrison said.

"But were they?"

"Rumors of their existence persist. One theory postulates that Hitler was a member of the New Minoan Order. But no one has ever proved that. If they are still around, they've kept their presence very clandestine." He shook his head. "But if Adam has translated their hieroglyphics, the papyrus scroll in the backseat could hold the answer to all the speculation."

"It's a seductive thought."

"Very seductive for an archaeologist." Harrison exited the freeway. The high-glare-headlight car that had been on their bumper since they'd left Jack in the Box took the same exit.

"So do you personally believe there could still be a Minoan Order?"

"Anything's possible."

"You don't believe in true love, but you believe there could be mumbo-jumbo weirdos running around trying to turn base metal into gold and brew up tornadoes?"

"I'm a cynic." He grinned and shrugged. "But I'm not totally closed-minded."

"Good to know you believe in something."

The light changed and he turned the corner. Maybe now they could escape the obnoxious driver who seemed determined to give her a migraine with those unforgiving headlights.

No such luck. The car also turned right at the light.

They were back in Fort Worth and drawing nearer to the Kimbell.

"Just drop me off at my car," she said.

"No way. I'm not about to let you go driving around on empty at one o'clock in the morning. I'll take you to your apartment and come back to pick you up tomorrow."

She started to argue with him but stopped herself. What the hell? If he wanted to cart her around Fort Worth, no skin off her nose. He made a left turn and darn if that blinded-by-the-light car didn't stay right on their tail.

"Harry." Squinting, Cassie glanced in the side-view mirror.

"Yes?"

"I hate to alarm you, but I think we're being followed."

CHAPTER
9

Harrison had come to the same conclusion about the Ford Focus in his rearview mirror long before Cassie expressed her suspicions. But before he made a move, he had to be certain.

"My head is burning again," Cassie said. "Hate to sound all woo-woo, but this isn't a good sign."

On that point they agreed. Harrison circled the block.

The Focus followed.

This was unbelievable. The driver couldn't be more obvious if he had a neon flasher light proclaiming, "I'm following you," perched atop his hood.

He slowed the Volvo.

The Focus decelerated.

Harrison navigated down a narrow side street.

Here came the compact Ford, practically kissing his bumper.

No doubt about it. Not only were they being followed, but the driver didn't care if they knew it.

Harrison crept along, analyzing the situation. Obviously, the person behind the wheel of the Focus wanted him to pull over.

Why?

He edged over to the curb. The Focus followed suit.

"What's happening? Why are you stopping?"

"I'm finding out who's following us and why."

His pulse kaboomed in his ears. After their conversation about the Minoan Order, he was feeling a little jumpy. *Get over it, Standish.*

They weren't being followed by members of some ancient cult desperate to get their hands on the ancient scroll. No way. It was too incredible. No matter how hot Cassie's brain got.

So who was following them?

His mind jumped to the thought of carjackers and highway robbers. Or maybe it had something to do with Adam's disappearance. Maybe he had taken money from mobster loan sharks to finance his dig and he hadn't paid them back and they'd been watching the crate, waiting for someone to pick it up.

Outlandish, yes. Impossible? Considering his brother, no. But far more believable than a killer secret brotherhood sect.

Stop with the speculation. Make a move, doober. You're not going to discover anything while cowering in the car.

Right.

"Here." He twisted a key off his key ring and handed it her. "Get the papyrus scroll from the backseat and lock it in the glove compartment."

Cassie did as he asked, retrieving the sheepskin-wrapped bundle, stowing and locking it in the glove compartment. She gave the key back to him.

He reached down at the side of the driver's seat and thumbed open the trunk release latch.

"Are you nuts?" Her eyes widened and her voice shot up an octave. "What if they have a gun?"

"I imagine that is a possibility."

He looked in the rearview mirror. The Ford Focus had not switched off its headlamps. The beams bounced off the mirror, momentarily blinding him.

Harrison could not tell how many people were in the car. It could be one person. It could be four or even more. He had no idea what they were up against.

"This isn't good." Cassie ferociously rubbed the back of her head. "My head is blazing. There's going to be serious trouble. Just drive away, Harry."

"And let them follow us home?" he said. "No thank you."

"I don't scare easily, Harry." She grasped his arm. "But I'm scared now. This doesn't feel right. Don't do it."

"Cassie." He met her gaze.

"Uh-huh." Her voice was barely above a whisper.

He was startled to see exactly how scared she was. Her hands were trembling and her mouth was pressed into a thin, anxious line. His gut twisted. He would protect her, no matter what.

"When I get out of the car, I want you to slide behind the wheel, hit the automatic door locks, and drive immediately to the nearest police station. Do you understand?"

"I don't like this. Don't go."

"I refuse to be intimidated by common thugs."

"What if it's not common thugs? What if they're uncommon thugs? Like members of the Wannamakeme-comealots."

He almost laughed at the way she mispronounced the name, but he didn't want to bruise her feelings. "There's no such thing. That cult no longer exists."

"Are you sure?"

"Right now, I'm not sure of anything."

"Whoever it is could hurt you," she said breathlessly. "My head's never burned this bad. Not even when I was in the rehab hospital."

"Yeah, well." He was trying hard to ignore the twinge of sympathy that sparked whenever he imagined sweet little nine-year-old Cassie in a rehab hospital. "That's why I popped the trunk. I'll use the tire iron as a weapon."

"What if they overpower you?" She laid a hand on his shoulder.

Was that concern in her eyes? Was she worried about his safety? Her touch struck a chord inside him, and then he felt stupid letting himself get so embroiled.

Stay calm, stay cool, stay detached from your feelings.

"That's why you're going to drive to the nearest police station as soon as I get the tire iron out of the trunk."

"I won't go off and leave you to fight them alone."

"You can and you will."

She lifted her hand from his shoulder to caress his cheekbone. Her fingers found the small scar he'd acquired playing Zorro with Adam when they were kids. Harrison's heart knotted. If she only knew how hard his knees were quaking, that venerating expression in her eyes would quickly disappear. He found it so much easier facing the unknown physical menace outside the car than intimate tenderness inside the Volvo.

Unable to deal with her admiration for his imaginary courage, he ducked his head and fumbled for the door handle. *Round the back of the Volvo, shove up the trunk lid, grab the tire iron, and start swinging.*

"Harry?"

"Uh-huh?" He hesitated.

"Take this with you."

"Wha—"

But that was as far as he got because Cassie unsnapped her seat belt, leaned across the console, and planted a kiss on his scarred cheek.

He was so startled that he jerked his head toward her, and her mouth slipped from his cheek to his lips.

The next thing he knew he was kissing her.

Full on.

It was hot and wet and moving.

For one endless second Harrison forgot about the Ford Focus parked behind him. He forgot about the Minoan hieroglyphics. He forgot about Solen and Kiya. He forgot about the amulet. He even forgot about Adam.

Whereas before there was danger, now there was nothing but pleasure. His full attention was focused on one thing and one thing alone.

Cassie Cooper's mouth.

Lush and full and ripe and sweet. She tasted of summer. Throbbing and heated and humid. Filled with life and intensity and drama.

He remembered swimming pools and lounging on the beach, smelled chlorine and suntan lotion. He thought of the Fourth of July, heard bottle rockets scream and Black Cats explode. He saw fireflies flickering through pecan trees, and he spied charcoal embers glowing white-hot in the bottom of a barbecue grill.

It all added up to a glorious *wow*.

His mouth sizzled as Cassie's tongue glided over his lips. Wow, wow, wow, wow.

Harrison floated. Caught, trapped, besieged. He was suspended in another time zone, another dimension, an alternate reality. Everything ceased to exist except the taste and shape of Cassie's mouth.

An eternity drifted past his consciousness, but rationally he knew it had been no more than a couple of seconds. He coped with the emotional impact the only way he knew how—by narrowing his focus and attempting to retreat into the sanctuary of his mind.

But it didn't work. He could not isolate his mind from his body. His penis hardened and his mouth moistened and his toes curled.

Pull away, pull away.

But he could not.

He reacted violently against his natural instincts. Something about her tugged at a long-denied, subterranean part of his psyche. Harrison flung himself into the kiss, restless, agitated, forgetful, crazed.

More, more, more.

His mind sped up. His anxieties flamed. Her lips were the single distraction from his escalating uneasiness. Where had his mind gone? Where was the essence of him? Where was Harrison Jerome Standish in all this?

Resist her! Resist her! Remember your mission.

Ah, but she was irresistible.

Her lips were wicked, her tongue even more so. Nibbling, licking, tasting, teasing.

Panic seized him, but Harrison was unable to fight off the very cause of his alarm.

His unquenchable desire for Cassie.

And then a fist knocking hard against his window slammed him straight back down to reality.

A rush of protectiveness, so strong he could taste the briny poignancy, suffused him. He had to shield Cassie.

He'd gotten her into this mess; it was his responsibility to extract her.

It was so deeply ingrained in him to mentally disconnect from his body's physical response that he couldn't help himself. He was barely aware that his limbs had gone rigid and his hands were curled into fists.

He jerked his head toward the driver's-side window, fully expecting to see either a knife-wielding carjacker or a brass-knuckle-wearing loan shark, or, bizarrely enough, members of the Minoan Order, their faces hidden behind Minotaur masks.

When instead he saw the smiling caramel-colored face of the *Star-Telegram* reporter who'd attended the Kimbell party, Harrison exhaled in surprise and rolled down the window.

"Hiya," the reporter said, waggling her fingers at him in a friendly wave.

"Hi." He smiled weakly.

"Remember me? I'm Lashaundra Johnson."

"Yes?"

"I know who stole the amulet."

"Pardon?" Harrison had detached his mind from his body so completely that he was having trouble processing what the woman was saying. She repeated herself.

"You know who stole the amulet?"

"Uh-huh." She bobbed her head. "I already figured it out."

"Who?"

"Cleopatra. The thin one. Not her." Lashaundra nodded at Cassie."

"What?" He had no idea why this woman was hanging on to the side of his car and babbling nonsense.

Cassie leaned over to whisper in his ear. "She's talking about the murder mystery theater."

Oh. He'd forgotten all about that.

"Yep," Lashaundra went on. "She doesn't want Solen and Kiya reunited 'cause she wants Solen's handsome bod for herself. I'm thinking old Cleo might even have stabbed the mummy as well, but I haven't quite figured out why or how. I don't trust her. She's too damned skinny. My mama always told me never trust a bony woman. They're just too hungry."

"Amen, sister," Cassie mumbled.

Harrison's pulse, which had jackhammered into the red zone when Lashaundra rapped on the window, dipped back to normal.

"So am I right?" Lashaundra asked. "It's the skinny bitch, isn't it? She's the thief."

"Sorry," Harrison said. "You'll have to wait until Saturday to find out."

"You won't even give me a hint?" Lashaundra gazed beseechingly at Cassie. "I've been following you guys around all night looking for a clue."

Cassie shook her head. "It wouldn't be fair to the others."

"Dammit," Lashaundra said. "Well, I figured it was worth a shot."

"I'll walk you back to your car, Ms. Johnson," Harrison offered, plus he had to shut the trunk. "You shouldn't be out alone at this time of the night."

"Okay," Lashaundra agreed. "I'll let you."

Harrison opened the door to get out and the dome light came on. That's when he got a glimpse of himself in the rearview mirror. His right cheek was branded with the imprint of Cassie's lipstick.

Perfect lips, sealed with a kiss. A stark reminder of how he had lost control.

He reached up to guiltily swipe the imprint away with a hand. The lipstick came off, but he could not so casually erase the taste of Cassie from his tongue or rid the smell of her from his nose or eliminate the primal stirrings in his body.

As he walked Lashaundra to her car, he mentally berated himself. *Kissing Cassie was a huge mistake. You will not let it happen again.*

What a mess!

He was stuck with Cassie until Saturday night, and yet it was almost impossible to resist her. He had to find a way. There could not be a repeat performance of what had happened in the car. He'd been so swept up by their passion for one another that if it had been a loan shark or a carjacker or even, as laughable as it seemed, a member of the Minoan Order at his window instead of the *Star-Telegram* reporter, both he and Cassie could be dead at this very moment.

From now on, for the duration of their time together, it was totally hands off. No matter what the sacrifice might cost.

CHAPTER
10

Keep your lips to yourself. Absolutely, positively no more kissing Harrison Standish.

Because when his mouth had landed on hers and his tongue had skimmed along her lips and her pulse had knocked with anticipation, Cassie realized she was traversing a paper-thin ledge in six-inch stilettos.

Tightrope act deluxe.

Her stomach quivered and her hands shook. Her brain scorched hot and her lungs squeezed breathlessly out of control. All the wonderful sensations she loved rained over her. It felt like romance, and nothing got Cassie into trouble quicker than the thrill of the chase.

She couldn't risk pursuing this feeling. There was too much at stake. Her job. Harrison's future. Maybe even Adam's life. They had to stay focused on the mystery. They couldn't afford the distraction of attraction.

They drove in silence. He kept both hands on the steering wheel, his eyes fixed on the road, unaware of what she was thinking, oblivious to the excitement throbbing inside her.

Maybe, she thought, her precognitive brain burn had

nothing to do with outside danger and everything to do with Harrison. Perhaps he was the threat.

They were inhaling the same air, sharing the same closed, dark space. He had never looked as sexy to her as he did right now. He'd been prepared to risk life and limb to protect her. Underneath the glasses and the mismatched clothes beat the heart of a hero.

Don't go there. Don't romanticize the dude. Remember how much he gets on your nerves? Just think about his dirty socks on your kitchen table.

Socks, smocks. Who cared about socks when a bona fide hero was driving her home?

And the very fact that he was so smart and private and respectful and he'd kissed her like he really meant it was a total turn-on. She'd never been with a brainy guy before, and she wriggled joyously at the thought of bedding him.

"You okay?"

"Uh-huh." She forced herself not to squirm. She could not let him know how much he affected her. She might have the hots for him, but she wasn't about to hand him that much power.

Harrison parked the Volvo outside her apartment. "I'll see you to the door."

"You don't have to do that," she said quickly, even though she was accustomed to men waiting on her, treating her like a princess.

Cassie had to get out of the car before she did something totally stupid.

Like lick him.

She jumped from the Volvo, red leather handbag slung across her shoulder, and was halfway up the sidewalk before he caught her.

"Whoa, slow down." He took her elbow.

She jerked away. "It's okay. I'm all right. No need for an escort. Ta-ta, bye-bye, thanks for everything. See ya tomorrow."

Babbling. She was babbling and she knew it. Babble, babble, babble. But the last thing she wanted was to let this man into her house. Because if she let him in, she absolutely knew she could not be trusted to keep her lips to herself.

"I'm not going to let you walk into an empty house at one-thirty in the morning."

"No big deal. I do it all the time."

"Not when you're out with me."

"Excuse me, but I did not hire you as my protector. Buzz off." She waved a hand.

"Give me your keys." He put out his palm.

"No." Damn, why wouldn't that sensitive spot at the base of her skull stop the infernal burning?

"Cassie," he said, "I'm going to unlock your door for you, wait until you get across the threshold, and then I'll take off. I'm not going to shoulder my way inside and rob you of your virtue."

No? Rats. She was big into having her virtue robbed by guys who flipped her switch.

"Listen, Harry . . . ," she started to argue, desperate to get him to step away before she kissed him again. But she stopped midsentence when she realized her front door was ajar.

He saw it at the same time she did.

Without another word, he grabbed her by the shoulders and moved her away from the door.

"Stay behind me."

She wrapped her arms around his slim, muscular waist and held on tight. Nice.

He moved forward and she went with him in a bizarre, backward waltz. He toed the door open wider and reached an arm around to search for the light plate.

A second later the kitchen lit up.

"My God." Harrison audibly sucked in his breath.

His muscles bunched and Cassie felt his tension slip right up her arms, to her shoulders, and then lodge hard against the fiery section of her brain.

What had he seen?

She stood on tiptoes and peeked over his shoulder with one eye shut to lessen the blow of what she might witness.

Aha.

This was the reason her quirky ESP had been sizzling off and on all night. The danger hadn't been at the airport. Nor was it in the car that'd been following them. Nor was it even Harry's sexy proximity that had lit up her brain like a Christmas tree. The menace had been right here in her home.

Her kitchen had been trashed.

Not that it was really all that easy to tell. Cassie wasn't much of a neatnik. The dirty dishes piled in the sink were hers, as well as the stacks of books, Blockbuster movies, and CDs crowding the kitchen table. The clutter of cooking hardware—blender, food processor, bread maker, etcetera—was strewn across the counter because she'd been too lazy to bother stuffing it into the cabinets after her last cookfest.

But what wasn't her own doing were the drawers hanging open and the dish towels tossed around the room and the bottle of Dawn tipped over and dribbling soap down the front of the microwave. Nor was she responsible for the box of smashed sugar-frosted cornflakes littered across the tile floor or the upended garbage can or the broken jar of Russian caviar pooling next to the open pantry door.

Dammit! An admirer had given her that caviar, and she'd been saving it for a special occasion.

And then all at once the reality of the situation smacked her hard. Her place had been ransacked. Her valuables either stolen or destroyed or both.

"My collage wall," she cried, shoving Harrison aside as she zigzagged around the land mines of spilled delicacies and sprinted for the bedroom.

Wishing she had a shot of tequila to brace her for what lay inside, Cassie flicked on the light.

Not even a quart of Cabo Wabo Milenio could have prepared her for this. The shelving had been ripped off the wall. Her collection of candles lay shattered, the collages yanked from their picture frames and scattered across the room.

Someone had been viciously searching for something. But she had no idea who or for what.

Helplessly, she stared at the destruction. She felt as if she'd stepped into a morgue, surrounded by the corpses of her previous relationships. She stumbled across the room, fell to her knees in the middle of the devastation, and bit down hard on her bottom lip to keep from crying.

The wall was silly nostalgia. She knew it. Maddie had lectured her for years about clinging to the past. But her twin sister had never really understood what the collage wall stood for.

It wasn't that Cassie lived in the past. On the contrary, she was definitely a live-for-the-moment kind of gal. But her memories of the men she had once loved echoed throughout the collages.

It was difficult to explain, but when she had been in those relationships, the anticipation and the passion and the intensity had prevented her from savoring the actual experience. It was only upon reflection when she looked at the collage wall that she realized what an incredible, fun, adventuresome life she'd led.

With time and distance, she could linger in the variety of her experiences. Relish what had been without the pressure of what could be. In a glance, the wall gave her a clear visual of who she was, where she'd come from, the things she valued, and what she believed in.

She'd dated tall men and short ones. Brunets and blonds and even a redhead. Slim men and chubby men. Atheists and Christians. Men from other countries. Men of other races. Scoundrels and saints. Rebels and reactionaries. Crusaders and crackpots.

Some of the relationships had been strictly intellectual. Others only emotional. A few had been purely sexual. But no one guy had ever been able to meet all her needs.

She was driven to seek fulfillment for all the different sides of herself. She could not resist. Her energy was cycled and replenished by the diversity of her men. She was always looking for something better. Scoping out her options.

Cassie knew she could never commit to just one guy. Marriage wasn't in the cards for her. That's why she bailed out of relationships before they got serious. She'd always been the dumper, never the dumpee.

And that's the way she liked it.

No one had to tell her that almost drowning when she

was a kid, spending three months in a coma and then nine months in a rehab hospital, had contributed to her need for variety.

She reached for a picture. Peyton Shriver. The charming art thief she'd spent several intense days with in Europe the previous year. She had known he was a very bad boy, and because of that, she'd never slept with him. But she couldn't say she'd regretted their time together. She'd learned a lot about herself from Peyton.

"This wasn't an isolated incident," Harrison said from the doorway. "This break-in is connected to what's been going on. Someone must think you've got something or know something that you're not even aware of, Cassie."

But she wasn't paying him much attention.

The invitation to her junior prom was ripped in two, as was the playbill to her first Broadway play, *Phantom of the Opera*. There was a partial sneaker print stamped across an old love letter, from the guy who'd taken her virginity. Cassie could even make out the brand name of the sorry scumbag's right shoe.

Nike.

Cruel bastard.

Who could have done this, and why? A tear slipped down her cheek. Then another and another.

Oh, crap. She wasn't supposed to do this. She swiped at her eyes and swallowed back a sob.

Distantly, she heard Harrison walk closer, but his presence really didn't register until he crouched down in front of her, his eyes level with hers. "It's okay. I'll help you piece everything back together."

But she couldn't look at him. She didn't want him to see her crying.

Carefully, he reached out and touched her forearm, as

if initiating such contact wasn't something he usually did and he wasn't quite sure if he was making a mistake or not. His fingers were hesitant yet firm, his palm warm. He stroked his thumb along the underside of her arm.

"Are you all right, sweetheart?"

Sweetheart.

Her chest squeezed. What a lovely, kind word and so unexpected coming from Standoffish.

Cassie raised her head, met his steadfast gaze. Here he was, offering to help her recreate her past with other men. His smile was faint, but considerate. He looked at her with such empathy that she knew, without another word passing between them, somehow, he understood.

"Thank you," she said.

"You're welcome." The look in his eyes, the touch of his fingers against her skin, the tenderness in his voice made her feel a lot better. For the first time since Maddie had moved to D.C., Cassie felt as if she wasn't alone.

And when Harrison knelt to pick up broken glass, mindful of the photos and memorabilia, Cassie just knew she had to kiss this man again.

He had to escape.

If he didn't, the mummy knew they would kill him. He realized this as surely as he could not remember his own name.

Faint fingers of daylight were pushing through the high, dirt-smudged windows of the warehouse. He had no idea when the men would return, but the consequences would not be good.

The throbbing in his back had dulled slightly, but the fresh wounds Demitri had inflicted upon him with the metal file stung with a fierce and fiery ache. He felt hot and sweaty and dizzy, and whenever he gazed into the distance his vision blurred.

He wondered if he had a fever. Was he delirious? Was this just some bizarre dream?

But no, the sharp teeth of pain tearing through him whenever he tried to drag himself to his feet assured the mummy that this was no dream.

It was a nightmare.

He gritted his teeth and rolled over onto his back. He ended up lying on his bound hands. His wrists were chafed raw from the too-tight duct tape, and his fingers were scarily cold.

Grunting against the pain, he made several attempts and finally managed to get into a sitting position with his shoulders propped against the wall. He sat panting from the effort that tiny accomplishment extracted.

The coppery scent of blood filled the air, and a warm wetness spread over the crusty dryness at the back of his shirt. Bile rose in his throat, and he gagged but did not throw up. He'd aggravated the stab wound, and it was bleeding again.

Once he'd rested enough that the dizziness and nausea abated, he glanced around for an escape route. After the men had tortured him and left the warehouse, he'd heard the heavy snap of a padlock latching the double-rollered doors.

He was locked in. The window was his only way out.

Up, up, up he stared. At the window looming far above his head.

It was only ten feet, but it might as well have been a million miles. He was that weak and debilitated. It was all he could do to keep breathing. How was he supposed to scale a wall with his hands duct-taped behind his back?

He was almost ready to say "Fuck it" and opt for death. At least if they came back and killed him, he would be out of his misery.

But something much stronger than the fear of those thugs and the pain in his body would not allow him to wallow in self-pity. A determination he didn't fully understand spurred him onward.

There was something very important he must do. He felt it straight to his bones. Unfortunately, no matter how hard he tried, he could not remember what it was.

Think, think. Who are you? What is it that you must do?

He closed his eyes. He needed a name. He needed a motivation to keep from giving up and surrendering to the relentless pain.

Froggy Voice had kept asking him about an amulet. Demanding to know where the thing was. He had no idea what the man had been talking about, but each time Froggy asked a question and he did not know the answer, Demitri would twist the metal file deeper into his skin.

A dark voice in the back of his brain murmured, *Find her.*

Find who?

Think, dammit. Think.

The harder he pushed, the more it felt as if his brain had broken into a thousand fragmented pieces, each walled off from the rest. He got snippets but could make no connections. He could not understand how it all fit into a whole.

The sound of a garbage truck rumbled in the alley outside the warehouse. The mummy tried to yell, but his voice stuck in his throat. When he finally forced out a sound, he was alarmed to discover he could not speak above a whisper.

On your feet.

He braced his shoes against the cement floor strewn with metal shavings and pushed himself up the wall.

Intense pain grabbed him in a vise. He stopped halfway to a standing position, hands bound behind his back, panting and sweating and sick to his stomach.

His knees wobbled. His stomach lurched. An icy-cold chill belied the sweat drenching his brow. His eyelids fluttered closed. He tasted the bile in his mouth again and almost lost consciousness.

And then a name popped into his head.

Kiya.

His beloved.

Heart strumming, he suddenly knew who he was and what he had to do.

His name was Solen.

And he had to get to Kiya.

He had to find his secret bride before she drank the poisoned wine.

CHAPTER
11

This time, he saw it coming.

The look in Cassie's eyes, the way she leaned close and puckered up those lush, glossy lips, left no doubt as to her intention. Panic-stricken, he sprang to his feet, leaving her blinking at the spot where he had just been kneeling beside her. She fingered her bottom lip, hurt and confusion on her face.

Had he been unconsciously leading her on? He shouldn't have touched her. He shouldn't express such sympathy for her plight. Intimate emotions just got you into trouble. Hadn't that message been hammered home enough times?

He cleared his throat. He wanted to tell her they needed to leave. That it was important they get a few hours' sleep so they could start looking for Adam again as soon as possible. But instead he said, "I'll help reconstruct your collage. But you have to promise you won't keep trying to kiss me."

"Why not?"

"Be . . . because," he sputtered.

"Because why?"

"Because I don't want you to."

"Oh." She considered that for a moment. "Do I have bad breath? I could go brush my teeth."

He raised both palms. Would he ever understand the way her mind worked? "It's not your breath. Your breath is minty fresh."

"So it's me? If I were someone else, then would you want to kiss me?"

"No. I don't want to kiss anybody."

"So it's you?"

"Yes." He would say anything to get the exasperating woman to stop talking about kisses. "It's me."

"You don't like kissing? Is that the deal?"

"I like kissing."

"Then what's the problem?"

"Kissing leads to other things."

"I know. That's the general idea."

This circular conversation was getting them nowhere. Not knowing what else to do to escape her chaotic reasoning, Harrison picked up a photograph of Cassie when she was about sixteen, draped all over some surfer-type dude on the hood of a station wagon. He was certain she must have made out in the backseat of that car. You couldn't miss the lustful gleam in the guy's eyes as he stared at her chest.

The jerkwad.

"Who's this?" He hadn't meant to ask that.

Cassie perked up and took the photograph from him. "Oh, that's Johnny D. He wanted in my panties so bad I thought he was going to explode."

"You didn't sleep with him?" Why Harrison should feel so relieved over something Cassie hadn't done a dozen years ago was beyond him.

"Are you nuts? The guy lived down by the river in his car. He had crabs like you wouldn't believe. Or that's what I heard from my pal Julie Ann."

"Why'd you keep his picture?"

"He was sweet, and I liked the idea of hanging with a musician. He wrote a love song about me and everything. But then again, the song sort of sucked. It didn't rhyme. He took me to a U2 concert when they came to Dallas back in the early nineties. If you see a U2 ticket stub, it goes in the frame with Johnny D."

"Cassie, we gotta hurry this up. I hate to rush you; I know this is important, but finding Adam and the amulet is even more important. We both have a vested interest in the outcome," he said, realizing the last thing he ever wanted to be was a memory on her collage wall. That's why he'd circumvented her kiss with some fancy foot-work.

She nodded. "You're right. I got caught up in my emotions. I can finish assembling the collages later. It was considerate of you to even offer to help, Harry."

He started to correct her, tell her to call him Harrison, but it hardly seemed worth the effort. If she liked calling him Harry, he could live with it for a few days.

"Good night," she said and extended a hand. "What time are you picking me up in the morning? Although technically it already is morning."

"Oh," he said, "I'm not leaving you alone in this apartment. Whoever trashed it might come back. Especially if they didn't find what they were looking for. We gotta get you out of here quickly, so pack a bag."

"What do you suppose they were looking for?" She took a backpack from the closet and tossed it on the bed.

"Adam? The amulet? The papyrus? Who knows?"

"But why come after me? I don't know anything." She headed to the bathroom. Harrison moved to stand in the doorway. He leaned against the jamb, watching while she hurriedly scooped up her cosmetics and toiletry items.

"Maybe you do and you just don't know it. One thing is for sure, it's not safe for you to stay, and as far as I can see there's only one solution."

"What's that?" She maneuvered past him to dump her makeup bag and toothbrush onto the bed beside her backpack.

He resisted making the suggestion. If he was smart he would just foot the bill and put her up in a hotel, but he needed to keep her close. Especially if someone was after her. Harrison took a deep breath.

"You're staying with me."

Harry's place turned out to be much like Harry. Bland, boring, and colorless.

Or rather that was the general impression everyone had about Harry. She'd once thought that about him too.

But the more time she spent with him, the more Cassie realized he was much more interesting than he appeared on the surface. He might be color-blind, but Harry was far from bland and boring.

He was deeply private and intense. The curious adventurer in her wanted to dig past the surface, find out what he was truly like. The adage "can't judge a book by its cover" certainly applied to Harry Standish.

His sterile, monochromatic white kitchen begged for a shot of color. Not to mention food. His pantry had a glass door, and all she could see were tins of tuna, boxes of whole grain cereal, and cans of tomato soup, all neatly stacked. The man was seriously in need of culinary intervention.

"I'm sorry," he said, "that my apartment is so small. I'm rarely here, and I've converted my bedroom into an office."

Cassie looked around and sucked in her breath. A bedroom converted into an office meant the narrow daybed in the living room was where he slept.

Whoo boy.

Why was she suddenly feeling out of her element? She rarely felt uneasy around men. What was it about Harry that rattled her cage? She wished she had something to calm the nervous flutters in her stomach.

"Let me just check my answering machine to see if Adam called," he said and went to the telephone in the corner of the room. He shook his head. "No messages."

"It's looking darker by the minute, isn't it?"

"Yeah."

His expression was grim, and Cassie had an almost irresistible urge to wrap her arms around him and tell him everything was going to be okay, but something held her back.

"Got anything to drink?" she asked.

It was either very late or very early, depending on your definition, but a glass of wine or a bottle of beer was exactly what she needed to help her fall asleep. And to quell her inexplicable attraction to Harrison Standish.

"Sure. I have bottled water and milk and orange juice in the fridge."

"No, that's not what I meant," she said. "Do you have something serious?"

"You mean alcohol?"

"Ding-ding-ding." She nodded. "Beer, wine. I'd even take a shot of tequila if you have it."

Harry frowned. "I know you're reeling from what happened at your apartment, but do you really think alcohol is the answer?"

"Yep, I sure do." She sauntered over to the refrigerator and popped it open. She sank one hand on her hip and studied the contents.

Well, here was a dearth of choices.

A carton of skim milk that had expired two days ago. A quart of orange juice with pulp—*yuck*—and a six-pack of mineral water. There was also a package of deli-sliced turkey breast in the meat drawer, a jar of maraschino cherries and a bottle of ketchup in the shelf on the door, and in the crisper a chunk of brown iceberg lettuce.

Eew.

She slammed the fridge door closed.

"I have a bottle of peppermint schnapps that Adam gave me for Christmas a couple of years ago," Harry said. "It's never been opened. Would that do?"

"Now we're talking. The schnapps sounds promising. Lead on, Poindexter."

"Poindexter?" He swiveled his head to stare at her.

His expression was deadpan. He might have been insulted or he could have been amused. There was no reading this guy when he didn't want to be read.

"Oops, sorry." She cringed apologetically.

"Sorry for what?"

"Calling you Poindexter."

"You do it behind my back all the time, why not go ahead and say it to my face?"

She opened her mouth to dispute his claim, but it was

true. She had called him Poindexter behind his back. And Standoffish. And Egghead.

"May I ask why you call me that?"

Apparently it was time for truth or consequences. "No real reason. Don't take it personally."

"It's because I'm a nerd."

"Yeah, well, kinda."

"Kinda?"

Way to go, Cassie. Pry that shoe out of your mouth. She had just insulted the guy who'd taken her in. She crinkled her nose. "It's not you, really. It's the clothes."

"Oh? What's wrong with my clothes?"

Nothing like brutal honesty to quash any budding romantic attraction into pulp. "You don't match, and everything you wear is out of style."

"I'm color-blind," he said.

"I figured."

"And I don't care about fashion."

"I figured that too, but that's what makes you a Poindexter," she explained.

"Don't forget the glasses." He grasped the nosepiece and lifted his spectacles up and down on the bridge of his nose.

"Here. Let me see what you'd look like without those." She stepped the few feet across the kitchen floor, reached up, and removed his glasses. That's when she realized just how close they were standing.

He held his breath and so did she.

Cassie was acutely aware of his masculine scent, the warmness of his temples where her fingers grazed, the serious set to his intense mouth. She stepped back, tilted her head, and studied his face in the overhead lighting.

"You've got amazing brown eyes. You shouldn't hide them behind glasses."

"I have to see where I'm going." He shrugged, acting like he was unaffected by her touch.

He was a self-disciplined guy, but Cassie was an expert at reading men. She recognized the subtle changes. His shoulders tensed up. His jaw muscles tightened. His fingers curled into his palms.

"You could get LASIK surgery." She set his glasses down on the counter.

"Maybe," he said. "But what's the point? You can't change who you are at heart. Guess I'll always be a Poindexter."

Cassie felt bad for having called him nerdy names. He really was a nice guy once you got to know him. And he was kinda sexy in a disheveled, absentminded-professor sort of way.

"I'm sorry," she said. "For calling you that."

"Don't be. I appreciate your honesty."

Why did his compliment warm her from the inside out? He was giving her that serious, bookish look of his, which she'd thought was due to the spectacles. But his eyeglasses were resting on the counter beside a peppermill. His chocolate eyes glistened with expression, and she could almost read his thoughts.

You interest me.

And that was the true compliment. A smart guy like Harry interested in a ditzy chick like her.

Cassie shook her head. *Don't get any funny ideas about this one, Cooper. With his brains, he's way out of your league.*

Yeah, but maybe he just needed someone to show him how to let loose and have fun. She was good at having fun, and Harry's curiosity seemed to suggest he might be game for whatever intriguing things she cooked up, either out of bed or in it.

Stop it! He already told you, no more kissing.

Aw, but he hadn't meant that. He just hadn't known how to handle his sexual feelings for her. So he'd put a moratorium on kisses. As far as she was concerned, moratoriums were made to be broken.

"The schnapps?" she said, eager to drown the runaway voice in her head that usually led her into one mess or another.

He dragged a step stool from the pantry and positioned it beside the refrigerator. Climbing up on the bottom step, he opened the small cupboard over the fridge and took out the bottle of peppermint schnapps still wrapped with a festive red ribbon.

"Got any shot glasses?" she asked.

He just looked at her. Dang if he wasn't downright cute without those pesky spectacles.

"Right. You're not the shot-glass type."

"I have coffee mugs."

"That'll do."

He retrieved a mug from the cabinet.

She looked at the lone mug and pursed out her lips in a sexy pout that came as easily to her as eating. "You're going to make me drink alone?"

"Cassie, it's three-fifteen in the morning, and we've got to get up early. We need sleep for our brains to function properly. Can't puzzle out a puzzle if your brain's not game."

"Cute."

"It's something my mother used to say."

"So why do you think they call it a nightcap? To help

you sleep. And you've got to admit we've had a rough evening. If the events of the day don't call for a strong bedtime belt, then I don't know what does."

He hesitated and then said, "Aw, what the hell."

"Attaboy." She grinned.

Harry poured a finger of schnapps into each mug.

"Stingy," she accused.

He added another finger's worth.

"That's better." Cassie raised her mug. "Here's to finding Adam safe and the amulet in mint condition."

"To finding Adam and the amulet," he echoed, and they clinked their mugs.

She swallowed the peppermint liqueur with a toss of her head. It burned nice and friendly all the way down.

"Whew."

Glancing over, Cassie saw that Harry had taken only a tiny sip of his schnapps and was making a face like he was downing castor oil.

"No, no." She shook her head. "You gotta shoot it down in one big gulp."

"It's going to burn."

"But then you'll feel warm and toasty inside. Trust me on this. Down the hatch," she wheedled.

He made a face.

She could tell he didn't want to shoot it, but the man needed to learn to relax. She gave him the college chant that had usually persuaded her to overindulge: "Chug, chug, chug."

More to shut her up than anything else, Harry slung back the schnapps.

"Way to go." She slapped him on the back.

She was leaning against the counter, her head buzzing sweet and easy, her breast just slightly grazing his arm.

She hadn't brushed up against him deliberately, but the results were the same as if she had. One quick glance down and she was honored to discover the bulge in his Dockers.

"You shouldn't have any trouble falling asleep now," she whispered.

"It's not the falling asleep that worries me," he muttered. "It's the getting up."

Cassie grinned at his unintended pun. She tilted her head and lowered her eyelashes for another peek at his fly. "Oh, I don't think you're gonna have any problem with that either."

Harrison flushed the color of ketchup. "I . . . er . . . um . . . sorry. I don't drink much, and it goes straight to my . . . er . . ."

He caught himself this time before he made another accidental pun. Poor guy knew next to nothing about sexual innuendo. She gave him a break and went to retrieve her knapsack from the foyer where she had dropped it when they'd come in. She slung it over her shoulder and padded into the living room.

"Okay," she called to him. "What are the sleeping arrangements?"

"I have a sleeping bag." He came into the living room to stand behind her. "I'll stretch out on the floor in my office. You take the bed."

"Thank you." She beamed at his chivalry. Her twin sister, Maddie, would probably have argued with him, insisting on taking the sleeping bag, but Cassie wasn't the type to bed down on the floor. She appreciated Harry's courtliness. A girl should accept considerate gestures graciously.

She went to kick off her heels, but misstepped and lost her balance. Harry reached out to keep her from tipping over and she fell hard against him.

He wasn't built like an Adonis, but he wasn't half bad. His chest muscles were firm, and the arm he wrapped around her waist was strong and comforting. Her knees weakened and she just melted into him.

"Are you all right?" His breath was warm against her ear.

"The schnapps made me a little woozy, I guess," Cassie admitted.

"Here. Sit down."

Holding her securely, he guided her to the daybed. She sank onto the mattress, and Harry perched anxiously beside her. He kept glancing around as if searching for an escape hatch.

What? Did he think she was going to rape him?

Yeah, well, he was the one with a boner. Can't rape the willing, buddy.

She sneaked another quick peek at his crotch. He was even larger than before. That was why he was so nervous. It wasn't because he didn't trust her, but rather because he couldn't trust himself with her.

Cassie hiccuped and slapped a hand over her mouth. "Oops, sorry," she apologized. "Sweet liqueurs sometimes give me the hiccups."

And then she promptly hiccuped again.

"I know how to stop them."

"How?"

"Rub your diaphragm."

"I use those birth control patches, not a diaphragm." She giggled. "And I carry condoms. Never leave home without 'em. That's my motto."

"Ha-ha. Funny. Does pretending to be an airhead really work on guys?"

She grinned. "You have no idea how well. The condom

line is one of the most popular, usually countered by an American Express joke. I learned a long time ago that a woman gets a lot more mileage out of being sexy than she does out of being smart."

"That's a sad commentary."

"Hey, I don't make the rules." She shrugged and spread her hands. "I just play by them. Intelligent women scare most men."

"Not me."

"You say that now." She wagged a finger. "But I bet if a woman you were dating challenged you on something about ancient Egypt and she turned out to be right, you'd dump her in a heartbeat. It's just the way most men are."

"I'm not most men." He glowered.

"I'd puzzled that out already."

"You don't have to pull that dumb-blonde act with me, Cassie."

"At this point, it's something of a habit."

"Habits were made to be broken."

She hiccuped again. "Oops."

"Rub right here." He placed three fingers in the center of his abdomen just below the level of his rib cage and stroked in a circular motion. "Like this."

Cassie leaned over and placed three fingers on his belly and stroked him in rhythmic circles.

Blame it on the schnapps, but oh, she was acting wicked bad!

"What are you doing?" He sounded scandalized, but she noticed he did not move away.

"You said to rub right here." In all honesty, where she ached to rub him was a bit lower.

"Now you're just causing trouble," he said.

"That's my middle name." Her eyes met his gaze and held it, but she did not stop massaging him.

"Cassie . . . you've been drinking." He forcefully took her wrist and removed her hand from his body.

"So? You've been drinking too, and we've only had one shot of schnapps, so it's not like we're snockered."

"I won't take advantage of you."

"Not even if I wanted you to?" She fluttered her eyelashes seductively.

"No!" he exclaimed, but she heard amusement in his voice. "Besides, I think you're just bluffing. You don't really want me to make love to you. You just like to tease."

Oh, really? Is that what he thought of her? That she was all come-on and no substance?

They stared at each other, eyes locked.

Her need for him was building faster than she could have imagined. Who'd have thought she'd be all hot and horny for ol' mismatched Harry?

But dammit, she was.

The glimmer in his eyes sent goose bumps marching up and down her arms, and she was wetter than a Slip'N Slide. Need for him, for his kiss, his touch, was a wild thing inside her, sending her heart thrashing wildly against her rib cage, throwing out all common sense.

"You think you have me figured out?"

"I do, or at least as much as anyone will ever have you figured out, Cassie Cooper."

"Go ahead. Get it off your chest. Let's hear it." She jutted out her chin, daring him.

"You sure you're ready for this? You might not like what I have to say."

"Go ahead." She raised a hand. "I'm all ears."

"Remember, you asked for it."

"Just shut up and analyze me."

"Here goes. You act like you're not afraid of anything. You hide behind your charm and your sex appeal and your gregarious talk. You have a hopscotch mind that often gets your body in trouble."

"Oh yeah?" she said, because she did not know what else to say. It was true.

"Yeah. But in spite of your plucky personality, you really have a fear of exploring anything too deeply. You keep everything on the surface, which you mask by a fascination with many subjects. Your flirtation with pleasure is actually a flight away from pain. Ergo, your attempts to get me into bed are in reality nothing but a bluff."

"'Ergo'? Who in the hell says 'ergo'? It's little wonder you get called Poindexter."

Cassie knew she was being defensive, but she was unnerved that he had figured her out so easily. Not even her own twin sister, Maddie, understood her motivations the way Harry did. It was amazing and a little disturbing.

She didn't appreciate being dissected so accurately, and she wasn't going to let him get away with it.

Cassie knew it was impulsive. She recognized that she was tipsy and that she was still vulnerable over her apartment break-in. And yes, maybe she was using pleasure to cloak her fears. She was on the verge of not only losing her job but potentially going to jail for the theft of a priceless artifact she didn't even steal.

But something deep inside her whispered that this time was different. Harry was an impulse worth acting on.

"Go ahead," she teased, reaching for the hem of her long-sleeved T-shirt. In one swooping motion she pulled it over her head. "Call my bluff."

CHAPTER
12

Put your shirt back on." It took every morsel of self-discipline Harrison possessed to say the words, but he had to stop Cassie's insane seduction.

He tried not to look at her breasts, but damn him, they were so *there*. The thin material of her skimpy black-lace bra barely supported them, and from where he was sitting they looked solely God-given, not bestowed by a plastic surgeon.

"What's the matter, Harry?" Cassie gave him a deadly wink. "Scared?"

Oh, hell yeah. His knees were knocking and his heart was rocking, but he wasn't about to let her know.

She reached out and walked two fingers over his arm. "See anything you like?"

What didn't he like!

Cassie had been blessed with full, round curves, a thick head of blonde hair, and luscious lips just made for kissing. She was the richest truffle at the confectionery, the fastest car on the showroom floor, the poshest vacation resort in the Caribbean.

Whereas Harrison ate low-carb, drove a ten-year-old

Volvo, and when he'd visited St. Lucia, he had camped out in a pup tent on the beach.

She was uninhibited about her body and quite obviously sexually experienced. He was outclassed and out of his league, and he knew it. His last few relationships had been with colleagues. Calm, studious women who could either take sex or leave it, with no particular feelings about it one way or the other.

The gleam in Cassie's eyes told him she cared about sex and cared deeply. How could he ever hope to measure up to her expectations? Or to satisfy her? She flourished on thrills and excitement.

Face the facts, you're not an exciting guy.

Besides, he had been studying her over the course of the past ten days, and he was slowly starting to figure her out. If he made love to her after her apartment was ransacked, he would just be feeding into her habit of using pleasure in order to avoid dealing with a painful experience.

Ha!

Look who's talking, accused a voice in the back of his head that sounded a whole lot like Adam. *You hide your fears behind the acquisition of knowledge. How come it's okay for you to cloak your fears, but it's not okay for her? That sounds like a double standard to me.*

He had to stop thinking about this. They had no future together whatsoever, and he wasn't a one-night-stand kind of guy. And there was the time crunch. Even if he could bring himself to let go of all his doubts, he simply couldn't afford the distraction.

"Put your shirt back on," Harrison croaked.

He picked up the long-sleeved T-shirt she'd dropped

on the floor and handed it to her. He was careful to keep his eyes averted from those mesmerizing breasts.

"Are you that prudish? Or are you just not attracted to me?" Cassie asked.

"How on earth could you possibly believe that I'm not attracted to you?"

"You're not taking advantage of a primo opportunity. There's gotta be a reason why. Is it me?"

"Are you that insecure?"

"Well, if it's not me, I don't get what it is with you."

"Woman, I have a Godzilla-sized boner and sweat is dripping off my forehead."

"So, what are you waiting for?"

"I just can't handle this right now, okay? I'm worried about my brother. Imagine if it was your twin sister who was missing."

"Oh. I see your point."

That was good, because if she didn't cover up soon he didn't know what he was going to do. The pressure was building inside him, low and scorching hot. His penis ached and throbbed. If he wasn't so adept at detaching from his emotions, he would already be pumping into her.

And getting yourself tangled in an intimacy that you can't handle.

Cassie, with her verve and her zest for living, would quickly drain him of his resources. If he couldn't even master his own libido, how could he hope to master anything else? If he lost control with her, he risked losing control in other areas of his life.

And if he lost control in other parts of his life, he would end up looking incompetent, useless, and incapable.

He couldn't take that gamble. He had to stay emotionally distant and mentally on top of things. His ability to disconnect from his feelings had served him well for thirty-two years. No point mucking around with success at this stage of the game.

Cassie, however, was not cooperating with his plan for self-domination. Not only was her chest still bare, but she was audaciously undoing the snap on her pants.

Whoa!

"What are you doing?" he exclaimed. If she took off those Cadillac pants right here in his living room in front of him, he was done for.

"Oh, settle down, Harry. I'm merely headed for the bathroom. I'm just going to take a shower and then pop into bed."

"Really?" He opened one eye, feeling both relieved and disappointed.

"I'm not going to jump your bones. I just unsnapped my jeans to scare you. You can stop sweating. I get the message loud and clear. Your body might want mine"— she flicked a sly smile at his crotch—"but your brain won't let you do the wrong thing, no matter how much fun we might have in the process."

"I . . . I . . ."

"No need to explain." She shrugged, hopped off the daybed, and reclaimed her backpack from the floor. "Long as you know, it's your loss."

"Button-pusher," Cassie mumbled into the darkness as she lay on Harrison's sofa. "Instigator, rabble-rouser, agitator."

But she wasn't talking about herself and the way she had tried to provoke Harrison into making love to her; rather, she was thinking about the way *he* had inflamed her without even being aware of what he was doing. The man was chock-full of untapped potential. If he ever decided to intentionally use his masculinity to his advantage, heaven help her.

He'd gotten to her so thoroughly, she'd wanted him so darned badly, she'd brazenly ripped off her shirt in front of him. She'd never done anything that inflammatory—and she'd done a lot of inflammatory things.

But she hadn't lit his fire. At least not all the way.

Just thinking about her behavior made her cringe.

She'd stared him right in the eye and practically begged him for sex, and he'd turned her down cold. What was the matter with her?

Or rather, what was the matter with him? Most guys would have been octopuses. But not Harry.

He'd been a complete gentleman. Drat him.

In her mind's eye she saw him as he'd looked, perched stiffly beside her on the couch. The man was graced with a razor-sharp mind, dark intelligent eyes, and an enigmatic way about him that commanded her attention. He was the trustiest horse at the stable, the wisest insurance policy at the agency, the calmest lullaby in the songbook.

Whereas she rode motorcycles, carried only liability insurance, and when she sang, she belted out rock and roll.

He was smart and quite obviously grasped concepts she would never understand. Half the things he said whizzed right over her head. She'd never been with a man more in touch with his mind than his body. He was brilliant. She could never keep up with him. He thrived on intellectual challenges.

And she was not a scholar.

She should forget all about what had *not* happened here tonight. She should ignore her body, still flushed from the excitement of kissing him. She should deny the ache low in her belly.

Frustrated, Cassie dug her fingernails into her palms. *Just go to sleep.*

But she couldn't.

She flipped. She flopped. She couldn't stand the torture. If she was going to get any sleep at all, she needed something to take the edge off.

Heave-ho went the covers. Her feet hit the floor. She retrieved her backpack and dug around inside until she found what she was looking for.

Ah, yes. Sweet relief.

Harrison couldn't sleep.

Instead of mellowing him out, the peppermint schnapps had revved him up. Although he was probably giving too much credit to the peppermint liqueur and not nearly enough to Cassie's inherent sexiness.

It was easier to blame the schnapps.

After twenty minutes of fighting the sleeping bag, he decided to get up and take a crack at trying to decipher the scroll. Just one problem. The scroll was still locked in the glove compartment of the Volvo. He would have to creep through the living room, tiptoeing past Cassie snoozing on his couch.

Knowing her, she probably slept in the buff. Without the benefit of covers.

He lay in the darkness a little while longer, but then curiosity got the better of him. He had to take another look at those hieroglyphics. If his brother—who was not the sharpest trowel at the dig site—had been able to decipher the Minoan hieroglyphics, there was no reason he shouldn't be able to figure them out too.

Except that ancient Egypt had been Harrison's only field of focus, whereas fickle Adam went on jags. He pursued whatever subject interested him at the moment. He had dabbled in everything from Egyptian to Greek to Mayan cultures. Grudgingly, Harrison had to admit his brother's versatility might have given him an advantage. Or maybe Adam's modern sensibility, his very edginess, had lent him the edge.

And, speaking of edgy.

Harrison felt as if he was hiking way too close to a steep canyon drop-off whenever he thought about Cassie. There was something compelling about her. Maybe it was her indomitable optimism that countered his natural pessimism. Even in the face of her ransacked apartment she had quickly rebounded. He wished he possessed such an elastic temperament.

I thought her exuberance got on your nerves.

Well, maybe he'd judged her a little harshly. Harrison had discovered his opinions often mellowed when he was in private. Maybe it was from growing up with a strong, domineering mother; maybe it was his instinctive loner tendencies; maybe it was just that when he got off by himself he really had time to contemplate. But it seemed his real enjoyment of being with other people came when he was alone. When he had adequate time to sit back and reflect on the interactions.

Alone, he could match up his memory with the feelings and try them on without the confusion and clutter of being expected to react in a certain way.

He thought of Cassie's winning smile, her saucy wink, the sexy sway of her hips, and he got a soft, warm feeling in the dead center of his chest.

Okay, stop thinking about her. Focus on what's important.

Resolutely, he turned his mind to the enigmatic hieroglyphics and his missing brother in order to keep it off his lovely houseguest.

But his resolution didn't last long. Cassie was the most—and he was being crude here, but no other word truly fit—*doable* woman he'd ever had the pleasure to kiss.

Which was exactly the quandary.

He wanted her. He couldn't have her. She was all wrong for him, and he was all wrong for her. He didn't do runaway lust, and she didn't do commitment.

He was just experiencing a physical reaction. Chemistry. It meant nothing.

You have a brain, Standish. Use it, for godsake, and keep your dick in your pants.

His dick, however, had a whole other agenda.

He tried to tell himself it was purely an intellectual pursuit that drove him from the sleeping bag, and not the insistent throbbing in his penis. He bought into his own line of bull. He would simply sneak into the kitchen without turning on a light, slip out the door, retrieve the scroll from the glove compartment of his car, and hightail it back to his office. He would not, under any circumstances, even glance over to see if Cassie did indeed sleep au naturel.

Two steps down the hallway and then he heard a soft, feminine moan.

Was Cassie dreaming? Or having a nightmare?

What if she was awake?

He almost pivoted on his heel and fled back to his office, but then she moaned again. It was a low, helpless sound.

Was she in pain? What if she needed his help?

He took a step forward but stopped, not sure what to do next. If she was asleep, he didn't want to wake her; but then again, if she was having a nightmare, she might appreciate being awakened

The moaning deepened, grew more frantic.

She had to be in distress.

Then he heard another sound. It was odd, out of place. A strange buzzing rattle. A shiver played down his spine like fingers on a keyboard. He'd heard that sound before.

On a dig. In the desert.

Rattlesnake.

But how could a rattlesnake have found its way into his apartment?

Harrison froze. His mind spun. He thought of Cleopatra and Cassie. Of asps and rattlesnakes. Of regal women and poisonous vipers.

The rattling buzz grabbed him by the ears and shook violently. Trouble. Danger. Someone had stabbed a guy in a mummy suit. His brother was missing, an ancient amulet stolen, an enigmatic papyrus found. Someone had ransacked Cassie's place. That same someone could have dumped a deadly serpent in his apartment.

"Harry." Cassie called his name in a rough, achy whisper. "Harry, Harry, Harry."

Had she already been bitten?

She must have heard him in the hallway. She was snakebit and calling out to him for help.

Galvanized, he rushed into the living room and flicked on the light.

And that's when he learned that Cassie was neither sleeping nor bitten by a snake.

She was in the middle of his bed, murmuring his name as she pleasured herself with the most sophisticated rattling, buzzing sex toy he'd ever seen.

"Cassie!" Harrison's scandalized voice broke through the sweet fog of her solo sexual adventure.

What? He had never seen a woman masturbating before? From the shocked expression hanging on his face, she deduced probably not.

"Good God, woman!" he exploded. "Have you no sense of personal decorum?"

Truthfully, Cassie was mortified to have been caught playing with the Rattler, but she wasn't about to let Harrison know that she was anything but honest, open, and straightforward about her sexuality. She tugged the covers over her waist and blinked at him in the bright light.

Oh God, this was the most humiliating thing that had ever happened to her.

"Well," she said matter-of-factly, totally ignoring that her body was burning up with embarrassment. "What did you expect? You turned me down."

The Rattler buzzed and vibrated beneath the sheets, and Harrison's gaze was fixed on the spot where it danced. "I . . . I . . . ," he stammered.

Cassie blew out her breath. It wasn't the first time she'd left a guy speechless, but it was the first time she'd ever had so much trouble collecting her thoughts. There was only one way to deal with this obloquy—turn it back on him.

"Come on, Harry. We're both adults here. It's okay to tell the truth—didn't seeing me like that turn you on?"

"No!" he denied, but when his gaze, quick and furtive, fell below her waist, she knew he was lying.

Buzz, buzz, buzz, went the Rattler.

"Could you . . . er . . . um . . ." He waved a hand at her sex toy slowly vibrating its way across the mattress. "Could you turn that thing off?"

She shrugged nonchalantly, trying her best to look casual and totally in control of the entire situation when she was anything but. Swallowing hard, she slipped a hand beneath the covers and pulled the vibrator out into the open.

Embarrass him. Make him feel uncomfortable. Can't let him know you're not as sexually liberated as you let on.

"See." Cassie winked, hoping against hope that he didn't notice how her hand was shaking and call her on it. "It's called the Rattler. It's got these little button heads that shimmy and shake and . . ."

His face was beet red. No fear that he was going to notice her own telltale flush. He cupped his hands over his ears and averted his eyes.

"That's way more information than I need. Thanks."

"Who knows? You never can tell," Cassie teased, while at the same time she imagined the earth cracking open and sucking her down inside and then slamming shut on her, forever keeping her safe and sound from the undignified backfire of her own audacity. "Someday you may end up with a woman who's just dying for a good rattle."

"I seriously doubt that."

She waved the vibrator. "Aw, come on, you're a man of science. You keep toying with that djed thing. This should interest you. Look: here's where you turn it on.

And here's where you adjust the speed. The faster it goes, the louder it rattles."

She was pushing him too far but couldn't seem to stop herself. If Harry had any clue exactly how unnerved she really was, he would quickly figure out she was not as candid about sex as she professed.

"Okay, okay."

She jacked up the dial. Now it sounded as if there were three dozen rattlesnakes in the room. "You ought to feel this sucker."

"No, that's all right. It's mechanics. I'm an archaeologist. Totally different sciences. Now put that thing away."

"Prude," she muttered under her breath, but it was only for effect. In reality she was extremely glad to stuff the thing into her backpack and out of sight.

They both simultaneously exhaled their relief.

"I've never met anyone like you," Harrison exclaimed, shaking his head.

She forced herself to grin impishly, when what she wanted to do was flee into the dark of night, never to face him again. "Is that a good thing?"

"Hell if I know."

He ran a hand through his hair and finally met her gaze. She did spy lust shining in those dark pools. She could also see that he was scared of his earthier impulses.

Right this moment, what she wanted more than anything was to pull him in bed on top of her. But the look on his face told Cassie that if she dared to do anything so bold, he would likely have a coronary on the spot. Never mind that he was young and in good shape. He obviously had no experience with daring women who knew their way around their own bodies.

"You flummox me, Cassie. I can't understand how you can be so . . . so . . ."

She tilted her head and studied him. He didn't seem judgmental. Not in the least. In fact, below his obvious embarrassment, he'd seemed quite curious about what she'd been doing.

"How can I be so what?"

"Uninhibited about your body," he finished.

"Hey, babe, I'm a *Cosmo* girl," she said saucily, finally regaining her natural sass. "Never miss an issue."

"I've gotta start reading that magazine." He grinned.

"You know," she said. "The two of us would make a spectacular hookup."

"What do you mean?"

"Look at it this way. I'm into romance, but I don't do commitment. You're into commitment, but without the romance-colored glasses. We've got sizzling sexual chemistry, although mentally we're polar opposites. Yet it's the perfect recipe for a lusty fling. Sorta like cinnamon ice cream—sounds like a bad idea, but it tastes really great. Say yes, and I'll give up the Rattler so fast it'll make your sperm swim."

He looked at her speculatively. "I'd have to be out of my mind to agree."

"That's the point, Harry. To get you out of your mind and into your body," she whispered.

He leaned down. Was he going to kiss her? Cassie's heart thumped. Please, oh, please, yes. She raised her chin, pursed her lips, and waited.

His lips hovered just out of reach; he wanted to. She could see it in his face.

"That's it," she egged him on. "For once in your life,

let go. Do something wild and reckless and irresponsible. Ask yourself, What would Adam do?"

It was the wrong thing to say.

He pulled back so quickly that he stumbled over the coffee table and fell squarely on his butt. "My brother would cause chaos. Just as he's already done."

"Okay, scratch the Adam thing," she said. "Forget all about Adam."

But it was too late. Harrison picked himself up off the floor and gave her a wry smile.

"While your offer of a wild sexual fling is tempting, here's the reality. We're running out of time. Adam is MIA, whether by choice or not we don't know for sure. Someone trashed your apartment. My livelihood is hanging in the balance and you're this close"—he measured off an inch with his forefinger and thumb—"to ending up in jail. This might not be the most prudent time to start an affair."

CHAPTER
13

Not long after dawn, the perky sound of Cassie's cell phone playing the digitalized notes of "Girls Just Want to Have Fun" dragged her from a very frisky dream about Dr. Harrison Standish.

In her dream, she'd been systematically dismantling his every sexual inhibition and enjoying herself immensely in the process. In reality, she cracked open one eye to discover she had a pounding headache. She fumbled for the phone and ended up rolling off Harry's couch, sheets tangled around her legs as she clobbered the floor with her hip.

And the cell kept ringing, taunting her.

Give it a rest, Cyndi Lauper.

She finally got the phone freed from her purse and flipped it open. When she saw whose number was on the caller ID, Cassie groaned. She depressed the talk button and, in the same tone Jerry Seinfeld used whenever he greeted his nemesis Newman, said, "Hello, Phyllis."

"Where are you, Cooper? I tried your home phone and got nothing." Don't you have your answering machine on?"

Should she admit she was at Harrison's apartment?

Cassie decided to evade the question. "It's only"—she paused to peer bleary-eyed at her wristwatch—"six-thirty. I don't have to be at work for three more hours."

"Be here in twenty minutes," Phyllis said. "Alone. Or it's your ass."

The dial tone hummed in her ear.

Witch.

She glanced up to see Harrison standing in the door-way. He was sans glasses, his hair sexily mussed, and he had the sweetest sheet crease ironed into his cheek. He wore boxer shorts and a T-shirt, and he was sleepily rub-bing his eyes. Dang, the man was downright adorable in the morning.

He stared. "You're not . . . um . . . I didn't . . . er . . . interrupt anything like last night?"

She realized that she was still lying on the floor with the sheet wrapped around her ankles. Memories of last night flooded her brain, and she got embarrassed all over again. Chagrined, she scrambled to her feet.

"Nope, nothing like that. I just forgot I wasn't at home, and I fell off your couch looking for my cell phone." She waved the phone to prove she hadn't been doing that other thing.

"Oh." He looked as if he didn't believe her.

"It was Phyllis," she said, desperate to get his mind off what he'd caught her doing last night. "She wants me at the Kimbell, ASAP."

"Uh-oh."

"Uh-oh is right. She sounded pissed off. I think we might be busted."

"I'll come with you," he said.

"No, that's okay, it's my problem. I'll deal with her."

"It's not okay. I got you into this mess. I'll get you out."

"I don't need you to save me. Phyllis was gunning for me long before this."

"Don't be stubborn," he said. "I'll go change."

Phyllis had told her to come alone. Although Cassie really wouldn't mind having Harry along for moral support, she didn't want to rile the curator any more than she already was.

"Harry," she said, stopping him halfway down the hall. He turned and looked back at her. "I think our search for Adam would be more efficient if we split up. We've already wasted a lot of time."

He paused, considering what she'd said.

"So you can just drop me off at the museum. I'll call you later and let you know what's going on."

"Or we can meet back here." He went to a drawer in the kitchen cabinet and pulled out a key. "In case you need to get in."

"You're giving me a key to your place. Harry, that's a pretty big step."

"Stop joking for once. Are you sure you don't need me to help out with Phyllis?"

"Positive."

"All right," he conceded. "I've been working on a search strategy. Adam occasionally stays at his father's house in Westover Hills whenever he's in town. I'll head over there while you go to the museum. I can interview the staff. See if anyone's heard from my brother."

"Okay."

Just two minutes shy of Phyllis's twenty-minute ultimatum, Cassie bounded out of the Volvo and hurried up the steps of the Kimbell. She skidded into the curator's office with thirty seconds to spare. She expected to see Phyllis looking like a thundercloud, which she was, but what she hadn't expected was to find Ahmose Akvar sitting behind Phyllis's desk.

When he spotted her, the Egyptian got to his feet and gave a courtly nod. "Miss Cooper."

"Mr. Akvar." Cassie extended her hand. He took it, raised it to his lips, and kissed her knuckles.

"Sit down, Cooper," Phyllis barked.

From the look on her boss's face, she was in much deeper trouble than she'd imagined. Help! She was seriously starting to regret not bringing Harry along with her.

Heart pounding, she sat, as did Ahmose. Phyllis remained standing, arms crossed over her chest as she leaned against the front of her desk, inches from Cassie.

"I'm confused," Cassie said. "Why is Mr. Akvar here?"

"May I address Miss Cooper?" Ahmose asked Phyllis. The guy certainly knew how to get on the curator's good side, asking her permission to proceed.

"But of course, Mr. Akvar." Phyllis flashed him a smile. "Please, go ahead."

Ahmose cleared his throat. "Miss Cooper, I understand that you and Dr. Standish have become quite close over the past few days."

Cassie shifted in her seat. What was he getting at? "I wouldn't say close. We barely know each other."

"But you have been working side by side on the star-crossed lovers exhibit, and you orchestrated this"—he paused—"murder mystery theater together."

"Um," Cassie hedged, not certain how to respond. She cast a sidelong glance at the curator. She didn't want to lie to the Egyptian official, but she didn't want to get herself in an even deeper crack with Phyllis. "I'm not sure what you're asking."

"Knock off the crap," Phyllis exploded. She leaned in close, glowered darkly, and shook an index finger. Cassie half expected her to grab the desk lamp off the table, shine it in her eyes, and mutter in a Gestapo accent, "Ve haff vays of making you talk."

"What?" Her voice came out in a whispered squeak. *Way to stay cool.* Oh man, this was much worse than she'd anticipated, plus she was such a lousy liar.

"Tell the truth. There is no murder mystery theater."

Cassie crumbled like a stale snickerdoodle. "Okay, all right, we made it up."

"Aha!" Phyllis crowed. "I knew there was no memo. I'm calling the police."

She reached for the phone, and Cassie was frantically trying to think of something to say that would make her put the receiver down when Ahmose Akvar reached over and pulled the phone from her hand.

"No," he said. "No police. Not yet."

"What do you mean, no police?" Phyllis glared at him. "We had the display case dusted for prints, and only two sets appeared. Cooper's and Clyde's."

"It is natural for her prints to be on the case. Personally, I believe neither Mr. Petalonus nor Miss Cooper are involved in the theft. The real thief would obviously wear gloves. I do believe, however, that Miss Cooper has unwittingly been manipulated by Dr. Standish and his brother, Adam Grayfield."

You could tell from Phyllis's expression that she was disappointed she wasn't about to see Cassie handcuffed and carted off to the slammer.

"Did you steal the amulet, Miss Cooper?" Ahmose asked.

This she could answer honestly. "No, I did not."

Phyllis snorted and started to say something, but Ahmose silenced her with a scathing glance. "I believe Miss Cooper could be a valuable asset to us."

"Excuse me?" She rounded her eyes and rolled out her best dumb-blonde routine. "I don't understand."

"Was the murder mystery theater Dr. Standish's idea?" Ahmose asked. "Did he ask you to go along with it only after the amulet disappeared?"

"Yes," Cassie admitted. "But I still don't see what you're getting at."

"Think about it, Cassandra," Phyllis said. "I fired you, and then Standish came to your rescue with this murder mystery theater idea. Now, why would he do that?"

"I don't know." Cassie shrugged, but a voice in the back of her mind whispered, *Why indeed?*

"Think, for once in your life," Phyllis retorted.

Ahmose frowned at the curator, and then he spoke to Cassie in a gentle tone. "Here's what I suspect happened. Dr. Standish was quite aware Ms. Lambert was looking for an opportunity to dismiss you. He and his brother, dressed as a mummy, staged a little drama for your benefit. Then Dr. Standish leaped to your assistance with an offer you couldn't refuse."

Cassie gulped. "I don't get it. Why would Harrison do something like this?"

"You are being set up to take the fall for the theft. You'll be the one going to prison, and they'll get off scot-free with the amulet." Phyllis snapped her fingers. "Put two and two together."

"But why would Harrison even offer to rescue me?

Phyllis had already accused me of taking the amulet. Why not just let me be arrested?"

"Timing," Ahmose said. "And Dr. Standish needed to plant evidence so the case against you would be airtight."

"Evidence? Like what? If they're keeping the amulet, what could they plant on me?"

"Another artifact from the exhibit."

The papyrus scroll? Cassie wondered. Was that what the baggage claim ticket and the crate had all been about? Was even Spanky Frebrizo in on it? She got a sick feeling in the pit of her stomach.

"I'm clean. Search me." She plucked up her handbag and shoved it at him. "Go ahead. Search me. Search my purse. Search my house. I've got nothing to hide." Then a sudden thought occurred to her, and she jerked the purse back into her lap.

"Hey." She pointed a finger at Ahmose. "Were you the one who ransacked my apartment last night?"

If he *was* responsible, the guy was cagey. His expression never changed. "Your apartment was ransacked?"

"Yeah? Know anything about it?"

"I do not. But perhaps your friend Dr. Standish faked a break-in for the opportunity to plant evidence."

"He couldn't have," Cassie said. "He was with me all evening."

"No, but his brother could have."

There was that.

Ahmose leaned back in his chair and steepled his fingers. "Miss Cooper, have you ever heard of the Minoan Order?"

Uh, not until last night, and Harrison had been the one to tell her about it. "Isn't it an extinct secret brotherhood cult?"

Ahmose shook his head. "Not extinct. The Minoan Order is alive and thriving in modern society."

"Hmm. Imagine that." She tried her best to look completely bored in spite of her racing pulse and mouth gone scarily dry.

"Members of this order believe that once the pieces of the amulet are reunited, a long-dead secret will be revealed. In fact, the Minoan Order has been caught several times trying to sell stolen artifacts. We've known for a long time they've been stealing them, we just haven't known how. Your friend Dr. Standish holds the key."

"What kind of secrets are you talking about?"

"I'm not at liberty to say."

"Alchemy? The ability to control the weather?" *Ka-thump, ka-thump, ka-thump* went her heart.

"Something much more provocative than that, Miss Cooper," he hinted.

"And you believe that?"

"I don't believe it, but that's not the point. The members of this order believe it, and they'll stop at nothing to get what they want. My countrymen and I suspect that Dr. Standish and his half brother, Dr. Grayfield, are both members of the Minoan Order."

"Really?"

"I can see you're having trouble processing this information. Do you know what the symbol for the Minoan Order is?"

"Yes. A double ring with the Minotaur."

"That is correct."

She and Ahmose locked gazes. "And?"

He reached down for the briefcase at his side, opened it, and passed her a college term paper with Harrison's name on it. She briefly skimmed the text. Her hand trembled, but she did her best to control it.

"So he wrote a paper about the Minoan Order. Big hairy deal. Who cares?"

"The Minoan Order cares. And Adam Grayfield has a tattoo of the Minotaur on his left shoulder blade."

"A lot of people have tattoos."

"The brothers own property together in Greece. A tavern. Want to know what it's called?"

"The Minotaur?"

Ahmose gave her a humorless smile. "I know this is not solid proof of their involvement in the Minoan Order, but collectively, these things make one wonder. That and the fact their mother was kicked out of Egypt fifteen years ago for performing a Minoan Order ritual at an excavation site."

No. Cassie couldn't buy into what Ahmose was telling her.

Could she say she trusted Harrison enough to side with him over a high-ranking member of the Egyptian Ministry of Antiquities? Could she so easily dismiss the possibility that Harry was not everything he seemed to be?

"For the sake of argument, say your suspicions are correct. None of that explains why Harrison and Adam would steal the amulet halves from the Kimbell instead of just taking them from the dig sites when they discovered them," she argued.

"You obviously don't understand how excavations work in countries like Egypt and Greece who've had antiquities pillaged for centuries. They're very sensitive about it."

"Please," she said. "Explain it to me."

Ahmose seemed endlessly patient, unlike Phyllis, who kept scowling deeply at her and pacing the carpet.

"There are armed guards at the sites. There's a great deal of paperwork, and everything must be approved and supervised by many people and recorded in many places. The Ministry of Antiquities takes immediate possession. It is very difficult to steal something, either at an excavation site or in the country of origin. The best opportunities for thieves occur when the artifacts are loaned to museums outside their homeland."

"Oh," she said.

"Then there is the political element," Ahmose continued. "One-half of the amulet was found in Egypt, the other in Greece. Neither country was willing to allow the other country access to their half of the amulet. In pieces, the amulet is useless to the Minoan Order. It is only through reunification that they can regain their long-lost secrets."

"Why didn't you come forward last night when the amulet first disappeared? Why didn't you call the police then?"

"For one thing, I do not trust the authorities in your country, and alas, I had no hard evidence against Dr. Standish. But that's where you come in."

"So what's the bottom line?" Cassie nervously drummed her fingernails on Phyllis's desk until the curator shot her a quelling glance.

"We need more evidence before we connect Dr. Standish to either the thefts or the Minoan Order. We want you to get very close to him. Gain his trust. If he thinks you are a fool, his guard will be down," Ahmose said. "It should not be so difficult for a beautiful woman like you."

"I don't know. It's underhanded. Sneaky."

"Your hesitation is understandable."

"I just need a little more time to think this through."

"Bullshit." Phyllis splayed both palms against her desk. "You want me to lay it on the line for you, Cooper? Here are your choices. Cooperate with us, and you'll get your dream job at the Smithsonian. Or side with Standish, and end up imprisoned for stealing priceless relics."

CHAPTER
14

Harrison couldn't help fretting as he drove to Ambassador Grayfield's mansion in Westover Hills. Why had Phyllis called Cassie at six-thirty in the morning? Had he made a serious error in judgment by letting her go see the curator alone?

It had seemed to make sense to split up. They were running short on time and needed to cover as many bases as possible, but in retrospect it might not have been such a hot idea.

One persistent question circled his brain. What if Cassie cracked and ratted him out? How much did he really trust her? After all, trust wasn't his greatest virtue.

He arrived at Tom Grayfield's front gate, entered the security code at the call box, and the gate swung open. He had expected to speak with the housekeeping staff, to see if anyone had seen or heard from Adam, but he was surprised to find Tom's personal chauffeur, Anthony Korba, puffing a cigarette on the back porch.

The minute Anthony spotted him coming up the driveway, he crushed the cigarette out beneath his heel.

"Harrison," he greeted and smiled broadly. "It's good to see you again. It's been a long time. No?"

"A long time, yes," Harrison said and embraced the man who used to drive him and Adam to and from the Athens airport whenever they visited Tom on holiday.

"You look good." Anthony sized him up.

"So do you. Is Tom here?"

Anthony nodded. "He came into town for the museum exhibit, and he's been invited to an event in Austin at the governor's mansion later today."

"Tom was at the museum for the exhibit? I didn't see him there."

"No, no." Anthony shook his head. "Plane delay."

"Harrison, how are you?" Tom's rich voice greeted him like a warm hug as he stepped out onto the back porch. "Don't stand on the stoop gossiping with the help, come in, come in."

"Hello, Tom." Harrison followed him into the house. Tom clapped him enthusiastically on the back. Over the years, the ambassador had been very generous to him, at times even assuming a surrogate father role.

"Let's go to my study." Tom led the way through the foyer, to the great hall, and on into his study. The lavish room was filled with expensive leather furniture, lots of animal trophies, and the finest aged scotch and Cuban cigars.

It had been several years since Harrison had visited the mansion, but not much had changed. He'd always felt uncomfortable in this house. It was too big, too ornate, too filled with dead things.

"Have a seat." Tom nodded at a chair and seated himself on the corner of his desk, fishing a Cuban from the humidor. "How've you been?"

"I'm doing great. How about you? How's the ambassador business?"

Tom laughed and waved a hand at his surroundings. His gold signet ring flashed in the light. "Obviously, I can't complain."

Harrison plunked himself down. A bull moose stared accusingly at him from the opposite wall.

"I did hear through the grapevine that you and Adam had decided to drag out the reunification ceremony with a little murder mystery theater concept. Good advertising ploy." Grayfield nodded and clipped the end off his cigar with special gold-handled scissors. "I'm guessing it was Adam's idea. He is gifted when it comes to bullshit. Takes after his old man."

"There's no murder mystery theater. It was a desperate stall tactic on my part." Harrison wondered exactly how much to reveal about Adam's disappearance. He didn't want to upset Tom unduly, but then again, if his son was in trouble, the man had every right to know what was going on.

"Oh?" Tom flicked his Zippo, lit the cigar, took a long puff, and then blew a smoke ring. "Why's that?"

He decided to tell him. Maybe Tom could help. "Adam never showed up at the Kimbell with Solen."

"What?" Tom groaned. "Don't tell me that kid is up to his old tricks."

"You haven't heard from him either?"

"No."

This had gone beyond pranks and publicity stuff. How could his brother just vanish into thin air? This was serious. "Adam didn't know you were coming into town for the exhibit?"

"It was last-minute. Wasn't sure I could make it in

time, and as it turns out, I didn't. My plane was delayed. There were storms over the Atlantic."

Harrison shifted in his seat and clutched the leather armrests with both hands. He thought of his brother. Of the underlying tension that had always existed between them. He had a sudden urge to start over, to absolve Adam. For having a father, for stealing Jessica, for being the fun, charismatic one.

Desperately, he wished his brother was in the room so he could apologize for having been so judgmental and withdrawn over the years. For not being the kind of big brother he should have been. He wanted to ask for a second chance. He didn't know if forgiveness was even possible now.

He felt despondent and somehow responsible.

If anything had happened to Adam, he didn't know how he was going to live with himself.

Tom studied Harrison's face. "Adam left you high and dry again."

"I really think this time is different. I have a gut feeling that he's in real trouble."

"I respect your concern, but let's not beat around the bush, Harrison. You're not a guy who's real in touch with his gut feelings. No offense."

"None taken."

Tom was right. What could he say? He'd been trained to shun his feelings in favor of logic. Anyone who knew Diana knew that. Except the training hadn't taken with Adam.

"Have you told your mother?"

Harrison shook his head.

Tom smiled. He loved being one up on Diana. "So you came to me first."

"Adam wouldn't want me to involve Mom unless I had no other choice."

"Wise move. No one wants an ass-chewing from Diana." Grayfield uncocked his leg and walked to the wet bar in the corner. "What makes you think Adam is in trouble?"

He poured himself a scotch. Drinking at seven-thirty in the morning? Tom must have noticed the look because he said defensively, "It's late afternoon in Greece."

Harrison ignored that comment and instead answered the question. "I can't reach him on his cell phone. I've left a dozen messages, and he's not calling me back. I'm really starting to get worried."

"Sounds like same old same old with Adam to me."

Harrison drew in a deep breath. "Okay. I didn't want to alarm you, but here's the whole story." Then, blow by blow, he told Tom everything that had transpired the previous evening.

Tom took a long pull of his drink. "Let's give Adam the benefit of the doubt, not that he deserves it, and we'll say that there is someone after him. What's your theory?"

"I was thinking he got in deep to loan sharks again. Maybe he gambled the money he borrowed to finance the Solen dig."

Tom shook his head. "Nope."

"Why not? It's happened before."

"Because I gave him the money this time."

Harrison was surprised. Adam had never taken Tom's money for a dig. He didn't like having to do things Tom's way. "Mind my asking why?"

The ambassador grinned. "Because of you."

"Me?"

"Couldn't let you take all the glory. Particularly after you found Kiya; that really fanned Adam's competitive streak. Why do you think I was trying to make it to this exhibit?"

"To see Adam show me up?"

Tom looked like a proud father for all of two seconds. "But once again, the kid let me down."

Conflicting emotions surged in Harrison. Feelings he used to be able to beat back, ignore. But ever since he had started hanging out with Cassie, he was having a harder and harder time suppressing his feelings.

"You're overanalyzing things again." Tom polished off his drink and got up. He came over to clamp a hand on Harrison's shoulder, his signet ring digging uncomfortably into his skin. "Don't worry. Adam will turn up. Always does. And usually with a very tall tale to tell."

Harrison started to ask if Tom knew that Adam had decoded the Minoan hieroglyphics, but he held his tongue. It was Adam's news to break to his father. Especially since Tom was such a Minoan Order buff. It was as big a deal as finding Solen. And for some strange reason, talking about it felt like admitting he might never see his brother again.

"I'm sure you're probably right," Harrison said, wanting to believe Tom's reassurances but deeply concerned that they weren't true. He got up to leave.

"If you hear from Adam, please tell him to call me. As much as he antagonizes me, I do love my son."

The minute Cassie left Phyllis's office, she phoned David, her brother-in-law with the FBI.

"Hey, Cass, how's my favorite sister-in-law?"

"I'm your only sister-in-law, David."

He laughed. "You're still my favorite."

"Flatterer."

"What's up?"

"I need a favor."

"For you? Anything."

"Run a background check on someone."

"Cassie, you aren't in any trouble, are you?" She could hear David rapping a pencil against something.

"Keyed up, Dave?"

"I'm always keyed up. It's dead around here. But stop avoiding the question. Are you in trouble?"

"No. Not really."

"Not really? I don't like the sound of that."

"Will you just do this for me and not ask a lot of questions, please?"

"Come on, don't make me promise that. I ask questions. It's my job."

"I thought you said you would do anything for me."

He sighed. "All right. Give me the details."

"He's an archaeologist named Harrison Standish. Someone in the Egyptian government just gave me bad news about him, and I want to know if it's true."

"What's the deal?"

"This Egyptian official suspects Harrison of being a member of the Minoan Order. You ever heard of them?"

"Yeah, and they're bad news."

"So the Minoan Order really exists?"

"Unfortunately, yes. Honey, I've got just one piece of advice. Run, don't walk, away from this guy. Why take the chance?"

"I can't walk away."

"Somehow I knew you were going to say that. You want to tell me why you need to know this?"

"I can't talk about it. Not now."

"All right," he said. "I'll look into it. In the meantime, if you get into any trouble, you call me. I'm a three-and-a-half-hour plane ride away."

"Thanks, David. I really appreciate it."

"No problem, kiddo."

"Um, there's just one other thing."

"What's that?"

"Please don't tell Maddie. She'll just think this is Duane Armstrong all over again."

Over at the warehouse, the mummy finally found his sarcophagus.

He'd spent the night gathering his strength, trying fruitlessly to recover his memory, and sawing the duct tape off his wrists with the sheet metal. He'd sliced his wrists to ribbons, but he didn't care. He had to get out of here before his captors returned to torment him anew.

And he had to find Kiya.

The men had hidden his sarcophagus behind a tall stack of corrugated tin sheet metal. Because he had been forced to make concessions for the piercing pain between his shoulder blades, it had taken him more than three hours to crawl his way around the warehouse looking for an escape route. His initial intent had been to grapple enough sheet metal over to the window and stack it high enough to reach the ledge.

Rationally, he had known that wouldn't work, that the sheets of metal were too large and unwieldy for him to handle. But he had no other plan, so he'd clung desperately to his illusion.

And then, when he was wrangling the metal, he'd discovered the sarcophagus.

A pleasant surprise.

If he could drag his ornate coffin to the window, it would make a much more effective ladder than sharp-edged, slippery, flat pieces of tin.

The unpleasant surprise came when he tried to move the damned thing. With his diminished strength, it wouldn't budge more than a few inches at a time. He sat panting on the floor and staring at the sarcophagus, his lungs almost bursting from the strain.

Kiya. He had to rescue Kiya. Had to get to her before Nebamun discovered his secret scroll.

He did not know where the thought about the scroll sprang from or what it meant. He closed his eyes and tried to concentrate.

Think.

A fleeting wisp of memory floated. Just out of reach.

Come on, come on.

In an instant the ephemeral remembrance was gone. And yet he could not shake the feeling of impending doom winding its way around his heart.

Why couldn't he remember?

Just get out of here. You can worry about your recall later. Out. Out. Out.

Get to Kiya.

He braced himself against the floor with his hands, bent his knees, and used his feet to push the sarcophagus forward through the narrow lane between the tall stacks of sheet metal. This time he moved it three inches instead of one.

Never mind the ripping sensation in his shoulder blades. He had to get out of here. The mummy wriggled forward on his butt, cocked his legs against the coffin, and shoved again.

And again.

And again.

And again.

An hour later, the sarcophagus was positioned beneath the window, a springboard to the world outside his warehouse prison.

He almost giggled. He felt that giddy. Grasping the gilded faceplate with both hands, he hauled his trembling body up onto the coffin. Once he reached that small four-foot summit, he lay resting, head tilted upward as he studied the window.

Sweet freedom.

He could almost taste it.

Except the window was still several more feet above the top of the sarcophagus. He stood on tiptoe, rested his chest against the cool wall, and stretched for the window ledge.

His fingers were just millimeters short of it. He was going to have to use the sheet metal after all. That meant climbing down, hoisting those hunks of sharp unfinished metal onto his raw, aching back, and dragging them across the warehouse space many, many times.

The wound in his back was already a boiling cauldron of pain.

He felt like crying. He clenched his teeth to stay the tears stinging the back of his eyelids. He'd never felt so alone, so empty, so hopeless.

At least not that he could recall. He had a hard time remembering.

To hell with self-pity. Get off your ass and get moving.

He didn't know where the tough inner voice came from, but it galvanized him. He slid off the sarcophagus, steeled his mind, and set off again.

Hours later, he was back atop the sarcophagus with a

stack of sheet metal draped over the top and dipping over onto the floor. It was enough to boost him an extra foot if he didn't slip off his precarious perch.

This time when he reached for it, his fingers found the ledge. Now all he had to do was drag his body weight up to the window.

Fourteen attempts later, he lay on the floor, bloody, sweating, nauseated, and ready to die.

Just let 'em kill you. Death couldn't be any worse than this.

But Kiya needed him. She was waiting. She'd always been waiting.

The thought bolstered his flagging spirits and he tried once more, crawling up on the metal-draped sarcophagus. He took a deep breath, gathered the very last ounce of his physical reserves, and lunged for the ledge with every bit of love for Kiya he possessed inside him.

He made it.

His chest hit the window ledge and his fingers found a secure hold on the window frame. He curled his feet against the wall, using them to propel him higher.

The metal sheets slithered off the sarcophagus and fell to the floor, but that was okay. He didn't need them anymore.

He was almost there.

And then he heard the ominous clicking and whirring rasp as the metal warehouse doors began to roll upward.

Cassie stood outside Harrison's apartment, staring at the key in her hand.

This was a defining moment.

Did she really trust him? Could she take him at face

value? Should she just walk away, pick up her cell phone, call him, and tell him what had happened?

Or should she believe Ahmose Akvar?

At this point it wasn't a matter of faith. If she did not do this thing that Ahmose and Phyllis were asking her to do, if she did not spy on the man who had trusted her enough to give her a key to his apartment, then she was going to end up taking the fall for the stolen amulet.

Besides, whispered that part of her that distrusted all men, *what if Ahmose is right? What if Harrison is playing you for a fool?*

There was only one way to resolve the issue. Go look for proof. If she found nothing incriminating, she could report back to Ahmose with a clear conscience.

But if you snoop, aren't you betraying Harry?

And yet, she had to know.

She pushed the key into the lock but didn't twist it, still hung on the twin horns of her dilemma. She thought of all the men in her life—her father, Duane, every guy on her collage wall. They'd all let her down in one way or another. How could Harrison be any different? She didn't owe him anything.

Resolutely, she unlocked the door and stepped inside. "Harry?"

The silence in the apartment was as deep as a moat.

"Yoo-hoo, Harry, you home?"

No answer.

Cassie's heart chugged and her throat went so dry she could hardly swallow. Like a sneak thief, she furtively edged down the carpet, headed for Harrison's office.

A floorboard creaked and she jumped half a foot.

Stop freaking out. He's not here.

His door was shut tight.

Another barrier to cross. Another wrangle with her scruples, but she'd come this far, she might as well see what was on the other side of that door.

The room, although crowded with books and papers and Egyptian artifacts, was tidy. Bookcases lined three walls. The fourth was taken up by a desk and computer equipment. A digital camera was perched on a shelf above his monitor, and stacked on the closest bookshelf were several photo albums. There was a mini-fridge positioned next to the computer desk. Cassie cracked it open to find nibbles and bottled water and soft drinks.

His space was his haven. He hid out here.

She studied the collection of artifacts but quickly understood she could be looking at evidence and not even recognize what she was seeing. She leafed through a few scholarly journals and her eyes glazed over. The material was way over her head. The room smelled of him, studious and worldly. It smacked her then, the extent of his intelligence, how much smarter he was than she.

Sitting here looking at his things, she felt so inadequate. A guy like Harry could never be interested in her for long. Once the sexual chemistry abated, there would be no common interest to hold them together. No glue to make them stick.

Who cares? It's not like you're into commitment.

Where the hell were these thoughts coming from anyway? It was probably nothing more than a case of wanting what she couldn't have.

Cassie thought about flicking on his computer and searching his files for evidence that he and Adam had orchestrated the theft of the amulet to set her up, but she wasn't quite ready for that.

Instead, she turned to the photo albums. She liked pictures. Photographs generally captured the good times in people's lives. She wanted to see Harry when he'd been happy.

The first photo album contained nothing but pictures of dig sites and artifacts. Here or there you'd see someone's shoe or an elbow, but this collection wasn't about Christmases or birthdays or summer vacations.

It wasn't even about people.

Disappointed, she stuffed it back on the shelf and opened the next album. Now this one was more interesting. These were pictures of Cairo. The shots were packed with people, but it was all crowds, no individuals, as if he'd been walking the streets of the ancient city snapping photos of buildings and vehicles and bustling streets. The pictures were artistic, displaying above-average skill with lighting and form and framing.

As she flipped through the books, it became clear that Harrison had a proclivity for observing life through a filter. Whether it was from behind a camera lens or through abstract theory or via ancient history, Cassie instinctively understood that he used these things to distance himself. His need for privacy isolated him. She felt at once sorry for him and ashamed of herself for intruding upon his sanctuary.

She almost did not pick up the third album, but in the end she was eager to find at least one picture of Harry with someone he loved. This album was older than the other two.

Inside, she found what she was looking for—baby pictures of Harry.

Her heart melted. He was such an adorable toddler in his diaper and a cowboy hat. Then a few pages later as a first grader with a missing front tooth. The glasses ap-

peared on his face in the next year's school picture and
her heart ached. It must have been tough having to wear
glasses so young. He'd probably gotten called "Four-
Eyes" more times than he could count.

There were a few pictures of him with a younger boy
she assumed was Adam. Frequently they were glaring at
each other. The pictures tapered off around his teenage
years. There was one shot of a sixteenish Harry beside a
battered Mustang, smiling his head off. Ah, so he hadn't
always been a Volvo aficionado. She noticed a clear absence of girlfriends. He'd probably been a late bloomer
when it came to dating.

Toward the back of the album she came across a
photo of what appeared to be Adam's graduation from
college. In the foreground stood Adam, wearing a cap
and gown, and Harry on the rolling green lawn of the
University of Athens in Greece. There was an older,
burly man positioned between them. She wondered if
this was Adam's father, Ambassador Grayfield. She'd
seen him in a few of the other photos too.

Adam, with his arm slung over the older man's shoulder, was grinning and making the V-for-victory sign.
Harry, as usual, looked rather taciturn. Cassie had an illogical urge to crack a joke and make him smile.

If she hadn't reached out a finger to trace the outline
of Harry's face, she wouldn't have seen the man lurking
there in the background. In fact, she almost didn't recognize him with a full head of hair.

She brought the album closer to her face and squinted.
He wasn't looking at the camera, but instead was studying Adam intently.

Alarm shot through her.

He was ten years younger and thirty pounds lighter, but she recognized him.

There, at Adam's college graduation, was none other than Phyllis's executive assistant, Clyde Petalonus.

CHAPTER
15

Right smack-dab in Harrison's parking lot, Cassie ran out of gas just as she was preparing to zoom over to Clyde's for a showdown. She sat in her Mustang, staring woefully at the gauge. She'd driven around with the empty light on plenty of times, and this had never happened.

Fine. Great. She could handle it. She would just call the auto club. She reached for her cell phone.

A car pulled to a stop beside her. She glanced casually over her shoulder and then did a double take when she spotted the white Volvo.

Uh-oh, busted.

Her pulse jumped. She had to stay calm and act as if she was completely innocent. As if she'd never been upstairs rummaging through his office. As if there wasn't an incriminating photograph in her pocket of him with Clyde Petalonus.

Harry sauntered over. Cassie rolled down the window.

"Hi," she said, trying her best not to look like a spy for the Egyptian government.

"Hey, you just drive up?"

"Uh-huh," she squeaked, hating that she had to lie, but taking the easy way out. She wasn't prepared to confront him head-on with the damning evidence.

"How come you didn't call and let me know you were leaving the museum?" Harry leaned against the door-frame and smiled down at her.

Her heart hammered. "I thought you were supposed to call me."

She hated this whole subterfuge. Especially since Harry was being so sweet. Damn, why was he being so sweet? He could not be a Wannamakemecomealot guy. He turned her on too much. She wouldn't get turned on by a bad guy.

Ahem? What about Peyton Shriver? And Duane? Let's not forget Duane.

"Guess we got our wires crossed," he said mildly.

"Did you find out anything about Adam?" She rushed to change the subject.

Harrison shook his head. "Tom Grayfield's in town, but he hasn't heard from Adam either. What about you? How'd it go with Phyllis?"

"Um, okay."

"Okay?"

Did he sound suspicious or was it just her guilt-ridden imagination?

She shrugged. "To be a pain in my butt. You know Phyllis."

"What'd she want?"

"What is this?" she wanted to snap, but instead she said, "She wanted to know more particulars about the plans for the second party on Saturday night. She told me to spend the day ironing out the details."

"So you're free to come with me to see Clyde Petalonus?"

"Clyde?"

"Yeah, in the nuttiness of last night I forgot that he lied for us about the memo. As I was driving back over here, I kept asking myself why," Harry said.

"I wondered the same thing."

The midmorning sun was beating down through Cassie's window, but that wasn't why she was starting to perspire. Rather, it was Harry's proximity and the topic of conversation that had moisture beading her neck.

"And he disappeared really quickly last night. I never saw him leave."

"You . . . um . . . didn't know Clyde before meeting him at the Kimbell, did you?"

Come clean. Tell me that, sure, you've been acquainted with Clyde for years and years, and then I'll know the photograph doesn't mean a thing.

He looked at her strangely. "No. What? Were you thinking he lied to protect me?"

"It crossed my mind."

"I was thinking he lied for you."

"Nope," Cassie said. "He wasn't lying for me." She met his gaze and telegraphed him a message with her eyes. *Please tell me the truth.*

Harry said nothing.

Apparently he wasn't going to confess. How could he stand there and fib to her? Crushed, Cassie fisted her hands. She felt as if she'd just learned her favorite chocolates contained strychnine.

What if he's not lying, her hope whispered. Maybe Adam was the one who stole the amulet. Maybe Clyde was protecting him, not Harry.

But Adam wasn't the only one in that graduation picture. Harry had been there too, and he had just denied knowing Clyde back then. The question was, Why would Harry want to confront Clyde about the fabricated memo if they were conspirators?

None of it made sense.

"Should we take my car or yours?" he asked.

Cassie swallowed. How was she going to play this?

He looked so endearing in his mismatched clothes and unruly hair that she just had to trust him. She would operate on the motto that had served her well throughout her life—when in doubt, smile and deny reality.

"Okay, Clyde, let us in."

Ten minutes later, Cassie was pounding on the door of Clyde's cracker-box palace in Arlington Heights, two doors down from a Taco Bell. The smell of breakfast burritos and lard wafted on the morning breeze. She knew where Clyde lived because she occasionally gave him a lift to work when his aged Buick Regal acted surly.

"We know you filched Kiya's half of the amulet," she said. "So cough it up."

Clyde did not respond.

She slid a sideways glance over at Harrison to see how he was reacting to the accusations she was hollering at the door, but as was often the case with Harry, she couldn't read his expression.

Holding the screen door open with one hand, she stood on tiptoe and tried to peer through the small diamond-shaped window at the top of the wooden outer door.

"You can run, but you can't hide, Clyde. Don't make us go to the police. Or worse yet, we'll sic Phyllis on you."

Cassie figured, if nothing else, *that* threat ought to have the curator's assistant swinging the door open pronto.

But no dice.

She couldn't see much through the window in the door. For one thing, even at five foot eight she was too short to get an unobstructed view. Obviously the cutout was for lighting, not for spying. Plus, the window was dusty and coated with grime. Clyde wasn't married, and apparently he kept house with a typical "Windex? I don't need no stinking Windex" bachelor mind-set.

"Spptt, Harry."

"What is it?"

"You're a good four inches taller than I am. Take a gander through the window and tell me what you see inside."

"To what end?"

"To the end of finding out what in the hell is going on around here."

He sighed, shouldered past her, and peered through the window. Cassie tried not to notice how he smelled like soap and toothpaste, or how cute and intellectual he looked in his round, dark-framed glasses. Sort of like a grown-up Harry Potter.

Stop ogling him. The guy could be a high priest in the Minoan Order. But even as she thought it, she still couldn't reconcile the Harry she knew with the cunning mastermind Ahmose Akvar had made him out to be.

"Well?" she asked.

"I don't see anything."

Cassie rolled her eyes. "What do you mean, you don't see anything? You have to see something."

"No," he corrected her. "There's nothing to see."

"You're kidding."

She muscled him aside, stretched as tall as her toes would allow, but she still couldn't see anything except the foyer wall. And it was a truly icky shade of latte. "We've got to get in."

"What?"

"How else are we going to learn anything?"

"We could be mistaken," Harry said. "Just because Clyde lied to Phyllis for us doesn't mean he stole the amulet."

Oh yeah? What does it mean when he's in an old photograph with you and Adam?

She waved a hand. "Look around and see if Clyde's the kind of guy who stashes a hide-a-key. Try under the welcome mat. We need to get inside and see if he left any clues."

Harrison grimaced. "This idea doesn't appeal to me."

"How come?" Was it because he might have left clues implicating him?

"I'm a private guy, and as such, I respect other people's right to privacy."

"Luckily, I don't have such misgivings. I'll do whatever I have to do to stay out of jail. I'm not taking the fall for Clyde's sticky fingers," she said.

"You've got to stop jumping to conclusions."

"Well, at least I jump. You spend so much time hugging the shore, too cautious to stick a toe in the water, that you never make a move."

"Yeah, well, what if there was a drop-off in the water? Or a deadly undertow? Who would be dead and who would be alive?"

"And who would have had fun while they were alive and who wouldn't?" she challenged.

"Why are we arguing about this?"

"You got me. Just check the welcome mat for a key."

"Fine."

"Fine." Hardheaded man.

Harrison lifted up the corner of the dusty welcome mat with two fingers. "Nothing here."

He let the mat flop back down, sending dirt scattering across the porch. Cassie peeked behind the mailbox and underneath an empty flowerpot but came up empty-handed.

"Looks like Clyde's not a key stasher," he said.

"Let's check around back. Maybe you can pry off a window screen so I can wriggle inside—and don't give me that long-suffering look."

"I don't see the point in breaking into the man's house."

"Hello? The guy stole Kiya's amulet and left me to take the blame."

"We don't know that."

She met Harry's gaze and he didn't flinch. What was going on behind those dark, enigmatic eyes? She didn't know what to think or whom to believe. "Clyde lied."

"People lie for all kinds of reasons." His eyes were locked on hers.

Was he lying to her? She was certainly keeping secrets from him. A tremor afflicted her, a slight thing, nothing terribly noticeable. At least she hoped he didn't notice. But it was in her legs and then her arms. She steadied the quivers by locking her knees, dropping his gaze, and nervously tucking a strand of hair behind one ear.

"You're acting differently," he said. "What's changed between us?"

Cassie hung a nonchalant expression on her face. "Changed? Nothing's changed."

"What happened with Phyllis?" He reached out a hand to touch her shoulder and she drew back. "See? That's changed. Yesterday you wouldn't have pulled away from me."

Dammit, why did she have to be such a lousy liar? She had to sidetrack him from talking about Phyllis. She couldn't keep fibbing, or she'd soon give herself away. She had to tell him something that was true to throw him off the scent.

"Maybe I'm still embarrassed about last night."

"Aw, Cassie, you don't have to be embarrassed about that. You were just being yourself. I like how open and honest you are."

If he only knew. Right now she felt about as open and honest as an alcoholic Enron executive. And as guilty.

"I'm going in," she said and nodded at the house, desperate to get out of this conversation.

"And what if some nosy neighbor decides to notify the police?" he asked.

"We'll just say we dropped by to see an old friend. He didn't come to the door. He's plump; he's middle-aged. He doesn't eat right. He's a heart attack waiting to happen. We were worried."

Cassie didn't wait for Harry to follow. She took off around the side of the house. The grass whimpered for a good mowing, and her sandals sank deep into the dewy foliage. The itchy Bermuda seeds tickled her ankles, and several narrow blades lodged between her toes.

Ugh. The sacrifices she made for her job.

She cornered the house and was pleasantly surprised to find the back door standing open. No breaking-and-entering charges needed. Well, no breaking anyway. Technically, she supposed she would still be entering.

She started up the back stoop, but a hand reached out and snagged her elbow.

"Are you crazy? Buy a déjà-freakin'-clue. Didn't we just go through this last night?"

She turned to look at Harry. "Hey, I like the déjà-clue thing. Way to reference pop culture. Didn't know you had it in you. Now let go of my arm."

"Woman, don't you have even a whisper of common sense? An unknown man in a mummy costume has been stabbed, an ancient amulet has been stolen, and your apartment was plundered. Figure out the appropriate response. Danger. Proceed with caution."

"Fiddle." She blew a raspberry. "If his place is empty, Clyde is long gone."

"There could be someone else inside instead of Clyde."

"Oh." He was right. She hadn't considered that.

"I'll go first. You stay right behind me."

"Can I wrap my arms around your manly waist?" she teased, to lessen the tension and to keep him from noticing any more changes in her behavior.

"Are you physically incapable of going five minutes without flirting?"

"Pretty much."

A grin tugged at the corner of his mouth, but he managed to fight it off. "Just follow me."

Harry ascended the stoop, Cassie at his heels. He pushed the door open. The hinges creaked ominously.

She made spooky horror movie noises.

"Shh." He frowned and whispered fiercely, "What if someone is in here?"

"The cow already got out of the barn on that one. I

don't think our presence is going to come as a news bulletin."

"Good point," Harry admitted and stepped over the threshold.

The kitchen was lit only by the morning sun dappling through the bare window. Except for the refrigerator and stove, the room was vacant. No dining table, no toaster on the counter, no dirty dishes in the sink. But there was dust on everything. It looked as if Clyde didn't live here anymore.

Very strange.

They moved into the tiny living room. Harry led the way, and it was all Cassie could do to keep from resting her hands on his shoulders. But she was still anxious about trusting him. She wanted to believe in him, but Ahmose had raised enough doubts in her mind.

They skulked down the narrow hallway and into the first bedroom. It was as dusty and empty as the rest of the house. They took a quick peek into the adjoining bathroom.

Nada.

One room to go.

The room at the end of the hall.

"If this was a horror movie, this is where the audience would be screaming at us not to go into the room. You realize we're the too-stupid-to-live people."

"I promise you that Freddy Krueger isn't in there."

"What about Jason?"

"Him either."

"Michael Myers?"

"Nope."

"Leatherface?" Cassie asked. "He's the scariest of all with that chain saw. Rrrrrrrr." She pretended to slice him up with a chain saw.

"Knock it off." Harrison squared his shoulders and moved toward the door. Cassie crept after him.

He turned the knob.

Blood swooshed through her ears.

Harry edged the door open.

Something darted out.

Something small and gray and fast.

A mouse!

Cassie shrieked, wrapped her arms around Harrison's neck, and jumped into his arms. "Omigod, omigod, omigod. I would have preferred Leatherface."

"You're afraid of mice?"

"Petrified."

"He's more afraid of you than you are of him," Harrison said.

"I seriously doubt that. You're incredibly lucky I didn't pee my pants."

He was holding her and chuckling. Cassie could hear his laughter deep inside his chest.

She didn't want to get down. It felt kinda nice in Harry's arms, and there was a mouse lurking in the house. But she wasn't a lightweight and she didn't want to break his back, so she let go of his neck and set her feet on the floor, all the while casting a suspicious gaze in the direction of the mouse.

"Let's wrap this up." He stepped into the room the mouse had come out of. Tentatively, Cassie crept in behind him.

It had a short stairway leading down into a cellar.

Oh no. She wasn't about to go down there. She quickly backpedaled.

"Where you going?" Harry started down the steps.

"That's okay, you go on, report back to me."

"What? You chicken to go down to the cellar?"

"No." Terri-fickin'-fied.

"Brock-brock." He made chicken noises and flapped his arms like wings.

"Don't make fun of me. I'm claustrophobic."

"And after that big speech about jumping headlong into the water."

Why did he have to call her on this? She hadn't been in a cellar in eleven years. She never wanted to be in one again.

"You know the only way to get over a fear is to face it," he said.

"I know."

Crap. He was going to goad her until she went into the cellar. With no windows and only one door to escape through.

"We'll leave the door open. I'll be right with you." Yeah, famous last words. Probably what Ted Bundy said to his victims.

Don't exaggerate. Harry's not a serial killer.

Maybe not, but he could very well be a thief who was trying to frame her for his crime. If that was the case, why had he brought her to his conspirator's house?

Maybe he had wanted to lure her here so he could lock her in the cellar. That thought froze her.

He extended his hand. "Come on."

Don't go!

"You can do it." His smile could have melted the polar ice caps. She was such a sucker for a great smile. How pathetic was that?

"Can't I just wait here?"

"That doesn't sound like the Cassie I know."

"All right," she said. "But if I do this, the next time I

want you to do something adventurous, you can't hold back."

"Deal."

She could do this. No problem. Just a simple cellar. She gulped and eased down the stairs.

"Now that wasn't so hard, was it?" He reached up and pulled the dangling cord on the bare lightbulb. It took every ounce of courage she possessed not to fling herself back up those steps.

"Hey, look here." He squatted on the dirt floor. Cassie could clearly see the imprint of what looked like a coffin delineated in the dirt.

Their eyes met. "Solen's sarcophagus."

Harry trod across the floor, headed for a cabinet positioned in the corner beside a cedar hope chest.

"Where you going?" she asked, quickly covering the gap between them.

"We're here. We've come this far. Might as well check out every nook and cranny."

"Such a thorough little scientist."

The expression on his face was somber. "I've got to be honest with you, Cassie. I'm really getting worried about Adam. What if he's"—she could tell he was having trouble even saying the word—"dead?"

His voice cracked, and the sound of it squeezed her heart. There was no doubt in her mind that he cared about his brother. He wasn't lying. This wasn't an act. Ahmose had to be wrong. Harry would never put either his job or his brother in jeopardy by stealing an ancient artifact.

Unless he's just a damned good actor. It's not like you're the best judge of a man's character.

But she could not deny the look of concern in his eyes. He was extremely worried about his brother.

Harry reached for the handle on the cabinet door.

"Ooh, wait, wait." She shook her hands like she was drying her fingernails after a manicure. "Let me brace myself in case there's another mouse in there."

"Tell me when."

She gritted her teeth and tensed her shoulders. "Go."

Harry wrenched the cabinet open, and they found themselves staring down at a bolt of white linen.

The mummy hit the ground rolling.

Ooph.

Stunned, he lay there gasping like a guppy. It was a long drop for a three-thousand-year-old guy with a leaky stab wound in his back.

Get up. You ain't got time to laze around.

He heard shouts from inside the warehouse. Knew his absence had been discovered by Nike and Froggy Voice. Frantically, he rolled over on his side, tried to force his legs to obey.

After a couple of wobbly attempts, he managed to drag himself to a standing position.

Get the hell out of here.

Right. Which way?

If he took off in the wrong direction, he could easily run into Nike and Froggy, and if he did, he knew there would be no getting away. In his present condition, he couldn't outrun an infant.

He swung his head around, spied a delivery van parked on the street at the end of the alley. Maybe he could hide behind it until the coast was clear.

Hurry, hurry.

Something brushed against his leg. He looked down and saw he was starting to unravel. A long strip of linen was dangling from his elbow. If he wasn't careful, he'd trip himself. Tucking the material into his fist, he took off at a lope, headed in the direction of the van, but just as he reached it he tripped in a pothole and went tumbling headlong under the vehicle.

He bit down hard on his bottom lip to keep from crying out. He was underneath the van's back tire, and when he rose up he bonked his head on the axle.

Son of a wh—

Something fell off the undercarriage.

He peered at it, blinking. It was a small oblong black box with a magnet on one side.

A hide-a-key. He smiled. He was saved.

Hope spurring his recovery, he scooted from underneath the van, slid open the box, and retrieved the key. He was just about to hop behind the wheel and take off when he heard a pounding noise coming from the back of the van.

Was someone in there?

You don't have time to mess around. Get moving. Get out of here.

Bam, bam, bam.

Get in the van. You can look in the back later.

He hopped inside, started the engine, and drove away just as Froggy Voice and Nike came bursting from the warehouse. Cutting the corner so short that the van bounced up onto the curb, he stomped the accelerator and careened three blocks through heavy traffic. All the while the knocking in the trunk was growing louder and louder.

Damn, shut up.

What if it was Kiya? The thought suddenly occurred to him.

Okay, that did it.

He pulled over to the shoulder, left the engine idling, and got out.

Vehicles blew past him. Someone honked.

Cautiously, he inched his way to the rear of the van. He grabbed hold of the door handle. Preparing to run at the first hint of trouble, he gingerly pulled the door open and peered inside.

The person bound and gagged on the floor looked familiar, but he couldn't place the name. Slowly, the mummy approached. A pair of gray eyes beseeched him.

"Hey," said the mummy. "Am I supposed to know you?"

CHAPTER
16

Clyde's the mummy?" Harrison fingered the bolt of linen.

"No." Cassie shook her head. It reassured her that he looked genuinely confused, and reinforced her trust in him. "There's no way. The mummy was stabbed in the back."

"Unless the stabbing was faked."

"No. It was real blood, and Clyde was in the museum looking fine just minutes after I found the mummy in the courtyard."

"Could he have stabbed the mummy?"

"Maybe."

"Or," Harrison said.

Their eyes met.

"Clyde and the mummy were working together," they said in unison.

Cassie was certain that Harry was as surprised by this insight as she was. Ahmose had to be wrong about him, that's all there was to it.

"I'm guessing the mummy created the distraction

while Clyde doused the lights and snatched the amulet," Harrison said.

"But if Clyde and the mummy were in cahoots, then who stabbed the mummy?"

"Could it have been a third party?"

"Somebody horning in on Clyde and the mummy's caper?"

"But who?"

"Maybe it's the same person who ransacked my apartment."

"Or maybe Clyde ransacked your apartment. Maybe the mummy double-crossed him. Or perhaps Mummy Man was the one who trashed your place." Harrison set the bolt of linen back in the cabinet.

"I'm telling you that mummy was in no shape to do anything more than breathe—and he was doing very little of that—much less ransack and double-cross."

"And then there's the central question." Harrison brushed his fingertips against his pant legs.

"Yeah," Cassie said. "Who's the mummy?"

"Adam?"

"What now?"

Harry took the djed from his pocket and fingered it, a faraway look in his eyes. He seemed to use the thing to help him think. "My brother's in trouble," he murmured.

"Call him again." Cassie handed Harry her cell phone. "I'll check out the cedar chest."

Palming the djed, Harry accepted her phone and pulled out the antenna. Cassie sank to her knees beside the cedar chest, praying there were no mice inside there either.

She undid the clasp and cautiously eased open the lid,

not sure what to expect. She was slightly disappointed to find sweaters. She lifted them out one by one.

"I can't get any reception down here," Harry muttered.

About halfway to the bottom of the chest, underneath all the sweaters, Cassie found something disturbing. It was a Minotaur mask and a wax seal with the sign of the Minoan Order engraved into it. She caught her breath. The implication was clear. Clyde was a member of the Minoan Order.

She started to call out to Harry to tell him what she found, but then she hesitated. As much as she did not want to believe Ahmose, the part of her that had trouble trusting any man whispered in her head. What if Harry and Clyde were in this together?

But then why had Harrison brought her here?

She pivoted in her squatting position to see where Harry was and if he was watching her, and that's when she realized she was alone in the cellar.

And the door at the top of the stairs was swinging closed.

It clicked shut with an ominous sound.

Cassie freaked. She totally lost it. Terrified, she flew up the steps and charged the door. No, no, she could not be locked in a cellar. She would die. No place to go to the bathroom. No food to eat. Not enough air.

Help!

Her knees were rubber, her body instantly drenched in sweat. She slammed both palms hard against the door. "Let me out! Let me out! You can't lock me in here!"

Two seconds later, Harry wrenched the door open and she tumbled out onto the floor, gasping frantically. He stared down at her. "It wasn't locked."

She swatted his leg. "I told you I didn't like cellars, and you left me down there alone."

"I thought you were following me. I had my mind on Adam and I—"

"You forgot me," she accused. She was *not* going to cry. She would not.

"Not on purpose. Why are you clenching your fist? You gonna hit me?"

"Maybe." No crying. Stop sniffling.

"Jeez, Cassie, I had no idea you were so claustrophobic." He bent down to help her up, but she squirmed away from him.

"You forgot me." Her bottom lip trembled.

"Okay. I forgot you. I'm sorry. I was focused on calling my brother, and when I focus on something I get absentminded about everything else."

He looked remorseful, but she wasn't letting him off the hook. Five minutes ago she'd been sure Ahmose was completely wrong about Harrison; now she wasn't so sure.

"Just calm down," he soothed. "Take a deep breath."

"Don't tell me what to do." She pushed past him, headed for the back door. For fresh air and freedom.

He followed her. "I didn't mean to make you cry."

"I'm not crying," she said, drawing in great gasps of air, the morning sun warming her face as she walked out into Clyde's backyard.

"What's this then?" He caught up with her and reached out to stroke her cheek damp with tears.

She jerked her head away and glared. "I'm not crying."

"Oookay, if you say so."

"You can be a big ol' jerk, you know that?"

"Do you want to tell me why you're overreacting?" he said calmly.

His calmness made her want to punch something. "None of your damned business."

He raised his palms. "All right, obviously you have a thing about getting locked in a cellar, and you don't want to talk about it."

"Damn skippy." She rubbed a tear from the end of her nose with the back of a hand.

"Please forgive me for leaving you down there. Sometimes I get so caught up in my mind, I forget what my body is doing."

"Gee, way to make a girl feel special, Einstein. Explains why you're not married."

"I suppose I deserved that."

She felt safer now, less haunted, more like her cocky self. The farther she got away from the cellar, the faster the past receded. She shouldn't have freaked out on him. It wasn't Harry's fault. He didn't know about Duane and the cellar.

Taking a deep breath, she opened her mouth to tell him about Duane, but got no further because a man darted out of Clyde's back door.

"Harry!" she cried as the man in Nike sneakers slammed into her and knocked her to the ground.

Immediately, Harry took after the guy. Cassie struggled to her knees. The guy was holding something in his hand that looked sort of like the keyless entry remote from a set of car keys. The man had a small head start, but Harry was closing the gap.

"Stop!" Harry hollered.

And to Cassie's amazement, the guy did.

But no one could have predicted what he would do

next. The man pressed the button on the remote in his hand, and Clyde's house exploded.

The force of the blast blew out the windows and knocked Harrison sprawling to the ground.

"Cassie!" He crawled back across the lawn.

"I'm here; I'm okay."

He reached for her and tucked her body under his, protecting her from the debris raining down around them. His heart was thumping madly and his mouth was bone dry.

Harrison had trained his mind not to react to his body's emotions so well that he was able to feel the spurt of adrenaline rushing through his system but still process his thoughts rationally. They'd checked every inch of the house, and it had been empty. The man had clearly slipped in the back door while they'd been in the cellar and set the bomb.

But who was he, and why had he blown up Clyde's house? What did all of this have to do with Adam and the missing amulet?

He didn't know, but he was determined to find out.

First, they had to get out of here. The police would be arriving soon, and they'd be hard-pressed to explain their presence here. They had no time for police questioning.

"Sweetheart," he said, the strength and clarity of his voice surprising even him. His chest was pressed into her back. "Are you all right?"

She nodded. He clambered to his feet. She rolled over and looked up at him, her eyes dazed. He held out a hand to help her up, but she scooted away from him on her butt.

"Stay away from me."

What was the matter? Was she shell-shocked? Had

something hit her on the head? She appeared to be okay. He took a step toward her.

"Don't come any closer."

"Cassie, I'm not the enemy."

"Aren't you?"

The look in her eyes rattled him to the bone. She was scared of him.

"You were going to lock me in the cellar so your accomplice could blow me up in the house."

"No!" He said it more vehemently than he intended because her fear of him tore a hole in his heart. When she cringed, he dropped his voice. "How can you even think that about me?"

"There was a Minotaur mask in Clyde's cedar chest and other things that looked like they could belong to the Minoan Order."

"There is no Minoan Order." Had she hit her head? Did she have a concussion? Was that why she was accusing him of such crazy things?

"Oh yeah? Then who detonated the house?" She stared at him as if he'd sprouted a pitchfork and devil horns.

"That guy in the Nikes—you just saw him."

"How do I know it wasn't staged for my benefit?"

"Look around. I think the bomb was real."

She blinked. "I'm so confused."

"Please believe me. I didn't try to hurt you. I'm on your side."

Siren screams. The emergency vehicles would be here soon.

"Let's get out of here. I'll take you somewhere quiet and safe. We don't need to get tangled up with the police."

"I don't know what to believe." She drew her knees to

her chest. She looked so lost sitting on Clyde's debris-strewn lawn with bits of grass in her hair.

He kept his hand extended. "You're just going to have to trust me."

"I'm not good at that." She shivered and rubbed her hands over her upper arms.

He squatted in front of her, took her chin in his palm, and forced her to look him in the eyes. "Cassie, I swear, I would never, ever hurt you."

Poor kid. She was shell-shocked. He couldn't blame her for jumping to ridiculous conclusions. He had left her alone in the cellar after she'd told him she was claustrophobic. He had been caught up in his own agenda, and he hadn't paid attention when the cellar door swung shut behind him.

He'd treated her like an afterthought.

When he thought about it from her point of view, he could understand why she'd come uncorked. A woman never wanted to feel trapped by a man. Had he learned nothing from having a mother like Diana? If she knew what he'd done, she would give him hell.

And then it hit him like a kick to the gut. Cassie had almost died in that house.

So how are you going to make it up to her? He had to do something to gain back her trust. He had to apologize. Big-time.

"I'm an ass," he said. "An A-number-one dillhole for being so insensitive, but we've got to get out of here before the police show up. Are you coming with me?"

He held his breath, waiting. The sirens screamed nearer.

Cassie reached out and took his hand.

*   *   *

A crowd had gathered on the lawn, but everyone was so intent on staring at the devastation that no one really took note of them as Harry gently escorted her toward the Volvo parked on the street by the Taco Bell. The first fire truck arrived just as Harry started the engine. By the time the second truck pulled to a stop, they were turning the corner onto a main thoroughfare.

"I feel like we've done something wrong, sneaking off like this," she fretted

"We don't have a choice. The police would question us for hours, and we simply don't have the time. We have to find Adam. Besides, how would we explain being in Clyde's house?"

He was right and she knew it. She did her best to throw off her anxiety. She'd never been much of a worrier. That was Maddie's job. Everything would turn out all right. She had to believe that, and since she'd chosen to go with him, she had to trust her instincts and believe in Harrison, no matter what Ahmose suspected him of.

"Where are we going?" she asked.

"It's a surprise."

"I'm not really in the mood for any more surprises," she said. She'd had enough of the unexpected for one day, thank you very much.

"It's nearby. Just a short detour. I want to go somewhere we can relax and catch our breath for a minute." He took University Drive to the Fort Worth Zoo.

"We're going to the zoo?"

"Uh-huh."

He parked the car, paid the entry fee, and they went inside. Cassie kept glancing at him, torn in two conflicting directions. Part of her wanted to break down and tell him everything Phyllis and Ahmose had sprung on her, but her ears still rang from the echo of the explosion, and she didn't know what to believe.

It was just before noon on Thursday. The crowd was light and consisted mainly of mothers with strollers, waving juice boxes and Lunchables.

"It's this way." Harrison took her elbow, guided her down the narrow asphalt path toward the rear of the grounds.

"There's nothing out here." She hadn't been to the zoo in a long time, but she was pretty sure they were walking away from the animal attractions.

"Special exhibit," he said.

A howler monkey screamed, and an eerie coldness blasted down Cassie's spine. She was still high-strung from what had just happened at Clyde's and feeling mistrustful.

She glanced over at Harrison.

He was sprouting a five o'clock shadow and his hair was scruffy, but he looked kinda good. And he smelled even better. Like soap and sunshine. She caught the aroma of cigar smoke on him. She liked cigar smoke. Her daddy smoked cigars when she was little.

Duane had smoked cigars too.

Well, hell, Duane had smoked a lot of things.

They had to circle around the construction zone, and just when Cassie was certain they'd reached the end of zoo property, she saw a temporary building constructed out of a tentlike material and mesh wire.

"What's this?" she asked.

He pointed at the sign that she'd failed to notice in her paranoia, and then she remembered reading about the two-week exhibit. In fact, there were banners up all over town advertising it. She'd just forgotten.

The building was a butterfly hatchery.

Harrison opened the screen door and they scooted into a small area, where they paid a small extra fee for the attraction and were greeted by a butterfly expert who gave them a short lecture.

"Go right on through." The perky lady guide handed them a color brochure. "Pick out a butterfly emerging from its cocoon, watch it hatch, and you get to name it. After that, walk on through to the butterfly garden. Please make sure the doors close securely behind you."

They walked into the hatchery area where another tour guide, this one a lanky male, greeted them. The humidity was high in this area. Cassie could just feel her hair frizzing, but she soon forgot about her hair as they watched the butterflies hatch.

"Which one do you want to claim?" Harrison asked.

Cassie heard the excitement in his voice and she was surprised to discover she was excited too, watching new life uncurl into the world.

"That one." She pointed.

"You've chosen Lepidoptera *Danaus plexippus*. The monarch." The guide grinned. "You've made an excellent choice."

A few minutes later, their butterfly was born.

"She's beautiful," Cassie breathed.

"She'll sit on that twig for a while to pump up her wings. What would you like to name her?" the guide asked.

Cassie looked at Harrison. "What do you think?"

"There's only one name for her." Harrison's eyes met and held hers. "She's a vibrant beauty who's only in your life for a short while. We'll have to call her Cassie."

"Cassie it is," the tour guide said and entered the name in his log.

Cassie's throat felt full and scratchy. She blinked and had to drop Harrison's gaze.

"Step on through into the butterfly garden," the guide said. "We'll bring Cassie in as soon as her wings have fully opened."

They moved into the garden ripe with lush fruit and vegetation. The climate was tropical, warm and damp, and the air was filled with all manner of butterflies.

Cassie had never seen so many of the lovely creatures. They were every color under the rainbow. Small, medium, large. Everywhere she looked she saw butterflies.

She glanced over at Harrison. Butterflies fluttered above his shoulders, landed on his head. One was even walking along the top of his ear.

"Look at you." His eyes crinkled.

Butterflies were all over her as well. Lightly kissing her skin with their spindly legs. She giggled and then pressed a hand to her heart. "It's so breathtaking. Thank you for bringing me here."

"My gift to you," he said. "To apologize for being such an inconsiderate ass."

"You weren't an ass. I went schizo."

"No. You had every right to be upset with me. In my single-mindedness I did let the cellar door close on you, and I'm sorry."

"Oh, Harry."

"Please, forgive me. I hate to think you're mad at me."

"There's nothing to forgive."

"You folks want a picture with Cassie?" The tour

guide came in from the other room with Cassie the monarch perched on his finger.

"Yes." Harrison nodded. "We do."

"Give me your hand," the butterfly wrangler tour guide instructed.

Cassie held out her hand, and he transferred the monarch onto her finger. Cassie the butterfly flexed her wings.

"Hurry," Harry said. "She's about to fly."

The tour guide snapped the Polaroid picture just as Cassie the monarch took flight. Harry was smiling and the tour guide was smiling and, aw hell, Cassie the woman was gonna cry.

CHAPTER
17

Harrison had wanted to do something nice for her, to apologize for being such a lunkhead and scaring her. But he hadn't expected this simple trip to the butterfly hatchery to affect her, or himself, so profoundly.

"That's the sweetest, most romantic thing anyone's ever done for me," Cassie said for the fifth time and stared down at the Polaroid in her hand. She'd kicked off her sandals and propped her feet on his dashboard. She had such adorable feet.

They had left the zoo and were headed down University toward I-30 in search of lunch. He wanted to find a quiet place where they could talk. They needed to hash out the significance of what had happened at Clyde's, but Cassie still had that goofy, sentimental expression on her face, and it was starting to unnerve him. He'd wanted to make her happy. He just wasn't sure he'd wanted to make her *that* happy.

"Obviously that creep who blew up Clyde's house was the same one who ransacked yours. Surely there aren't two Nike-wearing criminals causing us problems," he said. "What I can't figure out is why he blew up Clyde's place."

Cassie said nothing.

"Unless he was trying to kill us. What do you think?"

"Harry, I can't hide my secret anymore," Cassie said. "There's something important I have to tell you."

"What?" He jerked his head around to stare at her. "What secret?"

"I can't keep this up. Suspecting you is killing me, so I'm putting my cards on the table."

"Suspecting me? Of what? What are you talking about?"

She took a photograph from her pocket and laid it on the console between them. "I know about you and Clyde, so you can stop lying to me."

"What?" he said for the third time, and momentarily took his eyes off the road to glance down at the picture.

It was the snapshot of him and his brother and Tom at Adam's college graduation in Crete.

"Where did you get this?" he demanded.

"Don't make this about me. That's Clyde Petalonus in the background, and you denied ever knowing him before you came to the Kimbell."

Harrison picked up the photograph and squinted at it. By gosh, she was right. It was Clyde. "I swear to you, I had no idea Clyde was in the picture."

"And you expect me to believe that?"

"You were snooping through my apartment," he accused. "You got this photo out of my office."

"Yes," she admitted.

He stared at her, stunned. He couldn't fathom that she would violate his privacy. He clenched his jaw. "Why?"

"I'm going out on a limb by telling you this," she said. "You don't know how much it's costing me to trust you."

"No more than what it cost me to trust you." He waved the photograph at her. "And you betrayed me."

"Harry, I'm sorry."

"My name is Harrison."

She flinched. "I can understand your anger, but I had no choice. Ahmose Akvar and Phyllis told me I'd go to prison for stealing the amulet if I didn't spy on you. There were only two sets of fingerprints on Kiya's display case. Mine and Clyde's. So I spied and I found the photograph."

"And you impulsively jumped to conclusions about me."

"It wasn't a big leap."

"Why did Ahmose recruit you to spy on me? What does he suspect me of?"

Cassie's gulp was audible. "He speculates that you're a member of the Minoan Order."

"And you believed him?"

"No. Yes. I don't know," she said miserably.

"We're going to get this straightened out," he said. "We're going to confront Ahmose."

At just that moment, a customized chrome Harley zipped around them.

Harrison did a double take, unable to believe what he was seeing. "There he is! There's Adam!"

"Where? Where?"

"On that Harley."

"How can you tell? It zoomed by so fast, and the guy is wearing a helmet."

"It's the same motorcycle I saw outside the museum last night. I would bet my doctorate on it." Harrison made an erratic U-turn. Car horns blared. He tromped the gas pedal and followed the Harley out onto the freeway.

"Hey, slow down. I like adventure, but there's adventure and then there's foolhardiness."

"I'm not letting him get out of my sight." He gritted his teeth determinedly.

They were too far away for him to get a good glimpse of the rider to see if it was indeed his brother, but Harrison knew that was the motorcycle. He changed lanes, edging out a U-Haul with New Jersey plates.

"Get back over," Cassie shouted. "The Harley's taking the Rosedale exit."

Harrison obeyed, turning on his blinker and cutting sharply in front of the U-Haul, earning himself a double-whammy middle-finger flip from the driver and his passenger. Cassie blithely waved at them, smiled broadly, and called out, "Thanks for letting us in."

"When in doubt," she told Harrison, "assume that getting flipped the bird is just the way people say howdy wherever they're from."

Ah, the sunny, illogical philosophy of Cassie Cooper.

The street they drove down was littered with potholes. Vagrants squatted outside liquor stores. Many buildings were boarded up, vacant. Women in very skimpy outfits sauntered up and down the sidewalk, waving at passing vehicles.

"Don't worry," Cassie said, apparently not even noticing they'd entered an unsavory neighborhood. "We'll catch up to Adam. I can still see the Harley. Wait, wait, he's pulling into the parking lot of that bar. Lemme see." She rolled down the window and craned her neck out of the Volvo. "The place is called 'Bodacious Booties.' Hmm, is your brother into seedy strip clubs?"

"Not that I'm aware of," he said grimly, but then again, who knew?

Nothing made sense anymore. Harrison was the quintessential reluctant hero journeying through the mythological woods with his very own, very sexy Trickster sidekick. When or how his life had started diverging wildly out of control, he could not exactly pinpoint, but all roads led right back to Cassie.

And the scary thing about it: he was enjoying the ride. Until a man in a filthy overcoat threw a brown paper bag wrapped around an empty wine bottle at his hood when he stopped for a red light.

"Asshole," the guy swore at him.

Harrison honked his horn.

"Hey, Harry, don't get so upset. It wasn't anything personal. The guy was aiming for that trash can next to the streetlight. See, there." Cassie waved at a graffitied trash barrel positioned at the curb. "He can't help it if he's a bad shot."

Harrison glanced over at the bum. The guy bared his teeth and shook a fist. Yeah, right, he was just aiming for the trash can.

Not for the first or even the tenth time, he wondered how Cassie had survived well into her twenties with those rose-colored glasses glued so firmly to her face.

He didn't even wait for the light to change. Once he was sure no traffic was coming, he floored it through the intersection.

"Whoo-hoo!" Cassie sat up straight and grasped the armrests with both hands. *"Breakin' the law. Bad boys, bad boys,"* she sang, the theme song from *Cops*.

He wished she'd stop making him grin at the most inopportune times. He bumped into the parking lot of

Bodacious Booties and cut the engine, glancing over his shoulder to make sure the bum hadn't trailed them from the intersection.

The chrome-customized Harley sat out front along with numerous other motorcycles. In peeling paint, the silhouette of a naked woman adorned the side of the building. The provocative beat of pole-dancer music throbbed from inside the club.

"Are you certain that's the bike you saw Adam drive away on?" Cassie asked in a squeaky voice. She sounded as nervous as Harrison felt.

"Positive."

He had no idea why Adam was inside this den of iniquity, but he was determined to find out. No matter how scared he might be to walk through that door.

But what to do with Cassie?

He couldn't very well leave her alone in the car in this neighborhood. Yet the thought of taking a woman like her into a place like that shoved icicles through his veins. The men in there would be on her like wolves on a newborn lamb.

It's up to you to protect her.

Okay. He could do this. He would do this. Adam was inside. His brother could help if things got dicey. But he had to think this through, get it right in his head so he wouldn't make the wrong move.

Cassie, however, had different plans. Before Harrison even realized what she intended, the crazy woman was out of the car and heading for Bodacious Booties, her own bodacious booty bopping up the steps.

He leaped from the car and charged after her. Lord, she'd be the death of him. He caught her elbow just as she stepped over the threshold into the smoky, dimly lighted strip bar.

A lanky, bored woman with breasts she had definitely not been born with spun listlessly on a small stage. To one side sat three pool tables. A gaggle of guys in leather and chains stood around drinking beer, chalking their cues, and occasionally casting glances at the dancer.

Harrison spotted the Indy hat immediately. Adam was sitting at the bar with his back to the door. A burly dude with a bandanna on his head was seated on the stool to his right. The barstool to Adam's left was empty. Harrison decided to approach from that side.

"There's your brother." Cassie nudged him in the ribs. "Go get 'im."

He hated to be rushed, but he'd seen the way the men were eyeing Cassie. Best to claim his brother and get out of here as quickly as possible. But then he thought of all that had happened, how Adam had been leading them on a wild-goose chase, and anger took over.

Stay calm, stay cool, stay detached from your feelings.

To Harrison's confusion, his never-fail mantra failed. No matter how strongly he told himself not to do it, he could not seem to stop himself from stalking over and slapping a hand on his brother's shoulder.

"Just what in the hell kind of game do you think you're playing?" he demanded.

Adam turned his head.

Only it wasn't Adam.

The guy had a face like a car accident. His cheeks were crisscrossed with pockmarks and scars. His nose had been broken at least twice, and his eyes were so small and close-set that he looked cross-eyed. Life had not been kind.

Without a word, the man pushed off the barstool and rose to his full height. Harrison was forced to look up and up and up. At six feet, Harrison was by no means short. But this dude was a sequoia.

"You startin' somethin' with me?" The cross-eyed guy leaned down and blew his hot, beer-and-pork-rind-smelling breath in Harrison's face.

"No, no," Cassie rushed to say. "He's not starting anything. Case of mistaken identity."

Why couldn't she have let him handle this? He might be terrified, but he didn't need her to rescue him.

"You let your woman do your talkin'?" Pork-Rind Beer Breath asked.

"Hey baby," said the bandanna-headed guy on the barstool to the right. He made smooching noises at Cassie. "I wanna start a little sumpin' with you."

"Let's discuss this like rational men," Harrison said. "I thought you were someone else. Please excuse my blunder. I'm sorry if I caused you any inconvenience."

"Rational?" Bandanna Head hooted. "You think Big Ray is rational?" Then he winked at Cassie. "After Big Ray kills your boyfriend, wanna go out back and get it on with me, baby?"

"Before you pound me senseless, could you answer one question?" Harrison said to Big Ray, who was clenching his fists and grinding his small, crooked teeth. Harrison's mind raced, searching for a way out of this mess.

"Yeah?" Big Ray grunted, slamming his right fist rhythmically into his left palm.

"Is that your customized Harley out front?"

"No," Big Ray said, jerking his thumb at Bandanna Head. "It's Freemont's. But I borrow it sometimes."

"Did you borrow the Harley last night? Were you near the Kimbell Art Museum?" Harrison asked.

"Nah," Freemont supplied. "That wasn't Big Ray. That was me at the Kimbell last night."

"Were you wearing Big Ray's Indy hat?" Cassie asked.

"It's not Big Ray's hat. He likes to borrow stuff," Freemont volunteered. "Like other men's women."

"Whose hat is it?" Harrison asked, doing his best to ignore that last comment.

Freemont shrugged. "I met a guy in the airport who gave me that hat, a hundred bucks, and a white envelope with the name 'Harrison' printed on it. He said I should show up at the Kimbell wearing this hat and give the envelope to someone who worked there. What's it to you?"

"You said just one question," Big Ray said. "That's a bunch of questions, and they're starting to sound pretty damned nosy."

Harrison pulled five twenties from his wallet and slapped them on the bar. "How many questions will this buy me?"

Big Ray's eyes lit up and he reached for the cash. Just when Harrison thought that maybe they had a chance of waltzing out of there without Big Ray pounding him into talcum powder, Freemont picked that moment to grab Cassie's butt.

"Honey," Cassie said glibly and wriggled away from him. "I'm not up for grabs."

"Then you shouldn't have been wagging that gorgeous ass in front of me," Freemont said and then smacked her fanny so hard the sound of it echoed above the stripper music.

Harrison saw red.

And for a color-blind guy, that was quite a feat.

All logic flew out of his head. He was an animal gone wild. He ignored Big Ray and turned on Freemont. Curling his lip, he snarled, "Get your hands off my woman."

"Make me, Four-Eyes."

At that moment, Freemont was every bully who'd ever called Harrison a wimp. He was every jock who'd gotten the girl by pushing around a weaker guy. He was every petty tyrant who'd ever sexually harassed a woman.

Harrison smacked his hand around Freemont's wrist and yanked the man off Cassie. Then, before he even knew what he intended on doing, he punched Freemont square in the jaw.

Old Bandanna Head went down like a sack of cement.

Harrison blinked, amazed at what he'd done. Freemont sprawled on the floor at his feet, the bandanna half off his chrome dome. Harrison's fist throbbed, but Cassie was gazing at him like he was her own personal superhero. Archaeology Man to the rescue.

Unfortunately, everyone else in the place was looking at him too.

"Get him!" Big Ray hollered, and then it was a free-for-all.

They were beating the living crap out of Harry. Not only that, they were beating the living crap out of one another. Guys fighting for the sake of fighting.

The stripper and the bartender had taken cover, but everyone else was slinging punches and throwing beer bottles and bouncing pool balls off each other's heads.

Men.

Cassie stood in the midst of it, hands on her hips. She had to do something to save Harry, or they were going to kill him. She could call the cops, but that would take too long. She needed a plan and she needed it now.

Okay, think logically. What would Harry do?

Her mind tumbled with possibilities, but she quickly rejected them. She needed something that would make everyone stop fighting so she could grab Harry and make a clean getaway.

Think, think, think.

Big Ray grabbed Harry by the collar and threw him against the bar.

"Ooph," Harry grunted, and the pain in his voice tore a hole right through her heart.

Impulse urged her to jump on Big Ray's back and start slapping him about the head, but for once something held her back. Harry was depending on her to remain composed. She couldn't go off half-cocked and possibly land them in even more dire circumstances. Was this what it felt like to be prudent?

But she wasn't accustomed to thinking things through. Acting out was her basic defense mechanism. How did she make the shift from spontaneous to structured thought?

A beer bottle whizzed over her head.

Hurry, think quick!

Play to your strength, use your talents.

What the hell were her talents beyond flirting? Things had gotten a little too out of hand for that tactic to work at this late date.

Cassie groaned. What was she good at?

Everyone said she excelled at thinking out of the box. Terrific, what out-of-the-box solution could stop three dozen pissed-off, half-drunk, badass bikers in their tracks?

Harrison was on his feet, swinging wildly, desperately at Big Ray and missing his target completely. Big Ray laughed and punched him in the gullet.

A pool ball rolled under her foot. She could pick it up and bean Big Ray, or she could do something really spectacular and arrest the attention of the entire bar.

Whatever it is, do something, anything, before Harry gets clobbered to a pulp.

And then the answer came to her.

Cassie had left him.

When things had gotten too tough for her to handle, she had turned and run out the door. A small part of him was disappointed, but most of him was happy she was out of harm's way.

He told himself that her adiosing from the bar was a good thing. He wanted her clear of the fray. She'd done the only thing she knew to do, and he couldn't blame her for that. With any luck, she was out in the Volvo on her cell phone calling 911.

If only he could hold on until the cops got there.

His right eye throbbed where Big Ray had just planted his fist. His glasses were broken, dangling from one ear. Freemont had roused, and Big Ray was holding Harrison's arms behind his back.

Freemont was still a little wobbly but determined to get even. He drew back a fist, took a deep breath, and aimed for Harrison's sternum.

Oh, shit, this is going to hurt.

Harrison gritted his teeth, clenched his jaw, and braced for the fresh assault.

But the punch never came.

Instead, the front door slammed open and Cassie

strode into the room, carrying her backpack in front of her. The loud buzzing sound of diamondback rattlesnakes filled the room.

"Okay, boys," she yelled and held the bag aloft. "Y'all hear that?"

Everyone froze.

When Harrison realized what she intended, he almost started grinning at her craftiness.

Helluva creative woman. Using her vibrator to save his bacon.

"That's right," she said. "I have ten diamondback rattlesnakes in this knapsack. Everyone raise your hands and step back against the wall, or I'll let 'em loose."

Bzzz, bzzz, bzzz, went the bag.

No one made a move.

"Do it!" She unzipped the bag.

The rattling sound was much louder now. Dozens of hands shot into the air.

"Now step against the wall."

Like the usual suspects in a police lineup, the men all backed up.

"Come on, Harry," Cassie said. "Let's get out of this joint."

In spite of his jelly legs, Harrison sprinted happily toward her.

"Now, nobody do anything stupid, and we'll all get out of this without getting snakebit."

Slowly, buzzing bag still held aloft, Cassie and Harrison edged backward out the door.

CHAPTER
18

Your poor eye." Cassie made a soft hissing noise of sympathy and tenderly applied a chunk of cold beefsteak to Harrison's battered face.

His right eye was swollen shut and his head throbbed. Even his teeth hurt. But they were alive and in one piece, which after the bar brawl was saying something.

He was on Cassie's couch, and she was seated next to him with her soft, round breast pressed into his side. She'd taken a shower and changed into silky black lounging pajamas, and she looked good enough to eat. If he were to keel over dead at that moment, his life would be complete. Which was a totally stupid thought, but he couldn't help the way he felt.

Since when? You've always been able to distance yourself from your emotions.

What in the hell had the woman done to him?

"How did you think of using the Rattler as a decoy?" he asked.

She grinned and tilted her head at him in the cutest way. "I just asked myself, 'What would Harry do?' "

"And *that's* what you came up with?"

"Uh-huh."

"Wow, were you off base. I would never have thought of using a dildo as a weapon."

"Maybe not, but you would have thought first, reacted second. So that's what I did. Me, normally I'm the other way around."

"I think we made a good team."

"Me too." She beamed. "You hungry? I can fix us something to eat. I'm starving."

He wanted to say no because he didn't want her to get up. He wanted her to keep sitting right next to him. He wanted to feel her breast rise and fall against his arm as she breathed. But the mention of food made his stomach rumble and she heard it.

"Got the message." She grinned. "Food it is. Here, hold this." She took his hand and used it to anchor the raw steak in place against his eye. "Come into the kitchen and talk to me while I cook. I like company."

And he liked being her company.

Obediently, he followed her into the kitchen, trying not to wince against the jarring body aches, but he must have given himself away, because after he had plunked down at her dining room table, she brought him a glass of water and a couple of ibuprofen.

"Here, swallow these."

He didn't argue.

"Luckily for you and me," she said, digging around in the freezer, "I cook in huge batches once a month and then freeze the extras with one of those vacuum-sealer thingamajiggies. All I hafta do is drop the bag in boiling water and toss a salad, and voilà, instant home-cooked meal."

"I feel like we should be out there looking for Adam," he muttered. "Not eating dinner."

"We have to eat, and you have to recuperate, and we have to plan our next move."

"That's the problem. I have no next move. I'm all tapped out of ideas."

"Not for long. You're great at coming up with ideas."

"Not with this headache."

"We could try calling his cell phone again." She fished her own phone from her purse and handed it to him.

He didn't hold out much hope on that score, but while Cassie set a pan of water on to boil, Harrison called Adam's number.

No answer. He left another voice mail message and hung up. He sighed, pressed the steak against his eye with the heel of his hand, and looked up just in time to see Cassie bent over the vegetable crisper.

Nice. Very nice.

Even with a bum eye and blurry vision, there was no ignoring Cassie's fanny.

Great, now he was acting like that jerk-off Freemont. Just the thought of the way that guy had touched Cassie made him mad all over again.

She took the butter lettuce to the sink and rinsed it under running water. Harrison's good eye was glued to her fingers, watching her stroke the soft fresh leaves.

"You're not still thinking I'm a member of the Minoan Order, are you?" he asked.

"No. You've convinced me."

"Now I just have to figure out why Ahmose suspects me. I've known the guy for years."

"You're probably just the most likely suspect. Finding Kiya was your life's work. You have a lot invested."

"All the more reason not to steal her amulet."

"More and more, I believe Clyde is the one who's really in the Minoan Order."

"You're probably right," Harrison conceded.

"So let's go over this again, try to jog the brain cells and piece this jigsaw together. What did we learn tonight?"

"Stay out of biker-bar strip clubs and away from guys named Big Ray."

She giggled and sent the lettuce for a ride in the salad spinner. "No, I mean about your brother."

"He wasn't the one in the Indy hat who passed Gabriel the envelope."

"The next logical conclusion is that Adam is the mummy."

"Which means he got stabbed."

"He could be dead," Cassie whispered. She looked over her shoulder at him with such sadness that Harrison had to glance away. "I'm so sorry."

"I don't think he's dead." Harrison refused to consider the idea. "He's not dead."

"But then where did he go? What happened to him? He could barely walk. How did he get out of the courtyard?"

"Better yet, who stabbed him, and why?"

"And if he isn't dead, then why hasn't he tried to contact us?"

They looked at each other. They were no closer to the answers than they'd been last night at the masquerade party.

Had it only been twenty-four hours ago? That meant they had forty-eight hours left.

"Let's walk through it one step at a time," Harrison said.

The steak was getting warm, so he took it off his eye and went to wash up at the sink. As he leaned over for the hand soap, his hip casually grazed against Cassie's. He glanced down to where their bodies made contact.

"You're not fooling me." She chuckled. "I've been to Europe. I know when I'm being groped."

"I'm not groping you." He moved his hip away.

"Your eyes are."

"Correction, my eye is groping you. One eye is swollen shut. Besides, eye groping doesn't count. If eye groping counted, you'd have to slap nine out of ten men you came into contact with."

"Good point."

"I couldn't be married to you," he said. "I'd be blind from the black eyes and the busted glasses over defending your virtue."

"Nobody asked you to marry me."

"That's good." He snorted.

"You're mad. Why are you mad?"

"I'm not mad."

"Then why are you snorting?"

"I don't like the idea of all that eye groping going on."

"It's not your problem," she said. "Go sit back down."

He did. Not because she'd told him to. He just didn't have anywhere else to go, and he was starting to feel a little woozy. He managed to make it back to the table without breaking into a sweat.

Cassie placed a steaming bowl of ziti with meat sauce and grated Parmesan cheese in front of Harrison, along with a garden salad and a glass of red wine. He had no idea he was so hungry until he got a whiff of the food.

"That was fabulous." He pointed at his bowl with the back of his fork after he'd polished off the food. The wine was good too. He took another long swig. "You're a helluva cook."

"You want dessert?" she asked. "I'm up for dessert."

"Whatcha got?" He let the change of subject go.

"Strawberry shortcake."

"My favorite."

"No way." She beamed at him. "It's my favorite too."

Cassie couldn't say for sure how it happened, but one minute they were eating strawberry shortcake, and the next minute Harry was staring at her as if she were the dessert.

"Hmm," she said, knowing it sounded forced, but she felt compelled to cushion the sexual tension with a barrier of words. "Strawberries are really plump and juicy this time of year."

Great, that came out all wrong.

"Yes, they are."

She slipped him a surreptitious glance and her heart committed hara-kiri, slamming suicidally against the wall of her chest.

Every time she looked at Harry, he got cuter and cuter. She hardly noticed his mismatched outfits anymore. Clothes were just clothes, right? And she no longer thought of his unruly hair as unkempt, but instead found it just-rolled-out-of-bed sexy.

This was an alien experience, and she wasn't sure how to respond. In the past, she was either attracted to someone or she wasn't. If she wasn't instantly attracted, then things went no further. But if she was attracted, she would immediately romanticize the guy. In the beginning, the men she loved were always taller, smarter, better-looking than in reality, but as the relationship progressed, she bumped up against that reality and quickly lost interest.

But it was different with Harry. From the moment she'd met him, she'd found him irritating and elusive. And while his serene, self-contained isolation had initially intrigued her, she hadn't been bowled over by the sexual chemistry. He was the reverse of every man she'd ever been with. The more she got to know him, the more attractive he became.

Until, *pow!* All she had to do was look at him, and her libido rocketed through the ceiling.

Whoa. Slow down. What if Phyllis and Ahmose were right, and Harry was in this weird Minoan Order cult thing? She didn't want to get involved with a guy like that.

Except she couldn't imagine introverted Harry joining any kind of group organization, much less a secret society that probably dressed up in silly costumes with robes and hoods and such. No matter what proof Ahmose claimed to have.

Nope, Harry was not a costume-wearer. When she'd tried to get him to dress up as Mark Antony for the masquerade party, you'd have thought she had asked him to wear a purple tutu and march in a gay pride parade.

"Why are you looking at me like that?" she asked.

"Like what?"

"Like you want to eat me up."

"Maybe I do."

"Last night I would have been all over that offer," she said. "But tonight you're bunged up. You should be resting. You need to heal."

"I need TLC." He lowered his voice, lowered his eyelids, and gave her a sultry masculine stare.

"You've had too much wine." She took his glass away and deposited it in the sink with the rest of the dishes. "I can't take advantage of you when you're in a compromised position. Wasn't that what you told me last night?"

"I'm not drunk." He got up and walked toward her, palms held wide. "See, no stagger."

No stagger but lots of swagger. He looked so rough and rugged with that black eye. Like a proud tomcat. His battered face shouldn't have been a turn-on, but it was. Did that make her seriously twisted?

Probably.

He had gotten into a fight protecting her honor, and that's what was turning her on. Not his poor wounds.

All righty then.

She had to keep him out of her bed. As much as she wanted him, it wasn't the right time. He was beat up, and she was feeling too susceptible. It would have been okay if all she felt was lust for him, but things with Harry were too complicated to muck up with sex.

"You're much too inhibited for me, Harry. I need a spontaneous guy."

"I can be spontaneous."

His Godiva brown eyes glistened with a very masculine agenda. He had had too much wine. His mind was on serious mattress moves. She had created a monster. Where were those damned silver bullets and wooden stakes when you needed them?

"No, you can't."

"Yes, I can. See?"

He stripped his shirt over his head and threw it on the

floor. Immediately, her eyes were drawn to his chest. Not movie-star ripped, but not bad by any means.

"What are you doing?" she asked.

"I'm calling your bluff."

"You're going to regret this in the morning."

"Who cares about the morning? We've got tonight." He hummed a tune with similar lyrics.

"Oh, please, don't start singing."

"We've got tonight," he warbled and came toward her.

Cassie grabbed for the can of Reddi-Wip on the table. "Stay back, or I'll shoot."

He stepped menacingly around the table.

Cassie's heart galloped, and damn her, but she kept staring at his naked chest. "I'm warning you . . ."

"Warn all you like. You're the one who plied me with ibuprofen and merlot. And now, sweetheart, I'm taking you up on your offer."

"That was last night. The offer has been rescinded. The coupon expired."

Harrison unbuckled his belt and walked toward her. He pulled the belt off and it slithered through the loops with an erotic, whisking sound. "Oh, I get it. You want to be the one to call the shots."

"Stay back," she teased, when what she really wanted was for him to advance. But what had happened to change him? Why had he been so reticent last night, but now he was so frisky? Was it merely the wine? Or was it something else. Something more?

He grinned seductively, not looking the least bit nerdy, and unzipped his pants.

"Don't you dare take off your pants."

"Don't play coy. You want me."

"I don't." She giggled, completely blowing her denial.

He lunged for her. She jumped back. "Don't make me use this."

"Bring it on." He kicked off his pants.

Holy smokes!

"You're naked," she gasped.

"Don't ever let anyone tell you that you're not observant." The expression on his face was purely wicked.

She extended her arm, depressed the nozzle on the Reddi-Wip. A long white stream shot across the room, slapping his brow.

But getting a face full of sugary whipped cream did not stop his forward motion. He swiped the Reddi-Wip out of his eyes and flung a foamy wad at her. She ducked just in the nick of time. The goop hit the wall behind her.

She squirted him again.

It grazed the top of his head.

A third squirt and she was backpedaling for the door, but no dice. Strawberry shortcake topping was not strong enough to hold him at bay. She attempted another futile spurt in self-defense, but the aerosol can was out of oomph.

Harry strode across the room, his hair spiked up and sticky with whipped cream. "Come here."

She shook her head, exhilarated.

"Don't run from me."

But she was already running, skipping through the living room, body on fire with excitement and lust. What a game. What fun!

She wondered if Solen and Kiya had ever played "your pyramid or mine?"

"Your punishment will just be that much more severe the longer you postpone it," he threatened.

"How much worse?" she squeaked.

"I'm going to give you the most thorough tongue-licking you've ever received."

Omigod. She almost fainted on the spot.

Who'd have thought boring old Harry would be the most fun she'd ever had?

She bolted for the bedroom, but he was far quicker than she ever imagined. He scaled the back of the couch, climbing over and dropping to the other side, almost cutting off her wily escape.

But somehow she managed to wriggle past him. Her pulse was pumping with enough endorphins to kick-start Freemont's customized Harley. She was high on adventure and ready for action.

Without really meaning to, she had thrown down the gauntlet and invited him to engage in a sport guaranteed to supercharge any heterosexual man's libido—the pursuit of a woman.

He caught her arm just as she reached the bedroom door. Her excitement was like a bird bashing frantically against her rib cage, desperate to get out. To burst free.

A giggle exploded from her, high and nervous. Their eyes met and Cassie stopped breathing.

What was he going to do? Wicked intent was in his eyes. A jolt of pure, raw sexual energy rushed through her, and her world narrowed into agonizing slow motion.

They were ensnared in the web of each other's gazes, transported to an endless time and space. They had reached the point of no return. They were about to become lovers.

And she feared the intimacy almost as much as she craved it.

In the muted hallway lighting, his complexion glowed golden and exotic. With his shock of black hair (never mind the whipped cream, of course), his proud patrician nose, and his sinewy build, he could have been Solen.

But she was no Kiya.

Cassie was too blonde and too soft and too flighty. Harrison needed someone more like himself. Someone dark and exotic and cerebral.

Disturbed by her thoughts, she pulled away.

But he would not let her go. It was as if he'd read the trepidation in her eyes and understood it.

"Tonight," he said, "you're mine."

And that was exactly what she wanted to hear. The whipped cream glistened like new-fallen snow against his ebony hair. Cassie's gaze tracked down his face to his chest to his flat abdomen and beyond.

She inhaled sharply.

His penis and testicles, heavy with desire, dangled between his thighs. He was wholly, unreservedly male. The sight of him tightened her lungs until she could barely force the air out.

She inspected him from head to toe, but he stared only at her face. Finally, when she felt brave enough, she lifted her chin and met his gaze full-on.

He peered straight into her, his brown eyes shining so intensely they were almost black.

She realized he was trembling. It was subtle. Barely noticeable. But his little finger quivered oh-so-faintly against her skin.

How sweet.

She was blind for believing Ahmose Akvar even for a second. There wasn't a larcenous bone in this man's body.

His vulnerability yanked her up short. He might have initiated this game, but he was as scared about the follow-through as she was. He was totally exposed, standing naked before her while she was fully clothed. He was open to her. Hiding nothing.

Cassie realized at once what a precious gift he was offering, even though he did not speak of it. Harrison Standish wasn't a guy who easily dropped his guard. He spent a lot of time by himself for a reason.

And yet Harry had chosen to trust her.

She felt more privileged than words could express. Her body grew warmer, moister.

His shaft stirred thicker, harder, jutting up ferociously, arcing toward his belly.

Irresistibly, Cassie's eyes were drawn downward. Her knees melted and her mouth watered. She gulped but found she could not swallow. She hadn't expected him to be so impressive. She'd had her share of men in her life, but none of them had ever captured her imagination the way Harrison did.

His erection crooked slightly to the right. The shaft of him was fuller than the spherical throbbing head. His tip was already moist, ready for her. She heard a rough groan of desire and was startled to realize the sound had slipped from her own throat.

Her pulse throbbed in the hollow of her neck. Tentatively, she reached out and touched him there for the very first time. She was shocked at how big he felt in her hand. Her breasts swelled, grew warm.

He unbuttoned her blouse, undressed her with care. By the time he was finished and Cassie was standing naked before him, they were both trembling.

"You have the most gorgeous figure," he breathed, running a hand from the curve of her breast down the cinch of her waist to the flare of her hip. "Hourglass, curvy, a real woman's body."

"Thank you," she said.

"I love the way you love your own body. Most women don't, you know."

Her cheeks heated, and she suddenly felt shy. Impossible, improbable, illogical. Cassie didn't do shy. She ducked her head, confused by her feelings.

Why did she suddenly feel so incredibly weak-kneed and defenseless? What was this strange hesitancy, this unexpected quietness?

Harry caught her chin, lifted her face up, and forced her to look at him. "I want you," he said, and with those three words her shyness disappeared.

There was nothing slow or lingering about his kisses. They started out hot and hard and quickly jumped to a frenzied pace. Passion poured out of him, poured out of her; it mingled, flowed, and became one blinding, driving force.

He tenderly caressed her breasts, and the space between her legs went hot and wet. His kisses slowed, then turned languid. He was changing things on her. His tongue licking hers was like fire dancing in the darkness.

He walked her backward until her butt bumped the edge of the bed.

"Lie back," he commanded. "And wrap your legs around my waist."

She did as he asked, curling her spine into the mattress. Her pulse thundered in her ears. What was he going to do next?

His cock bounced playfully against her belly. He was standing on the floor, looming over her.

She was on the bed, her butt almost hanging over the

edge, her legs wrapped tight around his waist. She grinned. Once he was inside her, she would have control over his thrusting. What a great arrangement.

But then he surprised her completely.

He slipped his hand down and gently massaged between her thighs. She flinched. The sensation was so invariably sweet. He leaned down and his mouth fastened onto hers, kissing her as he tickled her slick feminine folds.

And then he inched his finger inside her, easing in and out until she thought she might scream from the superbness of it all.

Harrison slipped a second finger inside her while his pinky stayed on the outside, doing some very interesting tricks. His wrist swayed back and forth to a smooth, balanced rhythm. All the while, his ambitious pinkie was circling lower, around and around and around, increasing the tempo and thoroughly glazing her with her own wet, honeyed essence.

"Oooh," Cassie said and shifted her hips upward, definitely wanting more of that technique.

And then he took it one step further and rimmed her tight, puckered rosebud. Caressing it carefully, pressing in with a light, steady pressure.

She groaned and grabbed the bedcovers with both fists. He did not stop. He kept up the warm, provocative finger glide. In and out and over and around. On and on and on he went, until she was dazed with need and desperate to sate her hunger.

"Where," she gasped, and then had to stop to catch her breath before she could continue with her question— "did you learn how to do that?"

Never in a million years would she have guessed that

a guy who spent so much time with ancient artifacts would be so knowledgeable about a woman's body. She hadn't given Harry nearly enough credit for versatility.

"Poindexter reads a lot." He grinned.

Mental note to self. Date more intellectuals.

"But you ain't seen nothin' yet, sweetheart." Harrison eased his hand from her and then dropped to his knees so that her legs were wrapped around his neck and his mouth was level with her most tender assets.

She hissed in her breath through clenched teeth, and her entire body tensed with exquisite pleasure.

His hair tickled her inner thighs. He plied his mouth delicately over her tiny straining ridge. He sank his hot tongue inside her, licking insatiably.

Wickedly his tongue controlled her. She was his puppet. He could do with her whatever he wished.

The slippery sensation was beyond anything she'd ever experienced. His tongue glided into her molten center and he worked his diabolical magic.

She moaned and arched toward him, providing him with easier access. The quivering sensation was indescribably, scrumptiously private.

How had their relationship progressed to such intimacy so quickly?

The affair that burns the hottest, fades the quickest.

It was something her mother used to say when Cassie had asked why she'd dropped yet another boyfriend.

But Harrison's devilish tongue soon shook such thoughts from her head. He grasped her hips with both hands, holding her pinned to the mattress as she thrashed and writhed. Her body absorbed his heated breath.

Oh, she was done for.

She rode his tongue, pushing and pulling, rocking and

bucking. She was searching, grasping, desperate to make it happen.

Her orgasm erupted from the very core of her soul. Exploding outward through her center, flinging into her limbs. Her muscles tightened, then went instantly slack. Her pulse pounded, and she saw a rhapsody of red-white starbursts.

Wet heat spilled out of her, flowed over him as the sound of his proud laughter filled the room.

Well, she thought, dreamily. She'd done it. She'd kept him out of her bed.

He had been standing on the floor the entire time.

CHAPTER
19

"Thanks. I needed that." Cassie sighed contentedly.

"You're welcome."

They were piled up in the middle of her bed. Her head resting against his shoulder, her body curled into his side. A smug smile played across his lips.

She traced the smile with her fingertips. "You're pretty proud of yourself, aren't you?"

"Aren't you proud of me?"

"What do you think?"

His grin widened and her heart just sort of splintered into two pieces, and in that moment she knew she had to tell him about Duane, even though she didn't understand why.

"Harry?"

"Uh-huh?" He sounded drowsy, self-satisfied. She noticed he'd stopped telling her to call him Harrison. Slowly but surely she was wearing him down.

"Can I tell you something?"

He turned his head and peered at her with his good eye. "Absolutely."

"Would you really want to know why I freaked out on you today?"

"You don't owe me any explanations."

"Yeah, I do. You gave me that beautiful butterfly apology, and it wasn't even your fault."

"Shh," he murmured. "It's okay. Honest. Forget about it. I don't care."

"I do. I acted like a crazy woman, and I want you to understand why. It's important to me."

"Okay."

"I was married once."

Harrison didn't say anything. Cassie gulped back her fear and plunged ahead. It was still difficult to talk about, even after eleven years.

"His name was Duane Armstrong. And I was madly in love with him." She had been apeshit crazy for Duane in that sick-in-the-head-obsessive-teenage way. It was humbling to admit it now. That she'd been so wrong about what love was.

"Uh-huh." Harry didn't sound any too enthused to hear about this.

"I wanted to marry him more than anything else on earth. He was handsome and fun and daring. He was twenty-one and I was seventeen. Everyone in my family was against it. Even my dad, which surprised me, because he and Duane were two of a kind. But I was young and headstrong and wildly in love, so I married him anyway. For the first couple of months it was great. One good time after another."

"Then what happened?" On the surface his voice was teasing, but underneath she heard the tension. He was jealous. "After a while did you discover you didn't like picking up his socks off the bathroom floor?"

"It's not so much his socks I minded picking up," she confessed. "It was his crack pipe."

"Dammit, Cassie, are you serious?"

She felt his muscles tense beneath her. "I was an utter fool."

"No, you weren't a fool. You might have made foolish choices, but you were never a fool." He sounded so vehement. Like he really believed what he was saying.

"I was so ashamed. I didn't tell anyone what I was going through. Not even Maddie."

"It must have been really hard for you, handling that all alone, hiding such a secret from your family."

She nodded. "The drugs really took their toll, and quick. Duane got crazy jealous. Possessive. The straw that broke the camel's back was when he locked me in the cellar while he went off on a two-day drug binge." She shuddered, remembering.

"Damn my hide." Harrison hissed in his breath. "And I had my head so far up my ass I let the cellar door slam shut on you. And that guy could have blown you up inside there." His voice hung on a clot of emotion.

"It wasn't your fault, Harry. I was having a post-traumatic stress flashback. There's no way you could have known. I just wanted to explain so you could understand me better."

"How'd you get the courage to leave?" He softly stroked her hair, and his touch was so incredible her heart just ached from the sweetness of it.

"I tried to help Duane. I really did. Tried to get him to join Narcotics Anonymous, but he denied he had a problem. I couldn't stick it out. I flaked. I didn't have the stamina for the long haul."

"Is that why you don't want to ever get married again? Because you think you did something wrong?"

Cassie nodded and clenched her jaw to keep from crying. Revealing her most shameful secret to him was much tougher than she'd thought it would be.

He gently slipped her head off his shoulder, threw back the covers, and got out of bed. He marched over to the remnants of her collage wall, his bare buns flexing in the light from the bathroom. Her heart fluttered. He was so magnificent.

He fisted his hands. "Which one is he?"

"Oh, Duane's not on my collage wall. I only put happy memories up there." Cassie sat up in the bed, curled her knees to her chest.

He looked over at her. The expression on his face plucked at her heartstrings. "It tears me up inside to think that someone hurt you. I'd like to kill the bastard."

"You don't have to," she said. "He died in a car wreck the day after I left him."

"God, Cassie, sweetheart, I'm so sorry you had to live through that." Harrison stalked across the room, sat on the edge of the bed, and drew her into his arms.

She was trembling.

"It's okay," he murmured and pressed his lips to her forehead. His soul caved in for all she had suffered. He tried to mentally cut off his rational mind from his emotions, but he couldn't stop sympathizing with her pain. "You're all right."

She clung to him and buried her face against his chest. Harrison had never felt so needed, so manly.

"I felt so responsible," she said. "I kept thinking that if I'd never married Duane, never *committed* to a relationship, he might not have gotten drunk and driven into that bridge abutment. He might still be alive today."

"Duane was a troubled man. Surely you've figured that out by now. His death had nothing to do with you and whether or not you stood by your wedding vows. You were only seventeen, Cassie. A kid."

Harrison rubbed circles on her back, wishing he could make her see the problem had been with her ex-husband, not with her, not with marriage or commitment. He felt her tears on his skin. He took her chin in his hand and tilted her face up until she met his gaze. Then he kissed her.

Slowly, sweetly, gently.

But it didn't stay slow, sweet, and gentle.

Things changed quickly, as they usually did with his quixotic, quicksilver Cassie.

Her body loosened, but her grip on him tightened. She increased the tempo of their kiss, stepping it up several degrees when she slipped her tongue past his teeth.

Their body heat mixed, mingled. Sharp need for her buried under his skin, fiery and fierce, spreading through his veins, taking him over.

What had started out as a comfort kiss ripened into a frantic, insatiable coupling of their mouths.

His hand went to the soft curve of her waist and his fingers sank deliciously into her flesh. He liked her meaty ripeness, loved caressing her full, rich curves.

She threaded her fingers through his hair, murmured low in her throat. He paid attention to her sounds and moved his fingers accordingly, sliding up from her waist to lightly stroke her lovely breasts.

She was so gorgeous. He was fully aware of how

lucky he was to be here. He wanted her so badly. Wanted to bury himself deeply inside her and never emerge.

He dragged his kiss from her mouth, down over her chin, to the underside of her supple throat. He knew he'd discovered an erogenous zone when her body tensed and a small helpless moan escaped her parted lips. She arched against him, her body pleading for more.

Supercharged, Harrison dipped his head lower, his tongue seeking those sweet, rock-hard nipples she thrust at him. He wet them both with his mouth and then rubbed the pad of his thumb over one nipple, while gently suckling the other.

She gasped and writhed.

He was on fire for her. His body was an inferno; he was so hard he didn't think he could go one more minute without sheathing himself inside her.

And when she reached down and slipped her hand along his inner thigh, he had to close his eyes and fight hard to keep from losing control completely. He was so scared he was going to screw this up.

"You relax and enjoy this," she said. "Stop playing with my nipples, roll over on your back, and just relax."

Music to every man's ears. He groaned and rolled over.

"Do you like for me to touch you like that?" she whispered, kneading his leg, moving closer, ever closer to his hard, flushed penis.

"Oh, babe, yeah."

It was so extraordinarily erotic, her hand on him. He lifted his head and looked at her, watching the lusty emotions play across her face.

Inch by agonizing inch, she worked her way to his primal spot. When she finally arrived, she took firm hold, wrapping a hand around his throbbing shaft, while at the same time gently scratching his scrotum with her little finger.

He couldn't stand it. Wouldn't let things finish this way. He had to be inside her. Didn't want to come without her.

"Come here," he groaned and pulled her up to straddle his waist, his penis pulsating against her behind.

He kissed her again, building her up, raising the tension until they were both crazy for it. They thrashed against each other, breathing hard, trembling and tingling, their bodies filled with lust and passion and desire.

"Ride me," he begged.

Cassie pulled her mouth from his, her long blonde hair trailing over his chest.

"Condom," she gasped and splayed a palm against his chest. "We gotta have a condom. Hang on. I'll be right back."

He groaned and grasped his hair with both hands as she slid off him and padded away in the dark. Seconds later she came running back into the bedroom, fumbling with her purse, fingers grasping at the clasp.

"Ooh," she wailed. "You've got me so charged up I can't get it open."

He propped himself up on an elbow. "Here, let me help."

"I've got it, I've got it."

The clasp popped open and she dug around inside, pulling out lipstick and cash register receipts and ink pens. She excavated loose change and a set of car keys and a tin of cinnamon Altoids.

"I know I have a condom in here."

"Try the zippered pocket," Harrison said, amazed he could stay so calm.

"I never put anything in there." She frowned, but slid the zipper open anyway. "Ooh, ooh." She pursed her lips and her face lit up. "You were right. I feel something."

Me too, babe; me too.

And for once, Harrison did not want to deny what he was feeling.

Then Cassie pulled a round, flat object from her purse.

"Hey!" Her nose crinkled. "This isn't a condom."

She held the ring up to get a better look at it in the light seeping from the bathroom, and Harrison recognized it instantly.

It was one-half of the magical brooch amulet.

"But I don't understand. "Cassie ran a hand through her hair. "How did it get into my purse?"

Had she stolen it? Harrison immediately felt disloyal for the thought. How could he believe that about her after everything they'd just shared? There had to be another explanation. He knew in his heart of hearts that she was not a thief. Come what may, he was on Cassie's side.

They turned on the overhead light and sat in the middle of the bed. Cassie put on her bathrobe, and Harrison tugged the sheet over his waist. With their ardor cooling, he felt suddenly vulnerable being so naked in front of her.

"I'm guessing Adam must have put it in your purse. You took it with you into the courtyard when you went to meet him, remember? Osiris found it in the bushes after the lights came back on at the museum."

"That's right," she said.

"This is absolute proof that Adam is the mummy.

That's not Kiya's half of the amulet. The markings on the rings are different."

"So this is Solen's half." She turned it in her hand. "Adam must have had to put it in my purse before Kiya's half was stolen."

"I'm certain of it."

"And I've been running around with it in my handbag all this time?"

"I'm willing to bet that's why your place was ransacked and why we were followed to Clyde's place."

"I don't understand how anyone knew I had it."

"Maybe they didn't. Maybe it was just a stab in the dark because you'd been helping Adam make arrangements for the exhibit."

She met Harrison's eyes. "But then where's the other half?"

"That's the million-dollar question."

"We have to put Solen's amulet in a safe place," she said. "Right now."

"Yes."

"But where can we put it until morning? It's eight o'clock at night, the banks are closed, and so is the museum. I'm not about to get Phyllis or Ahmose involved. I want this thing as far away from me as I can get it. It's caused nothing but trouble."

"Tom Grayfield has a safe. We can ask him to keep it for us until we can get it back to the museum in the morning. Where's your phone? I'll give him a call."

"The battery on my cell needs charging. I'll go get the cordless from the living room."

"Never mind. I'll come with you." He threw back the covers and tried to act nonchalant as he slipped from her bed to search for his pants. He wasn't accustomed to strutting around a lady's apartment buck naked and having her appraising eye on him.

When they reached the living room, she picked her cordless phone from its docking station on the end table and passed it to Harrison.

"Hey," she said. "My answering machine's unplugged."

"It must have happened when your place got ransacked."

"No wonder I haven't been able to check my messages. I thought I'd forgotten to turn it on." Cassie plugged the machine in. The red message light winked.

"Look. I've got a message." She checked the caller ID. "Blocked call. It came through at four-fifteen yesterday afternoon, when we were preparing for the party. Hold on. Let me check the message before you get on the phone."

She hit the play button.

"Cassie." The voice was low and urgent, but Harrison recognized it right away. "It's Adam. Lost your cell number but luckily had your home number programmed in my speed dial."

On the tape, Adam hesitated. In the background they could hear the roaring sound of an airplane taking off.

"Adam must have been at the airport when he called," Cassie said.

"I've discovered something very disturbing," Adam continued after the plane had passed over. "This is vitally important, so listen carefully. I'm being followed, and my life is in grave danger. I'll be at the party wearing a mummy costume to give you the details. If something happens and I don't get to see you, then you've got to get a message to my brother, Dr. Harrison Standish."

Why had Adam called Cassie instead of him? Harrison wondered.

"Tell my brother the secret to the Minoan scroll is in the math. He'll know what I'm talking about. Don't say a word about this to anyone else. Harrison is the only one you can trust. Did you—"

The answering machine beeped and then fell silent. It had cut him off.

"Did he call back?" Harrison asked. "Was there another message?"

Cassie checked the machine and shook her head. "What was he talking about? What math?"

"I have no idea, but I'm going to find out."

He went out to the Volvo, got the scroll from the glove compartment, and brought it back up to Cassie's apartment. He spread it out on her coffee table atop the half-finished jigsaw puzzle of New York City.

The secret is in the math. The secret is in the math.

Harrison stared at the scroll, his fingers tracing the impenetrable hieroglyphics. Did his brother honestly expect him to decipher something no one else in history had ever been able to decode?

Adam had done it.

The secret is in the math?

What in the hell was he talking about? Harrison took the djed from his pocket and passed it from palm to palm. The electromagnetic properties helped him think.

Math had been the one subject Adam had excelled in over Harrison.

Okay. So? How did math help translate the scrolls?

He paced Cassie's living room, hands clasped behind his back rubbing the djed, his thoughts totally absorbed by the task. Cassie sat curled up on the couch, her legs tucked underneath her. She looked so gorgeous he had to remind himself to keep his attention on the job at hand.

The secret is in the math.

What math? Solen's birthday? Kiya's birthday? The day of their deaths?

Dammit. He didn't have time for parlor games.

Except it wasn't a parlor game. Adam was in serious trouble over whatever he'd learned from deciphering the scroll.

Think.

The secret is in the math.

The Minoans were seafaring people and merchants. Most scholars believed their hieroglyphics were nothing more than ledgers and accounts.

Math.

Harrison clutched a handful of hair in desperation and started to push his glasses up on his nose before he remembered that Big Ray had busted them in the fight and his extra pair was in his locker at the museum.

Solen had been a Minoan scribe. Until he'd been sold into slavery and ended up in Egypt. Until Ramses IV had recognized his talents and sent him to learn Egyptian hieroglyphics. Solen would have acquired much new knowledge in the pharaoh's house. He would have honed his skills, obtained new ways of communicating.

What if Solen had combined the old skills with the new? What if the scroll Adam found in Solen's tomb was a hybrid of Minoan and Egyptian hieroglyphics? What if the scroll had been written by Solen himself?

The secret is in the math.

Numbers. Numerology. The stars and moons and planets. Astrology.

The sun.

In the time of Ramses IV, the Egyptians had worshiped the sun.

Yes, so what, big deal.

Math of the Sun: The Immortal Egypt.

The title popped into Harrison's head. It was the name of a book Diana had given both him and Adam when they had graduated from high school.

"It's the seminal work on how math affected religion in ancient Egypt," his mother had said. "Read it."

He'd found the work deadly boring and never looked at it after the initial attempt. But he still owned it. It was on the top shelf of the bookcase in his apartment.

The secret is in the math.

Could the answer be in that book?

But the book Diana had given them was about Egypt. This was a Minoan scroll in Minoan hieroglyphics.

And Solen had been a displaced Minoan in Egypt, learning the culture, absorbing the religious beliefs. It was worth a shot. He didn't have anything else to go on.

"I think I might have a chance at translating this thing," he told Cassie.

"Okay," she said.

"The problem is that it could take me a long time, and even then I might not be able to translate it. Should I waste time even trying, or should we just be out there looking for Adam?"

"We don't know where to look, and at least you do have a clue on how to translate the hieroglyphics. I think you should do it."

"We also need to get the amulet locked up someplace safe before the people who were after Adam figure out we've got it and come after us. We already know they're ruthless."

"I could take the amulet to Tom Grayfield while you translate the scroll," Cassie offered.

He liked the idea. She would be out of her apartment. Both she and the amulet would be safe with Tom. Then he could totally concentrate on unlocking the secret of Solen's scroll, knowing Cassie was in good hands.

"I'll call Tom," he said, "and let him know what's going on."

While Cassie got dressed, Harrison called Tom's cell phone number.

"Ambassador Grayfield's phone," Anthony Korba answered in his distinctive gravelly voice.

"Anthony. It's Harrison. Am I disturbing you?"

"No, we're on our way back from a meeting with the governor in Austin."

"May I speak to Tom? It's urgent."

"But of course."

Thirty seconds later Tom came on the line. "Harrison, what's up?"

Quickly Harrison told him what had transpired, except he did not tell him about the scroll. It was pride that held him back. He would hate to admit defeat where Adam had succeeded if he failed to translate the hieroglyphics. "I need someone to look after Cassie while I take care of a few things. Can you keep her and Solen's amulet safe for me?"

"You don't even have to ask. I'm there," Tom said. "We're still an hour out of Fort Worth, but give me her address. We'll drop by and pick her up on the way."

"Thanks, Tom, I owe you big-time."

Tom laughed. "We'll work it out. See you later."

Harrison cradled the receiver and looked up to see Cassie in the doorway, dressed in her Cadillac jeans and a sexy turquoise tank top. Her hair shone in the light. Even without his glasses he could see she was a knockout.

She crossed the room toward him and his heart careened into his chest. He took her hand and pressed the amulet into her palm. "Tom's sending a car for you."

"Thank you for looking out for me." She curled her fingers around the amulet. "I promise to guard it with my life."

CHAPTER
20

Harrison's heart was pumping hard and fast when he let himself into his apartment with the scroll tucked under his arm. Part of his erratic pulse was due to the excitement of trying to translate the scroll, but most of it was attributable to his changing relationship with Cassie.

He was having feelings he shouldn't be having, and he didn't know what to do about them. He had always protected his heart by disengaging from tender feelings. He analyzed his emotions. He did not wallow in them.

Except he was wallowing now, and he'd never felt anything this intense.

It's just the thrill of the danger. Don't worry about it now. Find that book. Translate the scroll. Figure out what had Adam running scared. Later. You can think about Cassie later.

He hurried into his office, spied the book he needed on the top shelf. He stood on his toes, stretching to reach it. It hit the floor with a solid *thunk*. He picked it up and opened it on his desk. Then carefully, reverently, he unrolled the scroll. Somewhere, among the old books and the arcane knowledge, he was determined to find the answers.

He was determined to find his brother.

And he was determined to shut down these inappropriate feelings for Cassie before they got completely out of hand.

Cassie was in the backseat of Tom Grayfield's black stretch limo making small talk with the ambassador when her cell phone rang. Thinking it might be Harry, she smiled at Tom. "Do you mind if I take this call? I know it's rude to talk on the cell phone when you're having a conversation in person, but this might be important."

"Not at all." Tom smiled. "Go ahead."

What a nice man, she thought. Considerate and generous. Imagine, someone as important as the ambassador to Greece going out of his way to pick her up so she wouldn't have to drive around by herself late at night.

She pulled out the antenna and flipped her phone open. "Hello?"

"Cassie, it's David." Her brother-in-law's voice was low and rushed.

"Hi, David. Now's not really a good time for me to talk."

"You're with someone."

"Yes."

"Is it your friend Dr. Standish?"

"No." Cassie smiled at Tom and mouthed, *I'll just be a minute.*

"Listen to me, Cassie; this is very important. I know you have a habit of not fully listening, but please make an exception this time. Do it for me."

Had he found out something negative about Harrison?

Could Ahmose be right after all? But no, she could never believe that about Harry. Not after everything they'd shared.

"Is it related to what we discussed yesterday?" she asked.

"It is. I checked out your friend, and he's as clean as they come. The guy could have been an Eagle Scout."

What a relief. Cassie blew out her breath. "Whew, you really scared me there for a minute. So everything checks out?"

"Not exactly."

"What not exactly?"

"Did you know Standish has a half brother named Adam Grayfield?"

"Uh-huh."

"His father, Tom Grayfield, is the ambassador to Greece. Not a nice guy. He has a tavern in Adam's and Harrison's names. It's called the Minotaur. The Minoan Order holds meetings there. He's under investigation by the Greek government. He moves a lot of gold bullion out of the country and they can't figure out where he's getting it, but they suspect he's laundering it through the Minotaur Tavern and Grayfield's scrap metal companies in the U.S."

Cassie gulped. Alchemy. The ability to turn base metal into gold. Members of the Minoan Order were supposed to know the secret of alchemy.

"Um . . . ," she began, trying not to get nervous, "as a matter of fact, I'm in Tom Grayfield's limo right now as we speak."

"Aw, shit, Cassie, no." The timbre of David's voice changed so quickly, she felt her fingers grow icy cold.

"What is it?" she whispered. "What's wrong?"

"I don't want to panic you, but whatever you do, you must get out of that man's car!"

But it was too late. The back of her head burned fiery hot. Cassie turned to look at the ambassador.

Tom Grayfield was still smiling, but now he had a derringer clutched discreetly in his hand. "It's time you hung up the phone, Cassie."

Harrison worked feverishly, playing with myriad combinations of the number sequences that he found in the math book and drawing on his knowledge of Egyptian hieroglyphics.

Three hours into the ordeal, he finally broke the code.

The ancient Minoan Order had used numbers to represent the characters from the Egyptian hieroglyphics. Their system was obviously influenced by Solen's association with Egypt. Once Harrison understood which number related to which character, he was able to start translating the scroll.

It was a slow, painstaking process. He had to go from Egyptian hieroglyphics to Minoan number symbols to English. It was after midnight by the time he completed the conversion. He read what he'd written. Blinked. Rubbed his eyes and read it again.

No. He shook his head. *It could not be.*

There, in black and white, was the reason why the amulet was so important to the Minoan Order. It meant far more than reuniting star-crossed lovers, and it possessed much greater power than merely cursing a vizier's descendants. The secret was even more stunning than the ability to turn base metal into gold or to create thunderstorms.

And it explained everything.

With dawning horror, Harrison realized what his brother must have understood the minute he translated the scroll.

Tom Grayfield would kill for the amulet. Even if it meant murdering his own son.

The truth was a sledgehammer.

Harrison had not only delivered Solen's half of the amulet into Tom Grayfield's deadly hands, he'd also placed Cassie in imminent danger.

There had to be a way to put a positive spin on this.

No point feeling terrorized or distressed just because she was staring down the barrel of a gun. What good did it do to panic or freak out? Life with Duane had taught Cassie that the more you focused on negative things, the more they grew. No negative thoughts allowed. She wasn't going to end up in a ditch with a slug through the center of her head. No sirree. So she was just going to stop picturing that.

Being taken hostage by the U.S. ambassador to Greece was just a minor inconvenience. A little misunderstanding. A tiny blip in the huge scheme of things. It would all work out in the end.

Except no one else knew that Tom Grayfield was a homicidal maniac.

Stop it.

He wasn't a homicidal maniac. He was just misguided, misdirected, or misinformed. It was up to her to set him on the right path.

"Tom," she said, purposefully using his first name in hopes of putting him at ease. "You look really tense. Maybe you should have a tipple of something from that minibar." She nodded at the small fridge tucked in the back of the limo.

"I don't want anything to drink," he snapped.. "Just sit back and shut up."

"A little vodka and tonic? A slug of gin and ginger ale? A snort of bourbon and branch?"

"Nothing!"

"Jeez, okay." She raised her palms. "I was just trying to be helpful."

"Well, don't. Now, hand over the amulet." He waved the gun at her.

"Is that what this is all about? Well, why didn't you just say so? I would have given it to you without all the gun-brandishing. Sheesh."

Cassie reached into her purse, pulled out Solen's ring, and handed it over to him, because she didn't know what else to do and she didn't want to get shot. Not when she and Harry were just now getting to the good part of their relationship. The wild, hot sex.

"Seriously, Tom, you don't want to kill me. Think of your reputation. Think of everything you'll lose."

Tom Grayfield flicked the dome light on, and he was staring at the ring with such rapture that Cassie almost asked if he needed a private moment alone with the amulet, but decided against being flippant.

He actually licked his lips. "No, I'm thinking of everything I'll gain."

"So you're an optimist. Me too."

"Stop being friendly," he said and slipped the amulet into his pocket while still keeping the derringer aimed at her heart. "I don't want to like you."

"It's okay to like me. Everyone likes me."

Well, except for Phyllis Lambert, but she was in the minority.

And Harrison. He didn't like you either.

Maybe not at first, but he liked her now. In fact, he liked her a lot. She could just tell. Cassie grinned, remembering.

"Why are you smiling? You're in deep trouble, young lady. Stop smiling."

"I can't talk, I can't be nice, I can't smile. What can I do?"

"Face reality, woman."

"I've never been very good at that."

"How about this: if you don't shut up," he threatened, "I'm going to shoot you on general principle."

"If you're gonna get testy about it, all right, all right. I'll shut up."

"Thank you." Grayfield blew out his breath in exasperation and turned off the dome light.

"You're welcome."

"I thought you were going to shut up."

Cassie made a motion of zipping her lip.

"I'll believe it when I hear it." Grayfield sighed.

They traveled in silence. Cassie peered through the tinted windows and tried to see where they were going. She didn't recognize this part of Fort Worth. There were lots of warehouses and scrap metal places. It was a dimly lighted, secluded area.

For the first time, it hit her how truly isolated she was and that she might not make it out of this alive.

The driver turned down a narrow road filled with potholes. There were no streetlights. The darkness around the limo loomed thick, lumpy, and profound. Anything or anyone could be lurking around the next corner.

Harry, if you can read minds, I'm in deep trouble. I need ya, babe.

She sent the mental vibration into the ether, crossed her fingers, and prayed. She was tapped out of positive thoughts.

The limo stopped at the end of the road, next to a large warehouse with an empty parking lot. The headlights played across a man lounging against the dock. He was smoking a cigarette. When the lights hit him, he dropped the cigarette on the cement steps, crushed it out beneath his sneaker, and leered at the car with a sinister smile.

A chill shot straight to the heated core in Cassie's head. Here was a dangerous man.

The limo stopped and the man sauntered over. She recognized him at once. He was the man who'd come running out of Clyde's house and knocked her down. The one who'd detonated the bomb.

Tom Grayfield rolled down the window. "Do you have what we need?"

"Uh-huh," the man grunted.

For one surreal moment, it felt just like when Duane used to swing by his dealer's location to pick up drugs.

The limo driver cut the engine. Apparently they were getting out.

The ransacking bomber opened the back door.

"Demitri," Tom Grayfield said, "this is Cassie. I want you to take good care of her."

The way he said "good care" made it sound like anything but.

Demitri held out a hand to help her from the car. She shied. His fingernails were dirty, and the look on his face was even dirtier.

"You were the one who ransacked my apartment," she

accused, staring down at his scuffed Nikes. "And you set off a bomb in Clyde's house."

"At your service." He was still extending his hand, and she still wasn't taking it.

"That was a really crappy thing you did, wrecking my collage wall, blowing up Clyde's place. He doesn't make a big salary, you know."

He shrugged. "Had to make sure you hadn't hidden the amulet inside your pictures. What's that wall all about, anyway? Those all the guys you laid?"

"Demitri, there's no need for vulgarities," Tom Gray-field prodded. "Ms. Cooper, do as I say. Take Demitri's hand and get out of the car."

She didn't want to but she didn't have much choice, seeing as how Grayfield had just positioned the nose of the derringer right under her rib cage.

"I'm going, I'm going; don't get so pushy with the gun." Reluctantly, she took Demitri's grimy hand and he hauled her from the car. The limo driver was standing outside the car with a flashlight and what looked to be a garage door opener in his hand.

"What are we gonna do with her?" the driver asked. His voice was deep and croaky. He sounded like a frog with throat cancer. She knew the thought was uncharitable, but at this point Cassie was over being kind.

Tom Grayfield smiled. "She's going to be Kiya's stand-in."

"Good idea, Boss." Demitri snickered.

Cassie didn't even want to imagine what that meant.

The driver pressed the button on the garage door opener and the thick double-rollered doors on the ware-house rumbled open. The man moved into the warehouse and flicked on the overhead lights. Demitri strong-armed

Cassie, shoving her inside. Tom Grayfield followed and closed the door behind him.

Locked in.

Trapped.

No way out.

Shades of living with Duane Armstrong.

Cassie was trying hard not to flip out when she spied what was sitting in the middle of the vacant, foul-smelling warehouse.

At first she thought it was just an ordinary coffin.

Her coffin.

But when Demitri pushed her deeper into the room, she realized it was Solen's sarcophagus.

Harrison didn't even think to call the police. That's how insane with fear he was. He was a man without a plan, acting from gut instinct. Feeling and reacting instead of analyzing and evaluating. There wasn't time to think. If there was ever a time for action, it was now.

He goosed the Volvo, exceeding the speed limit. He looked down at the instrument panel. The gas gauge needle had dropped past half-empty. But in spite of his deeply ingrained habit of filling up at the halfway mark, the idea never even entered his mind.

Only one thought existed.

Cassie.

He didn't know if he was headed to the right place or what he would do when he got there. All he knew was that he was going to rescue his woman.

He had to find her.

Because if anything happened to her, he would die. He would cease breathing, his heart would literally stop beating, and he would leave this world a much better man for having known her.

Cassie sat on a stack of cold sheet metal, her hands and feet bound with duct tape. There was sheet metal to the left of her. Sheet metal to the right of her. And sheet metal behind her.

What was with all the sheet metal? Then she finally got it. Alchemy. That's how Tom Grayfield had gotten rich. So if he already had the formula for turning base metal into gold, why was he after Kiya and Solen's amulet?

Ahead of her, Demitri, the froggy-voiced limo driver, and Tom Grayfield donned Minotaur masks, black-hooded robes, and started performing some kind of bizarre ritual dance around Solen's sarcophagus.

What a lot of bull-loney.

After several minutes, Grayfield positioned himself at the head of the coffin, pulled a piece of paper from the pocket of his robe, and began to chant something in a very strange language.

Outside, the wind kicked up. It howled through a hole in the broken glass of the window above her.

So this was the Texas contingent of the Minoan Order? Frankly, she wasn't impressed. She had expected more. More people. More action. Something more *Eyes Wide Shut*.

Grayfield went on and on and on.

Lightning momentarily illuminated the warehouse in a hot blue flash. Thunder grumbled. Rain spattered the tin ceiling. Funny, the storm had gusted in awfully fast. The midnight sky had been cloudless when they'd hauled her into the warehouse. Must be an unexpected norther.

The chanting continued.

"Good grief," Cassie called out. "How long is this gonna take? I hafta pee."

"Silence!" Tom Grayfield yelled, and pointed a finger at her like the grim reaper on a really bad PMS day with no Midol in the house.

"Excuse me for living." She wondered if Adam knew his dad was such a huge jackass.

"Gag her," Grayfield said to Demitri. "We will have no more interruptions."

There was a brief time-out while Demitri came over, peeled a strip of duct tape from the same roll he'd used to tie her up, and slapped it over her mouth.

That was gonna hurt coming off.

"Anthony," Grayfield barked to the limo driver. "Help Demitri drag her over here."

Good grief, what now? Wasn't it bad enough she was trussed up like a Christmas goose, forced to watch a really bad floor show with the piquant taste of duct tape on her tongue?

Anthony trotted over and eyed her speculatively from beneath his mask. He tried to slip his hands underneath her armpits, but because she was bound he kept having trouble. He squatted, his chest pressing against the back of her head, his fingers brushing along her rib cage.

Dude, stop tickling me or I'll pee on you.

Finally he got his arms underneath hers. "You grab her legs," he said to Demitri in his froggy voice.

"No fair; her bottom half is a lot heavier than her top half," Demitri complained.

"Obviously," Anthony croaked, "you have not noticed the size of her bazoombas."

Okay, you bozos, nix the sexual comments. She glared at them, hoping to get her point across.

Grumbling under his breath, Demitri grasped her feet and they hoisted her off the floor.

Cassie considered wriggling around and making them work for it, but they would probably just drop her, and it wasn't like she had much chance of getting away with her ankles hobbled.

"She's heavy," Anthony grunted.

Ha! I'll have you know I have big bones. One sixty is not considered overweight for a woman who's five foot eight.

"You could drop a few pounds, sister," Demitri concurred.

What? She should be stick-thin and make it easier for these nimrods to lug her around? They were damned lucky she was gagged, or she'd have given them a protracted lecture about the unrealistic body images modern society projected onto women.

But she soon got over her pique when she realized Grayfield was standing directly over her, his eyes glowing darkly from behind the bull head mask. He raised the sarcophagus lid.

"Put her inside."

The Volvo screamed like a constipated banshee for a good three minutes before Harrison figured out that somehow he'd managed to bump the shifter into second gear while driving seventy-five miles an hour through pouring rain in Fort Worth's warehouse district, running one stoplight after another.

What if Cassie was already dead?

No. He couldn't afford to think like that. He wouldn't.

He would make it in time to stop Grayfield from carrying out his ritualistic human sacrifice.

On Cassie.

Harrison cringed, imagining the man he'd once considered a surrogate father doing something so unthinkably heinous. But the Minoan hieroglyphics told the truth. He'd found the answer lurking in the occult scroll.

Ambassador Tom Grayfield had named both his sheet metal business and the tavern in Greece after the Minotaur, the symbol of the Minoan Order. His interest in the order had not been strictly academic. Tom had financed Adam's excavation for the first time. Not because he wanted to see Adam best Harrison in competition, as he claimed, but because he wanted Solen found after Harrison had excavated Kiya. He wanted his hands on both pieces of the amulet. The rings themselves were the last step in an earth-shattering prescription.

Because the papyrus Adam had found in Solen's tomb had been the formula for immortality.

The last few cryptic lines of the translation were burned indelibly into Harrison's brain:

Whosoever commands the double circle holds the key. Believe it is true and it is. The one element that transmutes all others? Blood.

He rounded the corner. Drawing closer. Almost there.

Please, God, let me be there in time to save Cassie.

He squinted as the road narrowed. In the mistiness of a damp dawn, without his glasses, with one eye swollen shut, he could barely see where he was going.

From out of the fog a sudden shadow loomed.

The mummy!

Stepping right into his path.

He twisted the steering wheel hard. The Volvo

swerved, tires screeching. He slammed headlong into a deep pothole.

His front tires blew. The noise exploded in his ears. He felt the jolt to his teeth. He went for the brakes, but his foot slipped and he hit the accelerator.

On busted tires the Volvo shot forward and plowed into a stop sign.

CHAPTER
21

No, no, don't put me in a dark, cramped, airless space with a three-thousand-year-old dead guy! Shoot me, stab me, run me over with a car. Anything but this!

Cassie fought against them, arching her body, bucking hard, trying to crack Anthony, the froggy-voiced limo driver, in the face with the back of her head. She cocked her knees and aimed to kick Demitri in the gut but only ended up squirming like a helpless worm unearthed by torrential rains.

They swung her up and over the side of the coffin.

And she came down hard on top of poor old Solen. He crunched louder than a sack of Cheetos. He had an old, dusty, dirty-feet smell to him.

Eew, grotty.

But she really didn't have time to get grossed out, because Tom Grayfield slammed the lid and she was trapped.

Shut in.

Closed off.

Sealed.

Her wrists were bound in front of her, her ankles

taped. She was powerless, at the mercy of her captors. She was, as Harry would say, royally screwed.

She rapidly sucked in the fetid air through her nose, unable to expel it in her panic. A scream gurgled up to her lips, but the duct tape held it back. Terror lodged inside her mouth, knotted down her throat to her sore, aching lungs.

Ice sheathed her body.

No, no. What were they going to do? They couldn't bury her alive. She couldn't tolerate that. Never, ever.

She flashed back. To being restricted, restrained, controlled. To the time Duane locked her inside the storm cellar and left her for two days. She did not want to go back to that awful place. She'd come too far. She would not go back into the darkness.

But she was already there, and the coffin was even smaller and tighter than the cellar had been.

Cassie gagged on her hysteria and it was rough and chalky and sour.

No, no.

You have to calm down. You have to stop freaking out.

Tom Grayfield was talking to his henchmen, but the sarcophagus was thickly constructed. His voice was muffled. She could not make out his instructions.

What were they going to do to her?

Oh, Harry, where are you?

In her heart, she knew she couldn't count on him for rescue. He had no way of knowing his half brother's father was an evil, twisted monster. He thought she was safe. He thought he'd done well by turning her over to Grayfield.

Believe in yourself, Cassie. Maddie and David can't help you. Harry can't help you. It's up to you.

But how was she going to get out of this? She was bathed in darkness, unable to move, unable to shout. And some part of Solen's ancient anatomy was poking hard into her upper back.

Were they just going to leave her here, slowly suffocating to death on the bitter flavor of her own fear?

Frantically, she shifted from side to side.

Let me out of here. Desperately she heaved in more air. In her panic, she hyperventilated. Her heart thumped heavily. Her head ached. Her lungs felt twisted, drained of breath.

The sarcophagus moved.

Cassie realized she was being hoisted and carried. Breathe, breathe; she could not breathe.

You're hyperventilating. You're not running out of oxygen this soon. Get hold of yourself.

But she could not. She was too excitable, too manic, too hyperactive for her own good. If only Harry were here. He was good for her. He kept her grounded. Calmed her down.

Harry, I'm sorry I failed you. I was supposed to keep the amulet safe.

Hot tears wet her cheeks. She would never see her dear, steadfast Harry. She wouldn't kiss his tender, inquisitive lips again. Nor would she ever make love to him fully, completely, the way she longed to make love with him.

Oh, Harry. It could have been so good.

And that was the last thought that slipped through her mind just before Cassie blacked out and embraced sweet oblivion.

*   *   *

"Adam?" Dazed, Harrison staggered out of the crumpled Volvo. The mummy was up ahead of him in the fog. Harrison could barely see where he was going. "Adam, come back."

But Adam did not heed his call. Was the mummy not Adam after all?

The mummy stopped at the corner. Harrison squinted, desperate to see where he was going. He motioned for Harrison to follow.

He wanted to shout, "I don't have time for delays. Cassie could already be dead." But he didn't want to think about that, even though he knew it deep in his bones. Cassie was in trouble. The worst kind of trouble, and he was to blame.

"Where are you going? What is it?" he called as he trailed after the mummy.

He rounded the corner, in the darkness, in the fog, felt an arm slip around him and draw him flat against the cold brick of the warehouse.

"Shh," said the mummy, pressing a finger to his lips. "They've got Kiya, but if they don't know we're out here, we can take them by surprise."

"Kiya?" Harrison stared deeply into the mummy's eyes. It was Adam all right, but he seemed different, sort of dazed and out of it. His mummy linen looked like hell, grimy with dirt and blood. Plus he smelled a bit gamey. "Don't you mean Cassie?"

"Kiya," he said quarrelsomely. "Are you going to help me save her or not?"

Kiya it is then. Harrison nodded.

"Come on."

They crept toward the double-rollered doors of the warehouse. They whirred open.

"Don't let them see you," Adam murmured and pressed himself against the building, hiding in the swirling fog. Lightning flickered and thunder growled. Harrison imitated his brother, pressing his body against the wall and narrowing his eyes as two men in black hooded robes and bull masks exited the warehouse carrying a sarcophagus.

"It's Wing Tips and Nike with my sarcophagus," Adam whispered. "Where are they going with it?"

Wing Tips and Nike? Had his brother gone completely mental?

The men hauled the ancient Egyptian coffin to the car parked at the curb. That's when Harrison realized it was Tom Grayfield's limo.

His pulse leaped. What to do? He had no weapon. If the men had guns, they would just pull them out and shoot him if he tried anything heroic at this juncture.

More important, where was Cassie? Was she inside the warehouse? Inside the limo? Or—and the fear that blasted through his veins was blistering and thick—was she in the sarcophagus?

From out of the warehouse stalked Tom Grayfield, also wearing a black robe. He carried in one hand a bull's head like the one a college football team mascot might wear, a derringer in the other.

"Nebamun." Adam spit out the word.

Huh?

"I will kill him," Adam said.

Harrison had to grab his brother by the scruff of his swaddling linen and hold him back. "He's got a weapon; you don't. He'll kill you, and then where will Kiya be?"

He understood Adam's anger. His vehemence. It took everything he had inside him not to succumb to his rage and charge Grayfield. But he could not afford to act on impulse. Cassie's life was at stake.

What was his weakness was also his strength. While his ability to detach from his emotions might cause him problems in intimate relationships, in instances like this it was a valuable talent. He needed a plan and he needed it fast. Wing Tips, who was really Grayfield's driver, Anthony Korba, unlocked the trunk.

"My sarcophagus," Adam whimpered as the men loaded it into the trunk.

Don't just stand there, do something. Harrison froze. His brain froze. He couldn't react. *Do something, do something.*

Korba got behind the wheel. The other guy held the back door open for Grayfield to slide in, and then he hopped into the passenger seat.

They were going to get away. And his Volvo was smashed into a stop sign half a block over with two flat tires.

Adam took off running in the opposite direction just as the limo started.

"Where are you going?" Harrison called out.

"To the chariot. We must catch them."

The chariot? Something very weird was going on with his brother.

Adam disappeared into the fog, and Harrison had to sprint to keep up with him. He heard a car engine roar to life. From out of the mist drove a delivery van, the mummy at the wheel. He screeched to a halt beside Harrison.

Harrison jumped in, and Adam floored it before he even had the door closed. The delivery van leaped forward, in hot pursuit of the limousine.

It was only after they spied the limo's taillights glinting through the drizzling fog that it occurred to Harrison that Cassie might still be in the warehouse. No time for second-guessing, although it was his instinct to question, question, question. He was committed to this course of action. Cassie had to be in the sarcophagus.

A loud thumping noise came from the back of the van. Startled, he looked over at Adam. "What's that?"

Adam shrugged. "Boreas. Ignore him. He's been doing that all day."

"Boreas? The leader of the group of warriors who sold Solen into slavery?"

"Yes," Adam hissed. "That traitor Boreas."

Thump, thump, thump. Who was really in the back?

"Adam, you have to stop the car. You have to let Boreas out."

"Can't," Adam said grimly, bandaged hands clamped on the steering wheel, eyes fixed on the car ahead of them. "Nebamun's got Kiya."

He had a good argument.

Thump, thump, thump. What in the hell was going on back there?

They were approaching a railroad crossing. Harrison could hear the warning bells of an oncoming train. He saw the flashing lights glaring against the fog. In the distance, the train blew a long, mournful whistle.

The limo scooted across the tracks just as the signal arm started to descend.

Thump, thump, thump.

The train whistle blew again, louder, closer. The headlights cut through the rain and fog.

Adam never slowed. He stayed right on the limousine's taillights.

"Adam, no!"

"He has Kiya." Adam's jaw was a rock of determination.

The signal arm was level with the top of the car. The warning whistle was earsplitting, the headlights blinding.

Harrison stopped breathing as the train hit the intersection.

Cassie touched that dark, empty place inside her. An ugly place she hadn't been to in years and had hoped never to go to again. She was submerged by the fear. It consumed her and she was lost.

But then a funny thing happened.

She made friends with the darkness and the closed, cramped space. Came to grips with the fact that she was probably going to die without ever seeing her twin sister or her mother or Harry ever again.

But once she let go and accepted her fate, the fear vanished. She felt no attachment, only peace.

And forgiveness.

Pure, unconditional forgiveness for both herself and her mistakes and for the whole of humankind. She was filled to the core of her being with the wonder of it.

She forgave her father for running out on the family after her childhood accident.

She forgave poor old Duane, that lost soul, for locking her in the cellar.

She forgave everyone she'd ever known. Friends, lovers, enemies, and all those in between.

She forgave Demitri and Anthony and Tom Grayfield, who were so blinded by greed and lust for power that they did not understand what really mattered. She felt pity and she forgave them.

But most of all, she forgave herself. For the wrong roads taken, the foolish mistakes made, the people she'd unwittingly hurt.

Her heart swelled with forgiveness.

Forgive me, Harry, for not keeping the amulet safe. For not trusting you completely. For not fully appreciating you for who you are.

She lay in the constrained darkness of the sarcophagus and she was filled with a bright, expansive lightness.

Harry, she thought. *Harry, Harry, Harry.*

How she wanted to see him again. To touch him, kiss him, taste him.

Would she ever?

The limo stopped. She heard the men get out. Felt them lift the sarcophagus. Saw the gray swirling mist, the leering bull masks and black hoods as they opened the coffin lid and dragged her out in the rain.

Adam braked to a stop just in the nick of time. A second later, and they would have been delivery van roadkill.

But the limo had gotten away.

Cassie was lost to him. Harrison's heart wrenched.

The train sped by, *clickity-clickity-clack*. He watched the cars slide past, dread mounting as the train continued on and on and on and the clock on the dashboard went *tick, tick, tick.*

Would they be able to find the limo? Was Cassie lost to him forever?

Thump, thump, thump sounded from the back.

"While we're stuck here, we might as well let Boreas out." Harrison sighed.

Adam shook his head.

Harrison reached over and pulled the keys out of the ignition. "Yes."

"Hey." Adam glowered.

Harrison got out and unlocked the back door to find Clyde Petalonus tied up inside.

Anthony and Demitri had carried the sarcophagus to the middle of the spillway of the Trinity River. A metal mesh fence had been erected across the cement barrier to prevent misdirected boaters from falling over.

The water was shallow at the top of the spillway, but swift. It rushed under the coffin, which was wedged tight against the fence, tumbling over the embankment into a mist of steamy fog below. The sound was a dull roar in Cassie's ears.

They had taken her out of the sarcophagus and laid her on top of it, still bound and gagged. They dropped her in the water a couple of times in the process, and now she was shivering wet.

Tom Grayfield was positioned behind the sarcophagus, bracing himself against it to keep from losing his balance on the slick cement. Anthony stood to her left, Demitri on her right. The fence at her feet. Both Anthony and Demitri were clinging to the metal posts in order to stay upright. In their hoods and masks, they looked like dark creatures from a *Star Wars* movie.

Rain pelted them all. Lightning streaked across the bitter black sky.

"Do you have the rings?" Grayfield shouted over the noise of the river and the rumbling thunder.

Both Demitri and Anthony held up one-half of the amulet.

Grayfield spouted some more chants in a bizarre foreign language. Cassie inhaled sharply. He was performing his own perverse version of the legend of the star-crossed lovers' reunification ceremony.

Solen was here, but there was no Kiya. That's what Grayfield had meant when he'd said she would be Kiya's stand-in. She wasn't certain exactly what all that entailed. If the rings were rejoined now, would her soul forever be melded with Solen's?

But how could that happen when Solen was long dead and crunched up like a smashed potato chip bag and she was very much alive?

"Get ready to meld the rings," Grayfield cried and raised his right hand high over his head.

Lightning lit up the sky.

Cassie stared helplessly. A flare of lightning lit the knife blade clutched in Tom Grayfield's upraised hand.

"Your brother believes he's Solen," Clyde said.

"What happened to him?" Harrison had commandeered the driver's seat, even though he couldn't see worth a flip without his glasses. He preferred his own driving to Adam's kamikaze charioting.

"Adam's got amnesia or something. He doesn't recognize me a bit."

"Yes, I do." Adam scowled at Clyde. "You're Boreas. You sold me into slavery and stole my birthright."

"Boreas was a young and strapping warrior. Do I look like a strapping young warrior to you?" Clyde patted his paunch and ran a hand through his thinning hair. "I mean, honestly."

Adam narrowed his eyes at Clyde and then glanced over at Harrison. "He's Boreas. Right?"

"No, Adam, he's Clyde. Clyde Petalonus."

Adam pondered this, but said nothing.

"I don't know what happened to your brother," Clyde said. "But I can tell you what happened to me."

The train finally came to an end, and the signal crossing arms rose. Harry bumped the delivery van over the tracks. They were near Forest Park on the Trinity River. There was a break in the overcast sky. The full moon playing a quick game of tag with the churning clouds. One minute the park was illuminated in a glow of light, the next minute cloaked in a bath of shadows.

Cassie, where are you?

Harrison fought off the black depression weighing down his lungs. He thought of her and remembered what they'd been doing when Cassie had found Solen's half of the amulet.

They'd been so close to making love. Joining their bodies completely. Fused.

Now he might never get to be with her.

The sadness was too much to handle. He shut down his emotions, closed off his feelings, hid from himself. This was why he had stayed detached for so many years. It hurt too damned much to get close to someone.

"What did happen to you, Clyde?" he asked.

Anything to keep his mind occupied and off the stark reality that time was running out. Harrison guided the van through the park, straining his eyes to search for the limo. He wished for his glasses. He wished for a gun. He had neither. "How'd you end up in the back of this van?"

"Demitri," Clyde grunted. "He roughed me up and stuck me in the back. If Adam hadn't stolen the van out from under him and Korba, I don't know what would have happened to me."

"You know Demitri and Anthony Korba?" Harrison's hands were clenched tight on the steering wheel. They'd lost a good five minutes waiting for the train. Anything could happen in five minutes. Cassie could die.

"And I know Tom Grayfield. We roomed together in college when he was dating your mother."

"You knew my mother?"

"I knew you too," Clyde said. "Most serious toddler I ever met in my life. You never played with toys, but you were always taking things apart and putting them back together again."

"Did you know my father?" Harrison held his breath.

"No. I just knew he broke your mother's heart. Grayfield was a rebound fling for her. And Grayfield was just using your mother's passion for the star-crossed lovers to help him get his hands on the amulet."

"You were at Adam's graduation from the University of Athens," Harrison said. "You were in the photograph, in the background."

Clyde nodded. "I couldn't miss his graduation, even if he didn't know I was there. I was as proud of him as if he were my own son."

"Did you know about the Minoan Order?"

Adam perked up. "Minoan Order? I know the Minoan Order."

"I heard rumors about Grayfield. I tried to warn your mother, but he was financing her dig and she didn't want to believe the rumors. Later she did, and that's why she asked me to look after Adam whenever he was in Greece with Tom. Mostly I had to do it from afar."

"I didn't know my mother was in Greece looking for Solen when I was a baby," Harrison said.

"I'm Solen." Adam raised a hand. "I'm right here."

"You're not Solen. You're Adam Grayfield."

His brother just stared at him.

Hoo-boy.

"How come I never met you before?" Harrison asked Clyde, trying hard to ignore his sagging spirits. They'd come to the end of Forest Park, and there was no sign of the limo.

"Tom and I had a huge falling-out over your mother. I was in love with her, you see," Clyde said. "But Tom was the one with the money, and nothing meant more to your mother than her work." He sounded sad, regretful.

Harrison left the park and turned onto University Drive. He had no idea where to look for the limo. The streets were empty. Lightning streaked across the sky. Raindrops spit upon the windshield. He turned on the wipers. They squeaked against the glass—*Cassie, Cassie, Cassie.*

The streets were empty. No traffic anywhere. He took University Drive to the freeway. If he circled around the overpass and headed east, he would have a bird's-eye view of the park.

Cassie, where are you?

His heart wrenched. He could no longer deny his pain. He was going to lose her before he'd ever really had the chance to know her.

Adam tugged on his shirtsleeve and pointed out the window. "Look, look."

A thick, hot blast of lightning electrified the sky.

Harrison glanced south toward the spillway of the Trinity River and his heart lurched.

There, in the middle of the river, were three men and a coffin.

CHAPTER
22

Whipping the van around in a dangerous and highly illegal freeway U-turn, Harrison prayed as he'd never prayed before. He lumbered over the median, crashed down into the westbound lane, and took the University Drive exit at twenty miles over the speed limit, tires squealing in protest.

"What is it? What's going on?" Clyde exclaimed.

"Kiya," Adam said at the same time Harrison said, "Cassie."

What were Tom and his henchmen doing with the sarcophagus on the spillway?

A fragment from the scroll translation lodged in his brain:

In the elements lies the progression to immortality. Earth, air, fire, water. Two rings, two hearts, lovers reunited always. Life becomes death, death becomes life. Full circle.

He didn't fully understand what it meant, but water had to be part of the ritual. He wheeled toward the spillway, heart in his throat, pulse pounding.

"There's Grayfield's limo," Clyde yelled.

It was parked near the river's edge. Harrison pulled the van up beside it. Lightning speared through the air, thick with ions, and smacked with a horrific jolt into a nearby tree.

They jumped and ducked their heads.

The tree burst into flames.

"This way, this way," Adam said, running along the bank toward the spillway ahead of Harrison and Clyde.

Harrison knew what was happening. He felt the dread, the chill, the horror of it shoot straight to his bones.

They reached the spillway. The awful scene was back-lit by the flaming tree.

Cassie lay bound and gagged on top of the sarcophagus. Anthony and Demitri were positioned at her sides, each holding a copper ring, extending them forward. Tom Grayfield stood over her, wearing the bull's head. He had a large gold ankh on a chain around his neck. He was the Minotaur, and there was a vicious knife clutched in his upraised fist.

The wind whirled. The water swirled. The air was rich with the smell of damp, fertile earth; the lightning hot and brilliant.

If Harrison made one move toward Cassie, Grayfield could stab her through the heart before he was halfway across the water.

I can't save her, he thought, and the despair was too much to bear. But he couldn't let her go without a fight. Couldn't lose her forever. Couldn't let Grayfield win.

Think, think.

He had no gun. No weapon. No clue what to do.

The djed. Use the djed.

The thought rose in his mind, clear and strong. *Use the*

djed. He pulled the djed from his pocket and raised it over his head, aiming at Grayfield's ankh.

Harrison held his breath.

Grayfield finished his chant.

Anthony Korba and Demitri leaned forward over Cassie's body to connect the rings.

Grayfield brought the knife down.

"Kiya!" Adam screamed and dashed into the water.

"Adam, come back," Clyde called.

A bolt of white-blue lightning descended from the murky black clouds.

It hit the djed with a force so strong that it dropped Harrison to his knees, but he did not let go. Would not let go. Nothing could make him let go.

The lightning sparked, jumping the gap from Harrison's homemade djed to the ankh around Grayfield's neck. It shot veiny branches of voltage straight into his chest.

Grayfield's body quivered as the electricity passed through him, welding him to the water.

But the lightning did not stop there. The energy frequency snapped and crackled as it leaped both right and left. It struck the two copper rings that Anthony and Demitri held in their hands.

It also fingered down from Grayfield's legs, illuminating him in a ghostly blue glow that shimmered and danced over the water.

The water that Adam was trudging through trying to get to Cassie.

Horrified, Harrison watched as the electricity jolted up through his brother's body.

* * *

The heat around her was intense, as was the eerie blue-white light. Cassie blinked, not understanding what was happening. Tom Grayfield stood above her, his body shaking, his eyes rolled back inside his bull's head, the knife fused to his palm.

And then the blue electrical light was gone and Grayfield's heavy frame slowly toppled forward.

Cassie raised her bound hands in a defensive reflex to block the blade that descended as Grayfield fell. She rolled her head to one side to keep from getting smacked by his bullish brow.

The duct tape stopped the knife. Grayfield's head thumped against the sarcophagus and his body slowly slid into the water.

Lightning lit the sky again. Thunder cracked.

Frantically, Cassie began sawing her wrists back and forth against the knife blade, desperate to get free before Grayfield's hand slipped down into the water with him.

To the left of her came another thump as Anthony Korba collapsed onto the sarcophagus as well, his cheek coming to rest against her knee. She almost kicked him off her, but then she saw that Solen's half of the amulet was still clutched in his outstretched fingers.

The duct tape broke free, and she shook it off. She pried the knife from Grayfield's hand and then ripped the gag off her mouth. Plucking the amulet from Anthony's fingers, she tucked the ring into the pocket of her blouse. She was leaning down to cut the duct tape from her ankles when she felt an iron grip clamp around her wrist.

"Not so fast, sister."

It was Demitri, Mr. Nike himself. He looked a little dazed, but his eyes were deadly. In his other hand he held Kiya's half of the amulet.

"Cassie!"

She turned her head to the right, saw Harrison and Clyde splashing toward her in the swift running water, and spied the mummy floating facedown in the water several feet from the sarcophagus.

"Harry!"

She tried to twist away from Demitri, tried with everything inside her to get to Harry, but Demitri applied so much pressure to her wrist, she feared the bone would snap. Helpless, she dropped the knife. It splashed into the river.

Demitri yanked her from the sarcophagus and through the water. He dragged her toward the opposite bank, scraping her knees against the cement spillway in the process.

She gasped against the coldness, against the pain, confused and frightened.

"Cassie, hang on. I'm coming!"

"Harry!" she called over her shoulder.

Demitri jerked her hard. "Shut up. Keep quiet."

They'd made it across the spillway. She tried to look back, to see how far away Harry was, but Demitri kept tugging at her so hard, pulling her so fast, she could not see what was happening behind her.

Demitri's got Kiya's half of the amulet. I have to get it from him.

He was hauling her up an embankment, through a cluster of trees. Somewhere in all the madness she had lost her sandals. Thorns and twigs pierced her bare feet. Her knees stung from the cement burns. She kept stumbling and falling down. Demitri was relentless, never stopping, never even slowing.

What she needed was a plan. Unfortunately, she had

nothing. If she could just slow him down long enough for Harry to catch up.

"Hey, Demitri, wanna blow job?"

"Huh?" Demitri paused.

Just as she'd hoped, natural male instinct momentarily outweighed the urgent need to escape his pursuers. But a moment was all Cassie needed. As soon as Demitri turned to see if he'd heard correctly, Cassie plowed her knee into his crotch with as much force as she could muster.

Demitri screamed and clutched himself with both hands, letting go of her and dropping Kiya's half of the amulet as he sank to the ground, writhing in pain. The amulet made a faint clinking sound as it bounced off a rock.

"A blow to your man parts. Blow job, get it?" Cassie stepped over him and pulled back her hair with one hand so it wouldn't fall in her face as she searched in the pre-dawn haze for the amulet.

She spotted the ring and leaned down to pick it up. Just as she reached for it, a man's hand appeared from the shadows.

Breathing hard, clothes soaking wet, Harrison scaled the embankment.

Cassie. I have to save Cassie.

The ground felt like wet cement, dragging him down, slowing him. He pumped his arms and pushed himself harder. The river was directly below him. If he slipped and fell, he would plunge into the deep pool of turbulent water tumbling off the spillway.

Got to get to Cassie.

He crested the hill, heard someone moan ahead of him

in the copse of trees. Spurred on, he zigzagged around stumps and boulders, broke through into a small clearing. He found Demitri on the ground, holding himself and rolling from side to side. Cassie was kneeling a few feet away, clutching something tightly to her chest in her knotted hand.

Her face was lifted upward, and she was gazing into the barrel of a gun.

Harrison blinked, unable to believe his eyes, but he understood at once what had happened. She'd racked Demitri, he'd dropped the amulet, and when she'd gone to retrieve it, Ahmose Akvar had pulled the gun on her.

The question was, Where had Ahmose come from, and what did he have to do with Tom Grayfield and the Minoan Order?

"Give me the amulet," the Egyptian demanded, extending his palm.

"Cassie, sweetheart," Harrison called out. "Are you all right?"

"Could be better," she said ruefully. "I'm not a huge fan of having firearms pointed in my face."

"What are you doing, Ahmose?" Harrison stepped around Demitri, who whistled in a low, keening wail. Cassie must have gotten him good. He moved purposely toward Ahmose, acting as if he was unarmed, acting as if this were all perfectly normal. He didn't want to escalate the situation by injecting unnecessary emotion into it. But he wanted to rush Ahmose and pound the shit out of him for scaring Cassie.

"Stay back, Harrison." Ahmose waved the gun at him.

"What's going on? Let's talk about this."

"Nothing to talk about," Ahmose said. "Give me the amulet."

"No." Cassie shook her head. "I won't."

Ahmose cocked the gun. "Please, do not make me shoot you."

Harrison could tell from the determined set to his jaw that Ahmose would pull the trigger if forced. Harrison had no idea why, but he was certain Ahmose was deadly serious. Sweat popped out on his forehead despite the fact he was drenched and shivering cold down to his very marrow.

"Give him the amulet, Cassie."

In the distance, sirens wailed.

"Give me the amulet."

The sirens goaded the urgency in Ahmose's voice. The Egyptian stepped forward and pressed the nose of the gun flush against Cassie's temple.

Her eyes widened and she looked over at Harrison, the fear on her face ripping a hole through him more vicious than any bullet.

"Give it to him," Harrison whispered. "It isn't worth your life."

"But Kiya and Solen," she whimpered.

"To hell with Kiya and Solen. You're the one I care about."

"Do as Dr. Standish says."

Reluctantly, Cassie unknotted her fist and allowed Ahmose to pluck the ring from her hand.

Without another word, the Egyptian stalked to the top of the embankment and stared down at the churning river below. He cocked back his arm and flung the amulet into the Trinity.

They all watched it hit the water and quickly disappear into the thrashing foam. Ahmose stuck the gun in his waistband and turned to go.

Harrison stared in disbelief. His entire life's work had just been thrown away. Impossible, unbelievable. He couldn't let it go. He had to know. He moved in front of the Egyptian, blocking his way.

Their eyes met.

"Why, Ahmose? Why?"

"Ask your mother," Ahmose said and then shouldered past him and disappeared into the wet, stormy night.

The sirens screamed nearer.

Stunned over what had just happened, Cassie stared at Harrison.

"Ahmose threw the amulet away. Why would he throw it in the river? And what did he mean when he said to ask your mother?"

"It doesn't matter," Harrison said, moving to close the gap between them.

Her bottom lip trembled as emotion swept through her. "Kiya and Solen." She choked back the tears. "They'll never be reunited now."

"Shh, sweetheart, it's okay." Harry reached out to cup the back of her head in his palm, threading his fingers through her hair. "Are you all right?"

"Fine." She forced a shaky smile. "I'm fine."

He lowered his head and tenderly kissed her lips. She'd never tasted anything sweeter than the flavor of his mouth. Fifteen minutes earlier she'd thought her life was over, that she would never see him again. She wrapped her arms around his neck, and he scooped her, against him. She never wanted to let him go.

"We better break this up," he murmured softly against her lips. "Demitri's getting away."

She sighed and stepped back. Harrison went after Demitri, who was trying to crawl off through the trees.

"Not so fast, dirtbag." Harrison grabbed Demitri by the collar and started dragging him, kicking and clawing, back into the clearing. Then Demitri tripped Harrison, knocking him to the ground. They rolled around, punching each other.

"Stop it! Stop it!" Cassie cried.

"Don't anybody move," came a voice from the mist. "FBI."

"How did you find us?" Cassie asked her brother-in-law, David Marshall, several minutes later.

She, David, Harrison, and Clyde were standing on the banks of the Trinity. They'd quickly filled David in on what had happened, each telling their part of the story.

Paramedics loaded Tom Grayfield, Anthony Korba, and Adam into ambulances. All three were unconscious from the refracted electrical discharge of Harrison's djed transformer. Demitri, who hadn't been as severely affected by the voltage because he'd been wearing sneakers, was shackled and had been led off to a waiting police cruiser. None of the uniformed officers with David had been able to find Ahmose Akvar, although they were still scouring the nearby woods and the perimeter of Forest Park.

"The burning bush." David indicated the tree still smoldering from the lightning strike. "Someone saw it flaming and called the fire department. When they got here, firemen spied Tom Grayfield's limo and radioed the police. I had them put an APB out on you the minute you told me you were with Tom Grayfield. Do you have any idea how frantic I've been, Cassie?"

Cassie crinkled her nose. "I'm so sorry, David. I didn't mean to involve you in all this."

"Hey." David smiled and shrugged. "What are brothers-in-law for?"

"You didn't tell Maddie, did you?"

"I had to. Maddie's my wife. We don't keep secrets from each other. She's catching the next flight out from D.C."

"Maddie worries too much." Cassie sighed. Although she might complain about her sister's fierce protective-ness, she would secretly be overjoyed to hug her twin close after tonight's ordeal.

"Your sister just cares about you," David said.

"I know." Cassie nodded and turned to Harrison. Their eyes met and her stomach clutched. Here was someone else who cared about her too. And she cared about him in return. Cared more than she ever thought possible. "I owe you an apology, Harrison."

"What for?"

"For believing Ahmose's lie. For doubting you even for a moment."

"Why did you doubt me?" he asked.

"Because of the photograph with Clyde in the back-ground. Why did you lie about knowing him?"

"Harrison didn't know that I knew him," Clyde inter-jected. "He never realized it was me in the picture."

Cassie's eyes never left Harrison's face, and he was studying her just as intently. She couldn't wait to get him alone so she could show him exactly how sorry she was for misjudging him.

"What's going to happen to Tom Grayfield?" Clyde asked. "And his henchmen?"

"Both the CIA and the Greek government are waiting

to talk with him about myriad offenses and violations. He'll be going to prison for a very long time," David said. "Anthony Korba and Demitri Lorenzo will face kidnapping and attempted murder charges along with Grayfield."

Harrison gazed after the ambulance that whisked Adam away. "Do you think my brother will be all right?"

"Come on." David clapped a sympathetic hand on Harrison's shoulder. "I'll drive you to the hospital."

CHAPTER
23

It was eight o'clock on Friday morning when they got back to Harrison's apartment. David had raised an eyebrow when Cassie told him there wasn't any need for him to take her over to her place, because she was staying with Harry.

Adam still hadn't regained consciousness. The doctor had advised them to go home and get some rest. He said Adam's prognosis was good, and he expected him to make a full recovery.

But once the front door had closed and she was totally alone with Harrison, Cassie was surprised to discover she felt shy and a little awkward.

He smiled at her, stretched out a hand, and her uncertainty vanished. In spite of his black eye and bruises, or maybe even because of them. No one had ever taken her breath the way that he did. How was it she'd never really realized exactly how handsome he was?

"Let's get you tended to."

"Huh?" She felt dazed from staring into those rich brown eyes.

"Your legs." He nodded.

Cassie peered down at her feet. They'd given her a pair of paper booties to wear at the hospital, but there was dried blood on her skin from her knees on down.

Harrison filled the tub with water and quietly undressed her. She appreciated the care he took, tenderly helping her off with her blouse. When he dropped it to the floor, Solen's ring rolled out.

"You have the other half of the amulet," he said.

"Little good it does now." She felt incredibly close to tears again. "Solen and Kiya will never be together."

"It's just a silly legend."

"Still, you never know."

"I understand," he said. "I feel the loss too. I never believed in the legend, and until now I never realized how important reuniting those rings was to me."

"It's sad."

"Shh, let's not talk about it." He finished undressing her about the same time the tub had filled. He turned off the water and helped her into the bath.

Sinking gratefully into the warm water, she told him everything that had happened to her in the warehouse. He told her what he'd discovered in the scrolls. How the cryptic message had led him directly to Tom Grayfield.

She spoke of her fear of never seeing him again, her terror at being locked in the sarcophagus, and then she told him about the strange and wonderful peace that had come over her. The forgiveness she'd felt for everyone.

He whispered of his dismay at learning he'd delivered her into Grayfield's hands. Emotion caught in his throat when he spoke of the horror he'd felt when he realized Grayfield intended to use her as a human sacrifice in his quest for immortality.

Harrison undressed and climbed into the tub with her.

They said nothing more, just gazed into each other's eyes, fully experiencing the moment. Both happy that they were together and alive.

She stroked his cheek with a washcloth.

He soaped her breasts.

She massaged his tense shoulders.

He brushed his fingers through the strands of her hair.

When the water grew cold, they dried each other off. He had Cassie sit on the counter and he knelt on the floor, tenderly cleansing her wounds. After first applying antiseptic ointment, he then put Band-Aids on the cuts and scrapes on her feet and knees.

They were completely naked in front of each other in the stark bathroom light, and neither was embarrassed.

It felt too right.

He kissed her and she kissed him back. He took her hand and guided her into his bedroom, dropping kisses on her face along the way. His dear face was battered and bruised, but Cassie had never seen anything as touching as the expression in his eyes when he gazed at her.

They sat together on the edge of the bed, kissing, stroking, licking, tasting. The tempo increased as their passion escalated. They lay back on the mattress. Cassie broke his kiss and nibbled a trail down his chin to his throat to his chest and beyond.

When her mouth touched his jutting penis, he sucked in his breath. She raised her head and met his gaze. His eyes filled with wonder and fascination and desire as he watched her stroke him. He looked so vibrant, so alive, so unlike the standoffish professor she had first met. She'd misjudged him and his ability to experience passion.

The heat of desire in his eyes was so stark, so hungry, it took her breath away. He wanted her.

She could see it written across his face. She tasted it in his kisses. Smelled it on his skin. He wanted her in a way no other man had ever wanted her.

While she was stroking him with her mouth, he gently reached for her, his fingers skating over her hip bone. She closed her eyes as she felt energy melt up from her feminine core into her breasts and into her throat. She tasted her own desire, hot and rich, mingling with the earthy flavor of him.

A silky moan escaped his lips. He carefully twisted away from her, breaking her gentle suction on his erection.

Her eyes popped open and she saw he had shifted onto his side, propping himself on his elbow. He was peering at her, and she saw the raw, animal intensity of need in eyes the color of Guinness.

He kissed her, his mouth urgent. His energy filled her, shocked her. He was more powerful than a charge of white-hot lightning.

When he lightly grazed her most tender spot, a desperate sweetness suffused her body, full of sumptuous delight. And all the capacity of her desire sprang alive. She reached for him, clutching, devouring.

She had no more restraint. Abandon claimed her, and she thrust herself against his hard body.

But he was tender. So very tender. He acted as if she were going to break into pieces if he so much as breathed on her hard.

"I want to get lost in your eyes as I make love to you, Cassie," he whispered, and it was exactly what she wanted to hear.

"Condom?"

"Right here." He dealt with the details, then poised

himself over her. Harry looked down into her face. "You're so incredibly beautiful. So brave."

"Not too shabby yourself, Professor."

She wrapped her legs around his waist, and with a reverential groan he sank into her. She felt so incredibly safe with him. She was able to let go of control and allow him to sweep her along with his masculine rhythm. She gave herself away, fully, completely, without hesitation. Unleashed her heart and surrendered. Forfeited everything to him.

"Harder," she cried and bucked her hips upward.

He rode her hard just as she wanted. Pushing into her, giving her glorious, inescapable pleasure.

Give it to me, give it to me. I want to feel you come.

Then it broke. Her thunderstorm. Her lightning. Her hurricane.

It was large inside her. So large. Spreading and growing. The air was a choir. Singing, vibrating his praises. *"Harrison, Harrison, Harrison."*

The sensation rushed through her, sweet, deep, hot, intense, flaming, burning like a slant of brilliant light far up inside her, diffusing through her and fanning the telltale rash of passion spreading up and over her breasts.

She shuddered against him as he shuddered into her.

"Oh, Harrison," she breathed.

"It's Harry," he whispered into the curve of her throat. "Call me Harry."

Cassie woke before Harry. She rolled over onto her side, stacked her hands under her cheek, and watched him sleeping.

She studied the way the sunlight fell across his bruised face. She held her hand poised above his hip, feeling the power of his body heat radiating up through her palm. She paid attention to the texture of his skin, so smooth and thick and tanned. She noticed how the very quality of the air in the room seemed different because they were breathing in tandem.

Tears filled her eyes and a strange tightness swelled her chest. She was overcome with a melancholy so intense she feared she might die from it.

Her natural instinct was to laugh, to move, to sing. Anything to buoy her mood and block out the sadness. But she did not do that. Instead, she lay beside Harrison, letting the melancholy fill her up.

Their time together was at an end. It was over.

As she fully experienced the sorrow of loss, a very strange thing happened.

All these years what she thought passed for happiness, activity, fun, parties, dates was so different from this unflappable sense of certainty. Her understanding of real and lasting happiness had changed. She had changed.

Something clicked deep inside her as she reconnected with the self she'd misplaced so long ago. Her habitual goals, scripts, and agendas dropped away in the realization of this better self, and suddenly she could see and hear and feel, both internally and externally, with greater clarity.

In that shimmering moment, she knew what she had to do. She had to stop hiding her pain. Had to fully live it, experience it, and then let it go. What she had been running from had already happened, and she'd survived. She was still here, still living her life.

She had so much to be grateful for. She didn't need that job at the Smithsonian to be happy. Didn't need parties or fast cars or constant stimulation. Everything she'd ever truly wanted or needed was within her reach. It was all right here.

All she had to do was make room.

He woke at 2 p.m. to find his bed empty. Cassie was gone. She'd crept away while he slept.

His sheets still smelled of her, vibrant as a summer garden. He squeezed her pillow to his chest and inhaled the scent of her.

Where had she gone? Why had she left?

The bedside phone rang. He snatched it up, his pulse bumping. Was it her?

"Hello?"

"It's Clyde. I'm at the hospital."

Simultaneously, Harrison sat up and dropped the pillow. "Adam—is he . . ."

"Awake, and he's regained his memory."

"Thank God."

"He wants to see you. He won't tell us what happened to him. Not until you get here."

"Us?" Was Cassie at the hospital already? Was that where she'd gone? But why would she go without him?

"I called your mother," Clyde said. "She's here."

Ten minutes later, Harrison walked into Adam's hospital room. On the drive over, one specific memory from the night before had stuck in his brain.

Ahmose, flinging Kiya's amulet into the Trinity, and saying, "Ask your mother." He hadn't known what Ahmose meant, but he did know his mother had been keeping too many secrets for too many years. It was long past time for a showdown.

But first things first. He had to speak to his brother.

Adam was sitting up in bed. Dark circles ringed his eyes, and his cheeks were sunken. He had an IV in his arm and he wore a hospital gown.

"You look as bad as I feel," Adam said.

"Dude." Harrison grinned and touched his blackened eye. "If you feel as bad as I look, you are so screwed."

Adam blinked. "That doesn't sound like you. You never say 'dude.' Or tease me."

Harrison shrugged and felt his cheeks heat. "Guess I've been hanging out with Cassie Cooper too long, searching for your sorry butt."

"I like the changes. She's good for you."

"Where's Mom?" He plunked down in one of the chairs for visitors at the side of Adam's bed.

"Right here."

Harrison looked up to see Diana and Clyde walking through the door carrying a Burger King bag. Adam held out his hand. "Thanks, Mom, you saved my life. The hospital food is bad enough to kill a guy."

Diana handed Adam the sack, then turned to Harrison. "Hello, son."

"Hello, Mother."

This is how it had always been between them. Distant, tentative, wary. He wished it did not have to be this way. He used to long for the sort of mother you could throw your arms around and wrap in a bear hug. But Diana was who she was.

Diana took the chair next to Harrison. Clyde went to stand at the back of the room, his arms folded on his chest, his eyes on Diana. Adam focused on wolfing down his food.

"So tell us everything that happened," Diana said. "Start from the beginning."

"Well," Adam said, "I was born in a—"

"Don't be a smartass," Diana interrupted. "You'd think after everything you've been through, it would have taken some of the starch out of your sails."

"Or some of the spunk out of the punk," Harrison muttered.

His mother grinned at him. Hey, for once they were on the same wavelength. Adam didn't seem to mind that they were ganging up on him. He waved a hand. "You guys are just jealous because I have an amazing ability to bounce back."

"So talk."

"All right." Adam wiped a smear of mustard off his cheek. "Here's where it started. Dad put me up to searching for Solen. I wasn't really interested. Had a hot girl I was dating and she was trying to get me to move to France with her, but Dad kept telling me how I had to beat Harrison. He said he would finance the dig, no strings attached. He'd never done that before. I thought it might be a chance to mend fences between us." He polished off the last of his hamburger, and with a free-throw toss landed it in the trash can. "He shoots; he scores!"

"Don't get distracted," Diana said.

Adam sighed. Harrison could tell this was painful for him, vocalizing the truth about his father.

"Dad had a lot of detailed information about Solen's tomb and where it was located. He refused to tell me where he got the info, and for the longest time I thought the data must be totally bogus and I wouldn't use it. I kept reminding him that he'd told me no strings were attached to the money."

"Harrison," Diana interrupted, giving him the once-over. "You're not wearing your glasses."

"Broke them in a bar fight. Long story."

Diana looked taken aback. "A bar brawl? You?"

"Dude." Adam gave him a thumbs-up. "Way to go, bro."

"Sorry, go on. I didn't mean to interrupt." Diana shook her head but looked at Harrison differently, as if she suddenly respected him more.

"Anyway, I finally followed Dad's instructions because I didn't know where else to look, and hey, I found Solen right where he said I would."

"And among Solen's artifacts, you found the scroll," Harrison supplied.

"Yeah, written in Minoan hieroglyphics. And I translated it," Adam boasted. "Took me several weeks of trying, but I did it. Dad pressured me." His face sobered. "Once I knew what it said, I wished I hadn't."

Diana fisted Adam's covers in her hands. "And what did you learn?"

Harrison caught the recriminating look his brother sent his mother. "You've known all along about Dad," Adam accused.

"Not known. Suspected. But I never knew for sure."

Harrison was startled to see tears misting his mother's eyes. He could never remember seeing her cry.

A nurse came in to take Adam's vital signs, and they had to wait until she was finished before he could continue his story. The tension in the room was palpable.

"Everything was in Solen's scroll," Adam said. "The legend of the star-crossed lovers. The curse he'd placed on Vizier Nebamun's family. And the reason my father wanted Solen resurrected. The formula for immortality."

The room fell silent for a long moment as Adam's words echoed off the walls.

"There were sayings in that text." Adam took a swallow of water. "Things my father often said. And the symbols that match the signet ring he wears. Since the hieroglyphics had never been translated, only someone versed in the oral tradition of the Minoan Order could have possessed such knowledge. That's why he had funded my dig. That's where he'd gotten his information. I had no idea what he was going to do with the formula, but I knew I couldn't turn it over to him. Not if he was in the Minoan Order."

"Adam called me when he got in trouble. He remembered me from his childhood and thought I could help since I worked for the Kimbell," Clyde interjected. "His plan was to split up the artifacts. Ship me Solen in his sarcophagus. Hide the scroll in a crate with a false bottom and leave it for Harrison to find, and keep the amulet on his person."

"When I got to Fort Worth," Adam picked up the story again, "Clyde wrapped me in the mummy linen. I had to be unrecognizable. I went to the museum masquerade party to tell Harrison what was happening, but I was afraid to approach him directly because Ahmose Akvar kept hanging around. I had no idea whom I could trust, who might be watching, and the last thing I wanted was to put them on his tail too. In the meantime, Dad sent Anthony Korba and Demitri Lorenzo to bring me back to Greece. Demitri cornered me in the courtyard at the Kimbell and tried to get me to tell him where Solen's half of the amulet was. When I resisted, he stabbed me in the back with a knife he'd filched from the caterers. Only Cassie's arrival in the courtyard saved my life."

"I've got to meet this Cassie," Diana said. "She sounds special."

Special wasn't the half of it. "You'll like her," Harrison said.

Adam kept talking. "I was in the courtyard bleeding, slowly losing consciousness, and I saw this red leather handbag. I dragged myself over to it and hid the amulet inside."

"It was Cassie's handbag," Harrison said.

Adam brightened. "So she has the amulet? Everything is okay? We can still reunite the rings?"

Harrison glanced over at Clyde. "You didn't tell him?"

Clyde shook his head.

"What?" Adam looked from one to the other. "What is it?"

Harrison blew out his breath. "We have Solen's half of the amulet, but Ahmose Akvar destroyed Kiya's half." He looked over at his mother. "Ahmose said to ask you why."

"What?" Diana looked startled.

Then, because he was beginning to suspect the answer, Harrison asked her the question he hadn't asked her in sixteen years.

"Who's my father?"

CHAPTER
24

You've already started to figure it out, son. Why else would Ahmose Akvar destroy one-half of the amulet?"

Harrison's gaze locked with Diana's. "Because he's descended from Vizier Nebamun. Ahmose destroyed Kiya's ring in order to prevent the reunification. He was desperate to prevent the curse."

"Exactly."

"What does that have to do with me?" he asked.

Clyde came over and placed both hands on Diana's shoulders. She leaned against Clyde and squarely met Harrison's glare. "You're upset about losing the amulet."

"How could I not be? It was my life's work. Your life's work too. Aren't you upset? Your opportunity to disprove the legend is gone forever."

"What does it matter if Solen and Kiya are reunited? If you don't believe."

"What if I do?"

Diana smiled faintly. "Which is it, son? Do you believe in the legend or don't you?"

Odd, but when he tried to think of Kiya, it was laughing, outrageous, fun-loving Cassie who popped into his head. And when he tried to imagine Solen, he saw only his own face. He shook his head, feeling disoriented. What was wrong with him? He turned the tables, answering his mother's question with the eternal question that so badly needed answering.

"Who is my father?"

"Are you certain you want to know?"

"I wouldn't be asking if I didn't." Harrison curled his fingers into his palms, bracing for the news he'd waited thirty-two years to hear. His heart curiously slowed. "I've always wanted to know."

"He was Egyptian. As you've always suspected. That's where you get your olive complexion."

Reaching up, Harrison touched his cheek. Half Egyptian. Somehow he'd always known this. Egypt was in his blood. It was as much a part of him as his color-blindness.

"Your biological father is dead. He passed away four or five years ago. I think it was a heart attack." She said it so emotionlessly, as if she had never made love to the man, had never given birth to his child out of wedlock.

And Harrison realized he'd been like his mother for far too long. Holding back, denying his feelings, living too much in his head and not enough in his heart.

He had not expected the news of his biological father's death to hit him so viscerally. He hadn't known the man, but he couldn't shake the feeling of having been cheated out of something vital.

"What was his name?"

"Mohammad Akvar."

He sucked in his breath as the impact hit him. "The former Egyptian prime minister?"

"Yes."

"Ahmose is my brother?"

"Your half brother, yes."

The full implication finally sank in. "That means I'm also descended from Vizier Nebamun. The man who poisoned Kiya and Solen."

"You are. So I ask you again, son. Do you believe in the star-crossed lovers or not?"

He recognized what she was getting at. If he believed in the star-crossed lovers, then he must believe in the curse. You couldn't have one without the other. But he did not believe in the legend. There was nothing to fear from the curse. As his mother had once said, there was no such thing as soul mates and undying love. No such thing as love at first sight.

What about Cassie? whispered a voice in the back of his head.

"It's a moot point. Kiya's half of the amulet is no more. Ahmose threw it into the river. We'll never be able to prove the legend of the star-crossed lovers one way or the other."

"Don't be so sure about that."

"Enough secrets." Harrison jumped up from his chair, no longer able to tolerate his mother's games. "Just tell me. Tell me everything."

Diana hesitated.

"You've got to let me have control over my own life. Stop withholding information."

"Are you certain?"

"Positive."

"As you wish." Diana nodded. "After you discovered Kiya's remains, I couldn't help worrying. What if I'd been wrong about the legend? What if it really was true? And what if either you or your brother one day found

Solen and the other half of the amulet? You were extremely determined, and Adam is very competitive. Throw Tom Grayfield into the mix, and I knew it was inevitable that one of you would find Solen."

"What did you do?"

"I had a replica of Kiya's amulet made."

"You're telling me that you switched the amulet?"

"Yes."

"But when and how?"

"Ten days ago. When you first arrived. Clyde made the switch at the Kimbell while you were setting up the exhibit."

Excitement took hold of him. All was not lost. The pieces could still be brought together, the amulet made whole. Solen and Kiya reunited.

"Ahmose did not destroy the real half?"

His mother reached into the pocket of her sweater, pulled out a small white jeweler's box, and pressed it into his hand. "I can't protect you anymore. It's your decision to make. If you're willing to take the gamble, then reunite the lovers."

Cassie had just finished burning the last memento from her collage wall when the doorbell rang. She rocked back on her heels and watched the picture of Peyton Shriver go up in smoke. She had thought that burning the photographs and memorabilia would be bittersweet.

But it was not. She felt empowered. She felt excited. She felt free.

The bell chimed a second time.

She closed the fireplace screen, dusted off her palms, and rose to her feet. She figured it must be Maddie and David. She was expecting them any minute.

She was surprised but very pleased to find Harrison standing on the landing.

"Harry!" She flung her arms around his neck and hugged him tight. She was so happy to see him, she barely noticed he did not hug her back. "What are you doing here?"

He held out a white jeweler's box.

For one heart-stopping moment she wondered if it was an engagement ring and her hopes leaped with joy. But the box was wider and flatter than a ring box, something more like what a bracelet or a brooch would be in.

"You brought me a present? Aw, Harry, you didn't have to do that."

"It's not a present."

"What is it?"

"Open it up."

She lifted the lid and stared down at an ancient copper ring. Confused, she glanced at Harry. "What?"

"It's Kiya's half."

"The half Ahmose threw into the river?"

"No. The real half."

"Excuse me?"

"Can we sit down? This conversation is going to take me a while."

"Sure, sure." She ushered him into the living room.

He sniffed the air. "You had a fire."

"Yes." She wanted so badly to tell him she'd destroyed her collage wall for him, but the timing had to be right and she wasn't sure this was it. "I was burning a few things."

He sat down on the couch and Cassie curled up beside him, kicking off her flip-flops and tucking her legs underneath her.

"Have you talked to Phyllis yet?"

"No." Cassie shook her head.

She'd procrastinated, not wanting to face the curator and tell her that not only was the reunification ceremony not going to take place, but the amulet stolen from the display was gone forever. Her dreams for the Smithsonian were officially over. But she realized she didn't feel so bad about that. She studied Harry's face and her pulse leaped. She had other dreams now.

"Good," he said.

Then he told Cassie everything he had learned from his mother. How she'd been madly in love with his father and been heartbroken when she'd discovered he was married and she was pregnant. He told her how Diana had left Egypt and gone to Greece to search for Solen and had met Tom Grayfield. He had been the rebound guy for her, and she had been a means to an end for him.

Harrison told her that he'd learned he and Ahmose were half brothers and that they were descendants of Vizier Nebamun. He even told her about Jessica and his teenage feelings for her and how he'd caught her in Adam's arms.

"So if we reunite the pieces of the amulet at the reunification ceremony, then you will be forever cursed."

"I don't believe in the legend, remember? I don't believe in curses."

"You want to do this?"

"I want you to have everything you've ever wanted, Cassie. If we make this right with Phyllis, you'll get your recommendation to the Smithsonian. Kiya and Solen are reunited. Everyone is happy."

"Well, except for Vizier Nebamun's descendants.

Even if you don't believe in it, clearly they do. Belief can do strange things to people."

"Like the belief in immortality? Tom Grayfield was ready to kill his own son over it. Call Phyllis, tell her that everything is a go for the reunification ceremony. Your brother-in-law even got the police to release Solen and his sarcophagus. Clyde's gone over to pick up the mummy."

Cassie glanced at her watch. "It's five-thirty."

"We have plenty of time."

"No. I can't let you do this."

"I want to do it. I've spent my life chasing this legend. The rings belong together."

"But you could be cursed. Are you willing to take that risk?"

"Yes," he said. "I am."

He got to his feet and so did Cassie. "I'm going to miss you when you're off to Washington."

She looked at him, not certain what to say. She wanted to tell him that she wanted *him*, not the Smithsonian, but he was holding himself stiffly, hiding his feelings.

"I brought you something to remember me by," he said.

"Oh?" She didn't want to be a memory. She wanted to be part of his life. *But what if he doesn't want you?*

He took something from inside his jacket pocket. It was a photograph the nature guide had taken of them with Cassie the monarch at the butterfly hatchery and a copy of the brochure.

"For your collage wall," he said.

Cassie bit back her tears. This was good-bye. He was giving her the big kiss-off. She'd never been dumped, but she'd done enough dumping to recognize the signs.

"No." She shoved the picture back at him. "I can't accept this. I won't put you on my wall."

He looked as if she'd smacked him hard across the face. Well, she wasn't going to make this any easier for him. She wasn't going to let him salve his ego with a paltry picture and a butterfly brochure.

"Cassie, I—"

"No," she said again as the doorbell rang. Relieved to have a good excuse to end the conversation, she rushed to answer it.

Maddie and David tumbled through the front door. "Cassie!" Maddie squealed.

"Maddie!"

They threw themselves into each other's arms and hugged as if they hadn't seen each other in four hundred years.

"Guess what?" Maddie's eyes danced. "I'm pregnant!"

"With twins," David added.

Maddie and Cassie squealed and hugged all over again, dancing around the kitchen. Then they hugged David.

It was only after the excitement died down that Cassie realized Harry had slipped out the door without even saying good-bye.

CHAPTER
25

She had turned down his gift. Apparently he wasn't good enough for her collage wall. And the only other face that Cassie had not put up on her wall was the face of her abusive ex-husband. In Cassie's mind, he and Duane were in the same category. They were the ones who had caused her the most pain.

He squeezed his eyes shut as despair washed over him. He sat parked in Diana's car outside Cassie's apartment. He'd borrowed it from her at the hospital. He was weak-kneed and aching, suffering much more than when Big Ray had beaten him up at Bodacious Booties.

Why should her rejection hurt so much? So she didn't want him on the wall. What was the big deal?

The big deal was he felt as if his insides had been ripped out. The big deal was he couldn't conceive of the idea of not having her in his life.

The reality of his feelings hit him harder than the lightning bolt he'd channeled with his djed. That's when Harrison knew that in spite of all the jockeying he'd done to hide his emotions and keep his heart

safe, he'd fallen hopelessly in love with Cassie
Cooper.

Everyone had returned for the reunification ceremony.
The guests were there. Phyllis was there, as were Clyde
and Diana and Adam, sans the mummy costume. The
only one missing from the original group was Ahmose,
who was cooling his heels in jail for attempting to destroy
a priceless Egyptian artifact and Harry.

She feared Harry wasn't coming.

To stall, Cassie had given away the prizes for the faked
murder mystery. She'd planned to award first prize to the
most authentic solution, but since none of the guesses
could touch reality, she'd picked Lashaundra Johnson as
the winner for her sheer tenacity.

It was eight-thirty-five and still no Harry.

Everyone was gathered around the two sarcophagi positioned in the middle of the exhibit hall. The twin sec-
tions of the amulet were in separate display cases at the
head of the sarcophagi, and between the cases sat the
original djed unearthed from Kiya's tomb.

Cassie glanced at her watch again.

Eight-thirty-seven.

Adam leaned in close to her. "I can stand in for Harrison."

"That won't be necessary," Harry said. "I'm here."

Cassie looked at him and her heart leaped. He'd found
his extra pair of glasses and he was wearing mismatched
shoes again, but she'd never seen a more handsome sight
in her life.

His eyes met hers. "I need to speak with you in private."

"Now?" She glanced at the crowd, which was staring at them expectantly.

"Now."

"Can't it wait?"

"No, it can't." Manfully, he took her elbow and hustled her into the hallway.

"What is it? What's wrong?"

"This," he said and then kissed her with more passion and need than he'd ever kissed her. "I love you, Cassie Cooper."

Her heart flipped. "Then why did you try to give me that picture for my collage wall? If you loved me, why were you walking out of my life?"

"Because you don't do commitment, remember? And besides, you turned down my picture. The only other man in your life who wasn't on that wall was Duane. Explain that one, Cassie. Do I cause you that much pain?"

"You silly man. I turned down the picture because I want so much more from you than a stupid photograph. I tore down my collage wall. For you. I burned everything. That's what I was trying to tell you when Maddie and David showed up. What I would have explained to you if you hadn't gotten afraid of your feelings and taken off."

"I'm not afraid of my feelings anymore."

"How can I believe that, Harry?"

"You'll just have to trust me on this."

"I'm not sure I can," she said.

"Cooper." Phyllis poked her head into the hallway. "The natives are getting restless. Let's get this sideshow on the road. Chop-chop."

"We better go," Cassie said.

"This isn't over." Harry held on to her arm until she looked him in the eyes. "Mark my word."

"Move it," Phyllis bellowed.

They went back into the exhibit hall.

Adam was retelling the legend of the star-crossed lovers. "And now," he said, "for the reunification of the rings of the amulet."

As they'd rehearsed the way it was supposed to happen the first night, Cassie picked up Kiya's half of the amulet. But instead of Adam taking Solen's ring, Harry picked up his section.

They came together between the two sarcophagi.

"Are you sure you want to do this?" Cassie whispered. "You're Vizier Nebamun's descendant. Are you sure you're willing to risk the curse?"

"Are you?" His eyes met hers.

She shook her head.

Adam began to read from the scroll. When he came to the line about blood transmuting all, Diana stopped him. "Whoa, wait a minute," she said.

"What?" Adam looked at his mother.

"You must have translated that wrong. Let me see it." Diana took the scroll from him. The crowd murmured with speculation.

"The translation is fine, Mother," Harrison said. "I got the same thing."

"And you used the *Math of the Sun: The Immortal Egypt* to translate it?"

"Yes, we both did," Adam said.

"Here's your problem. Your sun calculations are off. The word isn't 'blood,' but 'love.'"

"What does that mean?"

"The one element that transmutes all others," Diana read, "isn't blood, but love. It's not a human sacrifice that's needed in the formula for immortality. But love.

And the way it is used at the end of this passage means that love transmutes everything else. In other words, the way to lift the curse is through love."

Cassie's eyes met Harry's. "We can transmute the curse through love."

"I love you," he said fiercely, and she could see the truth of it in his dark brown eyes. "Do you love me?"

"Just join the amulet," she said, "and find out. If you're willing to take the chance."

Harry stepped forward, slipping Solen's section of the amulet into Kiya's. The minute the amulet halves touched, a bolt of blue-white lightning shot from the djed and into the copper amulet.

The crowd gasped.

The rings melded.

Electricity shot through Cassie and Harry. Their gazes fused as surely as the amulet.

Cassie tumbled down, down, down into the glorious abyss of Harrison's dark eyes, and she was awakened. She had known him always. In a bridge across time they were joined.

Cassie was his Kiya, and he was her Solen.

She grounded him. With her sensuality, her earthiness, her authenticity. He'd always been like a kite, mentally flying high above his body, soaring over his feelings. Nothing much touched him. Nothing physical ever really got through. Until Cassie, he'd never reveled in food, never lost himself in the pleasures of the flesh. She was his anchor, his tether, the string that kept him from floating away.

Which was odd. Externally, he appeared to be the calm, centered one, and she was the flighty butterfly. But while her mind was mercurial, her body was not. She lived her physicality. Embraced her essential humanness.

Harrison could not take his gaze from her. Never had he been so captivated by anyone's face. Her eyes had such clarity, such depth. Here she was, his destiny.

All those old misguided beliefs that had caused him so much pain disappeared in the light of her love. There was no curse. Her love for him transmuted it. He realized now the truth he'd been denying for so long.

He'd been running from the thing he most deeply wanted. Through her love, she'd helped him realize his true self. He recognized, without any more doubts or misconceptions, his real nature. The external was transient, but that essence of who he was would live forever.

Like Solen and Kiya, their spirits merged for eternity.

In that moment, in his heart, Harrison realized he had believed in love all along.

ABOUT THE AUTHOR

LORI WILDE is the best-selling author of more than twenty books. A former RITA finalist, Lori's books have been recognized by the *Romantic Times* Reviewers' Choice Award, the Holt Medallion, the Booksellers Best, the National Readers' Choice, and numerous other honors. She lives in Weatherford, Texas, with her husband and a wide assortment of pets. You may write to Lori at P.O. Box 31, Weatherford, TX 76086, or e-mail her via her homepage at www.loriwilde.com.

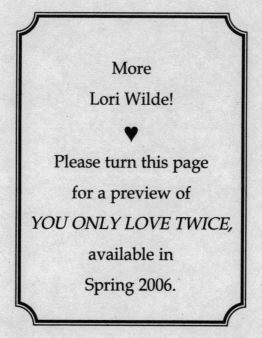

More

Lori Wilde!

♥

Please turn this page

for a preview of

YOU ONLY LOVE TWICE,

available in

Spring 2006.

CHAPTER ONE

Marlie Montague was right smack-dab in the middle of exposing a massive government cover-up when her front doorbell pealed.

As an inside joke, her computer geek ex–best friend, Cosmo, had programmed it to chime a snippet from the theme to *Mission: Impossible*. But that was before he had sold out his scruples and left Corpus Christi to go to work for the FBI in Quantico. Even though she'd grown accustomed to her odd doorbell sound, Marlie still missed Cosmo and wished she could be more forgiving of his career path.

She sat tailor-style at her white drawing board, black charcoal pencil in hand, surrounded by a bank of computers, some ivory, some ebony, all Macs. From a CD player wedged in the corner of the room, Alanis Morissette waxed philosophically about life's little ironies. An aroma therapy candle dubbed Inspiration flickered from its perch on the windowsill. It smelled like a cross between starched fresh white linen and black whip licorice.

Deeply engrossed in the comic book she was illustrating, Marlie continued to draw Angelina Avenger with her eyes blazing and her guns drawn as she confronted a top-ranking CIA agent about his part in a global oil conspir-

acy. Her pencil hollowed the lines of Angelina's cheekbones, accentuating her haunting beauty and steely inner
toughness.

She paused a moment to study her handiwork, then applied her eraser to perfectly arch her heroine's auburn
eyebrows. Angelina might be the most kick-butt crime
fighter in the comics, but she never neglected her groom-
ing. The woman was serious trouble in high heels.

Quite unlike Marlie.

Oh well, what was the point of having an alter ego if
she couldn't possess all of your good qualities and none
of your bad?

She glanced down at her rumpled black tracksuit that
she'd never once run track in and realized she'd been toil-
ing for almost fifteen hours without a shower, and only
her tweezers knew for sure the last time she'd plucked
her eyebrows. Whenever she got lost in the work, all
sense of time and space vanished. She flowed into the
creative zone, her ability to shut out the real world both a
blessing and a curse.

The doorbell played *Mission: Impossible* again.

Irritated by the interruption, Marlie sighed, reluctantly
laid her pencil down, and pushed back from the story
board. Who the heck was it?

Maybe it was UPS with a box of her free author copies
of *Defender of the Truth*, the latest edition of Angelina's
adventures in which she brings down a greedy pharma-
ceutical company for dumping toxic waste into the Mis-
sissippi River.

The bell rang again and curiosity got the better of her.
She padded down the hallway. When she reached the
front door, she had to go up on tiptoe to peer through the
peephole. Being five foot two was an inconvenience at

times; little wonder she'd created Angelina as a six-foot Amazon.

It was a man.

A stranger.

Her arm hairs lifted and her breathing sped up. Who was he?

He stood with his back to the door, gazing out at the moderately priced homes that made up her cozy little corner of Oleander Circle, just a mile from the Gulf of Mexico. Pushing her glasses up from the end of her nose, she squinted to get a better view. She didn't recognize him, at least from the back.

He wore a sweat-stained navy blue T-shirt and gray cotton workout pants that, in spite of their bagginess, couldn't camouflage his strong, muscular butt. In one hand he held, of all things, a Pyrex measuring cup.

Could this be her new next-door neighbor come to borrow a cup of sugar?

More like a cup of egg whites. Cleary, this guy never put a bite of the sweet stuff in his mouth.

If this was indeed her new neighbor, then she had watched him from her office window two weeks earlier when he'd moved in. Her imagination thrilled as she remembered him lifting those boxes with bulging biceps, stripping off his shirt when he got overheated and dazzling her with a righteous view of his six-pack abs.

He'd so captivated her fancy, Marlie had considered turning him into a cartoon love interest for Angelina. Hans Von Hunk. Honorable, brave, loyal, and, most of all, dynamite in the sack. Angelina had been all for the deal, but Marlie feared a romantic entanglement might cause the Avenger to lose her edge.

The man on her front porch wore his hair cropped

close to his head. Not quite a buzz cut, but almost. More like Richard Gere in *An Officer and a Gentleman*. She knew the look and abhorred it. Precision military.

Tessa James from across the street, newly divorced and on the hunt, said she'd heard rumors he was an ex–Navy SEAL. Marlie hoped not. She didn't trust military men. Not even ex-military. Not even sexy ex-military.

Don't sweat it, Marlie babe. A macho man like him would never be interested in a mousy woman like you, Angelina whispered in her ear. *He's much more my type. You should have hooked up with Cosmo when you had the chance.*

But Marlie had never been physically attracted to Cosmo. They'd been friends and nothing more.

The man on her doorstep turned, giving her a breath-taking view of his handsome profile. A provocative five-o'clock shadow ringed his angular jaw, and his hooded eyes were an intriguing shade of blue-gray-green. He looked demanding and resilient. Tough and shrewd and dangerous.

Definitely dangerous.

Leaning in, he rapped hard against the door.

Caught off guard by the unexpectedness of the sharp sound, Marlie gasped. She jumped back and almost fell over the coffee table.

What if she was wrong? What if this guy wasn't her next-door neighbor? What if his agenda was far more ne-farious than a cup of egg whites?

Her underground comic books were controversial. Just last week she'd gotten a death threat mixed in with her fan mail. And it had happened before. She'd even notified the police, but they'd blown her off, pooh-poohed her fears as unlikely, so she hadn't bothered calling them this time.

Could the man with the wolfish expression in his enigmatic eyes mean her harm? Could he be the crazy who'd written her the death threat?

Seven years spent researching, writing, and illustrating her conspiracy-theory comic book series had given her a suspicious mind. That, and the fact that her father had been a government whistle-blower killed under mysterious circumstances by the naval officer who was supposed to have been his trusted friend. That traumatic event fed her cynicism.

You're being paranoid again, Angelina said.

Easy for her to say. She was a fearless crime fighter.

You're not afraid he's come over to do you harm. You're just too chicken to talk to a good-looking man.

There was that.

Marlie's natural impulse urged her to slink back to her office and pretend she'd never heard the *Mission: Impossible* theme. She had a deadline looming and three pages left to illustrate before tackling the computer work.

That's right. Stick your head in the sand. Blame it on your work. Never mind that you're hiding behind your shyness, using it as an excuse to avoid getting a real life. And maybe, just maybe, a real man.

Shut up! Marlie gritted her teeth. Sometimes she regretted ever having made up Angelina.

"I'm not sticking my head in the sand," she muttered. "I'm not." She knew she had a bad habit of talking to her own fabrication. It was one major drawback to living along and working out of her home.

Prove it.

"Not interested in him. He's military."

You don't know that.

"Girlfriend, check him out. His posture is so perfect it looks as if someone nailed a two-by-four into his spine."

What's wrong with military?

"Come on, you of all people asking me that question."

Open the damn door, Mar. You think he's got a submachine gun stashed down the front of his sweat pants?

"I can't open the door looking like this." Her hair was unkempt, she wore no makeup, and there was a coffee stain on her white T-shirt in a strategically embarrassing spot.

Excuses, excuses.

"Hello? Anybody home?" The hypnotic sound of his voice, all sinful and chocolaty, lured her.

Double dare you to introduce yourself, Angelina challenged.

"Okay, fine, all right, I'll do it. Just give me a second to freshen up first."

So hurry before he leaves.

What suddenly compelled her (besides Angelina's big mouth), Marlie couldn't really say. It was an odd sensation, pushing up from somewhere deep inside her, daring her to open the door.

Maybe it was nothing more than the urge to get a better look at the supreme hottie. Maybe it was because she'd been feeling a little too isolated since Cosmo left. Or maybe it was because if this man was going to be living next door to her, she had to know exactly who he was and what he was about. When push came to shove, Marlie valued information over safety, because the right kind of information could ensure safety.

Stripping off her coffee-stained shirt as she went, Marlie dashed into her bedroom. She pushed back the beaded curtain that served as a closet door and somehow managed to dislodge her bowling ball from its case in the process.

The ball escaped, bumping away across the hardwood floor. She ignored the fugitive, snatched a clean T-shirt from a hanger, and hurried into the bathroom.

He rang the door bell again.

This is your mission if you choose to accept it, Marlie thought. *Open the door.*

"Coming, coming," she shouted. A surge of excitement, unexpected and joyous, snared her in its grip. She was startled to realize she really wanted to meet him and distressed that he might leave before she got back.

She rinsed her mouth with Scope, while simultaneously releasing the elastic band that kept her unruly brown hair pulled back. She pulled a brush through the tangles and then dabbed on a subtle shade of pink lipstick. One quick look in the mirror told her she was semipresentable.

She rushed down the hall, so focused on her goal that she did not see the bowling ball. Her ankle clipped it and the ball rolled between her legs. She ended up sprawling facedown on the floor and noticing it was way past time she got the vacuum cleaner after those dust bunnies.

Another peal of the door.

This mission will self-destruct in seven seconds.

"Hang on!"

Dragging herself to her feet, she hobbled to the door and flung it open to discover that her sexy next-door neighbor had vanished. In his stead stood the UPS man.

"Where'd he go?" She cocked her head, craning for a look around the man's body, but all she could see was the boxy brown delivery truck parked at the curb.

"Where'd who go?" The UPS man stared at her, perplexed.

"The guy who was just here."

"What guy?"

Marlie sighed. At some point between the Scope gargle and the bowling-ball mishap, her neighbor must have given up and gone home and the UPS man had appeared.

Oh well. She blew out her breath, surprised to find herself feeling so disappointed. She shook her head to dispel the feeling and reached out to take the box from the UPS man, only to discover he was also clutching a wicked semiautomatic weapon.

With a silencer attached to the end of it.

Naval Criminal Investigative Service Special Agent Joel Hunter took the measuring cup and strode back into his house. So much for his brilliant may-I-borrow-a-cup-of-shampoo ploy. Apparently, Marlie Montague wasn't about to open her door to a stranger.

Not that he could blame her. She was a young woman living alone and engaged in subversive activities. He'd be leery too, if he were in her shoes.

He knew she was home. Her Toyota Prius was in the driveway, plus when he'd returned from his run, he'd checked the surveillance equipment that Covert Ops had installed in her house. Marlie had still been holed in her office, working on her comic book. Joel had retrieved the measuring cup from the kitchen cabinet of the house he'd rented fully furnished and trotted over to carry out his new orders.

Initially, his assignment had been simple. Keep her under surveillance. Then while on his jog, he'd gotten a cell phone call from Camp Pendleton with additional instructions. Befriend the suspect and gain her trust. But under no circumstances was he to allow her to uncover his true identity.

But of course. *That* was a given. You couldn't exactly expect to get chummy with the daughter of the man your father had killed.

Joel wondered, not for the first time, if his connection to Marlie was the reason he'd been relegated to the case.

Even though he was career Navy and loved the SEALs with all his heart, his habit of questioning orders had led him to leave the SEALs for a career with NCIS. His habit of testing authority probably stemmed from a revolving door of stepfathers who'd tried to tell him what to do, when Joel knew good and well they wouldn't stick around long enough to see their discipline carried out. Hell, his own father hadn't stuck around.

What could he say? His mom was a butterfly, attracted to hard-asses. In order to survive childhood, he'd learned to stick to his guns and stand up for himself. As a Navy man, he was damned good at his job, so he was usually forgiven for his insurrections. But not this time. He'd spent the last two weeks trying to figure out which one of his higher-ups he'd pissed off enough to saddle him with this crappy babysitting assignment.

He flung off his sweaty clothes and stalked to the bathroom. If Montague wouldn't answer her door to a stranger, he had to come up with another way to meet her.

Twisting the shower faucet to a tepid temperature, he climbed inside the tub and yanked the curtain closed.

In the past thirteen days Joel had discovered Marlie rarely had guests (other than her mother), and she often didn't go out for days at a time. When she did venture from home, it was usually only to the grocery store or bowling on Wednesday nights. She led a very mundane life. Working, watching television, occasionally talking on the phone with a girlfriend. He was beginning to wonder if she was agoraphobic.

He was also beginning to think Mission Command was barking up the wrong tree. Marlie Montague looked like somebody's wide-eyed kid sister. The kind of wholesome girl-next-door so valued in 1950s sitcoms, like *Gidget* and *Donna Reed* and *Father Knows Best.* She even wore her hair in a ponytail.

A dissident innocent? Joel wondered. Was there such a thing? The only time he'd seen her act the least bit lively was at the Starlight Lanes. She mowed down bowling pins and racked up strikes with deadly precision. So what if she'd written a couple of conspiracy-theory comic books with antigovernment themes? Big deal. It was fiction.

But that's where he kept getting hung up. If her comic books were strictly fiction, then why did Navy Intelligence consider her a threat to national security? Could she actually have stumbled upon a real conspiracy within the ranks of the U.S. government? But the Navy was Joel's life, and he didn't want to give credence to such thoughts. He trusted his government, believed in everything America stood for.

He blew out his breath. Like them or not, his orders had been clear. His job was to get friendly with Marlie, and that's what he would do.

Now, he just had to come up with plan B.

Aw hell, Marlie thought, *what a day to get whacked.*

She needed a shower, her Visa bill was three weeks overdue, and, worst of all, she hadn't had sex in two years. *I'm going to die broke, manless, without clean underwear on, and living in a house I rent from my mother.*

Just as Mom had predicted.

Whenever Penelope Montague bemoaned her daughter's lack of a love interest, Marlie kept her mouth shut, even though she could have pointed out that Daddy had been dead for fifteen years and her mother hadn't dated since. But any mention of the late Lieutenant Commander Daniel Montague made her mother misty-eyed and then she would whisper, "My most heartfelt wish for you, Marlie, is that you'll find an eternal love like the one I have with your father."

Who needed a constant reminder that she was coming up way short in the everlasting-romance department? And what potential lover could measure up to those lofty expectations anyway?

Nor was today looking especially promising for locating a soul mate.

Not with Mr. Semiautomatic shouldering his way into her house under the guise of expedient package delivery.

"Step back," the man said and kicked the door closed with his foot.

In a weird way, she'd been waiting for something like this to happen. As if deep down inside she'd always known it would come to this. She felt at once calm and panicked.

He was a bland, nondescript sort of fellow. Thinning blond hair, ordinary features, medium build, steady hands. A perfect killer. Calm, cool, and unmemorable.

She clenched her fists. What to do? "Who are you?" she squeaked.

He tossed the box aside and raised the gun. "I'm your assassin."

This couldn't really be happening. It seemed too sur-real. Too laughably Hollywoodesque.

He stood there, deadly as a coiled rattlesnake, staring at her with absolutely no expression on his face. But his blue eyes were serious, hard, and blizzardardous.

Reality hit her. Her heart pounded and she felt as if her lungs had gone white, squeezed of air, constricted by fear, dread, and, oddly enough, curiosity.

What now?

"Shhh." His voice was low and steady. "Don't worry. It won't hurt."

Everything happened so rapidly.

Marlie hit the floor in a rolling dive at the same time as the gunman fired.

Keep moving; get behind something. It was Angelina, coaching her.

Marlie scrambled behind the coffee table. Rapid-fire bullets decimated the wood. Oak chips flew everywhere. Amazingly, she wasn't hit.

But you soon will be if you don't do something imme-diately! Move it.

That's when Marlie's gaze locked on the bowling ball. There was no time to think. One-handed, she stuck her fingers in the holes and raised it up to her head just in time to block his shot.

The bullet struck the ball and ricocheted off. The force of the impact vibrated all the way up Marlie's arm and into her shoulder. For a moment she was dazed, unsure what had happened.

The gunman yelped, dropped his gun, and clutched his hand. Apparently the stray bullet had struck him.

Marlie leaped to her feet and slung the ball at him like

she was bowling a perfect game. It caught him in the shins and he went down hard.

He screamed a vile curse.

Blindly, she ran, bracing herself for the earth-splitting pain of a bullet slicing off the top of her head. She flew across the kitchen floor, threw herself out the back door. The brick patio was rough and cold beneath her socked feet.

As she sprinted around the corner of the house, her shirt caught on the branch of a peach tree. It ripped and chilly air bit into the skin under her armpit.

Her breath came in raspy gasps and her heart hammered like a NASCAR piston. The ten extra pounds she was lugging around suddenly seemed like a hundred.

She panted, her mouth dry. She ran full throttle, her lungs crying out in pain, and yet it felt as if she were moving in slow motion, her feet mired in invisible syrup, her life flashing before her eyes.

Marlie, age three, the first Christmas she could remember, clutching the little red wagon Santa had brought and crying because the handle had flown up and struck her in the nose.

Marlie, age eight, at her first dance recital, tripping and falling on her chubby white-tutu-clad butt in front of a tittering audience.

Marlie, age eleven, dressed in black at her daddy's funeral, clinging helplessly to her mother's hand.

Marlie, age sixteen, her first heartbreak. Robbie Dorfman dumping her for Veronica Jackson because she had sprouted bigger breasts over the summer.

Marlie, age nineteen, tearing open the envelope containing a check from Underground Press for three hundred and fifty dollars for her first *Angelina Avenger* comic book. She'd been so proud of herself, so happy.

It was all there in a microsecond, her memories tumbling in and then going quicker than the time it took her to draw in a breath. Any second her world would go black forever. Her life cut short at twenty-six.

And I never even really lived.

She could hear the hit man thrashing around the peach trees behind her. She heard him grunt. Heard the deafening sound of her own blood whooshing in her ears.

Something hot and fast and quiet whizzed past her head.

Another bullet.

Yipes!

It bounced off the bricks on the house and a piece of mortar struck her cheek.

Get moving. Over the fence.

Marlie didn't exactly know how, but she managed to scale the six-foot wooden fence and fling herself over into the yard next door without getting killed.

She stumbled, fell to her knees in the straw-colored grass, and then quickly got up again. She risked a glance over her shoulder and saw that the hit man wasn't climbing the fence after her.

He must be hurt.

A perverse sense of glee overtook her, and she charged up the steps of her neighbor's porch. She turned the door handle.

Locked.

No big bad tough Navy SEAL was at home to save her. Marlie cried out, but it was a small sound, soft and helpless.

But she refused to admit defeat. Not yet. No matter

what, she had to get inside. Had to find a phone and call 911.

Stripping off her shirt, she bunched it around her fist and punched a hole through the paned glass of the upper part of the kitchen door. Heedless of the shards, she stuck her hand through the opening, twisted the lock, and pushed the door inward.

Marlie shoved her way over the threshold. Her feet, covered only by black-and-white toe socks, glided over the glass, miraculously uncut. Her heart was rapping so hard she feared it might explode right out of her chest.

It was at that very moment that a disturbing notion occurred to her. What if her neighbor and the UPS man were partners in crime? They'd both been at her front door just minutes apart. It was a possibility.

There you go with the conspiracy theories again.

"What the hell is going on here?"

Startled, she raised her gaze and met the hard-eyed scowl of the muscular man standing in the entryway between the kitchen and the hall, wearing nothing but a bath towel cinched around his gorgeous waist.

THE EDITOR'S DIARY

Dear Reader,

Ever notice that the best-laid plans have a funny way of crumbling like blue cheese, especially when you throw love into the mix? Come see what a ferocious man and a flirtacious lady do about it in our two Warner Forever titles this May.

Romantic Times BOOKclub Magazine calls **Amanda Scott's** previous book "a dynamic story," and they couldn't be more right. But her next book is even better, so prepare to be dazzled by **LORD OF THE ISLES**. Lady Cristina Macleod, eldest daughter of a Highland chieftain, is smitten with Hector "the Ferocious" Maclean. As a warrior fearsome enough to earn every man's respect and a man rakishly handsome enough to win any woman's affection, Hector is the perfect match for Cristina. The only problem is that he has just asked for her younger sister's hand in marriage. However, Cristina's father has a secret plan to fix everything. For throughout the western Highlands, marrying off one's younger daughters before the eldest is considered unlucky, and Macleod hates to be unlucky. So as guests arrive for the wedding, Macleod plies everyone, especially Hector, with a powerful Scottish whiskey. But what will "the Ferocious" do when he discovers he's married to the wrong sister? And can Cristina win his heart?

Much like Hector "the Ferocious" Maclean, Cassie Cooper in **Lori Wilde's MISSION: IRRESISTIBLE** knows all about plans going awry. Entrusted with planning a ball that honors the reunification of two halves of a priceless Egyptian amulet, Cassie Cooper knows her job is on the line. But really—how hard is it to plan a party for scientists? So when the lights cut out, half the amulet goes missing, and a mummy collapses with a knife in his back, Cassie knows she's in trouble. Desperate to save her job and find the artifact, she turns to her nemesis: Dr. Harrison Standish—or Standoffish as she calls him. So now this man who doesn't believe in romance and this woman who's in love with love must unravel the secrets behind this magic amulet while dodging bad guys and racing against the clock. But will love catch them first? Grab a copy and find out why *Rendezvous* raves that Ms. Wilde "has a unique voice that will soar her to publishing heights."

To find out more about Warner Forever, these titles, and the authors, visit us at www.warnerforever.com.

With warmest wishes,

Karen Kosztolnyik, Senior Editor

P.S. Are you hungry for more? Pick up these two treats that never fail to satisfy: Lani Diane Rich tells the witty and hilarious story of a woman whose mother is kidnapped with only an ugly parrot for ransom and a sexy ex-fiancé for help in MAYBE BABY; and Marliss Melton delivers an intriguing new romantic suspense about a Navy SEAL who uncovers the truth behind a stunning DIA agent's disappearance only to fall head over heels for her in IN THE DARK.